LIM

By

Hershel Howell

Hershel B. Howell

8-5-09

PublishAmerica
Baltimore

ISBN: 1-60563-063-2
PUBLISHED BY PUBLISHAMERICA, LLLP
www.publishamerica.com
Baltimore

Printed in the United States of America

This book is dedicated

to

Peggy, my late wife who for the last 58 years has shown me so much patience and love. This manuscript would not have been possible without her assistance and understanding.

Acknowledgments

I would like to recognize my daughters-in-law, Wanda and Shelley. Their encouragement and advice was invaluable.

Third, my son Rex, for his continued encouragement, and the use of his office and equipment. His advice and writing ability was such a great help.

I wish to thank my good friend Don Dewberry. How he deciphered my scrawled handwriting in typing the first draft was unbelievable. Some of the multiple words and choice lines are from Don. Without his expertise in editing, it would never have come off.

To the many others that helped with the story and advice that have not been mentioned here, I wish to say thanks.

Last, but certainly not least, I wish to thank my agent Sue Rogers. When I was ready to call it a "lost cause" she took the reins and got it done. Sue, you cannot believe how much I appreciate your advice and help.

Chapter 1

Lim drove the new Blazer off the road in front of the small Baptist church, got out and walked across the street. With only a glimpse, you could immediately tell by his stately manner that he was the true southern gentleman. Maybe it was the way he held his head, or the effortless steps he took; the snow-white hair and mustache, or the erect stance with his shoulders pulled proudly back. Whatever it was, Lim would be the first one you saw in a crowd, especially if you caught the twinkle of devilment in his steel gray eyes, offset by a stern don't cross me look. The tuxedo with ruffled shirt, bow tie, and shiny black shoes only enhanced his well-proportioned, yet slender physique. An "L" shaped scar over his right eye added an air of mystery to his dark complexioned face. Today his walk was steady and his eyes alert, not showing any sign of the one drink he had limited himself to for this memorable occasion. Seventy years was old, but somehow it did not seem to fit Lim, even with more miles than years, as there was not much he had not done or seen. He had held up well considering his fast lifestyle, leaving no mark of his true age.

Lim was old enough to be Bubba's grandfather, but he was more like Bubba's father and he was just as proud of him as he would have been of his own son. In fact, it was as if he were giving the groom away instead of Mr. Ranking giving the bride Stella away.

Bubba, walking out of the church, spotted Lim and cut across the church lawn to meet him. Smiling, he held out his hand, "Lim, you always were the best looking man in town. You sure look good in that tux. In fact, you look like you should be the one getting married, not me."

Lim replied with almost childish glee, "Bubba, most of us old fools can hide a lot of things with new clothes. It's when you take them off, then you know how old you are. You see all the wrinkles and dangling skin that used to be muscle and flesh. The clothes can hide it, but it's still there. It's kinda like painting an old car to hide the rust and dents, but the age like the mileage is still there. What time is it? I could use a drink."

Bubba, not looking at his watch, caught Lim by the arm and led him into the church. "Lim, I could use one too, but you know what we promised Stella. No drinking until we get to the reception. By the way, it was awfully nice of you to rent the Country Club for the reception."

"Aw Bubba," Lim replied, almost sounding embarrassed, "that was nothing. After all, you're the only family I got. I helped raise you and you're supposed to take care of your investments. Anyway, weddings make me nervous. Are you getting nervous kid?"

Smiling the easy smile that was as much a part of Bubba as his nose and eyes, he replied, "I guess marrying is sorta like dying. The past is over and gone and you don't know whether you're going to heaven or hell. If you're human, you're bound to have second thoughts and the waiting can weigh on you most every way."

"Yeah, Bubba I guess that's sorta true, but marrying's part of living not dying. It's growing up. It's what we're put in this world for, to marry and have a family," he stopped in thought for a second, and then continued, "of course some of us old fools never had sense enough to realize that."

"I wonder how Stella's doing," Bubba asked absently as he opened the door. "I bet she's wound up so tight she'd like a bracer too."

"Probably does," stated Lim in agreement, "but this is the biggest day of y'all's life, a day we'll all remember. I suspect the excitement is all she'll need. However, knowing Stella, I'm sure she's ready to get things moving. Probably has everyone walking a tight line."

Bubba rubbed the back of his hand nervously and laughed. "Well, I've been in a lot more relaxed places myself. I'd feel much better if we could have just eloped."

Both men turned as Brother Layton came up to Lim and shook his hand. "Lim, you look mighty good." The preacher turned to Bubba and seeing his nervousness, tried to ease him a bit. "Bubba, all the time Lim and I bird hunted together I tried to get him to come to church, but in over ten years I never could. Guess all it took was for you and Stella to get married."

"I been waitin' and wondering if the walls were going to fall in or something," Bubba replied poking at Lim.

Lim broke in, "Preacher, you know I could find me another bird hunting partner."

Brother Layton laughed and said, "We better get this wedding going before Stella calls it off. She's been as nervous as a cat in a dog pen." The organist walked by about this time and he called for her to wait, joined her and they walked down to the vestibule. The Preacher was having an animated conservation with her as they walked, waving his hands about.

The sanctuary was beginning to fill as the people came in; many were now standing on the church steps. The Mayor and most of the Board of Aldermen were present. Even Sheriff Tate and Deputy Hodge were there, along with a gaggle of reporters snapping photographs. With all the publicity this little town had received because of Lim, Bubba and Stella, there were more people here than at the Fourth of July barbecue. After all, there are not many towns the size of Taylorsville that have had local people become national celebrities overnight.

Brother Layton nodded to Bubba and said, "This is it. Let's go." Walking into the sanctuary, they stopped in front of the altar.

The preacher nodded to the organist and she began playing the wedding march. Bubba and Lim turned and watched Stella and her father walk slowly down the isle. The long white wedding gown added to the beauty of her beaming, suntanned face as she stopped in front of the altar.

Brother Layton asked, "Who giveth this woman in Holy Matrimony?"

Mr. Ranking stated his name and gave Stella's hand to Bubba.

The preacher continued the ceremony and a short time later Lim gave Bubba the wedding band. Bubba almost dropped it as he slipped it on Stella's finger. Brother Layton completed the ceremony and announced them as husband and wife.

"May I present Mr. and Mrs. Charles Davidson," the Preacher loudly proclaimed as he smiled at the crowd.

As Bubba pulled Stella in his arms and kissed her, one of his football buddies hollered from the back of the church, "'Atta boy, Bubba."

The crowd stood as one and erupted into spontaneous applause. The bridesmaids and flower girls barely got down the aisle before Stella and Bubba walked down the aisle holding hands.

The Country Club reception was more or less the usual; wedding cake, punch, and back slapping, throwing the bride's bouquet to her bridesmaids and Bubba throwing the bride's garter to his football buddies that were certainly enjoying the reception more than anyone else, especially the champagne that Bubba slipped to them.

Lim had found himself a drink stronger than the punch and gone out onto the Country Club porch. Bubba and Stella came out and spying Lim, they came across the porch to where he was standing.

Bubba put his arm on Lim's shoulder. "Lim, been lots of chasing and roping but I finally got my brand on her."

"Bubba, you've done *good*," Lim said acknowledging Bubba's statement as he turned to Stella, "Everyone needs somebody and you got the top of the line." He hugged Stella, "You couldn't look any more beautiful."

With tears in her eyes Stella replied, "Lim, I love you so much, thank you for everything."

Lim reached over and put his hand on Bubba's shoulder, "Stella, you and Bubba are the two finest people I know. Bubba may mess up every now and then, but all husbands do. Love him and he'll make the best husband any woman ever had." He looked at Bubba with a stern, fatherly expression, "Bubba, you don't know how lucky you are. Keep that in the back of your mind."

Bubba looked at Stella and smiled, his eyes speaking to her, but his heart talked to Lim. "Thanks, Lim. We best hit the road. We'll see you in a couple of weeks."

Dodging through the line of rice throwers, they headed for Bubba's car, jumped in, and sped down the Country Club drive with a string of cans tied to the bumper, throwing sparks from the pavement. Turning north on Highway 7, Bubba pulled over to the side, got out and untied the battered cans. Getting back into the car, he pulled Stella into his arms and kissed her saying, "Mrs. Davidson, you don't know how happy I am. This day took a long time coming."

She put her arms around his neck and replied, "You are my husband and I love you. This is one marriage that's going to last."

Bubba smiled and kissed her on the end of the nose, then turned and started the car. "I sure am glad Brother Layton put that statement, 'For better or for worse' in the ceremony," pulling the shift into drive with a laugh he continued, "and you agreed to it." The big car's wheels spun in the gravel of the shoulder, and catching the pavement it sped up the highway.

Stella moved closer to Bubba and kissed him on the cheek. "And you, big boy, made the same vow," she exclaimed punctuated with a naughty laugh!

Lim stood at the front of the country club and watched as the speeding car disappeared up the highway. He was happy for them both, but a feeling of loneliness came as he thought of the past few years. Remembering their close friendship and wondering what effect the new change in Bubba's life would bring. He stepped off the porch still wondering about his and Bubba's relationship as he walked across the parking lot to his car.

"Hell, they got their own life to live, now. That's what it's all about. That's what man and woman were created for—to get married."

Lim staggered a little as he got in his four-wheel drive. In order to appreciate Lim Appleton, one had to understand his heritage. I guess to get the full take on what makes him tick, you'd have to go back a long time, maybe even before the Civil War to the mid 1840's when Lim's great grandfather moved to the Union Community and bought up the bigger portion of the choice river bottom farm land. At that time, the small community of Union was just a crossroads seven or eight miles north of Taylorsville. During the buying, he bought a section of hill land along the boundary of the present Taylorsville Community. Lim was named after his great grandfather, Limbrick Appleton, and like old Limbrick, he didn't like the name either. So he went by the short name of Lim. He was like his namesake in other ways, too. He liked fast living, women, and liquor and didn't believe in making a living by the sweat of his brow. The only difference was that Lim, even though he was known as a gambler, was an honest man and his word was his bond. One couldn't say the same for his great grandfather, who made a fortune dealing in slaves, whiskey, crooked land schemes, and any other shady way he could figure to beat someone out of a dollar. However, even with his questionable character, old Limbrick Appleton made quite a name for himself during the Civil War.

There too, he lived up to his name becoming a Colonel over a cavalry unit that was called Appleton's Raiders. It was said they should have been named Appleton's Bloody Looters as the feared cavalry unit did most of its raiding on towns north of the Mason Dixon Line. The towns they raided didn't have any connection with the war, but had money and other valuable possession. The South could use the money and supplies, but there again, it was only shared by the Colonel and his men, with the Colonel probably getting the best cut. This greed and lust for money added to his growing fortune during the war.

After the war, when everyone was losing their farms, homes and life savings, along with whatever they had left in the reconstruction period, Limbrick Appleton, through his crooked dealing, amassed more land and money. Enjoying the luxuries of easy money, he built an extravagant home on his Union county plantation, which became a conversation piece to everyone that saw it.

The extravagant three-story structure, lavishly furnished with pieces imported from Europe and the Far East, was a landmark to Taylorsville and possibly even to the South. There again, old Limbrick added to his fortune by using the elegant mansion, servants, food, and liquor to entertain the crooked politicians and reconstruction leaders helping him to amass more wealth, land, and power. The same lust and greed followed him until his death in 1880. Leaving a name hated by many and envied by only a few.

The burial of Limbrick Appleton started a family cemetery, which was located in a white oak grove a short distance behind the plantation house. A second grave was added to the fenced family plot the same year, as Limbrick's wife passed away and was buried beside her husband. This left their only living child, Arthur, who was married and was living in the plantation home with his parents when the chain of deaths took place. You might say that overnight the operation of the plantation and the numerous Appleton enterprises were placed on his shoulders. Arthur possessed his father's traits of shrewdness, dishonesty and even possessed the same lust for power. He just wasn't as ambitious as his father had been. The land and money he inherited was more than ample to last the rest of his life, which was a good thing because working was not his calling. Liquor, women, and gambling were, but the hand of fate stepped in and took over. When old Limbrick died, the Lord, or the Devil, decided to have a say. Young Arthur had just completed the legal work on the inheritance when the luxurious plantation home burned. It was suspected that this might have been Arthur's doings as the upkeep on the mansion was very expensive and rumored to be well insured. Anyway, he moved his wife and newborn son to Taylorsville and built another house. It was big, but not nearly as elegant as his father's house had been.

It was a rambling, one story frame house with a plantation design, which was common in Mississippi after the war. It was built high off the ground with red brick underpinning and had a foyer, three bedrooms, a large living room, dining room, and kitchen with brick chimneys on each end of the house. The front porch ran the length of the house and was dressed with tall, square columns and steep banistered steps. In the center of the house was a small parlor with an outside entrance leading to the "L" shaped back porch that had entrances to the kitchen and back bedroom. All the rooms had ten-foot ceilings with tall windows that ran almost to the six-inch cypress tongue and groove floor. The original house had an outside privy, but in later years, the parlor had been converted into a spacious bathroom. The people of the town knew the house as the "Big House."

Unbelievably, Arthur had just moved his wife and son into the new house when he suddenly sold the entire estate—land, cattle, farming equipment—everything except the Big House and the section of land at Taylorsville. Not saying a word to anyone, he took the money and walked out leaving his wife and only son, Lim's future father, almost destitute, with only the house and land for consolation. He moved to Memphis, rented a suite of rooms in a fancy hotel where he spent his remaining days living it up gambling, drinking, and cavorting with fast women. Undoubtedly, the fast living was too much as he passed away a short time later.

After his death, the deserted wife and son brought Arthur's body back to Taylorsville and buried him in the family plot. Maybe not too proud, but he was still her husband and the father of her son. Naturally, after the funeral the widow began checking into his personal effects, but couldn't find a will, bank records or anything that dealt with his estate. Like everyone else, she assumed he had considerable wealth left from the sale of the plantation, but there was no trace of what happened to the money. The only thing his wife knew was that he made periodic trips back to Taylorsville, presumably to get money. This started the legend that he must have hidden the fortune somewhere in Taylorsville, as he never trusted banks. Arthur was smart and shrewd, and must have figured that if he put his money in the Taylorsville Bank that they, (his wife and son), would find out about it and attach it. Of course she wouldn't have, she had too much pride and felt it was blood money anyway and didn't want any part of it. Whatever happened to the money remains a mystery, even to this day. Well, it was a mystery to *almost* everyone.

Arthur's son, who was named after his father and called Junior, remained on the farm and didn't marry until in his later years after his mother died. Like his namesake, Junior had the same Appleton traits and about the only work he ever did was to look for the alleged lost Appleton fortune. Then Lim arrived on the scene, the only child and heir to continue the Appleton name. When he was old enough, he joined the search for the missing heritage same as his father.

Lim was surely all Appleton, and as he grew, he and his father continued the search for the treasure. Maybe the thrill of looking for it was in his blood, or it could have been the chance for easy money. Whichever, it was an obsession to Lim. Not only did he search for the Appleton treasure, but also looking for any lost treasure or old artifacts became his main interest in life, next to gambling, which took top priority.

Of course, the obsession marked Lim as a true descendant of those peculiar Appletons. His exploits became the center of local gossip and people took every chance to make fun of him. Lim didn't seem to be too concerned with what people thought and was quick to advise those that made questionable statements that it was best if they kept their remarks to themselves. His six-foot-two-inch frame, quick temper and questionable reputation was usually enough to keep the gossiping to a minimum, at least where he could hear them.

Junior died in 1920 and they buried him in the family cemetery. Lim's mother, a Christian and well respected lady, was determined that her son would get a college education if nothing else came from the Appleton Estate, which had by this time dwindled to three-hundred-twenty acres of land. So she sold three hundred acres, keeping the twenty acres with the Big House and invested the proceeds in a college education for Lim. All that remained of the once great Appleton Estate was the Big House and the twenty acres, which had a tenant house on the backside of the land where the last of the old plantation blacks, Jennie and her husband Tobe lived. And of course, the one-acre family cemetery plot up at Union. In less than seventy five years, a fortune of over ten-thousand acres of the finest land in the county, and no telling how much cash, had been squandered on…well, nothing.

(I had better say this right here. Jennie was black as night but Tobe was a much lighter color. There wasn't any question that he had white ancestors. Of course, back then it's the same as it is today, there are many signs of mixed blood most everywhere you go, it's an accepted skeleton in the closet for both races that neither race is proud of and very little is said about openly. There's always some whispering and low talk about who was in the woodpile with whom, but there's one thing for sure, the color sure didn't change by bleaching in the sun. I guess some people are going to take offense at me for writing what I just did, especially some of those organizations that seem to like to stir up trouble rather than stir down trouble, anyway, what I have just written is the truth and if I stepped on your toes, I just did. You can stick your head in the sand all you want, but when you look around it's staring you right in the face. It's important for you to understand the racial situation as it really was at the time this took place.)

Lim excelled in college, graduating with honors and was in the top ten percent by his second year in law school. All indications were that one Appleton was going to be educated and finally give the Appleton name dignity and respect. Adding to the brighter side, Lim had met this beautiful Delta girl and planned to take her as his bride as soon as he graduated.

It appeared that everything was going to work out just as it should. However, fate would have no part of this. Lim's mother died and everything started falling apart. Adding to Lim's worries, his bride-to-be changed her mind and began a romance with a rich Delta planter's son leaving Lim with a wound that would take a long time to heal, if ever. It was more than Lim could take. He lost all his ambition. Besides, college was what his mother wanted. He closed his law books and walked out of the University, moving back to Taylorsville.

He had some of the money left from the land sale but it didn't last long because he quickly took up his ancestor's habits of gambling, wild women, and liquor. The Appleton genes took over with a vengeance. No one knows much about Lim's life for a number of years after that except that he left Taylorsville, leaving Jennie and Tobe to watch after the Big House and the twenty acres of land. Some say he joined the army, others said that he went to prison and some even say he went to sea with a treasure hunting expedition.

Wherever Lim was and what he did took a long time, as Lim was in his late fifties when he came back to Taylorsville and moved into the Big House. It was pretty run down after all those years. The porch had rotted out, the roof and most everything was in drastic need of repair. Lim had apparently accumulated some money because soon after he came back he had the Big House repaired almost to its original condition. He bought a four-wheel drive Willis Jeep, built dog pens and covered chicken pens where he raised fighting cocks.

Lim wasn't one to make friends. He usually shied away from people, but he did become pretty close friends with Brother Layton, the Baptist Preacher who had begun visiting Lim in an attempt to get him to turn from his fast living habits and come to church. He wasn't successful. Something good did come from the preacher's faithful visits; he and Lim became friends and bird hunting partners. The preacher half way accepted the fact that Lim was going to continue his habits of drinking and gambling. Age had taken care of Lim's other questionable activities.

Even though Lim had numerous unacceptable traits, in his quaint way, he had many good traits that the community knew very little about. Even the people he helped didn't know where the money or food came from. In fact, there weren't many poor people in town, white or black that he hadn't helped in his own quiet way. Because of this, by the time Lim got old enough to draw Social Security he was broker than many of the people he had helped. However, like the good poker player he was, he kept everything to himself.

Lim's charity and goodwill was how he became friends with Bubba. Bubba's mother was a widow and had a hard time finding work. When Lim heard about her situation, she was trying to hold down two jobs. One was working as a clerk down at the 5 and 10 cent store, and her other was part-time help for Mr. Dale down at the tax assessor's office. Mr. Dale was like most everyone else, he wanted to help Bubba's mama but having just been elected he'd spent everything he had and what he could borrow getting into office and couldn't afford a full-time worker. Although things were trying, they weren't on welfare and this pleased her. Somehow, Lim found out about her destitute condition and wanted to help out. He hired Bubba to do odd jobs for him, such as mowing the grass, cutting firewood, helping with the fighting cocks and other chores around the Big House. With all the mysterious stories about Lim and his past, it didn't take long before he became Bubba's idol and Bubba spent all the time he could over at the Big House.

Lim took a liking to Bubba and spent time with him, taking him hunting, fishing and letting him drive his old jeep; he also helped him get his driver's license when he turned fifteen and even helped with his schoolwork. Lim was a long way from being a fool and there wasn't any subject he couldn't hold his own with especially math and history. Lim's big hobby, other than treasure hunting, was sports. He passed that interest on to Bubba, teaching him everything he knew of baseball and football. Lim encouraged Bubba when he was down and praised him when he was doing good. Football was Bubba's strong suit and along with ability, he had determination, especially since he was doing something that pleased his idol. Lim and Bubba's friendship grew strong over the years and this strength proved to be a binding commodity in the adventures they were to face in the future.

Bubba became Lim's chauffeur after he got his driver's license, especially on Saturday nights when Lim made his weekly gambling trip up near Memphis to a place called Bailey's. It was not unusual for the game to last all night ending the middle of the next day. Bubba was not allowed to sit in on the games. He would go to a movie, then come back and sleep in Lim's truck until Lim was ready to go home. Many nights Lim would have had too much booze to drive, so he would sleep while Bubba drove home. Lim was one of the best gamblers around, but the fellas he played with soon found his weakness for alcohol and most of the time took him to the cleaners before the night was over When Lim did win, it was by a sizable margin, sometimes being in the hundreds of dollars. On these good nights, he'd give Bubba twenty or thirty dollars depending on the total of his winnings. His big saying to Bubba was, "One of these days we're gonna drive home in one of them city slickers' Cadillac."

Bubba, whose real name was Charles Robert Davidson, was a big kid for his age, in his senior year of high school he stood a good six-feet tall, and weighed close to two-hundred pounds. He had a smile that would charm the birds in the trees and had a pretty good effect on the girls, too. He wasn't the most studious person, perhaps even a little on the slow side, but he wasn't slow when it came to running. He was by far the fastest boy on the football team and had strength and a natural ability to go with it. Lim's training and encouragement paid off. Taylorsville had a team of big and strong seniors. Being good players put them in the play-offs that year for the North Division Championship, slated to play Red Creek for the conference title. Red Creek also had a big team of oversized country boys that looked like a junior college team and the game was publicized to be quite a match giving the towns people plenty to talk about. Signs and banners were on all the doors, "Beat Red Creek—Go Taylorsville."

Lim didn't miss a game. His interest in Bubba made him one of Taylorsville's strongest and loudest supporters. You could hear him holler over most of the crowd whenever Taylorsville got the ball, "Give the ball to Bubba!" Usually right after that they would give the ball to Bubba, and you guessed it, most of the time Bubba would break through a host of tacklers for a touchdown. It was almost like Bubba was doing it for Lim.

School and ball practice took up most of Bubba's time, but to help support his mother, he had a part time job at Morris' Service Station. He usually got there right after ball practice and stayed until the station closed which on weekdays was somewhere around 9 o'clock and on Saturdays they closed at 6 o'clock. Of course, Morris let Bubba off early on the nights they had a game. That's enough background and history; this is where the story begins— Wednesday afternoon before the big game on Friday night.

Chapter 2

Lim drove his four-wheel drive into Morris' station and stopped in front of the regular pump. Bubba came out and greeted him with a large smile.

"Lim, what did you hit to do that to your front fender?"

Lim got out and walked around to the front of the truck. "Aw, I was up in Stogner's Slash the other afternoon and slipped into a tree. Just fill her up, Bubba, then I need to talk to you."

Bubba locked the nozzle with the gas cap and checked the oil while it was filling. Returning to the nozzle, Bubba worked it to even money. "Lim, looks like four dollars even." Lim gave Bubba a five and followed him inside. Bubba punched four dollars on the cash register and pulled the handle. "What you need to talk about Lim?" Bubba asked as he gave Lim the change.

"Bubba," Lim said as he glanced around to see if anyone else was near, "them boys up at Bailey's want to wager a little on the game Friday. I need to know what you think is gonna happen."

Bubba laughed nervously and hesitated before he replied, "Well, Lim, they're big and it's said that they look like a college team. I hear they're favored by as much as two touchdowns, but I kinda doubt they'll be that tough."

"You sound like you'd call it even money, or only one touchdown," Lim prodded his young friend.

"That's about right. Like I said, I'd go easy, at least until the half." Bubba remembered the last time Lim bet on a game. He had hedged or raised his bets during the game. "I believe we can win, but it's gonna be a close game."

"Bubba, give 'em hell," Lim said as he walked out the door putting his wallet back into his pocket. "I'll see you at the game."

Bubba watched Lim's truck drive up the highway and thought about the past. 'Lim's one hell of a person. I wonder how much he's going to bet. It'll be in the hundreds.'

Shaking his head, Bubba went back into the station to get a broom, came back out front, and started sweeping the concrete slab between the building and the pump island. His thoughts still on Lim, 'In the past two years, he's been almost like a father. He's done everything he could to make a man out of me. Made me feel like I was somebody.'

Leaning the broom against the regular pump, he took the oil rag out of his back pocket and wiped the dust off the pumps, while thinking of what Lim said about his working at Morris's, 'Bubba, everybody has to work, some with our hands and some with our head. Me, working with my hands is just not my calling, unless you call dealing cards work. Just remember this, if we didn't have people working, who would support those not working?' Shaking his head as he picked up the broom and went inside, "Lim's some peculiar fella," he muttered under his breath.

The game was a sell out and Lim and his two betting buddies were seated on the Taylorsville side about half way up the south end of the wooden bleachers. Lim felt pretty good about his two-hundred dollar bet on a seven-point spread, plus he was holding back a hundred of the three he'd borrowed against his Willis.

The crowd was fast filling the bleachers. It looked like every seat would be filled. The field lights were on adding to the festive, carnival like atmosphere. Out on the field, both teams were going through their practice drills and the cheerleaders and band had the excited crowd roaring. It was a perfect night for football. The weather was cool but not cold. It may have seemed a little cool to the spectators, but on the field, it should be just right for the players. The field lay east and west and over the east goal post, a full moon had just cleared the eastern horizon as the loud speakers came on and instructed the crowd to stand and bow their heads for prayer followed by the national anthem.

After the national anthem, no one sat down on either side. The frenzied crowd roared and with it, Lim's voice rose above everyone else's. "Let Bubba have the ball!"

Neither Bubba nor anyone else on the team could do much. In fact, Taylorsville had a pretty rough time in the first half and was down by fourteen points as the half ended. Lim left his betting buddies in the stands and was at the gate when the team went to the dressing room. He caught Bubba by the arm and walked up the hill to the dressing room with the team.

"Bubba, the first half didn't look too good. What do you think?"

Bubba flashed his trademark wide smile and replied in a slow voice, "Lim, I told you to go a little light, but it's gonna look better in the second half. The best things they've got are those two big ends. Either one could knock a mule down. We'll double-team them in the second half. I don't care how good they are, with A.C. and Red double-teaming them, they are gonna get a little hesitant 'bout coming at us before this game's over. Then you're gonna see our wide play start working. They've got the lead, but paid for it. We're getting through on their pass plays, putting pressure on the quarterback. It ain't as bad as the score. Look, we're coming after them in the second half. You can believe that."

Lim patted Bubba on the hind end, "Get after them Bubba." Walking behind the stands, he slipped a drink out of the half pint he had stashed in his coat pocket then went back up into the stands.

"Lim, you get them straightened out?" one of his betting buddies asked with a laugh as Lim sat down. "You want to sweeten the bet a little?"

Lim sat down and acted like he had to think about that before he could commit. After a minute he replied, "Guess you two got me down pretty good on the seven points, but I got a hunch it'll be different 'fore it's over. I tell you what though boys, since you two are so sold on taking me to the cleaners, give me three-to-one and I'll bet you a hundred Taylorsville will win."

This sorta set the two back and they discussed the matter privately a minute. Barney, who did the betting, turned to Lim and replied laughingly, "If you want to give your money away, we'll take it three-hundred against your hundred."

The third quarter was played more or less back and forth and neither team could get anything going. Then just at the end of the quarter, they carried Red Creek's big right end off the field. AC and Red had done their job. The other end didn't look too sporty either and wasn't near as spry as he was at the beginning of the game.

The fourth quarter started with Taylorsville's ball on their own thirty-yard line. Lim knew what was going to happen and it did on the very first play. Bubba took the ball wide around their replacement end for thirty yards, and then repeated the same play on the next down and he went into the end zone.

Lim's two partners suddenly weren't as talkative as they had been and as the ball game progressed, they seemed to get even quieter. Lim, slipping a little liquor into his coke, didn't let up. He was enjoying the game to its fullest and roared with the crowd, "Give the ball to Bubba!" And with almost every play they did. The game wound down to less than a minute and it didn't look as if

Taylorsville was going to pull it out. With the ball on their own fifteen-yard line, time was the big factor now, but maybe it played in Taylorsville's favor. With third and four, almost a sure passing down, the quarterback faked a pass then pitched the ball out to Bubba who crashed through two would be tacklers and completely ran over the right end, breaking loose for an eighty-five yard touchdown. The crowd came to its feet as Taylorsville lined up for the extra point with less than thirty seconds to play. Taylorsville, not going for the point after, lined up to go for two points. Win was their thought. It was do or die.

"Give the ball to Bubba," Lim hollered. They did and Bubba crashed into the end zone winning the ball game by a score of fifteen to fourteen.

The following week, Lim barbecued a 150-pound shoat and had the team up to the Big House for a feast. Things quieted down after that except Bubba was a hero and football scouts came from all over, all trying to persuade Bubba to sign a college football contract. But even with Lim's encouragement, Bubba didn't sign with any of them He decided he didn't want to go to college because his grades were not all that good. That disappointed some people, but didn't bother Bubba because at Christmas he gave his girlfriend, Stella, an engagement ring that he'd gotten Mr. Bell down at the jewelry shop to let him have on an installment plan. They didn't set any definite time for the wedding as Stella's father, Mr. Lee Ranking, let them both know in no uncertain terms that no girl of his was going to marry a boy that didn't have any more ambition than to be part-time help at a service station, especially when he could be in college on a football scholarship.

I guess Bubba and Stella were more interested in romance than in the future, which was something older people had to worry about.

Lim's thoughts didn't help too much when it came to college. He reverted to his theory that some people had to work with their hands and some with their heads. College only made it easier on those working with their heads. The big thing with Lim was what you did with the money you made. That was what success was all about.

Lim's theories certainly suited Bubba and Stella and they could find plenty of excuses to back it up. After all, who would hire the school graduate if people didn't quit school and go to work?

Bubba's not going to college was settled. He and Stella's least concern was making a living. Right now Bubba's main concern was Stella. Stella was a tall girl at five-foot-eight or nine inches and well built for her size, long legs and arms, bosomy, but not too much, had a light complexion with auburn hair, and a few freckles. She was tomboyish, could knock a baseball about as far as most boys, and was as tough as most. Don't get me wrong, she was all woman and when dressed in high heels, tight fitting skirt and blouse, she would turn any man's head.

Like Bubba, Stella wasn't the studious type. She liked the outdoors and plenty of excitement, which Bubba was only too glad to furnish—sometimes a little too much. Her parents tried to get her to go to college, but college wasn't for her either and she stayed in Taylorsville after graduating from high school. She went to work for her father who was a druggist and owned Taylorsville Drug Store, plus a large farm, which he used mostly as a tax write-off.

Bubba and Stella were like two peas in a pod and this slower pace was more to their liking. The romance between them was limited to petting as Stella's parents were "Hard-Shell Baptists" and had instilled in her that sex before marriage was a sin and would ruin a young girl if she indulged. With their guidance, Stella had developed a strong belief concerning sex and was determined that she was going to be a virgin when she married.

Bubba's up bringing may have been the same as Stella's, but it didn't take like hers. His feeling was that sex was made for having, and a girl was fair game if she could be persuaded. Stella knew Bubba's feeling and would put up with a little fondling as long as it was above the waistline, but would tell Bubba in no uncertain terms that it was time to go home when the lovemaking got below the belt.

Taylorsville School, like most schools, had some girls that had the reputation of being more liberal with their lovemaking than others. One of these girls was Martha Hatley, who had been Bubba's girlfriend before he started going with Stella. Martha still had a crush on Bubba and Stella knew it. Bubba didn't help the situation any by teasing that he could always ask Martha out and she would be considerate of his feelings. This certainly didn't set well with Stella and she let Bubba know right quick that if he ever went out with Martha he'd better plan on staying. She also let him know that if she ever looked at him with her sleepy-eyed haunting ways, she not only would scratch her eyes out, but would snatch every hair out of her head and his, too! Bubba, seeing the sharp flashes in her eyes, realized his little scheme had backfired and decided it best to let sex be something Stella could bring up the next time it was discussed As you can imagine, this pretty well settled the subject of sex, but it didn't keep Bubba's hands from roaming.

Chapter 3

Bubba was now the big hero in town, so the mayor gave him a job with the city Electric Department. From all appearances, it looked like everything was going to work out well for Bubba, which was usually a sure sign that you could expect that to change. It fact, it changed sooner than you could have guessed because a short time later Lim invited Bubba over to the Big House to eat quail.

Jennie, who did most of Lim's cooking, came over and prepared the birds along with homemade biscuits, mashed potatoes and gravy. It was sometime after the big meal that Lim and Bubba were in the living room talking when Jennie came in.

"Mr. Lim, will you need anything else? I got the dishes done."

"No, Jennie," Lim replied, slipping her a couple of bucks. "You need for one of us to drive you home?"

"Tobe'll be here in a minute to pick me up," she replied as she opened the door. "I'll wait for him out on the porch."

Bubba had gone over to punch up the fire. Hanging the poker on the mantle board, he noticed a strange looking object on the mantle. It was an odd, chrome-plated device with a handle like a pistol. The handle would let the barrel spin around when you held it.

Bubba picked it up and examined it closely, then held it out in front of him. "What in the world is this thing?"

Lim stood and took it from him. "Bubba this is a metal finding machine. It'll find any metal. Its strongest attraction is to iron, but it'll find gold, silver or copper."

"You must be putting me on," Bubba replied with an unbelieving grin.

"No, Bubba, that's the truth. It works." Lim took his gold watch out of his pocket and handed it to Bubba. "Here, I'll go into the next room while you hide my watch. I'll show you how it works."

Lim went into the dining room as Bubba looked around for a place to hide the watch. He walked over to the dresser and put the watch behind a vase, then walked over and opened the door to the dining room.

"All right, Mr. Gold Finder, show me how it works."

Lim walked to the center of the room, held the thing out like he was pointing a pistol and it began to rotate slowly in a circle. As it turned, it pointed to the vase and stopped.

"It's over by the vase," Lim replied with a satisfied grin.

Bubba couldn't believe what he had seen. "You ever find any gold with it?"

"Nope. I found a few coins and Mrs. Vaiden's ring she lost in her yard. However, I do know where there's a lost treasure buried. Well, I'm pretty sure it's there, but there's no way to get it."

"What do you mean you can't get it?" Bubba asked.

"Like I said, it's the location," Lim replied.

Bubba broke in, "Well, where in the hell is it?" Then he thought about what he had said and added, "You may not want to answer that."

"It's all right", Lim replied, "It's buried downtown in the city park."

Bubba looked confused, his eyes asking more questions than he could get his mouth to speak. Finally, he said, "In the city park? Why can't you go dig it up? All you would have to do is ask the mayor. You sure it's a buried treasure?"

"I'm sure it's there, least something is and I'm pretty sure it's a valuable treasure. I checked it out with this machine. It's something and it's a big stash of whatever it is."

Bubba thought for a minute, and then muttered, "Why would a valuable treasure be buried in the city park? A person would be a fool to bury something valuable there, especially gold. You sure that the something buried there is gold?"

Lim gave Bubba a sly smile. "I thought like you're thinking when I first detected it. I was down at the park looking around with the detector, looking for lost coins when the thing went crazy. In fact, I checked from every corner of the park and all it would do was spin and point toward the center of the park, to that speaker's pavilion. The finder had such a strong reading I got really excited. It has to be something big. So big in fact that I figured I had better keep it quiet 'til I found more about what it was."

Bubba got caught up in Lim's emotions and began to get excited himself. "What did you find out? Is it really gold and silver?"

"Yes, Bubba. I have every reason to believe its gold and silver and a big pile of the stuff at that."

"Are you sure it's not some old car motor or something else? Why would gold and silver be buried in the park?" Bubba asked.

"Like I started to tell you, I figured I better find out what it was before I stirred up a big thing with the city. So I started checking into it. I read everything I could about the history of Taylorsville. You know, who first settled here, how the town was laid out, about the city's involvement in the Civil War and what happened after the War right up till now. Not getting the answer I wanted, I read all the old newspapers I could and started checking with every old person I could locate. That's where I found my answers."

Bubba interrupted, "Found what answers? Is there really a treasure buried in the park?"

"Believe it or not Bubba, it's there. I got the information I was looking for from an old Darkie who was over a hundred years old. Soon as I asked him if he knew about any folk tale of a treasure being buried in Taylorsville, he immediately came back saying, 'You mean the one the Yankee's buried in the old city park?'"

Bubba broke in, "What the hell did he know? He said that?"

"Yes," Lim said with a smile, "the old fella told quite a story. He said he was a young boy, nine or ten years old during the Civil War, when the Yankees took over Taylorsville. They set up their headquarters, tents, wagons and stock corrals in the park. He said he got an eatin' job for watering the horses, mostly drawing water from the city well and keeping the troughs full. He also fed the horses and mules and did other odd jobs, so he pretty well kept an eye on what was going on. Like when they looted the town and took everything of value from all the town folks. He said he remembered seeing a wagon bed full of silver plates, pitchers, vases, and all kinds of jewelry, money, watches, everything. The looting went on two or three days and they got so much of the stuff that they had to put side planks on the wagons to hold it all. "Then one day the Yankees suddenly began taking down tents and loading their equipment on wagons. The old Darkie said he didn't know what was going on at first, but it didn't take long to find out, because before they got everything loaded, a Rebel cavalry unit came storming into town. There was a terrible battle all around the park and a lot of soldiers on both sides were killed."

Bubba sat with his mouth hanging open as Lim continued. "The old Darkie said it scared him so bad he hid under one of the watering troughs and watched the battle, which lasted up into the night. Finally, the Rebels got too much for the Yankees and the Yankees started digging a big hole right there in the middle of the park. He didn't know how many men came in to help, but they buried all that treasure in the hole. It was dark, but he could see the men dragging the stuff and throwing it in. The next thing they did was pull a couple of wagons with hay over where they buried it and set the wagons on fire."

Bubba broke in, "I can't believe it! All this time and the treasure's still there? Why didn't the old Negro dig it up or at least tell someone of its whereabouts?"

"I was curious about that too and asked him that same question," Lim replied. "He explained it this way. When the Yankees set the wagons on fire, they spotted him under the watering trough. Before he could run, a couple of soldiers snatched him from under the trough, tied his hands and feet and put him in one of the loaded wagons, then they high tailed it out of Taylorsville with the Rebels after them like a pack of fox hounds. The Yankees took him with them up into Tennessee then on up into Kentucky. Everywhere they went he became their water boy and handyman. He finally ended up in Peoria, Illinois when the war ended. Being a slave's son, he didn't know the whereabouts of his parents and didn't have any hankering to go back to Taylorsville so he stayed in Peoria. Some white folks took him in, gave him a place to sleep and something to eat for what little work they had for him to do." Lim went over to the table and replenished his drink.

"When did he come back to Taylorsville?" Bubba asked.

"He said it was up in the 1890's, almost the turn of the century. I asked him if he thought about looking for the treasure when he got back. His answer to that was, 'Lordy, Mr. Lim, after more than thirty years it weren't no use to look fer that stuff. It'd been dug up long fo dat.'"

Bubba stood up with his mouth hanging open not knowing what to say, then said in a low voice like he thought someone might be listening, "Lim, reckon that stuff is still there?"

"It's there," replied Lim, "I know for sure something's there. Every time I take this machine down to the park, it points right to the speaker's pavilion. It's there and it's got to be a big stash. Ain't no telling how much."

Bubba was really excited now. "Why don't you go to the mayor and get the city to let you dig it up?"

Lim smiled, "Bubba, this thing ain't fool proof and if we got the city to go to a lot of trouble and didn't find anything, people would laugh the mayor out of town. Besides, there's enough people laughing at me now saying I'm a nut."

Bubba thought it over for a minute. "Lim, are you sure it's there?"

"I know there's something there and would bet my last dollar on it," Lim replied.

That was good enough for Bubba, because Lim didn't usually make bad bets. Bubba left Lim's around ten with the story of the hidden treasure occupying his thoughts. Lim had said it would be all right if he talked to the mayor about it.

The next afternoon Bubba parked the Electric Department's truck in the city's warehouse and walked across the street to the mayor's office. The mayor was closing his door to leave as Bubba walked up.

"Well Bubba, how are you? Did you want to see me?" he asked.

"Yes sir, Mr. Mayor, if you have a minute."

The mayor unlocked the door and motioned for Bubba to come in. "Come in Bubba," and pointed to a chair for Bubba to sit. "What is it you need to talk about?"

Bubba found it hard to get his words started and squirmed in his chair. Finally, he got up enough courage to speak. "Mr. Mayor, I'm not crazy, but I know where a fortune in gold and silver is buried and I need your help."

The mayor slid to the edge of his chair. "A what?"

Bubba took his time, told the mayor all about Lim's gold finding machine and that the machine pointed to the speaker's pavilion in the city park. Then he told him about the old Negro's story of how the Yankee's looted Taylorsville and buried their loot in the city park as he watched from under the water trough.

The mayor laughed it off. "Bubba, you know we'll be the laughing stock of town if we dug up the park looking for buried treasure. That old Negro probably imagined he saw all of that stuff. You know how an old man's mind can wander."

Bubba interrupted him, "That's true, Mr. Mayor, but if you did find a treasure it would put Taylorsville on the map, and from what I hear, the city could use the money."

The mayor sat back in his chair and let Bubba's story sink in. He thought about the city needing to fix the foot-deep potholes in the streets; how bad they needed a new garbage truck, new streetlights, and all sorts of things.

"Tell you what, Bubba," the mayor said cautiously, "you get Lim to bring his machine to the park in the morning at six. Won't be anyone around then to laugh at us. I'd like to see that machine work. You have my curiosity up and it won't hurt to look. But we better keep this to ourselves. If this got out people would dig up the whole town."

The next morning Lim and Bubba met the mayor and he was amazed. Lim made his demonstration from every corner of the park. Each time the chrome detector slowly turned and pointed to the speaker's pavilion.

"You boys got me really curious," the mayor said as he got in his car. "I'll have to tell the board members. Maybe we just might figure a way to check this out."

Nothing was said about the treasure for a couple of weeks. Bubba was almost ready to check back with the mayor when the mayor sent him word to come by his office after work.

As Bubba walked in the mayor's office, the mayor greeted him, and then said, "I'd like to go see Lim. Reckon' he's out at his house?"

"We could go out and see," Bubba replied.

Lim was there all right, sitting under a large oak tree in his front yard. As they drove up, he got up from his lawn chair and walked over to the gate, stopping long enough to yell at his bird dogs to quit barking and shooed them back under the porch.

"Well Mayor, it's nice to have one of the City Fathers come for a visit. Come in and have a seat."

The mayor did not waste any time with formalities. "Lim, I really don't have the time. We're having a board meeting tonight, I'm going to talk to them about the city park project, and I want to be sure I know what I'm talking about. So I figured I'd get you to demonstrate again how that machine works."

Lim understood immediately what he meant by the *park project* "All right, Mayor, come on in the house. I'll be glad to demonstrate all I know about my machine." Lim let the mayor hide his gold watch a number of times and each time the detector pointed straight to it. The mayor even hid his gold ring and Lim found that, too.

Finally, the mayor said, "All right boys, I'm sold. I'll see what I can do to convince the board, but I want this kept secret. The town has enough to talk about as it is. They'll laugh us out of town if they heard about this before we had some results."

The next day the mayor sent for Bubba again, this time not waiting until he got off work. As Bubba walked into the mayor's office, the mayor closed the door behind him and said in a low voice, "Bubba, I've got everything worked out up at the park. We're going to move the speaker's pavilion, put down a new water line to it and repair the fountain. We'll be able to dig up the whole area and no one will suspect what we're looking for."

Bubba thought for a minute about what the mayor said. "Mayor, I kind of figured you'd find a way to do it. After we find all that treasure you'll have everybody talking about you."

Smiling, the mayor commented, "I hope it's not about me making a fool of myself. Tell Lim the board agreed to split any treasure we find sixty percent for the city and forty percent for him as a finder's fee. We'll draw up a contract to make it legal. I just don't want any talk or publicity of what we're doing to leak out until we find the treasure. I'll let you and Lim know when we plan to start."

Bubba could hardly wait until he got off work. At five-o'clock sharp, he had the city truck parked in its garage and was on his way to Lim's.

Lim was sitting on his porch having a drink when Bubba drove up. Bubba got out of his car with a big smile on his face and poked a little at Lim's beverage choice at this time of the day. "Little early for a drink ain't it? You fixin' to go out?"

"Naw, Bubba," Lim replied, swirling the whisky around in his glass. "Just sittin' around with nothing to do. I decided I'd have one to relax. Come on in and I'll give you one."

Bubba saw Lim's ice chest on the porch and replied, "I'll have a pop."

"There's one left from the fishing trip yesterday," and pointed at the cooler.

Bubba fished out an RC, opened it, and took a seat in a cane bottom chair next to Lim. "Just had a meeting with the mayor."

"How'd that turn out?" Lim asked.

"About like we expected," Bubba answered with a laugh, "they're ready to draw up a contract giving you a forty percent finder's fee."

"That all sounds good, Bubba," Lim replied with a gleam in his eyes, "but remember this; whatever we find I'm splitting my part down the middle with you." Lim reached down next to his chair, retrieved a bottle, and replenished his drink. "Stick with me, Kid, one of these days we're going to drag in the big pot, you wait and see. You can't win if you ain't in," Lim added with emphasis.

"Lim, ain't no use in you splitting the treasure with me," Bubba argued, "all I did was to talk to the mayor."

"That's enough to make you a full partner", Lim countered. "You got it set up. We wouldn't be doin' this if you hadn't. Shoot, the mayor would've probably laughed me out of his office. You're getting half and it's no need to say any more. After all, you're the only family I got."

"Lim, you know I appreciate it, but somehow I don't know if I'll feel right about taking it. If it's as big a stash as you think it is, what would I do with all that money?"

Lim laughed at his young friend. "Morris still wants to sell his station. You and Stella are fixing to get married and I got a feeling you'll find plenty of places to spend it. If you don't, I know Stella will."

Bubba laughingly replied, "Hell, Lim, it makes me nervous just thinking about it. I think I'll keep it as a surprise to Stella. She'll really throw a fit when she hears I'm part owner of a treasure."

Bubba left Lim's a little after seven, stopped by Stella's and they went out to the fish house and ate supper. It was all he could do to keep from telling her, but not a word was mentioned. Even when they went up to the County Line on Saturday night and took Lim with them, both men got to sipping suds pretty good and Stella had to drive them home, but not a word about the treasure.

Monday morning when Bubba went to work the mayor sent word for him to drop by his office. An hour or so later, Bubba was seated in his office and the mayor laid out the plans. "Bubba we're starting in the morning. Get word to Lim. I got it set up for you to help with the project, so there won't be any questions about you being there."

Of course, this suited Bubba and as soon as he got off work, he went out to Lim's and told him. Naturally, this brought on a little celebration and Bubba had enough to drink that he shouldn't have been driving. He ran in a ditch turning into his driveway. At least he didn't have far to walk and it didn't damage his mama's car.

Like the mayor had promised, the next morning a work crew started moving the speaker's pavilion and a backhoe started the digging. Everything was going as planned, except somehow it leaked out what was happening. Before the backhoe took the first dipper of dirt, a crowd had gathered. Everybody was joking and laughing about the city looking for buried treasure. The more they dug the more the crowd ragged the mayor who was there inspecting each dipper of dirt. Bubba and Lim, standing with the mayor, got their part of the heckling too. Suddenly, the crowd's noise settled to a whisper when the backhoe hit something. The mayor, Bubba, and Lim jumped into the hole and began digging with shovels. Someone on the edge of the hole yelled, "It's gold and silver bars. Must be a wagon load." Simultaneously, everyone was pushing and shoving trying to see and some fell into the hole. Getting the people cleared from the hole, the backhoe started digging again. Then someone hollered, "It's a piece of railroad iron or rails."

The crowd couldn't stand it and jeered the mayor something awful as the backhoe raked the heavy rails out of the hole.

No need to tell anymore. The Mayor and Board of Alderman became the laughing stock of town. Lim and Bubba got their share of the ragging, decided it best to get out of the lime light and took off on a fishing trip over to Stogner's Slash.

As you can imagine, things were messed up for quite awhile. Bubba missed a few days at work and the mayor, in a nice way, suggested it might be best if he gave up his job with the city. Bubba agreed and gave it up. Luckily, Morris needed help and gave Bubba his old job back at the station which did more business than ever, with people coming by to pick at Bubba and to see the person that could sell City Hall on digging up the entire park looking for buried treasure.

Stella was probably more upset than anybody else and gave Bubba back his ring telling him her father nearly had a heart attack when he heard about the fool thing he'd done. To make matters worse, her father found out Bubba lost his job and was back working at Morris' station. In no uncertain terms, he told Stella to keep Bubba away from his house and she could forget about marrying a nut that could make a fool of himself like Bubba had

Bubba took breaking up with Stella pretty hard and tried to drown his sorrows in whiskey. He almost let it get the best of him. It probably would have if Lim had not given him a talking to.

The talking came about one night when Bubba was out at Lim's and drank too much, forcing Lim to put him to bed. The next morning Bubba had a bad hangover and tried to get some black coffee down. Lim brought a bottle of whiskey in, poured Bubba a drink, saying, "Drink this. A drink is the best thing you can do for a hangover."

As Bubba forced the drink down, Lim tried to explain what Bubba had done wrong. "Bubba, drinking is all right as far as I'm concerned, and I'll probably drink it 'til the people say whiskey finally got old Lim. But Bubba, remember this, there's one thing about liquor; when you have to have it to hide your feelings or use it as a crutch or an excuse for something, you're done in. It's time to leave it alone. Drinking is something you do to enjoy yourself, not hide something."

The talking must have had the desired effect because Bubba straightened up. From that day on, there had to be a really special occasion to find that he'd drank too much. He would still drink a drink or two or even a few bottles of beer. It may have been losing Stella or his respect for Lim, but whatever it was; Bubba grew up a lot that day.

Chapter 4

Christmas came and things cooled down some. Most everyone had forgotten about the park incident. Even Stella and Bubba were back on pretty good terms and her father had agreed for her to go out with him as long as they didn't stay out past eleven o'clock and as long as Bubba didn't do any more fool things.

Bird season opened and Lim was spending most of his time hunting, which brought on another story that was quite amusing and it ties in with this story. Anyway, one morning Lim and a stranger came by Morris' station in a new Ford. Bubba didn't recognize Lim until he walked up to the car and asked if he could fill it up.

Spotting Lim he quickly smiled and said, "Why Lim, I didn't know it was you riding with this…" he started to say City Slicker then he changed it to "…gentleman in the sporty rig."

"Yeah, Bubba," Lim replied with a smile, "even old Lim gets to ride in one of these fancy four wheelers every now and then."

"You must be headed bird hunting with all them dogs," Bubba noted. "Old Lou and Jake don't know how to ride in a fancy vehicle like this."

"Thought we'd try a round. This is Mr. Brady White, a friend of mine from Memphis. He came down to show me his dogs and see if we could scrap up a mess of birds."

Bubba stuck his hand through the window and shook the man's hand. "Pleased to meet you. I'm Bubba Davidson." Bubba turned to Lim, "Those dogs of Mr. White's sure look like they can go. Reckon old Lou and Jake will find any birds?"

Lim smiled with a go to hell look and replied, "Mr. White said I might as well leave them home—said Old Lou and Jake won't find a single covey."

Bubba spoke to Mr. White as he handed him a five-dollar bill for the gas, "Those dogs of Lim's don't look all that fancy, Mr. White. They're so poor the

33

sun will shine through them, but they know how to find birds. Don't take no bets against them."

Mr. White laughed as he cranked the new Bronco. "We're gonna find out who has dogs and who doesn't. Lim will probably leave his dogs home this afternoon."

"Don't kill them all," Bubba said as the shiny truck sped out of the drive.

Bubba went inside and rang up the five dollars on the cash register saying to himself, 'That Mr. White seems like some kind of city slicker. He'll have to get up early to outdo Lim.' His thoughts continued as he walked back out to the front, 'That goes for his dogs, too. They'll be lucky if Jake and Lou let them find a bird.' He wiped the top of the regular pump. 'I'll have to give the dude credit for one thing, though. That sporty rig he has sure out-did Lim's old pickup.'

Bubba did not see Lim for the next couple of days and curiosity had him wondering how the hunt had turned out. Mr. White, being as cocky as he was, did not seem to set too well with Lim. Friday night Bubba got his answer when he and Stella were at the fish house and Lim came in and joined them.

Lim put a bottle in a brown paper bag on the table as he sat down and asked, "Stella, you and Bubba doing alright?"

"Best we can," Stella replied with a smile. "Lim, you know how it is keeping Bubba straight."

The waitress came up as Bubba started to defend himself, thought better of it, then placed his order. "Three orders of fish, couple of cokes and three glasses of ice, and bring Stella an extra onion."

Stella interrupted and said, "One of these days, I'm going to eat that onion."

Laughing Bubba asked Lim, "How'd them fancy dogs of Mr. White's stack up with Lou and Jake?"

"Hell Bubba, you know there ain't a dog in the county that can out hunt Lou and Jake. Those dogs of Brady's are good field trial dogs, but when it comes to putting birds in the sack, Lou and Jake could sit in the back of the truck and do as well."

"Tell me all about it. I've been pretty curious about how the hunt turned out. Mr. White was pretty cocky up at the station."

Stella poured the drinks and handed Lim his. "Bubba told me a little about it," she remarked. "He said Mr. White was ribbing you pretty good."

Lim laughed a little as he said, "Aw, Brady's all right. His biggest problem is he's got more money than he knows what to do with. Anyway, I've known

Brady for the last three or four years. Met him at Bailey's one night. I told him about bird hunting around Taylorsville and he's been hounding me ever since to come down. So this season I told him I'd take him. No telling what he paid for those two dogs. They're offspring of 'Memphis Joe' a past national field trial champion. In fact, both dogs have been written up in the major outdoor magazines and have won a number of field trials.

"Anyway, back to the hunt. Trouble started when Brady drove up to the house and let his dogs out. Old Jake took a dislikin' to his biggest dog named Sport. They fought all over the yard before I got out there and separated them. After that, he told me I should leave Jake and Lou at the house, his dogs would be all we needed. Well he started off wrong when he said that and I started to send him back to Memphis right then, but I passed it off saying that if I went bird hunting Jake and Lou were going with me. After we got that straight, we loaded the dogs in the back of his Bronco and Jake and Sport tied in again. I'd just gotten them settled down when we came by the station."

"Sounds like the day was shaping up pretty good," Bubba said as the waitress set their food down. "How'd they do when you got to hunting?"

"Oh, after we started hunting they did all right. After we got our first covey up, things settled down some. We hunted the ridge land over at Stogners across from the old Rogers house. Anyway, when we parked the Bronco and let the dogs out, those two dogs of his were almost out of sight before we got our guns loaded. They hunted that way most all day. Not knowing where his dogs were, we started hunting. We didn't get over a hundred yards from the truck when Lou and Jake pointed the first covey. Brady wanted to get his dogs in on the point so we waited 'til his dogs came in and honored the point. We walked the birds up, killed three on the rise, and then we really had a dogfight. Lou went out to retrieve one of the birds and Brady's other dog named Lady Sue tried to take the bird away from her. Well, Lou got upset and they got to fighting. Then old Jake and his dog Sport couldn't stand the excitement and got in the middle of the fight. You never saw such a fight. They were all over that lespedeza field."

"Hell, Lim, with all that fighting, you ever get any real bird hunting in?" Bubba asked laughingly.

"Yeah, after we got them separated, things went very well. His dogs hunted one way and Lou and Jake the other."

Stella laughed as she took a bite of her catfish. "What about the birds? Did his dogs find more than Lou and Jake?"

Lim grinned as he answered her. "Hell, Stella, like I told you at the start, ain't nobody's dogs can find more birds than Lou and Jake. We got points on ten or twelve coveys. His dogs may have pointed three of the ten coveys."

"You going to invite this Mr. White down next year?" Bubba asked.

Lim grinned and replied, "If I do, he ain't bringing those fighting dogs."

After the meal, Lim got up and picked up the half-full fifth. "If you don't need this with your courting, I'll take it with me."

"Bubba don't need anymore," Stella replied poking at Bubba. "I'll have enough trouble with him as it is."

"Hell Lim, all she wants to do is go park," Bubba said interrupting Stella, which solicited a dirty look.

"By the way," Lim said as he began to walk off, "I got some birds I'm going to cook up tomorrow night. Can you two come over and eat with me?"

"I'm sure Bubba can," Stella replied, "but I'm supposed to go to Memphis with Mama. I know I won't be back in time."

Getting up, Bubba said, "You mean you and Mr. White killed a mess of birds with those fighting dogs?"

"Yeah, Bubba, we even killed a good mess for him to take back to Memphis. Anyway, come on over, I've got something I want to talk to you about."

Chapter 5

After Jennie had cleaned up and left, Lim took the fifth of whiskey, a coke, and a couple of glasses to the living room telling Bubba to bring the bowl of ice.

Bubba set the bowl of ice by the whiskey on the coffee table. "Reckon I'll just have a coke. Want me to fix you a drink?" Bubba asked.

Lim nodded and Bubba fixed his drink. "Lim, you said you had something you wanted to tell me?" Bubba asked as he handed Lim the drink.

"Bubba," Lim said as he took the drink, "I know things didn't turn out too good on the deal down at the park, but you can't let stuff like that hang over you. So it turned out we were wrong. Do you know many people that ever succeed without having a few set backs or missed their bets on the first venture? Look at the people it pleased to see someone fail." He did not let Bubba say anything. "I bet you there's not one person in a thousand that hit it big that didn't have people laugh at him or think he was goofed up or knocked in the head. If the truth were explained, we found what we were looking for. Maybe it wasn't gold and silver, but it was buried treasure. That old black man wasn't lying either. He saw them bury the rails. It being dark, he thought it was the town loot. I did some checking on this up at the University in some Civil War records. The Yankees did bury the rails; took them out of the main line just north of town. At that time, the rails were probably more valuable to the Rebels than the loot the Yankees got away with. What I'm leading up to is what we did wasn't as bad as the town people put it on to be. The town was looted and a treasure was buried. It just so happened it was the railroad rails, not gold. There's always some people that's going to make a big to do or run down people that try, especially if it's something they'd like to do themselves but don't have guts enough. We tried and were wrong. So what? Think what it would have been if we'd found the town loot in place of the rails."

Bubba agreed with what Lim said, but was growing skeptical at what he suspected Lim was leading up to. "You done got something in your head and I don't know why, but I got a feeling it's going to be worse than City Park."

Lim refilled his glass trying to stall the conversation so he could work out how to say what he was thinking. He went over to the fireplace and punched the fire up. He turned back and looked Bubba straight in the eyes. "Bubba, like I say, stick with me and one day you'll be a rich man. You won't have to be greasy and dirty and work like a dog to make a living. Just use your brains. Most people work so hard they don't have time to make money."

Bubba drank his coke down, looked at Lim, then went in the kitchen and got another coke before he asked Lim what he was really up to, knowing all the time he shouldn't. "Lim, what are you on to? I know it's got to be something pretty far out or you wouldn't stall as long as you have."

Lim sat down after he'd lit his pipe and said, "Bubba, now hear me out. Might as well sit down."

Bubba sat down as Lim started the story. The expression on his face was doing the talking. "I guess you've heard all the gossip about the Appleton family?"

Bubba didn't answer. His blank expression did the answering.

Lim continued, "Well, there's been plenty of it and to me it doesn't make a damn what's been said, it's probably true anyway. Bubba, I don't know if you know it or not but at one time the Appleton family was about the richest people in this country and my no good great-grandpa was the kingpin of it all. Most everything he ever did was bad, selling slaves, stealing, lying, making whiskey, and doing most anything he could to beat people out of their money. He was no good from birth and I'll be the first to admit it. However, it seems everything he touched turned to money and he did leave a fortune in land and money to my grandpa Arthur, who was about as no good as his father, and was lazy on top of that. Then to make matters worse, when his son, my father to be, was sixteen years old, Grandpa Arthur up and sold everything except this house and a section of land lying north of here, took the money, which could have easily been a couple-hundred-thousand, and went up to Memphis, deserting his wife and son. He moved in one of the fanciest hotels that he could find and started living it up drinking whiskey, gambling, and running with loose women."

Hesitantly, Lim finished his drink and set it on the coffee table, picked his pipe up and re-lit it. "To make the story a little shorter, the fast living was more than old grandpa Arthur could take and it wasn't long before he passed. Well, they brought his body back here and buried him in the family plot up at Union where his father and mother were buried. That's when it was found that he didn't leave a will or note or anything saying what he did with the money he was suppose to have. My grandmother and father knew he couldn't have spent all the money, even a third of the money, so they went to work trying to find what he did with it. I guess you heard your part of the gossip. Anyway, all the banks in Memphis were checked and everywhere else, knowing he probably didn't have it in the bank, as he never did trust them. Plus he was too smart for that, knowing if his wife found out he had it in a bank she might have attached it or something. Anyway, not one penny of the money could be found, or anything that could give them a lead to where it was."

Bubba's curiosity was kindled. "What did he do with it?"

"It wasn't but one other possibility; he buried it and more than likely someplace around here. Someone came up with that idea because he kept making periodic visits to Taylorsville for something. Never came to see them, his wife and son, but they'd hear he'd been in town and figured he came home for more money."

Bubba interrupted again, "You mean to tell me he sold over ten thousand acres of land, mules, cows, farm equipment, and everything?"

"That's right, Bubba, and like I said, it could well have been over two hundred grand."

"Where in the hell could he have stashed that much money?" Bubba asked. "It must have been a suitcase full."

Lim smiled. He knew he had Bubba where he wanted him. "That's what I'm leading up to. My father looked for it most all his life. Then, when I got big enough, I helped him. We pulled up most every fence post on the Union plantation and dug up the whole foundation of the home that burned. We searched everywhere, even drained the stock pond. Never found nothing."

Lim hesitated before he went further, just looked at the simmering fire in the fireplace, then leaning back in his chair saying in a very casual way, "Bubba, I finally figured out where he hid the stuff."

Bubba came out of the chair, "Lim, if you know where it is, how come you ain't gone and got it?"

Calmly, like when he was looking over a poker hand Lim said, "That's where I need your help," he started to continue, letting what he said sink in.

Bubba butted in, "Lim, where in the hell did he bury it?" When he thought about what he had said, he quickly added, "I shouldn't have asked that."

"That's all right," Lim continued, "it's buried in Great-Grandpa Lim Appleton's grave."

Bubba sat back down, "You", hesitating…said in a low voice, "ain't planning on me and you digging up your great grandpa's grave?"

"That's right, Bubba. I've figured most every place I can think of and this is the most likely place he could have hid it. You know I don't bet 'less I'm pretty sure I'm gonna win. I'd almost bet all I've got it's buried in the cemetery. What better place could you find? Anyway, if it's there, I'll split it with you. Half of it'll be all I need for the rest of my life. I got a feeling you could put the other half to pretty good use. What do you say?"

Bubba sat for a minute, his mind running in all directions wanting to jump at the deal, yet deep in the back of his mind he tried to think of what could happen. Speaking slowly he questioned Lim, "What if we get caught or someone found out about it? I've heard that grave robbing is some kind of crime."

"Aw, Bubba you can't look at the dark side, you got to think you're gonna win to win. If you roll dice and think you're gonna crap out, you can bet you'll just about do it. By heritage, I own the cemetery and I'm the only heir to the money. We're not grave robbing, we're looking for something that belongs to me and we think it could be buried in the grave. We're not going to dig up my old great-grandpa's body only dig down a couple feet. No one will ever know. Besides, the only house close to the graveyard is a quarter mile. I know we go by the Benson's house going to the cemetery but I figured that out too. Tomorrow's Sunday and the Bensons' go to church every Sunday night. We'll wait till they've gone to church, then go in there, dig up the money and come out after they've come home from church and gone to bed. We can cover the grave back and the fresh dirt will just blend in with the cleaning me and Tobe's been doing at the cemetery the past few days."

Bubba poured some coke in his glass. "I've heard the Benson's own all the land around the old cemetery. I also heard that old man Benson is some kind of horse's butt. He won't let anyone hunt on his land and if he even sees a car on that road he wants to know who owns it and what business they got going back in there.

"Yea," Lim agreed, "he's a butt, yet that's a county road and old man Benson can't say a word about anybody traveling it. Plus, I guess I'm the only living heir to the cemetery and if he sees my truck, he'll think I got business back there. Get that thought out of your mind, him or his wife will never know we been back there."

The thought of all that money just laying somewhere overwhelmed Bubba. He visualized a suitcase full of tens, twenties and hundred dollar bills. He stood up, emptied his coke, went over and poured a small amount of bourbon in it. Holding it up to Lim, he said, "Something tells me I'm a fool, but fools got to have money too. Count me in. This is to the Appleton fortune, that me and you are gonna find."

Lim touched his glass, smiled and said, "Stick with me kid, and one day you're gonna be rich."

Bubba was a little light headed from the drink. He looked at the pendulum clock swaying back and forth and realized what time it was. "Hell, Lim," he blurted out in a startled voice, "it's twelve o'clock. We done got rich enough for one night." Reaching down and picking up the empty bottle, he poured a few dribbles in Lim's glass. "Besides that, we're out of whiskey."

Lim, a bit unsteady, pushed himself up from the oak rocker and said, "Bubba, reckon I did a bit too much celebrating. You all right to drive home?"

"Hell Lim", Bubba blurted, "thinking of all that money your old great-grandpa left, ain't no way I'll get drunk. You just get everything ready. We'll either find the money or your great-grandpa one, tomorrow night."

Lim walked to the door and turned on the porch lights. "I'll have the shovels, pick and lantern ready. Pick you up at a little after seven."

Everything worked as planned. It being Sunday, Bubba got to sleep late then go to church with his mother. Not seeing Stella at the morning worship, more than likely, she would go to Sunday night church with her mother. That would work out fine.

Lim picked Bubba up around seven-thirty. It was a windy, dark night, with a light misty rain falling. Passing the Benson's house, a light was burning, but it did not look like any cars were there.

"I told you they'd be at church," Lim said as he drove past. Pulling the pick up to a stop just south of the cemetery fence, Lim got out, went around, and was lighting the lantern when he noticed Bubba was still in the truck. Walking back and opening the truck door Lim said, "Something wrong, Bubba?"

"Yeah Lim," Bubba replied sheepishly, "I ain't never had a hankering to be around a cemetery, especially on a spooky night like this. Let's just go back to your house and have a drink and forget this."

"Aw Bubba, get out of there. There ain't nothing can bother you in a cemetery. Everybody here is dead except you and me."

Crawling out of the truck with the whiskey bottle in his hand, Bubba replied, "Yeah, that's what I was thinking."

Lim unlocked the gate and motioned with his arm at the dim outline of the cemetery. "Old Great-Grandpa must have spent a bundle on that fence. Look at those two-foot square brick gateposts with the decorative wrought iron gate and matching fence. Even the post got the fancy spear point design." Walking through the gate Lim stopped and waved his arm again "Bubba, see those graves, they're all Appletons. Old Limbrick was the first, then his wife Betsy Lou. Next was my Great-Aunt Elsia Appleton, Lim's sister who never married. Following her, my grandfather Arthur, then his wife, Grandmother Molly Bar." Waving his hand Lim continued, "Over there by the cedar tree is my father's grave, Arthur Jr. and next to him, of course, is my mother's grave, Katie Bell. She was the last to be buried."

Bubba looked at the misty outline of the battered tombstones and replied, "Lim, reckon one day you'll be buried here?"

With a chuckle Lim replied, "Yep, Bubba, guess I will. I got my grave site picked out over there by Mama's." He stopped a second, and then continued, "Old Limbrick was the Alpha, I'll be the Omega. Then, Bubba, you can lock the gate."

Bubba, looking greenish pale in the orange lantern light replied, "If you don't want to buy a new gate you better leave it open tonight. I just might decide to leave you here and if I do I'm going to be leaving in a hurry."

Lim held the lantern and led the way with Bubba so close he was breathing down his back. They cut across to the far side of the small cemetery plot to a large pointed grave marker. Lim stopped in front of the marker and held the lantern up so Bubba could see the tall pointed gravestone. It looked something like the Washington Monument, only smaller, around fifteen feet, give or take a foot either way.

Lim lowered the light down the marker, the yellow light reflecting the carved name and epitaph:

LIMBRICK L. APPLETON
Born June 2, 1801
Died March 4, 1880
He Lives In the Memory
Of His Fellow Man

Bubba read the faded eulogy. "Lim, from what you tell me about your great-grandpa, there could be mixed emotions about the memory he left."

Lim's face reflected the flickering lantern light, broke with a smile. "Reckon' old Great-Grandpa wrote that himself?"

Lim set the lantern next to the grave took the bottle from Bubba and downed a straight drink. "Bubba," he said as he turned and looked at the young man squarely, "I figure Grandpa Arthur buried the money a couple of feet deep, so start at the tombstone and dig back toward the foot marker. We'll find a box with the money in it somewhere in between. Sitting down by the lantern Lim continued, "After this night's over, your name will be in all the papers."

"I can see it now Bubba Davidson and Lim Appleton strike it rich and find long lost heritage."

Making a sweeping motion with his hand in the yellow lantern light, Lim continued the fantasy newspaper report. "Lost heritage, worth over a hundred thousand dollars, Davidson and Appleton, the same two people the City of Taylorsville made fun of a short time ago, have the last laugh. Yeah, Bubba, the next problem you'll have is figuring what you are going to do with your half of the money."

Bubba stuck the shovel in the ground a foot or so back from the tall marker, pressed it with his foot and dipped the shovel full out. "Being around a cemetery at night gives me the creeps enough, but digging makes me think something is going to jump out and grab me. If I die of fright I won't need the money."

Lim sat beside the grave holding the lantern and bottle, encouraging Bubba with each dip of the shovel. Bubba was steadily mumbling to himself and old man Appleton, "Lay still old man, I'm not going to bother you, lay still."

After digging for almost an hour, Lim had the whiskey bottle nearly empty and Bubba had dug down over waist deep, the full length of the grave.

All at once, things started happening. The ground gave way under Bubba and with a wild scream, Bubba fell through into the casket! The more he tried to get out, the more the casket caved in. In fact, by the time Lim could hold the lantern where he could see what was happening, Bubba had stomped old Limbrick Appleton's bones every way except the way he was laid.

To add to all the commotion going on down in the grave, right behind Lim a voice suddenly called out. "What you boys doing?" This scared Lim so bad he fell sprawling into the grave, lantern and all on top of Bubba, who was already half crazy. Bubba was so scared; he was just jumping up and down crushing what few bones were left of Lim's great-grandpa. You would think the devil himself had hold of his feet or was choking him. Lim knocked Bubba down in the crumbled casket, setting Bubba to screaming that much more.

The next thing that happened was a flashlight shining into the hole and a voice saying, "Lim, what in the hell are you doing?"

Lim, trying to get his wits straight, couldn't say anything for a moment. When he finally figured out it was Sheriff Tate, he said, "Cut that light out of my eyes, and get me out of this damn hole."

To add to the confusion, Deputy Hodge who had been slipping up on the far side shined his light from the other end of the grave saying, "Well, I'll declare. I ain't never seen nothing like this. Ain't them the funniest two birds you ever seen?"

The sarcasm stirred Lim up that much more. "Shut up and give me your hand!" Lim shouted.

Finally, the sheriff and deputy quit laughing long enough to get them out of the grave and promptly slapped handcuffs on them before they could stand up. This made Lim mad as a hemmed bobcat and he went for Sheriff Tate, almost knocking him into the grave. It took Bubba and Deputy Hodge both to pull Lim off the sheriff. No telling what would have happened if he hadn't been cuffed.

After a lot of arguing and pushing, they got Lim and Bubba to the sheriff's car and began putting them in the back seat. That's when they noticed the bright glow coming from the grave. No one knew what it was at first until Sheriff Tate hollered, "The damn grave's on fire."

"Get a shovel," Sheriff Tate called to the deputy. "That lantern must have set the remains on fire. We got to get it out!"

Well there is not much more to be said except the shovel was down in the grave too and by the time they got the fire out by throwing dirt with their hands, the biggest part of Great Grandpa Appleton had burned up.

It was noon the next day before old Kirk Wilson, Lim's lawyer and long time bird hunting and drinking partner, got them out of jail. This time Bubba knew what was coming. Stella threw a fit something awful, telling Bubba to never speak to her again. That, plus everybody ragging, kept Bubba and Lim pretty well hid out in the river bottom claiming to be fishing.

Lawyer Wilson tried to get the charges against Lim and Bubba changed to a misdemeanor. Sheriff Tate, who was upset with Lim for attacking him, would have no part of this and insisted he was going to press for criminal charges against Lim. The grave robbing was bad enough, but for the attack on him, he wanted Lim to serve some time.

This brought the Grand Jury into the picture and Lawyer Wilson did his best to get the charges dropped, however the sheriff put the pressure on again and the Grand Jury gave a true bill, the case would be tried.

Old Kirk, using his strategy, immediately started getting the trial delayed, hoping the delay would let the publicity die down. However, the delay more or less backfired. The story got in the newspapers and everyone was joking or making fun of the incident. Bubba and Lim got the brunt of the adverse publicity.

The judge set a new trial date. This time Lawyer Wilson didn't object and went out to Lim's and met with him and Bubba telling both as they sat in Lim's living room, "Boys, the trial's set for Tuesday, and Lim, I want you to forget about your weekly trip to Bailey's." Then looking at Bubba he said, "We don't have a lot of defense other than public sentiment and your past record," his eyes flashed from one to the other, "which is not to your best interest either." Getting up, he concluded with, "You boys could serve some time. I'm doing everything I can, but remember—no mess ups."

Lim acknowledged Kirk's advice. "Kirk, do all you can and if we lose it won't be your fault. Sheriff Tate is making a big thing out of this. He knows we weren't robbing no grave. He also knew we had no intentions of bothering old Limbrick's remains. The damn thing just caved in."

"I realize that and plan on bringing it out in the trial," Kirk answered. "Probably the worst part is you jumping the sheriff."

"Hell Kirk," Lim replied, "the old goat should have told me he was arresting me. I'd have gone with him and you and everyone else knows that. He just let his badge go to his head, and when he slapped the cuffs on, it made me mad as hell."

Kirk caught the part about the sheriff not advising they were under arrest. "We can probably use that to our advantage. Anything else you can think of, keep it in mind. We'll spend some time Monday going over everything."

Lim and Bubba followed Kirk out onto the porch and watched his car disappear up the crooked drive. "Look's like a good time to go fishing or have a drink," Lim said. "Let's start with the drink."

Naturally, Tuesday morning, with all the publicity, the courthouse was full. In fact, the judge had to threaten to clear the courtroom during the jury selection because the crowd was raising so much commotion. The prosecuting attorney was having a hard time finding people that Lim had not helped in one way or another, or that was not friends with Bubba. The jury was finally selected.

As the trial progressed, the whole thing became more of a joke. Especially when Lim was put on the stand and the prosecuting attorney started cross-examining him. It was during Lim's testimony that the court nearly broke up. The prosecuting attorney asked Lim if he wasn't ashamed and sorry about causing his poor old great-grandpa's remains to burn up and Lim told him he wasn't necessarily concerned about it. Then when the prosecuting attorney asked the question of why he was not concerned it almost put the audience in the aisles.

Lim replied, "I reckon' burning his bones didn't make that much difference. He's probably been burning in Hell since the day he died."

Even the judge had trouble holding his composure and called a recess.

Sure enough, the jury wasn't out over thirty minutes and came back with a guilty verdict, with a recommendation of leniency, which the judge must have already had in mind. He fined Lim three hundred dollars for the attack on the sheriff, which was not too bad, but the six months sentence he gave Lim and Bubba working at the city cemetery every Saturday, not only hurt Lim's feelings but the physical work surely wasn't to his liking.

After the trial, things settled down again. Bubba went back to work at Morris' Station and each Saturday he and Lim went to work at the cemetery cutting grass, cleaning around the grave markers with hoes, and when needed, helped dig graves. As time passed and they finished their sentences, most everyone had forgotten about the grave robbing. Everyone except Stella, who was back on speaking terms with Bubba, but that was about all.

Chapter 6

It was up in March, what people would call a cold day in March. It had been raining all day and the wind was out of the north. Lim pulled into Morris' station, wet and cold. His speech was a little blurred and his walk a little unsteady. You could tell he had had a drink or two.

Walking around the truck, Lim said, "Bubba, fill her up." Bubba asked Lim where he had been for the past few days. Lim said, "Bubba, that's what I need to talk to you about. Reckon you could come by when you get off?"

Bubba, not realizing what Lim was up to, said, "Sure, Lim. I get off about seven. I'll come by and have a drink. Ain't nothing else to do at night. Stella's still mad as a settin' hen."

Lim was ready for Bubba when he got there. He had a full fifth, two glasses, ice, and a chaser setting on the coffee table. Bubba had a couple of drinks before he questioned Lim. "What do you want to see me about?"

Lim sipped his drink. "Have a seat for a minute. This is gonna take a little time to explain."

Bubba sat down hesitantly, knowing all the time that he probably should go home. Lim was up to something and Bubba suddenly realized that he had messed up again.

Lim began. "What I'm gonna tell you about, happened back in the twenties and let me say this, I have been to the courthouse, newspaper office, and library and checked it out from A to Z. What I tell you happened and it's not just hearsay."

"I'm not saying my old great-grandpa Appleton's fortune was hearsay. I know it's buried someplace here, in or around Taylorsville. But right now, I'm at a loss as to where. I still believe it's in or close to that cemetery, but that's past. We goofed up and I'm admitting it. I just got a little over confident."

Bubba sat and looked at Lim, his eyes asking questions he knew more than likely he didn't want the answer to.

Lim continued, "What I'm fixing to tell you happened. I ran across the information while I was looking for clues of where the old goat may have hid the Appleton money. I found the story I'm going to tell you in an old newspaper. It was so interesting I started checking it out."

Bubba took a big swallow from his glass, and then asked, "Checked what out, Lim?"

"The story of the Stroader's Crossing train robbery. Here," handing Bubba his glass as he continued. "I guess you've heard about the robbery that was pulled off up north of Stroader's Crossing years ago. I've heard of it for years, most all the stories were different. But, I know it took place. Too many of the old natives know of it and passed their version of what happened down to their offspring."

Lim could tell from the blank expression on his face that Bubba had not heard the story. "Well it was in the fall of '24. Three men barricaded the tracks just above the crossing at Moody Creek Trestle, stopped the train and robbed the mail car of over ten thousand dollars in gold. During the robbery, there was a shoot-out and the train guards protecting the gold wounded one of the robbers but they got away on horseback just the same. The guards went after them as soon as they could get their horses off the train.

"In the testimony at the trial, the robbers came straight down the railroad to Stroader's Crossing, then headed west. The train guards captured them about four miles northwest of town at Peter Brown's Hill where they'd holed up in an old abandoned shack.

"One of the robbers was killed before they gave up and after the smoke cleared, they captured the other two, but one was badly wounded. The story was that they put them right here in the Taylorsville Jail, but they never found the ten thousand dollars in gold. The sheriff and everybody looked but couldn't find a trace of it. The only thing the two robbers would tell was that the loot was dropped during the get-away."

Bubba interrupted Lim. "What happened to the two fellas that were in jail?"

"Both were sent to the state penitentiary," Lim replied. "The one that was wounded died before he could finish his sentence. The other one served out his time. You might say, served his time. The last couple of years of his sentence were spent in the State Mental Hospital where he continued to stay after his release. He died a few years later. He was so sick he never was able to come back to Taylorsville. He had some kind of disease that affected his brain. I think it was syphilis."

Bubba left himself wide open with his next question. "Unless somebody found it, that gold's got to be somewhere between Moody Trestle and Peter Brown's Hill. That ain't over four or five miles. You got any ideas where it might be?"

Lim leaned back in his chair and finished his drink. He knew he had Bubba where he wanted him. "Bubba, I've studied the map of the area and even walked the route and I feel like I know the most likely place the robbers could have dropped it."

"Where in the hell could that be?" Bubba asked.

"In the old Stroader Well," Lim replied.

"Where in hell is the old Stroader Well?" Bubba asked looking confused.

Lim filled his glass with two fingers of bourbon and the rest of chaser. "You know where the old crossing is? It used to be a rail spur there. For years, there was an old water tank where the steam engines filled up their bunkers. Years ago there was a county road crossing there. It crossed the track and ran down the edge of the river bottom to the Union road, then crossed the river to Peter Brown's Hill. There's still signs of the old road bed in different places."

"I know where that road bed is," Bubba interrupted with a look of recognition. "I just didn't know it went all the way to Peter Brown's Hill."

"Yeah. It goes on down and crosses the Union road. There's some good bird hunting along the edge of the hills all the way to the Union road. The last time I hunted that route I found nine coveys. Some had thirty birds or more. The coveys looked like flights of black birds when they got up."

"I bet you killed a sack full," Bubba replied. "But you still haven't told me where the well or the old plantation house is."

Lim smiled that coy smile of his that usually ended in trouble. "I know, Bubba. I got off on hunting. Almost forgot what you asked me. Back in the Civil War days, the Stroader plantation house was located east of Stroader Crossing about a hundred yards or so. There's some big cedars still there. The well was located on the north side of the old plantation home. The Yankees burned the house in 1864, but for years people traveling that way used to stop at the well. It was still used on up into the early 1900's. It's hazy in my mind, but I remember it. It had a big-shingled roof cover and had two wood buckets. As you drew one up, the other went down. Seems like it was sixty or seventy feet deep. Anyway, I've been to it and it's still there. Honeysuckles and bushes have growed up so it's nearly covered over. I'm pretty sure it's caved in and people have thrown junk and stuff in it. But I got a feeling that down in the bottom of that old well is a rotten sack with ten thousand dollars in gold coins."

"Lim, that's some story," Bubba said rubbing his chin. "What you got in mind?"

Everything got quiet for a second or two, then Bubba added, "I can't stand no more foul ups. I just got Stella back to speaking to me and if we get into any more trouble I might as well forget about her."

"Ain't no way we can mess up," Lim replied. "Old man Hatfield inherited the remnants of the plantation where the well is. I'll get him to agree to let us look for the gold, if it makes you feel better. I'll get it in writing. Won't be no way to mess up."

Bubba didn't say anything for a minute or two as he tried to figure the pros and cons of what could happen. Filling his glass, he held it out to Lim. "I don't know how you keep coming up with these crazy ideas, but one of these days it's gonna work. I know I shouldn't but…we're going to hit one of these days. You can't keep going fishing and not catch something. Here's to the Stroader Well gold."

Lim touched Bubba's glass, and said, "Bubba stick with me. One of these days we gonna draw the right card and we're gonna drag the pot."

Business was slow down at Morris' Station and Morris agreed to let Bubba have a week off with the understanding it was without pay. Lim went to Mr. Hatfield and he signed an agreement to let them look for the train robbery gold with the understanding that he was to receive twenty percent of anything they found. Everything was set and working as planned.

On Monday morning, Lim, Bubba, and Mr. Hatfield went to look at the well. They found it without too much trouble. In fact, Mr. Hatfield led them right to it.

The well was located in a sweet gum thicket about fifty-yards off the old Stroader road. Mr. Hatfield had it fenced in with his pasture, but said as he crawled through, "If you want, you can put in a gap where you can drive out to the well."

There was an outline of old bricks that had probably served as a protection wall around the well opening.

"I remember the brick wall," Lim commented as he looked at the remnants of the old well top. "It was about four feet high and over to each side there were wooden post that seemed about a foot square that held up the wood shingled pavilion. The well pulley was bolted from a cross beam built into the roof and it had two buckets. I believe the buckets were wood and the rope was sea grass. Do you remember the well when it was still in use, Mr. Hatfield?"

"No, Lim. All traces of the old plantation home were gone when we inherited the place. I remember my grandmother telling stories of the plantation, but I don't remember anything ever being said about the old well. Anyway, Lim, you and Bubba go ahead, put your gap up, and cut what trees you need to clear out for your work area. You won't bother a thing. Just keep the gap up where my cows won't get out."

That afternoon Bubba and Lim brought their equipment and cleaned off a working area around the well, and set poles for an "A" frame. Tying a well pulley at the top of the "A" frame, they ran the jeep winch cable through the pulley and were ready to start.

The first day was spent pulling fence posts, brush and other junk out of the old well, killing a couple of snakes in the process. Things moved along pretty fast until they got to the dirt that had caved in and accumulated in the well. Lim worked the wench pulling the five-gallon buckets of dirt out which Bubba filled with a shovel at the bottom of the hole. This slowed them down considerably. However, the third day Bubba dug into the well curbing and hollering back up to Lim who was peeking over into the well.

"Lim, I hit a wood wall or something."

"That's probably a cypress curbing to hold the water bearing sand back. You're getting close to the bottom. Maybe four or five more feet and you'll be there," Lim called back.

This gave Bubba some encouragement and by dark, he was almost to the bottom of the well. Water had started to seep in. That's when his shovel made this metallic clank as it struck something. It being dark in the well, Bubba couldn't tell what he'd found. He emptied the shovel full of dirt in the bucket and called to Lim, "I'm coming up with the bucket. I found something."

The sun had gone down making it hard to see, so Lim took the bucket around in front of his jeep and turned the headlights on. Pouring the dirt out and going through it eagerly with his hands, Lim found a dirt-coated object. Holding it in front of the headlights Lim scraped the dirt away.

"Why it's a silver dinner knife," Lim muttered almost in disbelief. Then in the same breath, he let out a roar you could hear almost to Taylorsville.

Bubba didn't know what was happening. "Lim, what the hell's so great? That ain't no gold coins, just an old dinner knife."

Lim patted Bubba on the back. "Hell, I know that, but it couldn't be better. You realize what we've found?"

Bubba stared back at Lim with a blank expression. "I sure as hell do—an old dinner knife. What do you think we found?"

"Look Bubba," Lim replied excitedly, "this is a silver dinner knife. Think about what that means!"

Bubba tried to think but couldn't.

Lim began to explain. "Back during the Civil War, these rich Southerners knew the Yankees would loot their homes and take everything of value. So, naturally the people hid their valuables, and sometimes it was in wells." Reaching over in the back of the pickup for the fifth, he handed it to Bubba. "Here have a drink. Tomorrow we'll sure as hell hit it big. There's probably a bucket full of knives, forks, spoons, teapots, and candleholders in that well. Most everything you can imagine and all silver, with that train robbery gold mixed in for good measure."

Bubba couldn't sleep at all that night. All kinds of thoughts drifted through his mind. He even figured on buying a new pickup, getting married to Stella, buying a house, hell, he might even buy Morris' Station.

Finally, daylight came. He hurriedly gulped down his breakfast and was at Lim's before seven o'clock. By eight, they were back at the well. With each full bucket winched out, the visions of riches grew greater, but reaching the white water bearing sand late that afternoon, their dreams began to whither.

Sending the last bucket up, Bubba called to Lim, "I've reached the bottom of the curbing. Ain't nothing but water down here."

Lim leaned over into the well holding on to the cable. "You sure you're at the bottom?"

Bubba returned the call, "Reckon so. I've hit hard dirt below the sand and water's coming in so fast; I'll be swimming before long."

That's when the unexpected usually happened to these two, and this time was no exception. Lim, holding onto the cable, got over balanced and with a scream of terror tumbled into the well. He held onto the bucket as the winch let the cable unroll. Screaming at the top of his lungs, he sailed down the narrow passage. Just before reaching the bottom, squirming, kicking, and hollering, he let go of the bucket and came crashing down on top of Bubba, knocking him down into the waist deep water.

Bubba finally got out from under Lim and pushed himself up the side of the curbing. "Lim, what the hell happened?" he asked in disbelief.

Lim tried to straighten his mind out from the sudden downward excursion, hesitated for a minute, then said with a sheepish grin, "Thought I'd come down and have a look for myself."

Bubba didn't know how to take Lim's humor, replied, "Well, have a good look around then tell us how in hell we're gonna get out of here. That bucket is out of reach. You ever tried walking straight up?"

Lim fumbled around in his back pocket and pulled out a half-full pint of hooch. "Least we got a drink. Here, have one."

They tried everything they could think of to scale up to the cable but nothing worked. All the while, the water in the well kept getting deeper.

Finally, Bubba told Lim, "If the water keeps getting deeper, we can swim up to the bucket."

Looking up at the round hole sixty or seventy feet above, Lim said, "It's getting dark up there. Bubba, don't get your dander up. Someone will notice we haven't come in before long and will come look for us."

"I don't know who that'll be," Bubba replied sarcastically. "Mother probably thinks I'm staying over at your house and you ain't got no one expecting us in, except them hungry dogs."

"Well, don't get down," Lim answered. "We'll get out sooner or later."

Near midnight, Lim caught hold of Bubba's arm saying, "You hear that?"

Bubba, half-asleep and half-frozen, said, "Hear what?"

"I'm sure I heard a dog bark," Lim said. "Someone must be hunting coons or something." Then Lim let out a long and husky, "Help! Help!"

No one answered, so Lim called again. Well sure enough, the Sullivan Boys had just turned their dogs loose down at Moody Creek and the dogs had hit a cold trail leading toward Stroader's Crossing.

Ben Sullivan, carrying the lantern, walked in front of his brother Dave. Ben stopped. Dave Bumped into him and asked, "What is it?"

"I though I heard someone holler. Sounded way off, almost like in a well."

"Aw, you're hearing things. Call to old Bilbo and get him after that coon."

Ben let out a commanding yell, "Look him up, Bilbo."

Both Lim and Bubba heard Ben holler and both started yelling to the top of their lungs, "Help! Help!"

Dave caught hold of Ben's arm. "I heard it that time. It's down there close to the old Stroader Crossing."

The boys hurried on down toward the crossing, stopped and called. Lim and Bubba answered. Ben held the lantern up where they could see to get through the thick underbrush. "Over there to the right, somewhere, they still sound far off."

Breaking through the sweet gum thicket, the brothers came out almost on top of Lim's pickup. As the lantern light reflected the tail light on the pickup, Dave said, "Well, I'll be. That's Lim's old truck, ain't it? Reckon' he's got hurt or…," hesitating before he continued, "maybe hit that bottle too much and not able to drive?"

As Dave went around to the front of the truck, Lim hollered, "Down here, in the well."

The Sullivan boys trying to shine the lantern down in the well was something to see.

"That you Lim?" Ben called down the well.

"Yes, it's me. I'm down here in the well. Pull that cable out and lower the bucket. We're about to freeze down here in this water."

Dave was the bigger of the two and always full of hell, never missed a chance like this, "What you doing down there, Lim? Getting a drink of water?" Both boys giggled out loud like schoolgirls.

For a moment, Bubba thought Lim might decide to stay in the well. "You big beer bellied horse's butt. Lower that cable." That was close but not exactly what he said.

The Sullivan boys got the truck cranked and winched Bubba and Lim out of the well. Almost before the bucket stopped on the edge of the well, Lim jumped off and grabbed Dave by the collar and said, "If you tell a living soul about this, I'll break every bone in your body." The brothers laughed so much they were rolling on the ground.

What you're thinking is right. Lim had half a fifth of liquor in the truck and shortly it was gone and the empty bottle thrown into the well. You know the rest; before noon the next day, it was all over town about the Sullivan brothers finding Lim and Bubba in Stroader's well.

The news spread pretty fast and before night, Stella had heard about it too. Catching Bubba down at the station, she flew into him and let him know in no uncertain terms how he made a fool of himself and embarrassed her for the last time. Bubba thinking to himself, 'What the hell? They were almost rich and what happened, happened. No need to blame nobody. He ought to have known something was gonna mess up when he let Lim talk him into another wild goose chase.'

Bubba watched Stella get into her daddy's car and slam the door. As she drove off, he said to himself, 'Bubba, you're about the dumbest person in the whole world. You get out of one pot then jump right back into the fire!'

Bubba was confused as he went over and leaned his arms across the regular pump. 'I'm about as unlucky as a feist dog catching a bob cat. Ain't no way I'm going to get Stella back and to tell the truth, I can't blame her.'

He picked up the water bucket and carrying it into the station, thought, 'Well, it's closing time. I'll go out to Lim's and see what he's got to say. Least a drink may help. One thing's for sure, hot as Stella is, ain't no need to think about calling her'

Lim was sitting on the porch when Bubba drove up and he could tell just by looking at him that he was feeling pretty low. He put his arm across Bubba's shoulder and walked him into the house. "Bubba, things ain't all bad. Jennie's cooking a mess of spare ribs and cabbage. After a drink and a good meal, you'll feel better."

"Sure hope so," Bubba said mournfully. "Ain't nothing but bad happened in so long a time I'm beginning to feel that's all there is."

Lim tried to cheer Bubba up as he passed him a drink. "Bubba, things could be worse. We could be out of whiskey. You could lose your job. Hell, Jennie could quit and then we'd really be in a tight."

Jennie walked into the room and heard what Lim was saying. "And dats what I'm a fixing to do if you and Mr. Bubba don't get in that kitchen and eat them ribs."

"I see what you mean," Bubba replied laughing, which seemed to Lim to lighten the mood, or maybe it was the liquor.

Sitting in the living room after supper, sipping a drink, Bubba was still down. "Lim, does bad luck sometimes just follow a person?"

Lim thought for a spell, and then answered, "Bubba, old lady luck is a strange thing. You know if anyone's had his share of bad luck I have, but it seems like it's always darkest just before the dawn. Least it runs that way with me. Why, I remember one time in New Orleans, I was down and out and as broke as a busted mirror. Hell, I was so broke it looked like I was going to have to get a job. But then old lady luck came through. I pawned my watch for twenty dollars and before the night was over, I hit a lucky streak and pocketed better'n three hundred dollars. Yeah, Bubba, like I said, most of the time, it's the darkest just before the dawn."

Bubba finished his drink and got up to go home. "Lim, it's dark as a dungeon right now. If what you say is true, daylight has to be right around the corner."

Chapter 7

A few days later, Lim and Bubba were up at Stogner's Slash dunking crickets. They'd gotten there early and had a cooler full of bream by nine o'clock. It was a pretty, sunshiny day and Lim and Bubba had their boat anchored close to a big old cypress stump in the old Stogner run, more or less taking it easy and were about ready to go home.

Bubba pitched his line over next to the stump and it hardly hit the water before a bream popped his cork out of sight. Bubba pulled it in, took the hook out and dropped the fish in the icebox. Putting on a fresh cricket, he pitched it back over next to the stump.

"Look at that big hole in that stump," Bubba said casually.

"A good place for a big catfish to be laying up," Lim answered as he pulled in a hefty bream and pitched it in the cooler.

Bubba moved his line over to the side of the stump and commented as he snatched out a keeper, "Lim, you ever do any grabbling?"

Lim moved his line and replied, "Did a little bank grabbling when I was young. Caught some pretty good fish."

"I heard about grabbling all my life, but still don't understand how you catch fish with your hands."

Lim dropped another fish in the cooler. "Well, I guess most people don't, but the main thing about grabbling, whether it's in a hollow log, stump, or a hole under the bank, is hemming the fish up. Of course, about the only time you grabble is when the fish are laying their eggs and have to find secluded holes to protect their eggs. That's what the grabbler looks for and when he finds one of these holes, he'll block it off where the fish can't get out and his partner will ease around the stump, or log, or hole in the bank and see if there are any other holes where the fish can get out. If he finds one he'll stop it up with a sack or chunk or maybe his foot." Lim paused his instructions long enough to snatch out a spraying brim. "After you get all the holes stopped up, you run a stick or

56

cane in the hole and see if you can feel a fish. If one's in the log, he'll let you know pretty quick by slapping his tail at the stick or cane and come busting down to the front of the hole trying to get out. This is where the grabbler does his hand fishing by pinning him to the side of the hole, or man-handle him with his hands long enough to get a rope through his gills."

Bubba broke in with a laugh, "Hell, Lim, a big fish could bite a man's hand off, couldn't he?"

"Naw, they're not that bad. However, they can strip the hide off your arm and hand in a hurry. That's why most grabblers wear gloves and long sleeve shirts."

"What about snakes? Looks like they'd be in there with the fish."

"Well you do have to watch out for snakes, but most holes are under the water and snakes have to have air and can't stay in there too long. The place you have to watch for snakes are the holes or logs that protrude above the water and have air pockets. An old cottonmouth can hang out there and pop you."

"What about a big fish tied with a rope? Looks like he'd be pretty hard to handle."

"Yeah, they can get to be a little ornery, especially if he's big and you're in deep water. There's this story I've heard most of my life about an old commercial fisherman that grabbled by himself. He used a hay hook tied to his wrist. The story went that the old man didn't come home after he'd gone grabbling one day, so some friends went searching for him and found his boat but no signs of the man. Anyway, to make a long story short, a couple of weeks later another fisherman found his remains and the remains of a large catfish; a hay hook tied to the man's wrist was sunk in the side of the monstrous fish."

Bubba pulled in another brim and replied, "I can see why it take's a certain type of person to be a grabbler. I can also see why most of them drink whiskey. I'd have to get pretty drunk myself to get up enough nerve to even try it."

"Aw, it's not that bad, Bubba, once you get into it and catch a fish or two it gets to be exciting and lots of fun. Of course, it's hard work. A person has to be a good swimmer and in pretty good shape. It's not an old man's sport."

"What's the biggest you've ever caught, Lim?"

"Well, Bubba, the biggest fish we ever caught we never did weigh, but he was a whopper. I figured he could have gone over a hundred pounds."

"Damn, Lim!" Bubba exclaimed, "That must have been the biggest fish ever caught around here, or did you catch him around here?"

"Yeah, Bubba. We caught him not over a mile up the bottom where the old Stogner run takes off from the channel."

Bubba dropped another spraying bream in the cooler and asked, "How come you didn't weight the fish? One that big, I'd not only weight him, but I'd show him off for a week."

"It's quite a story, Bubba. We were bank grabbling—that's where you wade or swim up and down the river looking for holes under the riverbanks. Usually one man walks along the bank and carries the fish, cigarettes, whiskey, or whatever you don't want to get wet while the rest search the river. We used a mule for this. One man would ride or lead the mule keeping up with the grabblers."

Lim reached into the cooler, slipped the fifth out and took a hefty drink, chasing it down with coke. "Anyway, we found this fish up under a clay bank. The water wasn't all that deep, up under your arms maybe, but the fish was a good ten or twelve feet back under the bank. We knew it was a big fish by the way he shook the ground when we first punched him with the cane pole. The fish was so far under the bank no one wanted to dive back under there and try to manhandle him, so we decided to dig a hole down from the top of the bank and catch him. We called that dry landing a fish.

"There was a shovel back at the truck. You remember Miller Stone don't you, Bubba?"

"No", said Bubba shaking his head. "All this must have been before my day."

"Well, anyway, Miller rode the mule back to get the shovel while the rest of us drug logs and whatever we could find to stop the long slit under the bank where the fish couldn't get out. Miller got back about the time we got the hole stopped up, and then everybody crawled out on the bank and started sipping a little corn liquor while the digging took place. It wasn't long before we dug through into the watery, underground cave. This is when all hell broke loose. Miller and I eased off in the hole and that fish liked to have drowned us. He would have if he'd had more room. Finally, we wore him down and tied him with a plow line, and then we crawled out of the hole and dragged the monster out onto the bank. It took three of us to get him out. You never saw such a fish switching and flopping his tail. Looked like an alligator."

Bubba broke in as he dropped a bream into the cooler. "I bet you hit that corn then. I can't believe you didn't weigh it."

"Bubba, you'll understand when I finish the story. Anyway, me and Miller dragged the fish up the bank and started tying him on the mule. He was so big, we had his head tied to the saddle horn and his tail was still dragging the ground." Dropping a bream into the cooler, Lim continued with a smile, "That old mule got a bit fidgety when we tied the fish to the saddle. It kept looking around at the fish rolling his eyes and backing his ears like something wild. Then Miller took the corn whiskey jug around on the other side of the mule and started tying it to the saddle. That mule got as nervous as a mouse in a snake din and I guess that old fish must have known it or something; anyway, all of a sudden he switched his tail and slapped it up under the mule's belly. That old mule went crazy as a Betsy Bug, jumped sideways, knocked Miller down and took off running down a cotton middle. He ran the full length of the cotton field, and then turned off on a field road that forded the river. Running like hell, the mule hit the river, lost his footing and almost turned a flip in the river. Then, you're not going to believe this, but that fish took off swimming down the river dragging the mule."

Bubba sensed he was being told a fish story and interrupted Lim. "He what? You mean the fish was swimming down the river with the mule?"

"That's right, Bubba. You never heard such neighing and braying. He'd have drowned that mule if we hadn't got to him when we did."

Bubba was so worked up that he pulled his pole in and laid it in the boat. "What the hell did you do then? How'd you get the mule out?"

Lim replied with a sheepish grin, "That's the sad part. We saved the mule and the jug of corn liquor, but somehow in all the commotion the rope holding the fish came loose and the damn thing got away."

Bubba just sat there with his mouth open and a blank stare in his eyes. "He *what?*"

Lim reached into the cooler for the fifth and said, "That's the truth. I ain't putting you on. That fish swam off down the river pretty as you please."

Bubba didn't say anything, but just sat and looked at Lim for a long minute. "Lim, you are putting me on."

Lim finished his drink and chased it, replied with a big grin, "Bubba, you know I ain't never put you on."

Bubba turned around and put his line back next to the old cypress stump. "Yeah, you ain't never put me on where I can prove you did, nor where you can prove you didn't."

Lim dropped a bream into the cooler and laughingly said, "That's what makes a good poker player."

Shaking his head, Bubba threw his cricket back in front of the hole in the stump. "Well, Mister Poker Player, if you're not putting me on, tell me this, if there was a fish in this stump how in the hell would you catch him?"

Lim answered as he took a bream off his hook and dropped it into the cooler. "You could block off all the holes and go down through the top. It's sticking up about six feet or so. One person would have to block that hole in front. Then one man would take a rope and slide down from the top and just wrestle the fish 'til he got a rope tied through his mouth and out his gills. Wouldn't be a problem for a good grabbler."

Bubba pulled up anchor and paddled the boat over to the stump, looking at the two-foot hole, which was about a foot below the water line. How would you find out if a fish was in there?"

Lim pulled his line out and turning the pole around. "Take a stick or cane or something like this one and poke around in there 'til you punch the fish." All the time, he was working the big end of the cane pole down through the hole in the side of the stump.

Suddenly, the action started. Lim poked a fish. The fish made such a ruckus it almost busted that old cypress stump in two. In disbelief, Lim and Bubba looked at each other for a second not saying a word. The expression on their faces did all the talking that was needed.

Bubba started taking off his clothes. "Hell Lim, if that's a fish, he's as big as the one that swam off with your mule. Let's go in there and catch him. Come on, you're not putting me on now."

Lim was a little more reserved and collected. "Feels like one hell of a fish," he said as he eased the cane out of the stump. He pulled the half-full fifth out of the cooler and took a long pull "From the sounds he made, we might ought to go get help if we're gonna try to catch him."

Bubba got his clothes and shoes off and slipped out the end of the boat in his birthday suit. "Hell Lim, you stay in the boat if you want to, I'll catch the fish. We'll weigh this one."

Well, it's questionable if Bubba caught the fish or the fish caught Bubba. Anyway, Bubba waded over to the stump with the water up under his arms and started feeling around the sides. Sure enough, he found another hole on the backside and called to Lim, "What am I gonna do about this hole? It's about half the size of the other hole."

Lim pitched Bubba two boat cushions and said, "Here, stick them in the hole. If one don't stop it up, use both of them."

Bubba crammed both cushions into the hole and worked his way around to the big hole in front of the stump. "Ain't any more holes. What do I do now?"

Lim probably had an idea about what was going to happen next, told Bubba as he turned the bottle up and took a hefty swallow, "Slide your feet over in the stump and sit in the hole. You'll have him blocked off then."

Bubba did what Lim told him and slid his bare feet over in the hole, squeezing up against the stump. He'd no more than got set, when the fish grabbed him by the foot.

A dog caught in a steel trap can holler, but you couldn't have heard two dogs caught in traps if they'd been on the other side of the stump. Bubba screamed so loud, he would've drowned out anything. It was an awful, bloodcurdling scream. By then, that old fish had Bubba's foot swallowed half way up to his knee. He spun around and Bubba screamed again yanking his foot out of the fish's mouth, stripping the better part of the skin off as he did.

Bubba hugged the stump with his feet stuck up above the water. Inside the stump, sounding like something wild, let out another yell as that fish decided to come out of the stump and you know where he caught naked Bubba.

Lim had worked up to the front of the boat and caught hold of Bubba, trying to give him a little encouragement. "Hang in there, Bubba. He'll settle down in a minute. You just got him excited."

Well, Bubba had decided grabbling wasn't his way of fishing. "I'd get out of this damn hole if I could."

Lim had to get his kicks in. "Bubba, that fish ain't all that big. Run your hand in there and see if you can feel him."

"Hell Lim, I can't do anything but sit here and hold my feet up. You're the grabbler, get in here and stick your hand in that stump. You can feel him all you want. All I'm going to do is sit here and pray."

Lim took his shirt off and his wallet and watch out of his pants. He picked the anchor rope up and pitched the anchor over the top of the stump. It came down on the inside close to Bubba's feet.

"See if you can feel that anchor with your feet", Lim said.

"I feel it," Bubba said as he raised his feet up. "It's about a foot from the water."

Lim stood up on the end of the boat. "You stay put. I'm going to climb down on the inside. I'll show you how a grabbler catches a fish."

Lim worked his way up to the top of the stump, got one foot over the side, and started down. That's really when the action started. Somehow, Lim slipped and went tumbling down inside that stump hollering worse than Bubba. He landed on top of Bubba's feet and on top of the fish at the same time.

Bubba squalled something awful as that fish grabbed his foot again. Then Lim squalled like a panther as the fish let go of Bubba and grabbed his hand stripping the hide from the elbow down. You never hear such a commotion inside that stump. You'd think Lim had an alligator hemmed up in there or one had Lim.

Finally, Lim hollered, "Got my arm through his gills, work that rope down here where I can tie him."

You can guess how that worked out. Bubba hollered to Lim on the inside of the stump, "Hell, the boats done floated around on the other side of the stump. I can't reach the rope."

Things quieted down on the inside of the stump for a minute. Bubba got concerned and asked Lim, "What you doing? You all right?"

"I'm getting my belt off," Lim replied tightly. "I'm going to tie him with it." Then the commotion started again. Finally, between bubbling yells Lim hollered, "I've got him tied Bubba. You can lower your feet."

Hesitantly, Bubba lowered his feet slipping them across the fish's head. "My God, Lim, that fish's head is two feet across!"

Lim was about out of breath. "Quit measuring and get out of the hole. I'm going to hand you the belt and you pull him through."

Bubba didn't have to pull the fish through. He'd no more than wrapped the belt around his hand when that fish came out of the hole and started down the river taking Bubba with him.

Bubba screamed for Lim to get the boat as he held on to the belt. Both the fish and Bubba were fighting for their lives.

Lim grabbed the anchor rope and pulled himself up inside the stump. He hollered at Bubba trying to give him all the encouragement he could. "Hold on, Bubba! I'm coming! Hold on Bubba!"

Bubba answered from down the river, whenever he could get his head above the water. "Get the boat, Lim! Get the boat! This damn thing is going to drown me!"

Lim knew he needed to hurry, climbing out of the stump as quickly as he could. With a bloody scream, he went tumbling down the side of the stump, going almost to the bottom of the river when he hit the water. Snorting and blowing water, he came to the top and hollered to Bubba, who was going around the curve of the river.

"Hold on, Bubba, I'm coming! Hold on!"

It didn't take but a few seconds for Lim to get in the boat and start paddling down the river. He kept giving Bubba encouragement as he paddled.

"Hold on, Bubba, I'm coming! Hold on!"

Lim paddled for all he could, finally turning the bend. He could see Bubba bobbing up and down like a fishing cork. Lim maneuvered the boat so Bubba could finally get hold of the side of the boat. He didn't try to get Bubba or the fish into the boat, just paddled for the bank and jumped out in the water to help Bubba pull the sloshing and twisting monster out onto the bank. Both men fell on top of the fish to keep it from flopping back into the slough, about as exhausted as the fish.

After a couple of drinks, and lots of whooping and hollering, they got the fish tied in the boat and paddled down to Lim's truck.

With the boat loaded in the back of the truck and the fish in it, they headed out of Stogner's Slash, which was about a mile from the main road, laughing, bragging and enjoying the booze. They met this green pickup truck about half way to the main road.

"That's Carl," Lim said as the truck pulled over to let Lim pass. "I wonder what he's doing down here?"

"Being a game warden, I guess he's trying to catch someone breaking the law," was Bubba's answer.

A cold chill ran down Lim's back. "My god, that's probably going to be me and you!" In a whispering voice, he added out of the side of his mouth, "Grabbling season is over."

"It's a-what?" Bubba exclaimed.

Carl pulled his pickup alongside Lim's and stopped. "Lim what are you and Bubba doing down here?"

Lim worked the gear down in low and answered, "Been trying to catch a few bream. What brings you down to the Slash?"

"Heard the boys up close to Union been doing a little late season grabbling in the old run. Thought I'd check it out. You and Bubba hear or see anybody grabbling? The season's over, but there's still a few fish laying up. There's always a few people who can't abide by the law," Carl concluded.

Lim gave the pickup a little gas. "No Carl. Me and Bubba's the only one's fishing here today." Laughing he continued as he eased the truck around Carl. "I'm too old to grabble and Bubba's too afraid of snakes."

Bubba held his breath and finally let it out as Lim punched the truck up in second. "Hell Lim, I didn't know it was against the law to grabble. I didn't even know there was a season."

"There's one all right," Lim laughed, "and it closed the last of June. It's been so long since I grabbled I guess I didn't think about the season."

"Hell Lim," Bubba laughed, "from the way that fish grabbed my leg I don't know if I caught that old fish or if he caught me. Here, give me a shot of that stuff," Bubba said pointing to the bottle. "One thing's for sure, we ain't going to turn her loose."

I guess the bad part of the story was Bubba and Lim could not show the fish off. They thought about saying they caught it on a trotline, but with Bubba's foot and leg like it was who'd believe that? Add that to all the hide being stripped off Lim's hand, that wouldn't fit with the story either.

Tobe took some pictures of them with the fish and it weighed in on his cotton scales at 86 pounds.

Of course, Stella got her laughs in when she saw Bubba working at the station the next day, one shoe off and one shoe on. She did not comment about it, just laughed and drove off, as she and Bubba still were not speaking.

Finally a couple of weeks later, Carl, the Game Warden, put two and two together when he came by the station and saw the picture of Bubba with the big fish pinned on the station wall. "I knew you and Lim didn't look right when I met you coming out of Stogners that day. Came within a hair of looking in that boat," he said.

Of course Bubba didn't help relations with Carl any when he smiled and said, "It wouldn't have made any difference. We caught that fish on a bream hook. It was perfectly legal. We just used a two pound grasshopper for bait."

Chapter 8

The little town of Taylorsville was rather peaceful for the next couple of months. Nothing happened, except the town's motel almost burned. It happened kind of strange like, and fit in with everything else unusual happening in Taylorsville.

It started when Ruby Horton, who runs the beauty shop in back of her husband Ralph's Barber shop, got word that there was a new, snappy walking young chick in town making out with her husband. Not letting anyone know what she was doing, she set a trap to catch them. She told her husband that she was going shopping in Memphis on Wednesday afternoon, the day all the stores in Taylorsville closed at noon.

Everything must have worked out as planned. She got all dressed up like she was leaving town, then hid out, parking her car in an alley up the street but across from the motel the chick was staying in. Sure enough, about the middle of the afternoon, here comes Ralph driving up in front of the motel. He got out carrying a fifth in a brown paper sack and knocked on the door.

Ruby saw the girl when she let him in the room and decided to give them plenty of time to get whatever they were going to do going good, then drove down to the motel and parked right in front of the room. She jumped out of her car holding a 32 revolver, ran to the door and started kicking and yelling.

Ralph didn't answer the door soon enough for her, which made her that much madder, so she held the gun with both hands and put two shots through the door. No sooner had this happened, when the door flew open and out came the young filly dressed in nothing but her panties and a brassier with Ralph right behind, half loaded and half dressed. At least he had his pants on, but his coat, shirt and tie were bundled in his arms. He came out of the room so fast that he ran over Ruby knocking her to the ground. After a second or two, she regrouped and emptied the 32 as she sat on the sidewalk. Her aim wasn't too good. She never hit Ralph or the girl, but she did put a bullet through her car's gas tank. Naturally, all the shooting drew quite a crowd and in the commotion, someone lit a cigarette and dropped the match on the pavement. Of course, all hell broke loose and before the fire truck could get there, three cars had burned, plus a big part of the motel. No one was hurt except Ralph. He looked real bad by the time Ruby got through with him. The young lady, I understand, left town and no one has seen her since. Ralph didn't open his barber shop for over a week and when he did, he didn't look in the best of health. There's mixed opinions about whether the gossip hurt or helped his business. Anyway, it gave the town a new subject to talk about.

Taylorsville is like most small towns, I guess. There's always something new to talk about. Anyway, what happened at the motel took the talk off Bubba and Lim for a while. In fact, Bubba enjoyed being on the giving end in place of receiving and did his part of the gossiping and whispering like everybody else.

Lim just laughed it off. "If everybody got caught that was fooling around, probably the whole town would catch on fire."

Everything quieted down again for the next few months. It looked like Bubba and Stella were going to get back engaged and Lim was staying out of the lime light. That was until Lim worked out the big cockfight with the boys up at Bailey's. Lim told them he'd put the fight on if they could get enough roosters. As you would expect, with their connections, this was not a problem and some twenty or thirty fighting cocks plus "Pete" were engaged to fight.

Which reminds me, I never did tell you much about Lim's fighting cocks except that he raised them. Lim not only raised fighting cocks, but he had this one special rooster named Pete. Pete was as important to Lim as his bird dogs and as you know, his dogs were his most valuable possession. Pete was not only valuable to him as a pet, but he was known to have whipped most every rooster in Mississippi, Louisiana and Arkansas. Besides having a long pedigree and bloodline, Pete was a beautiful bird. Pete was a little bigger than a Bandy rooster, with brownish-red feathers streaked with bright red, white, and black. You've heard of being the "Cock of the Walk", well Pete was just that and somehow you might even suspect he knew it. Once you saw him, you'd never forget his beautiful markings.

The fight date was set for Saturday, two weeks away. The week before the fight, Lim got Bubba to help him build the fighting pen, which was about five feet high and twenty feet square, made of chicken wire. Strands of wire were strung across the trees to hang lanterns on and fixed bench seats were built around the pen. All this was located on the backside of Lim's twenty acres so there wouldn't be anybody nosing around that would let it leak out about them having a cockfight. Of course, cockfighting was strictly outlawed in Mississippi and Lim knew that. He also knew that nothing would suit Sheriff Tate more than to catch them and put the whole bunch in jail.

Lim decided he'd barbeque a small hog to kick the function off and that way the crowd for the cockfight would be less suspicious. With that idea, he decided to cook the hog over an open pit right there at the fighting arena.

Bubba and Tobe dug the pit about the size of a grave, but only a couple feet deep. They lined it across the top with steel reinforcing rods then stretched concrete wire across the top of the rods.

On Friday before the fight, Tobe and Lim started cooking the hog, and of course, any function Lim had any dealings with had plenty of spirits. It took most of the night and plenty of spirits, but by mid morning Saturday Lim and Tobe had the meat cooked, cut up and in iceboxes ready to serve. The guests were expected to start arriving about three that afternoon.

A worktable and bar was set up on one side of the fighting arena. Lim made a final inspection and told Tobe to start icing down the beer and pops. He was going to the house and take a bath and freshen up before his "guests" started arriving.

Bubba was in charge of parking the cars, which started arriving around three that afternoon. Most everyone had arrived by six when Lim and Tobe started serving the food, which consisted of baked beans, barbeque, and cabbage slaw.

Bubba didn't eat, but left as the guest started eating, telling Lim, "I'll see you around 8:30. I'm taking Stella up to Toney's to eat spaghetti. I told her you'd be needing me to help with the barbeque. Hopefully I'll be back in time to see Pete fight."

"How'd that set with her?" Lim asked flashing a stupid grin.

Bubba pulled a coke out of the iced tub and grinned, "She had a few questions along with some dangerous flashes of those green eyes, but she finally settled down."

Everything seemed to be working as planned. It was a good meal and Bubba took Stella home around eight then hurried out to Lim's, knowing the fights would have already begun. But with as many roosters as were fighting, he'd still get there in time to watch Pete take on the big named rooster the groups up at Bailey's were backing.

The area was rocking and feathers flying when Bubba arrived. Most everyone was liquored up and feeling no pain. Lim was in the wire fence area taking bets and spoke to Bubba as he stuck the bet money in a cigar box. "Glad you could make it Bubba. Hand me a drink off the table over there."

"When's Pete going to fight?" Bubba asked as he handed Lim the drink.

"Got two more fights, then the main event."

The presentations were made before each cockfight and the owners of the roosters would bring their birds to the ring, hold the cage up so everyone could see the bird, then tell or brag about the rooster. After that, everyone would place their bets. The owner handed the roosters in wire cages over the fence to Lim who was the referee. After placing the two cages on the ground, Lim would open the cage gates and the fight was on. Usually the fight lasted until one rooster killed the other, the winner put back in his cage the dead rooster put in the trash sack and the bets paid.

After the next two fights, Bubba worked his way around to the far side of the fenced off area. Lim told him to go get Pete out of the back of his truck and raised his hands to quiet the crowd. As the crowd quieted, he addressed them.

"Now we will have the main event. Will the owner of the bird called Whirl Wind Joe bring his bird and come to the arena and give us the history of his bird?"

A short fat man in a black shirt, open at the neck and exposing a gold chain that hung almost down to his belt with some sort of medallion sporting a large diamond in the center, pushed his way through the crowd. He looked like a gambler, most anyone could spot him walking down the street and know his kind of business. The man walked up in front of the wire enclosure smiling, exposing a number of gold teeth that matched his neck chain. He took the cage and held it up so the crowd could see the bird, then quietly said, "I got one thousand dollars I'm betting on this bird. I reckon' there ain't nothing else to say except he ain't never been whipped and he'll cut that scrawny bread fed rooster of Lim Appleton's to pieces before he can get out of his cage." All the time he talked, he was pointing toward Bubba who was holding up Pete's cage. The crowd laughed and roared as he handed the bird over the fence.

Bubba handed Pete over the fence to Lim, who made his speech from inside the fighting arena, holding the cage above his head.

"Well, old Pete may be bread fed, but he sure as hell never lost a fight," he paused as the crowd responded with laughter, "cause a fighting cock wouldn't be here if he lost a fight." Then he announced, "I fought a number of birds and Pete ain't no amateur. What you boys don't take of the thousand dollars, I'll cover." The crowd raised six-hundred dollars including Bubba's twenty and Lim covered the four-hundred.

Bubba watched Lim's face as he took Pete to the center of the pen. You could tell how much he cared for the bird by watching his eyes soften as he gently spoke to it. Bubba could have sworn he said, "Win this one Pete and you'll never have to fight again."

Pulling the cage door open, the two birds sprang forward and the crowd roared. The northern bird, a little younger, quicker and somewhat larger than Pete, knocked him into the side of his cage before Lim could move it out of the way. Pete's experience helped him dodged the two inch razor sharp spurs and sprang past his opponent, but the quicker northern bird managed to turn and rip a gash in Pete's side, stripping out a hand full of feathers. The two birds fought back and forth, feathers and blood flying, both showing signs of the other's long spurs. It appeared that Pete was becoming weary and the loss of blood was affecting his strength. The excited crowd didn't let up as the northern bird came in for the kill. Skill and Pete's experience paid off. Flapping his wings, he came up over the younger bird and caught him in the neck with his razor sharp spurs, almost decapitating Whirl Wind Joe. The dying bird flopped across the arena and finally fell over. The fight was over. Pete, weary and weak, flapped his wings in the victory salute, which the crowd acknowledged with a roar of approval.

Everybody was laughing and slapping each other on the back as Lim sorted out their winnings. Before Lim could give Bubba his, someone hollered, "The sheriff is here." Then over the noise of the crowd, Sheriff Tate hollered, "Everybody's under arrest." Lim being in the pen couldn't do anything but hand Bubba the money box over the fence and whisper, "Run"—which Bubba did along with everyone else. Bubba almost ran over Deputy Hodge who tried to tackle him, which would have been like a car-chasing dog actually catching a car. Bubba sidestepped him and let out for the river bottom. He must have run a mile before he stopped to get his breath.

It was dark and Bubba was running as if he was running for his life. The vines and bushes scratched him pretty bad and he fell into the creek which made him look like he'd been caught by a bear. Bubba finally came out at a crossroads and caught a ride that got him home around midnight. Unluckily for Bubba, his Mama was still up when he got home and he had some explaining to do. His mama must have asked a million questions. This was bad, but things got worse the next morning when Sheriff Tate came around with a warrant for his arrest and put him in jail with Lim and Lim's cock fighting cronies.

I guess it was best Sheriff Tate took everybody to the J.P. Court and fined them in place of going before the Judge, because he'd probably have given Lim and Bubba a jail sentence in place of the $155.00 fine. Lim paid Bubba's fine, which helped, but that wasn't the worst of it. Stella was one of the first to hear about Bubba being in jail and told him when he walked down the jail steps on the way to the J.P. Court that this was the last straw. She was through with him and never wanted to see him again

You would think nothing more could happen, but it did. The sheriff confiscated all the surviving gamecocks and to make matters worse, he said he was going to have them all killed and feed them to the prisoners.

Soon as Lim heard what the sheriff was going to do he went down and did everything he could to get Pete, even hired Kirk Wilson to try to legally stop the sheriff. Which delayed the thing, but that couldn't stop it. The sheriff was going through with his plans and he could legally do it. A couple days later word leaked out the sheriff had taken the birds out to his farm and one of his tenants, Bulla Morgan was going to kill and dress them for the sheriff.

Of course, this was supposed to be all secret, but Bubba found out about it when Bulla's husband let it slip down at the station. Bubba knew he'd have to work fast because if the sheriff took them out there one day, he'd probably have them dressed the next. Whatever he was going to do, he had to do it fast.

As soon as Bubba got off work at a little past nine, he went out to Jennie and Tobe's house. Lim was upset enough about Pete so Bubba decided it would be best not to tell him what he was up to. Anyway, Jennie was a close friend of Bubba's, the same as she was to Lim, so Bubba told her his plans.

"I don't know what Bulla will do, but I'll help," Jennie said. She immediately went to her back porch, got an apple crate then went to the chicken house and caught one of her largest pullets. Putting the bird in the apple crate, she told Bubba, "You take this up to the car. I'll go through the house and tell Tobe I'm going with you. He came in a few minutes ago. I been holding his supper fer him, just put it on the table when you drove up."

"I didn't know Tobe liked work that well," Bubba laughed. "You better keep an eye on him."

Jennie didn't answer Bubba, she just disappeared through the door. When she came back and got in Bubba's car, she started in. "Mr. Bubba, you know Tobe's too old to be messing around. I don't pay that no mind. I know he ain't gambling cause he ain't got no money. What he's sneaking around doing, I don't know, but whatever it is I got a feeling he's up to no good. He comes in late every night dirty as a hog. You'd think he been working in the field, but I know better than that, too. I don't know what he's up to. All I know is it ain't no good and he sho' ain't tellin'."

Bubba grinned as he shifted to second gear. "Maybe he's got a change of heart and got a job, going to make you a living."

"That ain't even funny, Mr. Bubba. Humph, he ain't never worked and he ain't gonna start now."

The sheriff's place was about four miles out in the country and as they rode, Bubba gave Jennie the forty dollars he'd gotten on the chicken fight, telling her to try for twenty but if she had to, go the full forty. The bird was worth more than that.

"Lawsey me," she said, "ain't no chicken worth forty dollars."

"It is to Lim," Bubba replied, which brought a thoughtful nod from Jennie.

It was past ten when Bubba and Jennie got to the farm and of course, Bulla was asleep. Luckily, her husband wasn't home yet. Bulla was scared to come to the door at first and kept asking. "Who is it? Who is it?" Finally, Jennie convinced her who she was and turning the outside light on, she opened the door. Bulla was dressed in a long baggy nightgown and her hair was tied with cloth strips. She asked Jennie, "What in the world is wrong? Is Sheriff Tate done caught Tobe?"

"Ain't nothing like that Bulla," Jennie replied, "me and Mr. Bubba need to talk to you."

Bulla acknowledged Bubba with a flash of her eyes and a nod. "What y'all want to talk about this time of the night? It must be awful important and it can't be no good. What you want to talk about?"

Bubba answered this time saying that it was important. "Bulla, we need to get one of the fighting roosters Sheriff Tate sent out here for you to kill and dress."

Bulla almost slammed the door in Bubba's face when he said that. "It ain't no way I'm going to mess with them cock chickens of Sheriff Tate's."

71

Jennie broke in, "Bulla, one of those fighting chickens belongs to Mr. Lim and what we want to do is swap you a pullet for Mr. Lim's chicken. Ain't no way the sheriff will know anything about it after it's dressed."

Bulla refused, saying, "If Sheriff Tate found out about this he'd sure as the devil put me in jail. If'n my man found out, he'd beat me half to death. Sorry Jennie, I can't do it."

Jennie tried offering her the twenty dollars telling her, "Here's twenty dollars. Ain't no way Sheriff Tate gonna find out about it. Take the money and buy yourself a new dress."

The twenty caught her eyes, but it took the forty dollars to convince her. Getting her coat on over her nightgown, she led Jennie out to the barn, all the while shaking her head and swearing that she was going to get caught. Bulla found Pete and swapped him for the pullet. Bubba heard her tell Jennie as she helped put the crate in the back seat of the car, "I'll have to ring all them chickens necks and start dressin' them before daylight to be sure Sheriff Tate don't get wise to what's goin' on. He comes out here a little ways after sun up and he's sure gonna be here early in the mornin'. He's been guardin' them chickens somethin' awful. First thang he does is count 'em soon as he gets here. Ain't no tellin' what he'd do if he knowed what's goin' on."

"Humph," said Jennie, "You dress and cut them chickens up and the sheriff or nobody else will know the difference."

Jennie gave her the forty dollars. "Bulla, you won't be sorry you helped out. You know Mr. Lim has helped us folks. He needs us to help him now."

"I knows that's right and that's why I'm doin' this," Bulla replied. "Forty dollars is a heap o' money, but if'n Sheriff Tate catches me, it'll take mosta dat to get me out of jail. What's left, if any, would go to pay my hospital bill if'n my husband finds out about it. What I's doing is fer Mr. Lim, and I knows I'm gonna get caught. Lawsey me! I wish you and Mr. Bubba had'a stayed home!"

It was near midnight when Bubba let Jennie out, offering her his last five dollars, which she refused, saying, "Didn't cost me nothing but a pullet." She wanted to do it for Mr. Lim.

"I bet Mr. Lim's going to have a fit when he sees that chicken," she replied beaming. "You gonna stop on the way out?"

"Sure am," said Bubba. "I'm headed for the Big House now."

Of course, Lim was asleep and Bubba kept knocking until he got Lim up. Lim came to the door in his BVDs and when he saw Bubba standing there with the apple crate under his arm he asked with a bewildered expression, "Bubba, what the devil you doing out this time of night? Are you in some kind of trouble?"

"Naw Lim, I brought you a present. Thought we might have a drink."

Lim looking at the apple crate then at Bubba, "You ain't drunk, are you Bubba?" Then in the same breath, yawning and scratching, he turned around and went into the living room saying, "Come on in."

Bubba sat the crate down in the middle of the living room. "Brought you something. Go ahead and open it."

Lim fumbled with the wire latch and finally got the crate open. "What you done caught, a coon or something? You sure you're not drunk?" Pulling the top back, Lim exploded, "My God, it's Pete! How in the hell did you do it?" Then saying as he picked Pete out of the crate, "We sure as hell gonna have a drink. Might even get drunk!"

Lim sat down and held Pete in his lap speaking to the bird as he gently stroked his shining feathers. "Pete, ain't going to be any more fighting for you. Like old Lim, you've had your day. Now I'm going to get you a flock of young hens and you can live the rest of your life like a rooster should."

Bubba returned from the kitchen with a fifth and two glasses of ice. "Lim, that's what I've been thinking you ought to do," he said as he set the bottle and glasses on the coffee table.

Lim took one of the glasses and answered Bubba with a grin, "I'm older than Pete, you know."

Chapter 9

I guess to this day, Sheriff Tate don't know what happened to Pete and the prisoners certainly enjoyed the pullet more than they would have a tough old rooster. Once again, it took a while after the cock-fighting incident for things to settle down. Except Stella, who always took a little longer. Lim was back to his usual self and if anything, he was more talkative and seemed happier.

A couple of weeks passed, then one afternoon Lim came driving into the station in a big hurry. He got out of his pick up and hurried up to where Bubba was standing. "Bubba, got to talk to you. It's real important."

Bubba didn't know what to expect, asked, "Want me to come over after work?"

But Lim pressed the point. "Ask Morris if you can ride down the road with me a minute. I really need to talk now."

Of course, Morris agreed and Bubba got in with Lim. They drove north out to the edge of town where Lim pulled over and parked. Bubba knew something pretty important had to have happened. Lim was acting strange, even for Lim.

"What is it?" Bubba asked showing genuine concern. "I ain't seen you this excited in awhile."

Lim didn't waste words; he went right to the point. "Bubba, I figured out where that silver knife we found in the well came from."

Bubba butted in, "You what?"

"Yes," Lim said with a big smile. "I don't know why you and I were so dumb, but the stuff's right there in the well."

Bubba couldn't believe what Lim was saying. "Lim, you been hitting that bottle this early in the day? We dug below the curbing to hard ground. Where in the hell do you think it could be? Ain't no way nothing is in that well."

"Bubba, you remember where we found the knife?"

Bubba thought that was a crazy question. Lim must be slipping or something, but he didn't reply.

"We found it about three feet or so down from the top of the well curbing on top of the debris that had fallen into the bottom of the well. That means it couldn't have been in the bottom of the well. It had to have come from up above. You said it looked like the well had caved in a few places."

Bubba immediately caught on to what Lim was saying. "You mean they may have hidden it in the walls of the well?"

"That's right, Bubba. Whoever hid it probably figured the Yankees would look in the bottom of the well, so they dug a hole in the well's wall and stuck the silver and valuables in the hole; filled it back with dirt and over a period of time it caved in taking the knife with it. Or it could have been dropped when they put the silver in the secret hiding place. All we got to do is lower someone in the well with a crow bar or sharp shooter and poke holes in the well wall 'til we find it."

Bubba knew who that someone would be, but what the heck, it sounded possible. "When do you want to go look?" he asked Lim. "I sure as hell can't get in any more trouble than I'm already in."

"How about Sunday?" Lim asked. "You'll be off and the "A" frame's still up. All we'll have to do is hook up the pulley. Shouldn't take that long."

Bubba thought for a minute. 'How the hell can we mess up doing this? Ain't no way.' Bubba looked at Lim and said, "Lim everything we do, one way or other we mess up. I've been calling Stella for days. She won't even come to the phone when I call. Hell, Lim, I want to go help but if I do, one way or the other something is going to happen."

"Aw, Stella will come around in a few days," Lim said knowingly. "She's just like most women. They get upset and then in a few days start realizing things weren't as bad as it first seemed to be. I bet you before the week is through she'll find a way to straighten things out between y'all. Love does strange things to people."

"Tell me about it," Bubba replied, then thought a long minute about what Lim had said. "Hell Lim, it sounds possible. All except Stella. Love don't effect her like it does most people. I'll be ready Sunday. Who knows this may be the one time something's really there. Things can't always be bad and what's the difference? Stella acts like she'll never get over this anyway."

They drove back to the station in silence. When Lim let Bubba out he said, "Bubba, it's always the darkest just before the dawn."

Smiling, Bubba answered as he got out of the truck, "Maybe the sun is going to shine this time. But right now, it's as dark as a coal cellar at midnight."

It was a little past eight o'clock Sunday morning when Lim picked Bubba up. As he drove, Lim's excitement rose and he was yakking away, however, Bubba was nursing a headache from Saturday night and couldn't get pepped up.

Lim handed Bubba the fifth and said, "Here Bubba, take a drag of this. You'll feel better."

Bubba choked the drink down. "I hope I don't fall off that cable. I'll die as sure as hell."

"Bubba, a'fore this day's over, you'll be the happiest person in Mississippi," Lim said as he turned off the road. "That hangover will be the least of your worries. Anyway, think of it this way, you'll be feeling better all day and I'm going to feel the same."

Lim lined the truck up to the "A" frame as Bubba uncovered the well. "Sure glad Mr. Hatfield put all these boards over the well," he said as Lim got out of the truck to help. "It would be some kind of mess if one of his old cows had fell in there."

Lim smiled and replied, "Yeah, Bubba that would have messed up the drinking water."

"But it might have broken my fall," Bubba replied trying to get into a better mood.

He pulled the cable out of the wench and looked down the hole. "What you going to have for me to sit on while I'm doing all the hole punching?"

"I already thought of that. I got you a board seat in the back of the truck. It's no recliner, but at least it'll support your behind."

"Got to be more comfortable than that bucket," Bubba said as he got the seat and fastened it to the cable. "Hand me that sharp shooter. If we're gonna find this stuff, we best be gettin' to it."

Lim handed Bubba the crowbar. "Use this at first. Start probing about every two feet all the way around the wall then I'll let you down a couple feet and you can do it again."

Bubba gently got onto the seat. "Don't mess up and let that wench get away from you. I'm not interested in taking an early morning bath."

Lim cranked the truck and came around to the front bumper. He eased the winch release off and Bubba slowly disappeared down the well shaft. "Holler when you want to start digging," Lim said.

It was almost noon and they had checked down over half way when Lim called down to Bubba, "I'm gonna pull you out. We'll open a can of pork and beans and sardines. Leave your crowbar stuck in the wall to mark where you stopped looking."

After eating lunch, Bubba felt better, but he still seemed down. Lim noticed Bubba's mood and questioned him. "Bubba, you've been quiet as a church mouse all day. What's wrong?"

Bubba didn't want to discuss his problems. "Ain't nothing. Just over did it last night."

Lim didn't go for such vague reply. "Look, Bubba, I practically raised you and I know when something is bugging you. Now what the hell happened last night?"

Bubba knew he might as well come out with it, because Lim was going to keep at him until he did. "It's Stella. You know she won't speak to me, that's not so bad. But what is bad, I found out she went out with one of them Sanders Boys' last night. I started to go over there and run him off, but then I decided it would probably make things worse."

"Then you decided to throw one on, huh?"

"Yeah, and I guess I must have over did it a little."

Feeling Bubba's pain, Lim replied, "I'm not the one to tell you about women. I had my part of heartache with them. Women are something else. They can love you to death one moment then tear your heart out the next. I know what's going on in your mind and I know it ain't easy to shake." He paused a minute trying to decide if he wanted to bring up painful memories of his own past, but if it'd help Bubba, why not? "I don't know if I ever told you about the girl I was supposed to marry?"

Bubba had never seen Lim get so serious. "I wondered why you never got married, but I figured it wasn't any of my business to ask."

Lim sat for a minute and looked off into space like he was reliving what he was thinking. "I know how you can get hurt. Some times, it can affect your whole life. I guess it can dig you deeper than anything else and make you do all kinds of fool things that'll haunt you the rest of your life."

Lim didn't say any more for a spell, he just sat there and puffed on his pipe, letting the smoke drift lazily up across his face. Bubba didn't know if he was through with what he was trying to tell him or if the memories were just too painful to go on.

"You were saying something about why you never did get married?" Then he wished he had let it go. He knew old memories hurt the most and Lim probably didn't want to talk about it.

Lim took his time answering and then as serious as Bubba had ever seen him, he told the story about his girl marrying the rich Delta boy and how it had caused him to quit school. He told him most everything except what happened in New Orleans. Bubba never thought he would see Lim so touched. He even thought he saw a tear in his eyes. When he got through, he looked at Bubba and said, "Bubba I guess I didn't realize you were old enough to be as serious as you are about Stella. I'm the one who's a fool. All I got to say is if you love her, get yourself straightened out, get a job and quit fooling around with the likes of me. Marry her before it's too late. I guess I'm too selfish or I'd already have told you. This time I'm serious. You better marry her if you can. If you don't, something *will* happen. You'll lose her and be kicking yourself like I am now."

He didn't say anything else. Bubba could tell there were lots of things being remembered just by the pained look on his face. He and Lim just sat there on the tailgate of the truck until Lim started knocking his pipe out on the jeep's bumper.

Getting up, Bubba said, "Lim, if we're gonna get rich before dark, we better get at it. Who knows, I may not have to get a job." For some reason Bubba felt better, as Lim lowered him down into the well.

It wasn't long after Lim lowered Bubba into the well that things began to happen. Bubba had worked down as far as he could reach and hollered for Lim to lower him down a couple of feet. Lim let off the wench and lowered Bubba down. He locked the wench and went over to look into the well.

Bubba adjusted himself, leaned forward and punched the dirt wall. The crowbar went all the way up to his hands making a clanking sound as it did. Bubba hollered up to Lim, "Lim, I hit something." Then not waiting for an answer he started punching the dirt away. The dirt came out easily fluffing off into the water at the bottom of the well. All of a sudden, a section caved off exposing a wood walled cave. Bubba sat there dangling on the end of the cable. He couldn't believe what he was seeing.

Lim hollered down, "What have you found? Bubba, answer me, what have you found?"

Bubba stuttered as he tried to answer. "Lim, Lim lower me a lantern. I swear before the Man upstairs, we done found it." Bubba let out a yell you could hear half way to Taylorsville.

Lim was so excited he couldn't get the lantern lit. Then, when he did get it lit, he almost dropped it into the well before tying it to the rope, all the time hollering down to Bubba, "I knew we'd do it. Old lady luck had to shine on us. Can you see? What does it look like?"

Bubba spun around on the cable. "Lower me a sack or something. We done struck a silver mine."

Lim lowered Bubba the sack and as Bubba pulled each piece out, Lim would holler down asking what it was. Bubba called back, "Everything you can imagine. A silver platter, coffee pot, knives, forks; hell, here is some stuff I don't even know what it is. Pull it up and look for yourself."

Lim hurriedly pulled the sack up asking as he did, "Is that all?"

"Lim, that ain't half of it," Bubba answered back excitedly. "This hole is as big as an out house."

Lim opened the sack and with shaking hands he talked to himself all the time he was taking things out and looking them over. "Lady luck, Lady luck." Then placing the silver in the back of the pickup, he let out a yell, "Bubba, you can't believe what's all here."

As soon as Lim emptied the sack, he lowered it back in the well. "Fill her up Bubba the sun's started shining."

For the next thirty minutes, half a dozen tow sacks full of the finest silver you ever saw was pulled out of that well. Bubba put the last of the glittering objects in the sack and called up to Lim, "Wind me up, Lim. I got all of it and open that fifth, we're going to celebrate."

Lim was so excited he almost let the winch go the wrong way dumping Bubba into the water at the bottom of the well. Finally getting it reversed, he reeled Bubba out. Hugging Bubba as he swung off the cable seat and almost shouting, he pulled him around to the back of the truck, "We did it! We did it! Ain't nothing but sun shining from now on."

Both men looked at the shining truckload of silver. Lim put his arm around Bubba's shoulders and said, "Bubba there must be as much silver as old King Solomon had."

Bubba looked at the gleaming treasure and let out a war whoop, grabbing Lim, both men danced around shouting like Indians doing a war dance. A couple of happier fools you never saw. But now, rich fools!

By the time the cable was unhooked, wound back in the wench, the empty fifth bottle was thrown into the well, and the second bottle was cut down pretty good before they got to Taylorsville.

The commotion of their arrival in town spread fast and before dark most everyone knew about the find. You'd think oil had been discovered or a flying saucer had landed.

The first stop was at Mr. Hatfield's who couldn't believe his eyes. He called his wife out to see the treasure. "Halma, come quick, Lim and Bubba have found a pickup load of treasure in that old well."

Halma handled the items and exclaimed, "There must be a fortune in silver here!"

Lim walked around the truck and said, "Mr. Hatfield, we're gonna be showing it off for a couple of days. We'll take good care of your part and get back with you later."

Mrs. Hatfield broke in, "You boys be careful with this. It's priceless."

Then Mr. Hatfield, not knowing how minds can change said, "Lim, I never thought you boys would find a thing. I sure am proud of you."

Lim and Bubba made their next stop at Bubba's house, showing the silver to his mother plus a large crowd that had gathered. Getting back in the truck, Lim drove straight to Stella's house. Bubba asking Lim, what in the hell he was doing as he drove up to her house and cut off the key.

"Bubba, if you're gonna get restarted with Stella, best you start right here at her house."

Bubba looking at Lim, not knowing what to say, blurted out, "I sure hope you know what I'm doing."

Hurrying to the front door, Bubba knocked and Stella's mother answered, "Why Bubba is something wrong?"

"No, Ma'am, Mrs. Ranking. Me and Lim found the Stroader treasure and I wanted to show it to Stella," he hesitated a moment, "and to you too."

Mrs. Ranking didn't say a word but pushed the door back and called, "Stella come quick. Bubba's here and they've found a buried treasure."

Lim certainly knew what he was doing, as both Stella and her mother came out to the truck. Seeing the truck bed covered with silver, Stella hugged Bubba and Lim both, exclaiming how proud she was for both of them.

By the time they got to Lim's house, people had gathered to look at the treasure and kept coming until well into the night. Lim and Bubba had to store the treasure in Lim's living room, but that didn't matter. People just came on in the house and stared in amazement. Finally clearing everybody out about midnight, Lim cut the lights out, took Bubba back to the kitchen, and fixed a sandwich.

Early the next morning, people were back at Lim's house again. Then the people from the newspapers came. Even a reporter from the big Memphis paper came down and took pictures of Lim and Bubba standing by their find. The mayor and most of the city's aldermen came. Everyone exclaiming this was about the biggest news Taylorsville's had in years.

Finally, up in the afternoon it seemed that everybody in town had been to look at the silver, when Sheriff Tate and Deputy Hodge drove up. Not wanting to be inhospitable, Lim invited them in to look at the treasure, but Sheriff Tate said, "Lim, I'm sorry. I didn't come out to look at the treasure." He hesitated as Lim stood there with his mouth open, "We came to pick it up."

"What do you mean pick it up?" Lim asked suspiciously.

"I mean Mr. Hatfield done had the treasure attached. So says the papers right here," which he handed to Lim. "It's not yours by an agreement signed by you. Your agreement time has expired, plus it also states you had an agreement for the train robbery gold. Nothing else was mentioned."

Lim took the paper and read it through. Sure enough, it referred to the contract Lim had signed with Mr. Hatfield, it was pertaining to the train robbery gold only, and it stated the contract was for thirty days. It didn't say anything about anything else they may find. There was nothing in the agreement that extended the time.

You talk about being taken aback, Lim and Bubba were about as low as a human could get as they watched the sheriff load the treasure and drive off. Of course, as soon as Sheriff Tate and Deputy Hodge left, Lim and Bubba went straight to Lawyer Wilson's house and told him the story, asking him to go to court and do anything he could to get it back.

I'll let you and Bubba know what we can do in a few days," Lawyer Wilson advised, "In the meantime, I'll request it be stored in the bank vault until we have a hearing. If it's stored in the jail, some of it's liable to come up missing."

Lim and Bubba, like two whipped dogs, went back to Lim's house. Lim invited Bubba to come inside; he said he wanted to show him something. Taking Bubba back to the kitchen, Lim opened the pantry door, took a water dipper hanging on the pantry wall and dipped the dipper full out of one of three churns covered with cheesecloth.

"Lim what the devil is this?" Bubba asked after tasting the contents.

"It's corn mash I'm going to run me off a little corn whiskey to put in the charred barrel over there in the corner." He pointed to a five-gallon wood keg standing by the door. Then before Bubba could say anything else he said, "Come over here to the sink. Let me show you something else." Opening the cabinet door, Lim pointed to a pressure cooker with a welded copper tube leading off the top. "That's my cooker. Gonna cook it off right here on the stove using the water from the sink for the condensation."

Bubba couldn't believe what he was seeing. Getting his wits finally, he said, "Lim, what in the hell are you gonna do next? You know you can be sent to the penitentiary for even owning a whiskey still, much less making whiskey."

Lim smiled as he replied, "Aw Bubba, just making some for my own use. It might be a little shady, but ain't like making it to sell."

"When you gonna run it off?" Bubba asked.

"It's about ready now. I figure in a couple of nights it'll be ready. It won't take all that long to run it off once I get it going."

Bubba, worried about the outcome of the silver, forgot about Lim's whiskey making. He talked Stella into going out to the fish house. Stella, for the first time, was on Bubba's side about the coming lawsuit telling Bubba, "That Mr. Hatfield is some mean person, doing like he has after how hard you and Lim worked to find the silver. Now acting like this. I can't believe he'd be that greedy." Then in a snuggling way, she asked Bubba if there was any way she could help.

Bubba reached over, gave her a peck on the end of her nose and replied, "Just don't get upset with me when I mess up. I don't want to ever have you mad at me again."

Stella reached over and kissed him as he drove. She replied, "I get mad at you because I love you so much."

Bubba though about that and said to himself, 'She sure must love me a lot.'

At least things were looking better. Stella's father agreed to let Bubba pick her up at her house. He even questioned him about the treasure when he came by to get Stella a couple of nights later. It was real progress for him to speak to Bubba, much less ask a question. There was one thing for sure; he was going to do everything he could to keep from messing up in the future.

Well that held true until after he had taken Stella home Saturday night and decided to stop by and visit Lim for a few minutes. He hadn't seen Lim in a couple of days. "He's bound to be wondering what's happened to me. Maybe he's got some news from Lawyer Wilson."

Bubba had forgotten about Lim's still and when he knocked on the door, he reckoned it was the first time he'd ever seen Lim ease the crack of the curtain back to see who it was before he opened the door.

Bubba went in a little confused at first. Lim acted a little nervous. "Bubba, you got here just in time. I just got through running off the first churn of mash."

Bubba suddenly remembered the still and thought to himself, 'Oh hell! What made me come out here?' He asked Lim, "Have you tried any of it?" He knew it wasn't much he could do now, but do the best he could.

Taking Bubba back to the kitchen, Lim handed him a glass saying, "Bubba, it's good with a grapefruit chaser. Go ahead. See what you think."

Pouring a moderate drink, and topping it out with some grapefruit juice, Bubba tried the brew. Adding more grapefruit juice, he commented, "Man, it's got a good taste, but it sure is hot."

"Yea, I know the first you run off is almost pure alcohol, but once I get it in the keg with the rest and age it a couple of months, it'll mellow out."

In the next few hours the second churn was run. Both did plenty of testing and were feeling pretty good. Laughing and joking, Bubba had forgotten any possibility of messing up. They'd just started on the last run, when it happened. Lim had gone over to turn the heat down on the cooker but didn't get there soon enough. The whole thing blew up with a big WHOOM! The kitchen was full of smoke, steam, and mash was everywhere.

The first thing Bubba remembered seeing when he finally picked himself up off the floor where he'd been knocked out of his chair was the top of the pressure cooker stuck in the ceiling.

Staggering across the room to Lim who was knocked down too, he tried to help him up. Lim was on his knees holding his hand over his eyes. "Lim, you all right?"

Pulling Lim's hand back, Bubba hesitated for a second, then said, "Boy, Lim you got a pretty ugly cut over your eye. Let me see how bad it is."

"We better take you down to Doc Cox and get a stitch put in it," Bubba said as he took Lim into the bathroom where he could wash the mash off.

"Hell Bubba," Lim said as he held a wet bath rag over his eye. "We can't go down there now. We got to clean this mess up and hide those jugs of whiskey. If nobody heard the noise when it exploded, they'll sure as hell smell it."

Lim was right about the smell. The place put out a strong, peculiar aroma that anyone living back in those days would know immediately.

Bubba gave in, "All right, you sit down in that chair and I'll go hide the liquor. Then I'm taking you to the doctor."

Lim sat down. "Get the shovel out of the hen house and dig a hole and bury it in the corner of Pete's pen."

Bubba took the two-gallon jugs, which was all that was left after the explosion, and went out the back door. Lim wrapped his head in a towel, found a mop and started trying to clean up some of the mess.

It wasn't long before Bubba got back. Lim had the remains of the still in a tub and handed it to Bubba. "Take this up to the pond and throw it in. If'n the sheriff comes nosing around he sure don't need to find this."

Bubba took the tub from Lim. "I thought I told you to stay put in that chair. I'll take care of this mess."

Bubba dumped the tub like Lim told him and returned to find that Lim was still bleeding like a stuck pig. "Come on," Bubba said as he took him by the arm, "This mess is cleaned up enough. We got to get you to Doc Cox's before you bleed to death. We'll finish it after we get back."

Since it was past two in the morning, Bubba had to almost beat the door down before Doc opened it. He came to the door dressed in a long flannel nightshirt, fumbling trying to get his glasses on as he opened the door. "Bubba, what you doing out this late?"

Bubba knew that the Doc had to have smelled the mash since it was all over his clothes. "It's Lim. We were cooking a stew and the pressure cooker blew up. It cut him pretty bad over the eye."

"From the smell of it, it wouldn't have been fit to eat," Doc said shaking his head, "bring him around to the office so I can get a good look at him."

Bubba went back to the truck, got Lim and helped him around to the doctor's little office on the side of his house. In a few minutes, Doc came through the house door that led into his office. He still had on his nightshirt, but had pulled on a pair of baggy pants. Half the nightshirt was tucked inside his pants with the rest hanging out. His hair was bushed out over his horn rim spectacles making him look like the mad professor in the Sunday morning comics. Doc looked at Lim as Bubba helped him sit on the examining stool; the old doctor smiled and said, "Lim, you and Bubba sure cooking late."

Lim smiled back and didn't miss a beat. "Yeah, Doc we got in kind of late." Knowing all the time that Doc knew what they had been doing.

Looking at the cut, Doc said, "Lim you're lucky. Another half-inch and it would've got your eye. Looks like it's going to take a few stitches, but it'll be all right. Going to have a scar, but at mine and your age it won't hurt your looks."

Lim laughed and replied, "Guess you're right Doc. No doubt I'm past the age of worrying about my looks."

Doc took a needle and told him to lie back on the table. He gave Lim a couple of shots around his eye, then got Bubba to hold the light so he could see better. The doctor skillfully put little stitches in the gaping cut. When he'd finished, he dabbed a little disinfectant over the stitches and put a piece of gauze and tape over the wound. "Bubba, did you eat any of the stew?"

Bubba flashed a wide grin, "No, sir, Doc, most of it blew all over the ceiling."

Laughing, the doctor replied, "Just thought if you did I might ought to doctor on you while you're here. Lim, that'll be five dollars."

Lim slipped Doc a five saying, "Sometimes a stew ain't worth cooking."

It was almost three in the morning when Lim and Bubba left Doc's office and walked back out to Lim's truck. The one person they didn't want or need to see right then was Sheriff Tate, and there he was parked behind Lim's truck.

"Saw your truck here at Doc's. Figure you must have had an accident or something, it being so late."

Lim tried not to get too close to the sheriff as he opened the truck door and got in. "Nothing wrong. Just had a stew pot blow up in my face. Took a couple of stitches to sew it up."

The sheriff came up to the truck window and shined his flashlight on Lim. Bubba knew this was going to make Lim mad. He held his breath hoping Lim would hold his temper.

"Look, Sheriff," Lim said, "I don't see no reason to shine that light in my face or in the truck either."

Sheriff Tate lowered the flashlight saying, "Cooking a stew you say?"

"That's right," Lim replied as he dropped the shifter down into first gear and pulled off. He turned to Bubba as he drove away, "One of these days I'm going to bust Sheriff Tate right in the face." He stopped talking long enough to change gears. "We better get Jennie and Tobe to help us clean up that mess tonight. You mark my words, the sheriff will be out to the house by daylight or before whichever, as soon as he can wake up Judge Webster and get a search warrant."

It was almost four in the morning when they got to Jennie and Tobe's. Jennie summed up the situation pretty quickly. She sighed and said, "Me and Tobe'll be on over in a few minutes."

Lim and Bubba drove home and started mopping by the time Jennie came in. "Lawsey, Mr. Lim, what done happened here?" Then she looked up at the ceiling. "What's that?" she asked looking about as confused as Bubba had ever seen her. She was used to Lim's peculiar ways, but even this was something else!

Lim poked the pressure cooker lid with the broom and it fell with a loud clanging noise at Jennie's feet. "Jennie, just making a little Christmas liquor and the damn pressure cooker blew up. Wouldn't been nothing to fret about, but I got cut over my eye. When we went down to get Doc Cox to sew it up, we ran into Sheriff Tate. I just figured he'd be here by daylight. I didn't want to give him anymore ideas than he already had."

"Lawd-hep', Mr. Lim. I don't know what I'm gonna do about you. Hand me that mop, and you and Mr. Bubba go and take a bath. You both smell like you done spoiled. I'll take them clothes over to my house and wash them."

It was daylight when Jennie and Tobe left and to look at it, you'd have to admit they'd done one heck of a job cleaning up that huge mess. That was when Sheriff Tate and Deputy Hodge drove up. Lim, expecting their visit, met them on the porch.

"Well Sheriff, what brings you out so early?" Lim asked eying the sheriff.

The sheriff handed Lim the search warrant saying, "Lim, you know I been around that stuff enough to smell it a mile away."

Lim opened the door and smiled defiantly at the sheriff. "Well, Sheriff, if you think you'll find anything, go right ahead and search."

By mid-morning, everything from the house to the old barn had been searched; all except the hen house and Pete's pen. Of course, they would have searched it, but when Sheriff Tate walked up to the pen and saw Pete walking around in the middle of his harem, he stopped and stared, then grunted toward Deputy Hodge, "That damn rooster has to be the one we confiscated at the rooster fight. How in the hell did he get back here? I'd know that rooster anywhere! Ain't no other rooster around here marked like him."

Deputy Hodge looked at the rooster scratching in the loose dirt in the corner of the pen. "Well, I'll be. It's the spitting image of the one we fed to the prisoners."

"Hell, I don't believe any chicken could be marked the same as that," Tate replied, then stomped around the house past Lim and Bubba without saying a word and went out the gate. He just got in his car and left, without looking at Lim or Bubba.

Lim watched the sheriff drive away. "Bubba, you know Sheriff Tate sure looked disappointed. Almost as if he found something he didn't want to."

For once Bubba and Lim got a break, even Stella didn't find out about the mishap. Stella did ask about the bandage over Lim's eye and Bubba explained it about as truthful as he could.

"Aw, Lim was cooking with his pressure cooker and got a little too involved with other things and the doggone thing blew up in his face. Almost got him in the eye," Bubba answered looking concerned.

When she saw the look on Bubba's face, Stella figured she knew the other things too. She just passed it off and nothing else was said about the whiskey making. As far as I know, Lim never asked Bubba where he buried the two jugs of liquor. All he knew was that it was buried somewhere in Pete's pen."

The next day, Lim went into town and bought Jennie a new pressure cooker. A couple of days later, he went to Memphis and bought two cases of whiskey. On his way home, he stopped by Morris' Station to talk to Bubba.

"Bubba, I've decided it's cheaper to buy the stuff than it is to make it. It'd be cheaper still if these hypocrites that drink it and then vote against legalizing it in the county would wake up."

Bubba gave Lim his change. "Guess you're right. Might help clean up the county, especially the roads where people throw their beer cans and empty bottles."

"Yea, Bubba," Lim replied, "if it was legal, you could go to the store and buy it, take it home, drink it and not be dubious about putting the bottles and cans in the garbage. Afraid someone will see them."

"That's right," Bubba replied laughing. "Except maybe them straight-laced deacons down at Brother Layton's church. They'd still be a little skittish about putting theirs in the garbage, even if it was legal."

As Lim started out the door Bubba added, "Old Whispering Willie would be about the only one it would hurt. But I guess he could put in a liquor store, if he wanted. He'd probably sell as much legal as he does bootlegging."

"You got that right," Lim replied and walked out the door.

Chapter 10

You'd think that Lim and Bubba caused all the Taylorsville talk. They did their part, but the Sullivan boys certainly were not angels. I guess in place of calling them *boys*, I should say *men* as Ben was thirty-eight and Dave was forty.

They were like two peas in a pod. Where you saw one the other was there or close by. Both were big men, six foot one or two and weighed in the two-hundred-thirty or forty-pound range. Both had brown hair, blue eyes, and as pleasant a smile as a sleeping kitten They were almost like twins, two big, happy, carefree boys that really never grew up. They wore the same type clothes, which was mostly overalls and denim shirts. Both wore an out of shape black felt hat and brogan work shoes. They ate like hogs and drank anything they could find that had alcohol in it. Neither had ever married; however, this didn't mean they hadn't done their part of womanizing, especially during the war. Both served in the Marine Corps and this was about the only time they were separated for very long.

Dave was two years older than his brother, and back in '42 was about to be drafted, so he joined the Marines and did a tough tour of duty in the South Pacific. He was wounded in the invasion of Guadalcanal and received a purple heart, ending his service time as quite a hero.

When Ben was eighteen, he volunteered for the Marines the same as Dave and served in the South Pacific. The war was about over when he volunteered and he didn't see as much fighting as his brother. However, he did get wounded. But, the truth finally came out that it was in a bar room fight. He got his ear almost bitten off. I'm sure he didn't get a purple heart.

After the war was over, they came back to Taylorsville. Dave came out as a Sergeant and Ben as a Corporal, both somewhat of heroes and moved back in with their parents, who were getting up in age. Both parents were still in pretty fair health, just too old to tend a farm and gave this responsibility to

Ben and Dave. Enjoying their hunting and fishing, they let the majority of the farm lay out. However, they did farm thirty or forty acres of corn and about the same amount of cotton each year. It was enough to make them a moderate income. The farm lay south of town with most of the cultivatable land between the creek bottom and town. The main highway to Taylorsville cut across one end of their largest field. Across the creek was the country club, the hospital, grammar school, hosiery factory, and ten or twelve houses, all part of town.

Well some things start small and just blow out of proportion. What I'm fixing to tell did just that, with chain reactions. Maybe whiskey caused it, I don't know. Some people say whiskey should be considered the root of all evil instead of money. If they were fighting over money, you can bet someone wanted to buy whiskey with it. Anyway, I'm sure it had a part in what happened.

To get on with the story of the Sullivan boys; there was this big white oak stump right in the turn row of their field next to the highway. It was five or six feet across the top and caused the boys some nagging troubles. Many cuss words were aimed at that stump. No telling how many plows had been busted on it or tires or radiators it had damaged. One Wednesday afternoon, the boys got caught up on their plowing and decided to get rid of the old white oak stump. First, the boys tried digging around it and pulling it out with their tractor, but the tractor couldn't budge it. Then it was decided the next best way was to blow it out with dynamite. With this new plan in mind, the brothers went down to the co-op to buy some dynamite. When the man at the co-op asked how many sticks they wanted, Dave didn't know how many sticks it would take.

"I guess a dozen will do," Dave replied scratching his head.

Back in those days, it wasn't a big deal if a farmer wanted to buy dynamite. So the man at the co-op let them have the twelve sticks, a couple feet of fuse and one dynamite cap along with some good advice. He explained to them to be careful because there was enough dynamite to blow up half of Taylorsville.

Reassuring the store manager that blowing the stump with dynamite was no big thing, the boys left the co-op and stopped at Whispering Willie's and bought a couple of pints of booze which was their first mistake, then headed back to town. By the time the brothers got to the field, one pint was empty and thrown out the pickup window and they'd started on the second. I guess both figured they'd need the booze to boost their nerves because neither had ever had any dealings with dynamite before.

Turning off the highway, Dave pulled down into the field and parked a short way from the stump. Getting out of the truck, Dave stuck the half gone pint in his overalls, then got an old truck axle out of the back and told Ben, "Come on, you bring the dynamite."

Well, both of the new dynamite experts worked around that old stump on their knees punching holes with the truck axle and sticking dynamite in the holes until they'd drunk the rest of the pint and run out of dynamite.

Dave attached the cap and fuse to the last stick and stuck it in the hole leaving about a foot of fuse sticking out, then asked Ben to give him his lighter.

Ben handed over his Zippo lighter and Dave flashed it a couple of times getting the flame started, lit the fuse, and both took off running. As I said to start with, sometimes things have chain reactions. At the same time that burning fuse disappeared down into the hole and got closer to the cap and the first stick of dynamite, old Doctor King was lining up a birdie putt on the third green next to the creek. He'd just country clubbed a shot up on the green that stopped an inch or two out of the leather, maybe two and a half feet from the hole. In case you don't know what country clubbing a shot is, it's a shot us older golfers use when we can't hit a golf ball far enough in the air to reach the green. We have to hit it short and let it bounce up on the green. No need to tell you, but this was a very expensive putt. Doc's group was playing scats (double on birdies) and six of them were playing. That putt was worth more than Doc got for pulling a tooth. At the exact same time Doc was pulling that putter back, Mabel Hughes who lived across the road from the Country Club was standing on a rickety kitchen chair getting a bowl off the top shelf of her pantry. Roosevelt Morgan was plowing his garden a hundred yards or so up the road from Mrs. Hughes house, with a stubborn old mule that he was having trouble getting to go. At the same time, the new city garbage truck was crossing Town Creek Bridge. Then all of a sudden there was a "WHOOO HUMMM!!!"

The Sullivan Boys got the stump out when the dynamite blew, but you never heard such a noise. Old Doc jerked at the sound just as he putted and that ball went across the green, out in the fairway, and almost to the spot he'd made his country club shot from.

Poor Mabel Hughes got the bowl all right, but she was straddle that chair as she brought it down and at the sound of the explosion she let the bowl go and it crashed onto the floor breaking into a million pieces. On top of that, she got an awful gash in a mighty embarrassing place.

"WHOOO HUMMM!!!," and Roosevelt Morgan's mule took off running and went through the garden fence taking the plow and a portion of the fence with him. It went around the corner of Roosevelt's house, the fence or plow one caught the front corner post of his porch and it took that post and three more down, then the whole porch came down. It closed the front of Roosevelt's house like a turtle snapping his shell shut.

The chain reaction continued.

When that stump came out of the ground, it really came out! It must have gone a hundred feet into the air. It went rolling, twisting right up through the telephone and electrical lines next to the road, and took most of the lines with it. You never heard such a hissing and popping in your life.

The stump turned and came down; you can guess where—right in the middle of that new garbage truck, mashing the big round garbage bed flat as a flitter. It scared the men driving the truck so bad that they let it get away and it came rolling down the bank where Ben and Dave were lying. If they hadn't gotten up and run like hell, it would have rolled right on top of them.

You'd think that after all this, the chain reaction would be over, but there's more. With the electricity knocked out, the people working down at the factory got paid for the rest of the day without having to do a thing. The school kids got to go home early. The mayor, who had been trying to get a call through to Washington all morning, got to say, "Hello, this is Mayor Henry…" And last, but certainly not least, young Doctor Walker, who had just started his new practice and was delivering a baby on his first maternity case, got to learn how to deliver a baby by flashlight.

Of course, there was some good to come from getting the stump out. It gave Lim and Bubba a gossipin' breather and Mr. and Mrs. Sullivan got the boys out on their own. Ben took off for Louisiana and got a job on an offshore oil rig. Dave ended up somewhere in Kentucky working for a construction company. The stump didn't break any more plow points and the hole where the stump had been gave the fish and frogs a new home.

Chapter 11

With all the different stories I've told about Taylorsville, you might think that it had more going on than most small towns. I challenge you to visit any town in Mississippi, large or small, spend a Saturday night at the police station or sheriff's office. You'll get your eyes opened. There is more happening than one can imagine; from some old lady losing her cat, to an alligator in the middle of the street, a stabbing down on the block, or a drunken brawl on Silk Stocking Row. You might hear about the preacher's daughter running away from home, or a seventy five year old man attempting to rape one of the patients in the nursing home. It would probably be a good idea if the police and sheriff departments invited the preachers, teachers, and town parents down every weekend to see what's going on in their supposedly peaceful town.

To add to all this confusion, during the period this story was written, integration had come to the Great State of Mississippi. The two separate school systems were being done away with. There'd be no more segregated restaurants, bus lines, public facilities, water fountains, or rest rooms. In fact everything public would be integrated.

Taylorsville was like most of the other towns. This was a big transition and there were some hard-core segregationists that said it wasn't going to happen in their town and didn't mind letting their feelings be known. Most of the true southern blacks were put on the spot They wanted all the new privileges, but didn't want to get the whites down on them. The plain truth was that the whites controlled the money and in their own way, took care of them. The blacks knew this and didn't want to lose the easy picking. Plus, everyone knew how mean some of those rednecks were. All in all, it put a strain on everyone.

To add fuel to this newly kindled fire, the Federal Government said that integration would be done immediately. To prove they meant business, when the schools of the South said, "We're not ready," the President of the United States sent thirty thousand soldiers to one of the major universities of the state to enroll a black student and said we *were*.

To the hard-core South, this was a slap in the face, was certainly uncalled for, and decided not to bow to the federal demands without a fight. Looking back, I bet it was like that in 1860 when the Federal Government and the Northern Abolitionist said the slaves should be freed. To prove the government meant business then, they were ready to fight a Civil War. One thing is for sure; when the Federal Government makes a stand, you had better get ready because something is fixing to happen.

Back in 1860, most southerners felt that slavery was wrong and even agreed that the slaves should be freed, but over a period of time. This was unacceptable to the North. The U.S. Congress said it would be done immediately and didn't care what trouble it caused, how many people it would break, or how many lives would be lost. This is how it was back then and the people of the South might as well get ready. Congress had spoken and was ready to make its stand.

I guess there are many reasons why the South took the stand it took against integration. Many important questions went unanswered in the 1860's; like how freeing the slaves immediately would affect jobs and the cost of labor or the money that would be lost. Everything in the South was geared to slavery. Many people had tremendous obligations and needed time to adjust. The only answer they got then was to do it immediately or else. They chose to take the, "or else," and the "or else" was the wrong decision. We've come a long way in the South, well, most of us have. More than likely, many of the same questions are being asked today.

Now again with integration, the South was offered the same alternatives— do it or else. Most of the people had the same feeling and knew it should be done, but this was a major transition being forced upon proud people. There was going to be many problems. Most everyone admitted that the black schools were inferior, and the arguments against integration fell short. It would lower the standards of education for quite awhile, but everyone knew it must be done. The morals were different. What would happen if the two races were suddenly thrown together? How would the social functions be held—school dances, parties, athletic programs? Then, there were the drastic differences in the housing and living standards. What would happen if a black moved next door, went to the same restaurant, same school, or same church? Finally, the major question in all their minds—would integration bring on interracial marriages? There were reports of this happening in some areas of the country and this literally scared some people. How would the people take this transition? Would it do away with the white and black race? Would we just have one blended race? The transition proved to be a tremendous challenge. It has taken years and will take years more. Time and patience are needed. The South asked for time and patience, but the liberal Congress and President turned them down. Maybe it's not like the Civil War, where hundreds of thousand of people were killed, but lives would be lost and everyone knew it. In the end, what those people that were pushing so hard didn't realize was that it didn't matter to the one person who lost his life if a thousand more had died for the cause. It was all he had.

Sure, there was a feeling among everyone of guilt and shame and that integration was a good thing, but it was like telling everyone they were going to have the same religion. Can you imagine how this would affect the Catholics, Jews and Protestants? It would take some working out and if the government said it was going to be done immediately, can you imagine what kind of war that would bring? Many people thought the same thing of integration. Customs and beliefs that had lasted for hundreds of years couldn't be changed overnight. Neither could two races as different in economical standards as their colors become equal in each other's eyes with the jot of a pen.

We had been working for equality since the Civil War, but it had been gradual. Now it was going to be done immediately. Where before, things had been almost totally segregated, now there would be black people working with white people. Black law enforcers, black officers in the regular army and there was talk of relocating people, same as bussing students to school, to equalize the number of people. This would certainly put blacks in political offices; already the blacks were playing on the professional baseball teams. Soon all sports would be integrated. Many were doubtful that integration could be accomplished. Now those doubts were changing, but still needed more time.

To make hard feelings worse, there were organizations on both sides, the hard-core integrationist were pushing for forced integration immediately. On the other side of the argument, there was a revived version of the white supremacist saying it ain't gonna happen. There were those of both races that had moved north and were used to the new way of living; it didn't help either side when they came south to "visit" and ended up causing trouble. As the saying goes, "There's one in every crowd." Taylorsville had one too.

Sylvester Morgan, Jennie and Tobe's nephew, was the one that came to Taylorsville. Sylvester lived in Chicago and each summer he came to visit

Auntie Jennie and Uncle Tobe. He usually stayed a month or more and each summer brought with him more of these liberal views. He made it a point never to say, "Yes, sir," and "No, sir," to his elders. He was always smiling and speaking to the white girls. He used the white restrooms and kept his teenage brothers stirred up.

The younger boys looked up to him. He owned his own car It was a 1950, four-door Mercury that he kept polished like new, decorated it with white sidewall tires and too much chrome for the mannerly folks of Taylorsville. It even had a foxtail tied to the radio antenna.

The car was a major problem and the way Sylvester flashed around in it not only got the law upset, it got Tobe, Jennie, and a number of the black in the community to shaking their heads. Everyone knew it was just a matter of time until something had to happen.

A confrontation was eminent between Sylvester, Tobe and Jennie, which happened one night at the supper table.

"Jennie, that boy is headed for some kind of trouble," Tobe said as he sat down at the dinner table.

"Yea, Tobe. You's right. I been doing a heap of worrying 'bout him. Is something new done happened you ain't told me 'bout?

"'Fraid so. This morning Sheriff Tate flagged me down and we had us a long talk."

"About Sylvester?" Jennie asked with a concerned look on her face. Having lived in the South she knew what could happen when the sheriff knew you and especially if he was down on you.

"Yep," he replied unevenly. "He said Sylvester was flashing around in dat car trying to stir up trouble with them young bucks he'd been hanging out with. He said they're no good and Sylvester's trying to be a big shot telling them about all the stuff that's going on in Chicago. He said if we don't get him to stop stirring up these people, or send him back home, he's going to put him in jail."

"Well," Jennie said, "I just heard a car drive up. That's him now coming home for supper. We better talk to him as soon as we get through eating. Sheriff Tate can be mean."

As Sylvester came in the back door, Jennie was all sweet. "Sylvester, we just sat down. Wash up and come eat. We gonna need to talk soon as supper's over."

Sylvester sat down at the table with a smirk on his face. "Is them white folks raising hell again? I ain't done no harm."

Jennie looked hard at Sylvester for a moment before she spoke. "Don't use that smart talk at this table. Sit down and eat. We'll talk after supper."

There wasn't much said during the meal. As soon as they were finished, Jennie started picking up the plates. Tobe pushed his plate over to Jennie then said, "Sylvester, I told you. You gonna have to remember you living in a different world to up North. Now you got Sheriff Tate all stirred up. This morning we had us a long talk and he said you been causing trouble all over town. What you gotta say about that?"

"I tell you what I got to say, Uncle Tobe. That Sheriff Tate is a black hating, mean old white man. I ain't done a thing to him or nobody else. Its just he's white and he's trying to give the black folks a hard time. He done run over you, Aunt Jennie, and all the black people so long, everybody thinks that's the way it's supposed to be. Well, it ain't, and I don't care if he be white or purple. None of us has to bow and scrape to no white man, and that goes for saying 'yes, sir' and 'no, sir' to 'em too."

Jennie butted in. "Boy, you don't even say 'yes, sir' and 'no sir' to me and Tobe and we's ain't white. It don't hurt nobody to be polite from time to time."

Sylvester got up from his chair and glowered over them. "You and Tobe just been living with them White Lords so long you both done forgot you got just as many rights as any of them. You don't have to ride in the back of no bus or drink at a different water fountain. I'm not, and I'm going to use the same restrooms, too. In Chi-town I don't, and I ain't here."

Tobe broke in, "Well, Sylvester, you better be getting yourself ready to go back to Chi-town. Jennie and I not planning on starting no trouble with the whites. We got us a home and we gets along with everybody in town. When time comes, things'll change. Right now, some things may not suit us, but there's plenty of things that do, and if you gonna live down here, you gonna live the way we do."

"You know, Uncle Tobe," Sylvester replied with a sneer, "if I was as white as you, I'd move to Chi-town. People wouldn't know if you had black blood or not."

Jennie butted in before Sylvester could complete what he was saying, "Boy, it don't make no difference about the color of the skin, the blood's all red. What you going to have to understand is there's good white folks and there's good black folks."

"Aunt Jennie, you call me 'boy' just like dem rednecks does. Can't you see that's what them white folks doing for you? You bow and scrap around old man Lim just like you his servant."

Jennie's temper began to show. "I'll 'boy' you and you better say Mr. Lim in place of 'Old Man Lim'. He ain't never done nothing to none of us but help us when we need him and you better not show him no disrespect if you knows what's good for you."

Well the talking did about as much good as pouring water on a ducks back, so Jennie decided she'd ask Lim to have a talk with Sylvester, which Lim did when Jennie brought him over to the Big House one day. Lim told him in no uncertain terms, it would be best if he went back up North before he got in bad trouble. He emphasized what he said by adding, "Sylvester, if you don't listen to Tobe and Jennie and go back home, one of these mornings someone is going to drag you out of the river with an anvil tied to your neck." The talking may have helped some and Sylvester seemed to have changed for a few days, but went right back to agitating.

I guess you would say Lim had some liberal views himself, but he was smart enough not to express them except maybe to Bubba, who he told one night when he'd hit the bottle a little hard.

"Bubba," he said, "in my opinion, this whole segregation mess has been wrong all the way back to slavery. As for my belief and I'm sure no one gives a hoot, the two school systems have been a fool's thing all the way. It hasn't done one thing but cost everybody money. Trying to hold on to separation of the races has made Mississippi the poorest and dumbest of all the forty-eight states. Far as I'm concerned, the preachers, good little ladies, and hypocrites, want the law to do the biggest part of their religious work and child raising. Such as keeping people from drinking, or husbands and wives from carousing, even trying to force children to respect the law and mind their parents. They want the law to do this when a stick on the child's behind and making the grownups pay for their sins would have done a whole lot more good. The answer is not sticking your head in the sand and making excuses, hoping it'll go away. You know I normally keep my thinking to myself, but we'd be better off with open saloons, legalized gambling, and cathouses—just let people run with who they want. They're going to anyway. Why pretend it's not happening when it is and let the law supervise it. Least you'd get a safe drink, fair roll of the dice, and have less chance of catching a disease."

Like I said, Lim kept his views to himself, Sylvester didn't. Instead, he kept things more on edge than it would have been with just the government interfering. With the situation being wound up as tight as it was and Sylvester not helping by shooting off his mouth every chance he got, there had to be an incident, and there was. Sylvester spoke to the wrong white girl, Tony Bartlow's sister. He even asked her to go out with him. She not only told Sylvester where he could go, but told her brother, who had the reputation around town of being no good. Tony gambled, drank, and stayed in trouble with the law. On top of everything else, he was a *real* redneck.

Just as soon as Tony's sister told him about Sylvester's propositioning her, Tony got his gun and a couple of cronies and started after Sylvester. The chase ended at Tobe and Jennie's place. The boy saw them coming and skipped out the back door, hightailing it over to Lim's house. By the time he got to Lim's, he was out of breath. He almost shook the door down before Lim could open it.

"Sylvester, what the hell's wrong?" Lim asked as he opened the door.

This time Sylvester used the right words. "Mr. Lim, Mr. Tony Bartlow's after me. He's got a gun and he's going to kill me, sure as the sun rises."

Lim was taken aback by Sylvester's appearance, he was genuinely scared. As Lim let him in the house, he asked Sylvester what he'd done to get Tony so mad. This wasn't any time for lying, so Sylvester told Lim what he'd done.

Lim looked at Sylvester in disgust. "I ought to take you out there and give you to them myself. I would if it weren't for Tobe and Jennie. You stay in the kitchen and I'll talk to Tony when he gets here. It'll give me time to make up my mind about what I'm going to do with you."

Sure enough, almost by the time Lim got to the front porch, Tony Bartlow was getting out of his car.

Not passing the time, he spoke to Lim, "Lim, I want that nigger. I know he came over here."

Lim didn't care much for Tony anyway and told him where he could go and to start the trip right then. He'd handle things in his house. "If you want the boy, go get the sheriff and do it legal. Don't come raising hell around my house."

Tony cussed and fumed a minute or two; all the while, he was pacing back and forth in front of the yard gate. When he saw that Lim meant business, he went back to his car, slammed the door, and spun gravel all over the yard as he left.

Lim went back into the kitchen where Sylvester was hiding behind the freezer and advised the young man to go to Jennie and Tobe's, get his clothes and not let sundown catch him in Taylorsville.

I guess to most people the warning Lim gave, along with Tony Bartlow's threat to kill him, would have sent most anyone running and hiding, but not Sylvester. He had a point to prove, so after things died down some he went right back to town carrying on as if nothing had happened. It doesn't take a genius to figure out what was going to happen next. Not long after this happened, Sylvester came up missing. A week or so later they found him; not in the river with an anvil tied to his neck, but in Stroader's well with a bullet through his head.

There's never a good time for something like this to happen and certainly, this was the worse thing that could have happened in Taylorsville. Both races were already crossed and on edge. Any spark, like Sylvester's murder, could very easily have caused a catastrophe.

Just when it looked like nothing else bad could happen—it did. Outsiders came...from both races and stirred up more trouble. A civil rights leader named Hazel Cat Jefferson brought in a group of professional troublemakers whose only job was to cause trouble. The first thing Hazel Cat did was call a meeting at one of the black churches, which got everyone attending in a bad mood, especially when he said they'd loose all their rights if the blacks didn't march and show the white's and the federal government that they meant business. The next thing, and by far the worst thing he did, was talking the blacks into boycotting the white businesses. This got into most everyone's pocket book and feelings really got strong.

What happened at the church leaked out. A white segregationist leader named Colonel Philip Trapp arrived from Louisiana and used the church propaganda, along with some choice reminders of reconstruction days, trying to rally the whites behind him. Most everyone knew he ranked high in a white supremacist organization. He wasn't the Grand Wizard or anything like that, but he was high enough to rally the strong segregationists of Taylorsville and succeeded in stirring up everyone else in town that wasn't all ready stirred up.

A few days later a black church burned. This brought the blacks out in force and Mayor Henry ordered a ten o'clock curfew put into effect. Every pickup truck had a gun rack, each full of guns and it wasn't because squirrel season had just opened either. After the church burned, the blacks retaliated by posting their men in front of boycotted businesses making sure everyone honored the boycott. Those that didn't were either beaten, their clothes were torn off, or their purchases, mostly groceries, were yanked from their arms and strewn across the streets.

A white-owned cafe with a big sign stating "Whites Only Allowed" mysteriously burned. Some people thought the owner had burned it for the insurance, as well as to fan the flames. Regardless of the circumstances, it happened, and the blacks got the credit.

The city had to do what it could to control the situation, but most everything it did seemed to stir things up more. Like closing the swimming pool, passing a no-marching ordinance unless the marchers had a permit. Even the public restroom had out of order signs on the doors. This may have caused more tension with both sides. A number of windows were broken and some shots were fired. More marches and meetings were held. The Federal Government decided it'd get in on the act and sent in the U.S. Marshals. The Marshals promptly let both sides know of their presence by posting signs in the Post Office and other public buildings saying that any racial disturbance was a Federal crime and violators were going to jail accompanied by Federal charges.

The Marshals and the curfew calmed the situation some, but the arrest of Tony Bartlow for the murder of Sylvester started everything again. This time the blacks were pleased and the white's were upset. The white protestors, led by Colonel Trapp, started causing trouble. A cross was burned and a black family's house was shot into. No one was arrested for the shooting, so Hazel Cat and his marchers hit the streets with a sit down demonstration and said that they were going to sit there until the Bartlow trial was over. The mayor and city officials tried to get them to change their protest location to the out skirts of town, but this didn't work. So the state sent in the highway patrol and broke up the sit-in with water hoses and a number of arrests. This pleased the whites to no end but only served to rile the black community. Things were beginning to get out of hand. More windows were broken, shots fired, another white business burned mysteriously. Things were getting worse everyday.

Lim had been pretty calm through the whole thing; claimed that he didn't have much to say either way. That was until the start of Tony's trial. He was subpoenaed by the prosecuting attorney to testify about his run-in with Tony, and of Sylvester coming to his house a few days before he was killed.

The subpoena wasn't so bad. What did get to Lim though was a number of anonymous calls telling him to keep his mouth shut or he'd be in trouble. This didn't set well with Lim at all. He not only testified against Bartlow, but laid it on pretty good, adding in the part about the anonymous calls.

The trial lasted the better part of a week. Tony Bartlow was convicted of murder and given life in prison. This should have ended the crisis, but some of the black community, those mostly influenced by Hazel Cat, thought the life sentence was too lenient. Hazel Cat claimed that the all white jury was prejudice and that Bartlow should have been given the death penalty. This started the marching and the boycotts again.

Colonel Trapp couldn't sit idly by, so he agitated the white's by starting a rumor that a black man in Chicago had confessed to killing Sylvester, so the Colonel and his followers demanded a retrial. Again, crosses were burned, bricks thrown, and shots were fired. However, a cross was burned in the wrong yard, or at least a number of people thought so. Regardless, a cross was burned in front of the Big House. This started a mystery that is unsolved to this very day. Who were the masked villains that sent everybody home; especially Hazel Cat and Colonel Trapp, who suddenly decided that Taylorsville could settle their own problems and it was best if the outsiders left while they could. The big question was; who was the masked hangmen that left both men standing naked under Moody Creek Bridge. One man on each side of the narrow creek, their hands tied behind their backs with a hangman's noose around each one's neck. The rope was drawn tight across the overhead bridge sills so that neither could sit down nor move. All Hazel Cat and the Colonel could do was stand there facing each other hoping the other didn't fall asleep or fall into the creek. The sheriff found them after receiving an anonymous call stating that it was possible the two men were having a set-tee under the bridge. Their testimony, and it was about all that was given before they left town, was that two men dressed in black had abducted them in their sleep and tried to hang them from under the bridge. In their testimony, both said their abductors wore stocking masks and had on gloves but you could tell both were white because they could see white skin above the gloves. Only one of the assassins talked, but his voice sounded like he was white.

Both men must have been pretty miserable after their night under the bridge. Whelp marks were all over their backsides from mosquito bites, and they were wet and about to freeze to death. Neither seemed to care to discuss anything that happened, except they both thought it best that they leave town.

A weak investigation of the abduction was made, but nothing became of it. Everyone seemed relieved, both whites and blacks, that Colonel Trapp and Hazel Cat were finally gone. Who were those men in black? Rumors leaked out that Lim and Tobe were the masked villains, but then again no one could prove anything.

Bubba got to thinking about what the sheriff said about both Hazel Cat and the old Colonel claiming the men that kidnapped them were white because both saw white wrists above the gloves, but that didn't mean much. If Tobe was one of them, they sure could have thought he was white.

Bubba confronted Lim about the fact that he and Tobe had come by the station pretty late the night of the hanging. Lim laughed and said that he and Tobe had been fishing over on Stogners and were just a little late gettin' in.

"Bubba, if you think me and Tobe had any connection with the Moody Bridge incident, well that's foolish thinking. I think ole Colonel Trapp and Hazel Cat must have figured it was about time to leave, and put that hangin' on themselves where they'd have an excuse to get out of town. Both could have been in cahoots all along, had some kind of money making scheme."

That answer set pretty well with Bubba until he got to thinking after Lim had driven off. He just couldn't figure out how in hell the ole Colonel and Hazel Cat could've tied their own hands behind their backs? Plus, Lim ain't never been fishing with Tobe that he could remember, and there sure as hell wasn't a fishing pole or a boat in the back of Lim's old truck that night.

Wiping his hands with a dirty grease rag, Bubba watched Lim's truck disappear up the street and grinned as he thought, 'That Lim's a hell of a person. I guess he'd tell me if he wanted me to know. 'Til then, guess what I know and think is nobody's business.'

Chapter 12

The courts sent Tony Bartlow off to prison. Everyone went home and Taylorsville got back to normal, as much as it could with the integration situation. The big talk around town and in the newspapers was the upcoming trial between Bubba and Lim, and Mr. Hatfield. Everyone had a take on how the courts would decide on the silver treasure. The publicity of the trial and about how Lim and Bubba had originally found the treasure brought on the next incident, and it could have hurt Bubba and Lim's friendship.

Lim's old flame, the one Lim told Bubba about and was so much in love with back in his college days, read about Lim's good fortune in the newspaper. A widow now, she decided to write Lim a letter expressing happiness over his good fortune and to wish him luck in the upcoming trial.

Bubba had gone out to see Lim after he got off work, and both were sitting in the living room talking about the trial when Bubba noticed a letter lying on the coffee table. He picked it up, not thinking anything about meddling or anything else, and read the name, Barbara Tanner, Clarksdale, Mississippi. Still not realizing its importance, Bubba remarked to Lim, "See you got some fan mail."

Lim turned blood red. He didn't say anything for a minute, then realized that Bubba didn't grasp its importance. He replied in a voice Bubba later realized was much more serious than it sounded. "Yeah, Bubba. It's from my old girlfriend; the one I told you about. Sort of brought back old memories."

Bubba could tell by the look on his face that Lim was still living the hurt of the past. He wished to hell that he'd left the letter lying there and never picked it up. However, after putting his foot in his mouth he felt he had to say something to maybe smooth things over. "I bet you were glad to hear from her after all these years. You're gonna write her back, aren't you?" Bubba asked.

Lim didn't reply, he just reached over and picked up the bottle and replenished his drink. Bubba felt like he'd been left dangling, so he blurted out, really sticking his foot in his mouth this time, "Hell Lim, you've been bleeding your heart all your life over her. She's got to be divorced or some other way unattached. One thing's for sure, she must still be in love with you or she wouldn't have written."

Bubba could tell from the hurt look in Lim's eyes that he'd probably do anything to rekindle that love affair which had once burned so intensely. But knowing that Lim would never write her back, said, "I'm sorry, I opened my big mouth. I should have minded my own business."

"It's okay Bubba," Lim replied smiling at his young friend. He changed the subject of their conversation to the trial, which was okay with Bubba, and they talked about that for the next hour or so.

Over the next few days, the letter kept coming back to Bubba's mind, and knowing Lim was so proud he'd never do anything about it no matter how bad it hurt. Bubba decided he'd do something, so he wrote a letter to Mrs. Tanner. I guess he laid it on a little too much and after it was done, Bubba knew he'd messed up the minute he put it in the post office. But it was too late then. Wasn't nothing to do but wait.

Nothing came of the letter until the week of the trial then Bubba got his answer. Lim came driving into the station a little too fast. Bubba as usual, came out in a friendly way and greeted him. Lim didn't return the greeting, just said, "Get in Bubba, I want to talk to you."

Bubba knew from the tone of his voice, and the look in his eyes he was mad about something. He'd never seen Lim quite so upset. Bubba didn't ask Morris if he could leave or anything, just got in and Lim drove off to the side of the station and stopped where no one could hear. Then he lit in on Bubba.

"Just who in the hell do you think you are?" Before Bubba could answer, he continued, "When you wrote that letter to Barbara, what in the hell did you say?" Still not giving Bubba a chance to speak, he went on in his anger. "You didn't have any business doing what you did and now you've got a mess started." He cranked up the pick up, "Ain't no need to have a friend if you can't trust him."

Bubba got out of the truck trying to explain, but Lim would not pay him any mind and drove off.

Bubba was so hurt and upset that Morris told him to go on home, he had to be sick or something. Bubba did, but didn't stay but a short while. He had to talk to someone, so he went over to Stella's and told her what he had done and how he had lost the closest friend he'd ever had. Explaining that he was just trying to do what he thought was right because he knew Lim had never gotten her out of his mind and undoubtedly, Mrs. Tanner still cared for Lim.

Stella didn't agree with Bubba that he'd done the right thing about answering the letter, but she did say, "At least both know the other still remembers. I can't see why Lim would get so upset."

Bubba went home feeling a little better, but still feeling mighty low. He told Stella he'd pick her up later and they would go out to the fish house and eat. He had no more than gotten out of sight, when Stella got in her father's car and drove out to Lim's. Lim saw her drive up and came out onto the porch, saying as Stella reached the steps, "Why Stella, what brings you to my humble abode?"

Stella, never one to waste words when she was upset, told Lim before he could even invite her in, "Lim, I came out here because of the way you treated Bubba. You ought to be ashamed of what you've said to him. I have never seen him so hurt in my life and all he was trying to do was help."

Lim tried to say something, but all he could get out was, "Wait a…"

Then Stella got right back in the middle of him, "You and Bubba have been friends over five years, and now you've hurt him like you have. I don't see how you can face yourself in the mirror. You'd better swallow some of that foolish pride you've got and go call that lady, not write her, and tell her the truth. Tell her that you're still in love with her and get off your butt and go see her." Not stopping to let Lim answer, and almost yelling by this time, she continued, "As for Bubba, you've hurt the best friend you ever had and that ought to hurt you more than anything. Nobody loves or thinks as much of you as he does, except maybe you."

With that, Stella stormed out of the yard, got in her car and threw gravel all over the place as she left. She almost ran over one of Lim's bird dogs who scurried out of the way of the fast departing car. Lim was so surprised at how Stella had talked to him that all he could do was just stand there on the porch with his mouth open as if he were still trying to say something.

Bubba picked Stella up about the usual time and they went out to the fish house. On the way, Bubba was unusually quiet and Stella knew why. She decided not to tell him about her trip out to Lim's. They'd just gotten seated when Lim walked in. He came right over to their table and without asking to join them, just sat down and placed a pint of hooch on the table. Without waiting for anyone to say anything, he turned to Bubba.

"Bubba I came out here to apologize to you. I went home after I made an ass out of myself up at the station and got to thinking things over." He looked at Stella with a slight smile, "That, plus being enlightened a little, I figured out what a fool I was by acting the way I did. I want to tell you Bubba that ain't nothing or nobody ever going to destroy our friendship."

Bubba smiled a smile as big as the moon, reached for Lim's bottle. "Lim, I'm the one that did wrong and I'm the one going to do the apologizing."

Stella broke in and pushed Bubba three empty glasses. "Ain't nothing no one needs to apologize for. All you need to do is pour us a drink and forget anything ever happened. You both know what's in your heart."

As long as those two lived, I reckon' there was never a harsh word spoken between them again. If anything, Bubba's meddling may have brought them closer and strengthened an already strong bond.

The trial started on Thursday. First, it was just going to be a judge's decision. Then after getting the silver appraisal, plus a bonafide offer of $22,000, the judge decided that due to the amount of money involved it would be best to have a jury trial, which meant selecting a jury. As usual, it was hard to find people that were not prejudiced in favor of Lim and Bubba. But a jury was finally selected and the trial began.

Everything looked like it was going in Lim and Bubba's favor until Mr. Hatfield's high priced lawyer got Lim on the stand and presented to the court the contract he had signed that stated Bubba and Lim were only looking for the train robbery gold. He also pointed out that the contract had expired and they were trespassing when they found the treasure. The slick lawyer added that Lim and Bubba did not ask Mr. Hatfield's permission to go out to the well when they found the treasure, accusing them of sneaking in.

Naturally upset, Lim lost his temper. This was what the lawyer wanted and he ate Lim alive. For a moment, it looked like Lim might tell Mr. Hatfield and his lawyer what they could do with the silver, but Lawyer Wilson came to his rescue and got Lim calmed down. However, the damage had been done.

The rest of the day went by without too much happening, except things got to favoring Mr. Hatfield. The next day the trial heated up again when the prosecution put the Sullivan brothers on the stand. Dave almost broke up the courtroom when he told about finding Lim and Bubba down in the well. Dave never missed a trick and told the whole thing from the part about them shining the lantern into the well and asking Lim what he was doing down there, to the part where Lim swore that he'd break his neck if he ever told anybody. Even the judge got tickled and had to call a recess.

After court was over that afternoon, Mr. Wilson said he wanted to come out to Lim's that night and talk to both of them, which he did about eight. Like Lim and Bubba, he enjoyed a drink and after Lim fixed one, he sat back in the rocking chair between the two of them and went over most everything that had happened in the trial.

"Tomorrow's the last day and I want to tell both of you, unless we come up with something else, we are liable, sure as I'm sittin' here, to lose this thing."

Lim lit his pipe and sat back, blowing a big puff of smoke up toward the ceiling. "Well Kirk, you know you and me have been friends a long time. I think you've done a hell of a good job trying to get the silver back for us, but if you don't, won't be any hard feelings. We sure as hell ain't going to lose any friendship over it." Before Lawyer Kirk could say anything, Lim added, "Me and Bubba didn't have anything before we started and all we'll lose is a little time. No one can take away the thrill of finding the stuff and all the fun we had looking for it."

Lawyer Wilson laughed as he replied, "Well, I'll have to admit that it's been an exciting trial what with all the publicity in the newspapers. Nobody wants to lose any fight they've started and I know the stuff would be there till doom's day if you and Bubba hadn't been so determined. That's got to be taken into consideration."

Lim laid his pipe down on the coffee table and searched his pockets for a match. "You know Kirk," he said looking up, "I can't believe Mr. Hatfield would have done this." He re-lit his pipe. "The night I went by their house and got him to sign the contract he said that he'd thought about having the well cleaned out. As he started to sign the paper, Mrs. Hatfield handed him a pen and said, 'Honey, what you waiting on? You know Lim's not going to damage anything and if he finds anything at all, we'd be better off than we are now.'"

Kirk broke in, "You mean Mrs. Hatfield said that?"

"Sure did, and Hatfield agreed with her when he signed it. That's why I can't understand them making the complete turnabout."

"Hell Lim," Kirk broke in excitedly, "what you just said means that the Hatfields agreed on anything you find regardless of what you signed." He stopped and thought about it a minute, then said, "I got to get Mrs. Hatfield on the stand. She could be the answer. Do you remember anything else?"

Lim thought for a minute, and then replied, "The only thing I can remember that's even connected with the well was when I went out to take the "A" frame down a short time before we found the treasure."

"What was that?" Kirk asked.

"I got to thinking," Lim said, "the well being open, I might should go out and cover it up before a cow or someone falls in. Of course, this was before I thought of where the silver might be. Anyway, I went out to the well and Mr. and Mrs. Hatfield were there when I drove up. Mr. Hatfield was drawing water for a sick cow. I told him of my plans about taking the "A" frame down and covering the well and he said that it was okay. He'd take it down in a few days that he already had some tin and boards to cover it with."

Kirk thought for a minute and said, "That might have some bearing on the case. He say anything else?"

Lim thought for a minute, then said, "By golly come to think of it, he didn't say anything else, but Mrs. Hatfield did make some kind of joke about leaving the "A" frame there. Yeah, she said, 'May as well leave it up, Lim. Who knows, you may want to come back and look some more.'"

Kirk almost jumped out of his seat, "You mean she said that?"

"Yeah, she was joking, of course, but said it sure as I'm sitting here."

"Lim, you and Bubba get ready," Kirk said as he abruptly stood, "we're going to get that silver back tomorrow."

Well, old Kirk Wilson may have been up in his years, but he still had a lot between the ears. The first thing he did was put Lim back on the stand and had Lim to testify that Mrs. Hatfield was present when Mr. Hatfield signed the agreement. Then over the objections of Hatfield's attorney, he brought out what Mrs. Hatfield said when he went out to cover the well and take down the "A" frame. When he said this, there was a murmur over everyone in the courtroom. Even the jury seemed to sense a dramatic change. Old Kirk didn't let up, but went in for the kill. He quietly asked the judge if he'd permit a hearing in his chambers to avoid any embarrassment for anyone. Of course the Hatfield's could object and he'd put Mrs. Hatfield on the stand, or, they could agree to the private hearing. Either way it went, they were in trouble and their lawyer knew it, so he went into a huddle with Mr. Hatfield. After a short discussion, Mr. Hatfield's lawyer agreed to the hearing in the judge's chambers.

In the Judge's chambers, Lawyer Wilson used his experience and before anyone could object he told the judge, "We don't want to have to go through a long cross examination of Mrs. Hatfield. It'll be too embarrassing. I request that Mr. Hatfield withdraw his case and let Lim and Bubba have what they actually have found. Mr. Hatfield will have gotten everything he has asked, his well cleaned and twenty percent of the find."

Mr. Hatfield and his attorney went to the corner of the office and in a murmur discussed the pros and cons of Kirk's offer.

After a short while, the attorney came over to the judge and announced, "Judge, due to the circumstances of Mrs. Hatfield's health, and being brought to the stand to testify, Mr. Hatfield had rather drop the case and settle on the twenty percent as the contract calls for."

Lim looked at Kirk who winked at him. The judge asked Kirk if he had any objections to the decision, to which he quickly replied that there were none. The judge went back to the courtroom and after everyone was seated and quieted down, he announced to the court the case had been settled and the terms of the contract would be upheld. No need to say any more, except the courtroom certainly agreed with the judge's decision. Even Stella came down and hugged Bubba in front of everyone.

Lim told Bubba he would take him and Stella out and buy them the thickest steak in Taylorsville, but they settled for the fish house, and before the night was over Bubba and Lim had laid one on. Stella had to drive them home. She had a bit of explaining to do with Mr. and Mrs. Ranking the next morning about why Lim's truck was parked up on the curb in front of their house.

The big question came now—what to do with the silver? The Judge had it moved to the bank and put in safekeeping until it was decided who really owned it. There's always someone that can tell you how to do anything, and before long, a group of ladies decided that the town should buy the silver and build a display room over at City Hall. This called for a number of town meetings with the city board, who felt the city couldn't buy it but would build the display room if the people could raise the money to purchase the silver. After everything was agreed to, a number of fund raising events, raffles, auctions, cakewalks, and most anything thought of was done to legally raise money, finally going to the old standby contributors, the businessmen. After a couple of months $20,000 had been raised, which was offered to Bubba and Lim in place of the $22,000 offer already made. Lim and Bubba didn't want to be hard, and the city said that their pictures and the story of how the treasure was found would be displayed in the new museum along with the silver. This made the deal and the sale price was immediately accepted. Strange as it may seem, Mr. and Mrs. Hatfield went along with the price. Lim said he figured Mrs. Hatfield had made that decision.

After Lawyer Wilson's part and the twenty percent out for the Hatfield's, Lim and Bubba divided a little over $15,000. Bubba immediately took his money down to the bank and deposited it. He felt like a rich man for once in his life and this should be the answer to many of his problems. Being able to pay off his debts, he could make Morris an offer on the station and maybe Mr. Ranking would finally agree on his and Stella's marriage, which he intended to get settled that night.

Lim didn't say much either way about the money, except he was going to get caught up on bird hunting. He did say that finding the Stroader Silver renewed his belief that one day he would figure out where his grandpa Arthur had hid the Appleton fortune.

"Bubba, one of these days, I'm going to figure out where the old goat hid that stuff and me and you are going to go get it," Lim said confidently. "You still got a claim to half of it."

"Lim," Bubba replied as he sipped a drink in Lim's living room, "the only claim I'd have to it would be if I helped you find it. That money is part of your heritage. Just don't go getting anymore ideas about digging up the rest of your relatives."

Lim laughed, "I still believe it's buried in or around the cemetery. When I figure where, I'll let you know," he said with a wink as he sipped his drink. "Come to think of it, it could be buried in old Limbrick's wife's grave. Grandpa Arthur would have had no qualms about hiding it in his mother's grave."

Bubba didn't say anything, just took a swig of his RC cola and shook his head.

Chapter 13

Bubba got to Stella's house a little after seven dressed in his new suit. Stella was surprised when she came to the door. "Hello, Bubba. You're mighty dressed up with that new suit. Sure looks good on you."

Bubba was a little embarrassed about the suit. "Thanks, Stella. You know, this is the first one I've ever owned and I feel a little uncomfortable in it." Before she could reply, he asked. "Is your dad in?"

His request surprised her so that she didn't quite know what to say. "Bubba, you want to talk to him?"

"If he's not busy, I'd like to talk to him."

"Come on in," she replied hesitantly. "I'll call him. I think he's in the den." She called her dad, returned to Bubba, and gave him a questioning look. All she could figure, Bubba was either drinking or had lost his mind.

Bubba could tell that she was just bursting to ask what he was up to, but ignored her looks and with another surprise he said, "When he gets here, let me talk to him alone."

This really got her curiosity up, but as Mr. Ranking came in, she got up to leave. "I'll be back in a minute," she said giving Bubba one of those, 'You asked for it looks.'

Mr. Ranking took a seat in the big living room lounge chair and motioned for Bubba to have a seat on the couch. "What do you have on your mind Bubba?"

Bubba suddenly wished that he had forgotten the whole thing. He called his own hand, so now he had to go through with it. "Mr. Ranking," he began nervously, "you know me and Stella have been wanting to get married for a long time. I know you've been against it." He thought for a second about what to say next. "With the good luck me and Lim had, I got a little money and I'm going to try to buy Morris out down at the station. I couldn't blame you for how you felt in the past, but now I feel I can take care of her and I...I'd like your permission to marry her."

Mr. Ranking sat in the big chair thinking about all the things involved in a wedding, wondering most of all if Stella would be happy. He got up without saying anything to Bubba and called Stella, who was waiting in the next room.

"Stella," Mr. Ranking began, "Bubba has asked for your hand in marriage." He waited a minute to let this revelation sink in. Stella just stood there stunned, as if she didn't know what to say. He smiled when he figured that Stella didn't know Bubba was going to ask for her hand. "Even though things have been rather hectic, I think he'll make you a good husband." Stella ran and hugged her father, then Bubba. She was so happy that she was crying.

I guess the story could end right here, with everyone happy and all the problems worked out, but it doesn't About the same time Bubba went over to Stella's, a long black Lincoln pulled up in front of Lim's house and a small man in a trim dark suit got out. He walked up to the gate and Lim's bird dogs spotted him. They almost tore the fence down trying to get to the strange looking fellow. Lim heard all the commotion and came out onto the front porch. When he saw the distinguished looking stranger with the fancy car, he hollered for the dogs to leave the fellow alone. Hesitantly, the little man opened the gate and came to the porch. The dogs sulked back under the porch, still growling. The man walked up the steps with his black brief case and asked, "Are you Lim Appleton?"

"Yes, that's me," Lim reluctantly replied offering him his hand. "What can I do for you?"

The man walked to the top of the steps and took Lim's hand saying, "I'm Thomas Breckinridge."

Lim shook his hand. "Mr. Breckinridge, what's the purpose of your call?" thinking as he shook his hand, 'Hell, this has got to be some government tax man or some nut trying to sell me something.'

The little man looked up at Lim's six foot, two inch frame and replied, "Mr. Appleton, I have a business proposition I would like to discuss with you."

Lim didn't want to invite him in, but he felt it'd be unsociable to tell him to get the hell out of there, that he didn't want to hear his proposition, so Lim reluctantly invited the man in and offered him a chair.

The man sat in a straight-backed chair by the coffee table and put his briefcase down beside the chair. Lim sat across from him in the recliner.

"Mr. Appleton I know you are wondering what my business is and probably wish I'd get the hell out of your house same as I would if I were you."

The man stopped to let what he had said sink in. The statement relaxed Lim some. At least he wasn't a government man. But what the hell has he got up his sleeve?

The man continued, "I've kept up with you and your partner's story in the papers. I've followed the recent trial you were in as well as the story of how you found the silver treasure, and I must say I've been very impressed with your determination and 'stick-ability'."

Lim leaned back, a little more at ease as the man talked, but he still wanted the gentleman to come to the punch line. Lim thought as he tried to sum up the situation, 'He must be some kind of con man.'

Lim was totally unprepared for what the man said next. "I am President of the Baton Rouge Delta Bank. I know you're probably getting ready to eat dinner and I need to get back to Baton Rouge so I'll come right to the point.

Lim thought to himself, 'Yeah and I'm Joe Palooka. Now this jerk is really going to put the con on.'

"I am looking for a reliable and trustworthy person or persons such as you and your partner to look for a very valuable treasure. Due to the secrecy I must demand concerning this matter and the value being what it is, truthfully I must tell you that I have had you and your partner, I believe you call him Bubba, investigated."

This really threw Lim off. Lim didn't like folks meddling, especially with a personal matter like his character, however, he tried to hold his temper, but still cut the man off, "And what did you find with the investigation?" Lim didn't hide his distaste at being investigated.

With a smile the man answered, "Oh, there were a few minor incidents with the law in your past, but nothing that would concern me. The part I was concerned with checked out perfectly."

"And just what might that be?" Lim replied still annoyed.

"My investigation proves you are a man of few words, you've done a lot for your neighbors and community and your honesty and your word is your bond."

Lim leaned back in his chair somewhat eased. At least the character report pleased him.

Mr. Breckinridge took a small cigar out of his coat pocket and offered Lim one, who held up his hand in a gesture of no. "What I will tell you will be documented with letters and affidavits," he started. With that, he picked up his briefcase, opened it and took out a copy of an affidavit saying as he did, "This affidavit from Colonel Robert P. Hampston was taken in 1907 by my father, who started the search for the Confederate treasure. Colonel Hampton was in an old Confederate Soldiers' home in Biloxi, MS."

Lim broke in, "You mean this treasure you are talking about has to do with the Confederacy?" Suddenly his opinion of the little man began to change as he realized that what he was talking about was real, especially if he could document it. At least what he'd said so far could be verified.

"That's right, Mr. Appleton," he replied blowing out smoke, "the story took place while Vicksburg was under siege by the Union army in May and June of 1863."

Lim, interested in the strange man's story, twisted his chair around to see better as he handed him the documented testimonial.

"Before you read the Colonel's statement, let me give you some of the Colonel's background." Lim laid the paper back onto the coffee table and with a puzzled expression leaned back in his chair. Mr. Breckinridge snuffed his cigar out in the ashtray and started the story in earnest.

"Colonel Hampston was General Pemberton's personal aide and advisor at Vicksburg. General Pemberton, as you know, was in command of the Confederate forces. What I'm going to tell you took place around the time the siege of Vicksburg was just beginning and they didn't know how long they could hold off the Yankees. Seeing the desperate situation of a possible siege of Vicksburg, President Jefferson Davis sent a very secretive message to General Pemberton. The messenger just made it into the town before it was fully surrounded. Because of its importance and the intense level of secrecy, the Captain that brought the message brought only a letter of introduction that stated that the captain's loyalty and honesty could not be questioned and because of the extreme importance and utmost haste, it was to be delivered orally to General Pemberton, and was signed by President Davis.

"I believe this should enlighten you as to the following affidavit, you may read it now."

Lim picked up the two-page testimonial and looked at it. Before he could even start reading it, a worried feeling came over him, as if he was back in 1863 and was standing there with the General suddenly feeling the anticipation that what the Captain might say would change the destiny of the war, maybe the world. Lim started reading the affidavit slowly and carefully:

I, Robert P. Hampston, now residing in the Beauvoir Confederate Soldiers' Home, Biloxi, Mississippi, am of fair health and sound mind swear the following statement to be true. The exact date and time could vary, but neither have any bearing on the truth of this statement. Which is as follows:

Lim stopped reading and asked, "Is this *Beauvoir* Jefferson Davis' home down on the coast?"

"Yes," Mr. Breckinridge replied, "I assume you are familiar with Beauvoir?"

Lim nodded his head. "Years ago I had the occasion to spend some time down in New Orleans. I remember driving through Biloxi and passing by the old home. Never gave it much mind at the time. I do remember seeing a sign that it was Jefferson Davis' home and something about it being an old Confederate Soldiers' home or hospital."

"That is correct," Mr. Breckinridge replied. "It was converted to a Confederate Old Soldiers' Home by Jefferson Davis' wife as a shrine to President Davis and the Confederate cause. Through stipulations stated in a token price sale to the Son's of the Confederacy, she arranged for the home and a certain amount of land be preserved as a perpetual shrine to the failed cause. I've been there a number of times. It's a beautiful place. In fact, the word *Beauvoir* is a French word meaning a 'beautiful view.' The home is located right there on the coast surrounded with, large two-hundred-year-old Live Oak trees, beautiful flower gardens, and manicured grounds. Behind the home, a number of acres were set-aside as a Confederate cemetery. My memory is it had over seven hundred graves. It too is well preserved and manicured. It's a beautiful final resting place for so many gallant soldiers."

"Sounds like a beautiful and interesting place," Lim commented. "I guess I was too interested in doing my thing back then to stop and smell the roses."

"I've had some of the same problems," Mr. Breckinridge replied laughing. "Go ahead and read. I won't interrupt you again."

Lim returned to the affidavit.

On or about May the 20th, 1863, I being a Colonel in the Confederate Army and legal aid and advisor to General John Pemberton, General in Command of the Confederate forces at Vicksburg, surrounded and under siege by the Union Army, was given a message by a Captain Chris...Chambers, I believe, his last name is hazy in my memory, to be delivered to General Pemberton. I told the Captain to wait and took the sealed letter to the General. The General read the introduction and instructed that the Captain should deliver the message orally. I showed him in.

The Captain was hesitant about delivering the message in my presence until the General assured him I was his legal aide and advisor, and then he quoted the message as follows, give or take a few words:

I, President Jefferson Davis, President of the Confederate States of America, for the sake of the Confederacy do command you to seek by request, or force if necessary, the $500,000 dollars in gold and silver the Confederacy has in safe keeping with the Vicksburg People's Bank, along with the diamonds and other contributions held by you. I further order you to deliver the same to Colonel Robert J. Willington at Tillsdale Point, six miles below Port Gibson. (The exact details of the rendezvous I do not remember, but the time set for the transfer was the morning of June 1st, 1863.) The captain continued President Davis' message; I cannot stress the urgency of this request and its importance. It is imperative that we deliver this money to our allies. Intervention by the Royal Navy will open the lifeline to our ports. I stress the importance of this mission and order the destruction of these most valuable contents before the Union Army confiscates it. Again, I stress the importance of this mission; the destiny of the war could be with its success. The captain concluded the message with Captain (whatever his name was), and will advise *final instructions of disposition and details of the rendezvous with Colonel Willington, as stated by the words of President Jefferson Davis.*

I further state in this sworn statement, that the captain advised General Pemberton the gold and silver be melted into fifty pound gold bars for safe handling in transportation. The delivery attempt would be by a boat running the Union blockade.

I further state that General Pemberton advised Vicksburg People's Bank to turn over the Confederate gold and silver holdings and within the day, it was delivered to General Pemberton's headquarters. The following day it was melted into 20 gold and silver bars, 10 each, their weight stamped on the ends of the bars ranging from forty-nine to fifty-two pounds. The weight I am sure is correct, or very close to being correct, as it was I who witnessed the weighing of the bullion. The silver and gold bars were placed two to a box that was built of rough cypress timber and had wording burnt in the side of the boxes, "50 Caliber Musket Balls" The jewels, diamonds, and rubies (a teacup full) were placed in a copper box, sealed in the same size cypress box, and filled with 50 caliber musket balls. The box was stamped the same as the bullion.

I further state that on or about May 22, 1863, the Merrygold Paddle Wheeler, previously in use as a ferryboat for the Confederacy, was stripped of all unnecessary weight and it's sides protected with iron plating. Within the week, the work was completed and on May 30 the silver and gold bullion, along with the jewels, was loaded aboard the vessel and it departed in the dark of the night, under the command of Captain Frederick L. Breckinridge and a crew of two men.

I further state that the Merrygold encountered heavy gunfire as it went through the Union blockade. Eyewitnesses reported to the General the following day that she took a water line hit. However, severely damaged, the Merrygold broke through the blockade and proceeded on her mission.

I further state that before the week was out, the General received a report that the Merrygold had sunk and that Captain Breckinridge and the crew were either killed or drowned.

I swear by witness of the adjoining signature that I am in good health for my age and of clear mind and the above statement is true and correct to the best of my knowledge, this date July 8, 1907.

Signed,
Robert P. Hampston, Colonel
Confederate States of America

Sidney Breckinridge and Thomas L. Overstreet witnessed the affidavit.

Lim read the witness' name and figured that Sidney Breckinridge must be this gentleman's father. Handing the document back to Mr. Breckinridge, he said, "Quite a story. I guess no one has ever found the boat, the Merrygold was it?"

"Yes. There was a report in the Vicksburg newspaper in 1890 that remnants of the Merrygold washed up on a sandbar twenty or so miles below Vicksburg. The reports in my father's record say part of the hull remained there until a large flood took it away in 1910. There were never any records of the cargo she was carrying. The newspaper report stated that she was on an important mission for the Confederacy when she sank running the Union blockade during the siege in 1863. It didn't say anything about her cargo."

"Then your father was fortunate enough to have witnessed the Merrygold?"

"No, unfortunately, he did not. He later told me the location of the Merrygold was uncertain and only remnants were left of the hull when the flood came in 1910. However, he does have in his record a testimonial of a tugboat captain that had seen remnants of the hull that still had the Merrygold name on it. Unfortunately, though, Dad did not have the opportunity to meet the captain until after the flood claimed her.

Lim sat for a moment in silence, and then stood up. "Mr. Breckinridge, would you care for a drink? I think I'll have one."

"Why, yes, I would enjoy a drink. Make it half and half with water."

Lim had to get away so he could think. He went into the kitchen thinking to himself. 'That's the damnedest story I ever heard. The little man seems all right. A phone call to the Baton Rouge Bank is all I need to check to see if he's lying. Probably some escapee from a lunatic home.'

Lim fixed the drinks and went back to the living room and handed the gentleman his drink. He sat down and leaned back. "That was quite a story. Is that all the information you have of the whereabouts of the silver and gold bars?"

"No, Mr. Appleton, but the rest will have to come after any decision you and I might make."

Lim leaned back as he would in a poker game and studied his next move— whether to draw or stand pat. "The information you have isn't enough to go on. Someone could have confiscated the treasure. It could have been in the boat when it washed ashore. You'd have to have more information before I'd be interested."

Mr. Breckinridge looked at Lim saying, "I like the way you talk. It shows sound judgment. I'll tell you this; the Captain of the Merrygold was my great uncle. He was critically wounded and a Yankee gunboat picked him up down the river from where the Merrygold sank. He died that same day, but before he died, he wrote a letter to his wife. The captain of the Union gunboat delivered the letter after the surrender of Vicksburg. In fact, the letter was written by the Union Captain that delivered it."

Lim leaned forward and sat thinking. 'He's withholding the main part until he finds out if we'll take the job looking for the treasure.' Lim rubbed his chin and spoke slowly and evenly.

"I assume you have that letter and it gives a close proximity to where the gold and silver was dumped, or whatever the disposition?"

"Your assumption is right and if you and I come to terms, all the information I have will be turned over to you."

"Just what is your proposition?" Lim asked.

Mr. Breckinridge declared his hand. "Mr. Appleton, I am almost certain the treasure has never been found. However, I must be truthful with you. We have had other people look for it in the past and no trace has ever been found. I feel it may take as much as a year, maybe longer to find it. However, I certainly hope you find it in a shorter time.

"This is the proposition I will make, I will give you a signed contract giving you fifty percent of the find, plus any and all expenses you incur to be taken out of the find. The contract will be for one year. It can be extended if necessary, but if you don't find it, you will still be bound by the contract—even if you find it ten years from now. Also, if unsuccessful in locating the treasure, you are to divulge the contents of the information I give you to no one."

Lim sweetened his drink, then handing the bottle to Mr. Breckinridge. "Mr. Breckinridge, I like the challenge of the proposition and would tell you here and now I will take the job, but I do have a partner. I'll have to discuss it with him. I'll let you know within a week one way or the other."

"Fine, this is my card. If you decide to undertake the project get in touch with me," he paused thinking a minute, "It would be best for you and your partner to come to Baton Rouge and we'll go over the data I have and sign the contract there."

Mr. Breckinridge finished his drink and stood up. "I must be leaving. I feel I've taken too much of your time already, and besides, by the time I get to Jackson it'll be late. Figured I'd spend the night in Jackson and drive on to Baton Rouge tomorrow."

Lim shook his hand saying, "I've enjoyed the company, and the story. Looking forward to seeing you in the near future."

Lim stood on the porch and watched the little man drive off in the big car. His thoughts drifting as he stood there, 'How in the hell can I tell Bubba with him fixing to get married and all? Hell, this'll blow everything.' Thinking to himself, as he went out to the pickup, 'I best go find Bubba if I can and get the matter settled.' Getting into the truck, Lim thought, 'He's probably out at the fish house, I'll stop and get a bottle and check there.'

He pulled into the fish house and spotted Bubba's car. 'Good, they're here,' he thought. 'Now how in the hell am I going to handle this? May be best to just forget the whole thing.'

Bubba and Stella were sitting in one of the little private dining rooms. They saw Lim and motioned for him to come and join them. Walking to the table, Lim thought, 'Least we'll be in private where we can talk.'

Lim asked if he was butting in and of course they told him he wasn't and to sit down and order that they had just made their order. Lim handed Bubba the bottle and started to ask how things worked out with Mr. Ranking, but Stella told him before he could get the first word out.

"Lim, Daddy agreed to our marriage and we have set the date. He was a real prince about it." She clutched Lim's hand. "Everything's settled. We're getting married June 10th."

Lim smiled as Bubba handed him his drink, "That's great. Bubba is the luckiest person in the world to get a girl like you," and holding his glass up continued, "here's to the two finest people I know."

Laughing, they all touched glasses, and then before they put the drinks down, Bubba made a toast to Lim. "Here's to the best man at the wedding."

All during supper, Lim kept trying to think about how he was going to tell Bubba and Stella about Mr. Breckinridge's proposition. Then the thought would come to him, 'Hell, if I tell them, it would postpone their marriage, maybe forever. Ain't no buried treasure worth messing that up.'

Bubba noticed Lim's pondering. "Lim what you in such deep thought about? One would think you were thinking about another buried treasure."

Laughing, Lim reached over and poured another drink.

Stella broke in, "Lim, you do have something on your mind. Is something wrong?"

"Now you both listen," Lim answered smiling. "What old Lim's thinking is not important. You two are going to get married and are not going to let anything get in the way."

Bubba, still puzzled, put it straight to Lim. "You don't usually come out to eat fish on Tuesday night. I can tell something's bugging you. What the hell's wrong?"

Lim thought about it. 'What the hell? It won't hurt to tell them about the proposition. I just won't let it mess up their plans. We'll do the looking for treasure after they're married.' He sipped his drink and said, "All right both of you, I'm going to tell you what it is. But before I do, I promise you both that what I say is not going to stop you from getting married."

Stella and Bubba looked at each other then set back in their chairs and braced themselves for what might come.

Lim went through the whole story, even to the dogs almost getting Mr. Breckinridge at the gate. After he got through, Bubba and Stella just sat there not saying anything, looking from one then the other.

Finally, Bubba broke the silence, "You mean it could be worth as much as a million and a half dollars?"

Lim didn't say anything, just nodded.

Stella turned to Bubba and said, "Bubba you couldn't possibly turn this down. We can put off the wedding if it has to be."

"Wait a minute now Stella," Bubba stammered, "it's been too hard getting your father to agree to this as it is. We're going through with the wedding." Bubba turned to Lim, "Hell Lim, sounds like the chance of a lifetime, but I'm afraid something will happen and I…I just can't take that chance."

Lim motioned for the girl to bring the check. He looked at Bubba and said, "Best we forget about it. Odds of finding the treasure would be against us anyway. It'll keep till after the wedding. We can talk about it then."

On the way home, Stella kept talking about the treasure and all the things they could do with their part of the money.

Bubba could see how worked up she was getting. "Stella, you might as well forget about it. I'm not going to let anything mess up our marriage. In fact, I'm supposed to go see Morris about the station tomorrow. It being April, I won't have but a couple of months to get it going before June 10th."

"Besides, what Lim's talking about will cost a good bit of money, probably as much as I got in the bank—just for my part. Hell, Stella, I got that money set aside to buy out Morris. He told me this morning maybe as much as four or five thousand dollars, and Stella I'll be lucky to have that much left in the bank after I pay what debts I owe."

Stella didn't answer for a long time, her mind working in all directions. Finally, she said, "Bubba, you know I love you and I promise you we're going to get married if we have to elope, but you and Lim need to go look for that treasure. The amount of money involved would be enough to live on the rest of our lives. It's just something we can't afford to turn down."

"Yes, it sounds real good, but you haven't thought of us not finding the treasure and losing all the money we got. The odds are against us. We're going to forget it for a while, maybe after I get Morris' Station and we get it going we can try then. Right now, there's no way we're going to try it."

"But Bubba, what if this Mr. Breckinridge gets someone else to look for the treasure? Can you imagine how you'd feel reading in the paper that someone else found the treasure and divided a million and a half dollars?"

Bubba didn't answer; he just turned north towards Union. His thoughts were mixed every way they could mix. A short time later, Stella was snuggled in his arms and the lost Breckinridge treasure was the least of their concerns.

That night Stella couldn't sleep. She kept tossing and turning. The treasure and her marriage held her thoughts. There had to be an answer. She'd doze off, and then awaken suddenly thinking she had the answer. Finally, sometime before daybreak, the answer came to her. Getting out of bed, she went to the phone and called Bubba. Of course, the phone call at four-thirty in the morning woke Bubba's mother. She was a little hard of hearing and half-awake and had a hard time trying to figure out who in the world would call at such an early hour. Stella finally got her to understand who it was. "My child, are you sick or in trouble or something?" she asked motherly.

"No, ma'am. I just need to talk to Bubba." Putting the phone down, she went to Bubba's room and told him Stella was on the phone. Well it scared Bubba half to death. He jumped out of bed half-asleep and stumbled to the phone.

"Hello, Stella. What in the world has happened?"

"Nothing has happened. I couldn't sleep all night and knew you were lying there sleeping like a kitten. I just thought I'd call and talk to you."

Bubba didn't know how to react to that. "Now Stella, what the hell is going on? Do you know it's four in the morning?"

"Sure, I know what time it is. Think I called to find out what time it was?"

"Stella, are you drunk?"

"No honey, I'll get serious now that you're awake."

"Please do. What's going on?"

"Look, Bubba, I just figured out how you and Lim can go find Mr. Breckinridge's treasure."

"You *what*?"

Stella giggled and replied, "Get yourself dressed and come over to the house. I'll have you some breakfast cooked and a hot cup of coffee poured."

Bubba hesitated; wanting to say it could wait till daylight, then grumbled, "This must be awfully important. I'll be over in a few minutes."

Well the two Mamas got in the picture. Bubba's mother wanted to know all that was going on and saying at the same time, "You sure that girl's not drinking?"

Stella's mother came into the kitchen and questioned her. "Stella, was that Bubba you were talking to at this hour in the morning? Is he in jail or drunk?"

"No mother," she replied trying to calm her down, "I called Bubba to ask him over to have breakfast with me."

"You what?" she asked disbelieving what she was hearing.

"That's right, now go on back to bed, Mother. There's not anything wrong. Guess I'm just in love."

Mrs. Ranking, half-talking to herself and half talking to Stella, went on back and went to bed. Of course, Mr. Ranking wanted to know what was happening asked, "What the devil is all the commotion?"

Snatching the covers up over her head, Mrs. Ranking answered, "Love has affected your daughter's head. Go to sleep."

Since the light was on in the living room, Bubba pushed the door back a little and quietly called, "Stella?"

She opened the kitchen door and motioned for him to come back to the kitchen. At least she was right about having breakfast. Sausage was cooking, biscuits baking and the coffee was already poured.

"You don't have this kind of a night very often do you?" Bubba asked defensively.

Stella laughingly replied, "Sit down and have coffee. I'll have the eggs cooked shortly."

"What is so all-fired important?" Bubba asked as he sipped his coffee.

"I'll tell you after we have breakfast," Stella answered.

It was a good breakfast. When they got through, Stella put the dishes in the sink and poured them both another cup of coffee. She came over and sat next to Bubba.

"Now, I'll tell you. I couldn't sleep all night. The thought of Lim and Mr. Breckinridge and the treasure kept haunting me. Bubba, if you and Lim don't give that deal a good chance, it'll be on our minds as long as we live. I know it's a gamble, but if you were to find it, it would be the answer to all our problems."

"You may be right Stella," Bubba replied looking at her evenly, "but the chance of us finding that treasure is almost nothing and I don't plan on losing you over it. It's like Lim told me up at Stroader's Well, if you love someone, you better go on and get married or someday you'll wish you had. Just like he messed up."

"Look Bubba, we are gonna get married, no matter what. Father has agreed to it and we love each other, so you get any foolish idea out of your head otherwise." She got up and brought the coffee pot over to the table. Heating up Bubba's coffee she continued, "If you'd listen, you'll agree I've got it worked out how we can go look for the treasure."

"Did you mean to say 'We' look for the treasure?" Bubba asked.

Stella knew it was now or never. "That's right. I'll go with you and Lim. We can spend all summer over there if we want to. Besides, you two will need someone to keep camp and watch over you. I won't be in the way. You know you have to set up a camp, tents and all. I'll be in a separate tent, won't anything be wrong with that."

Bubba could see that she had it all worked out. "Stella, you must have lost your mind. The first thing, your father will have a fit when he hears about this." Then, thinking that Mr. Ranking may have heard what he said, he stopped and listened thinking to himself, 'Hell he might come out of that bedroom any minute throwing a fit, wouldn't blame him if he did.'

Bubba tried to hold his voice down. "Look, Stella," he answered quietly, "you don't know what you're talking about. This summer it'll be so hot you can't sleep and then in the fall so cold you'll freeze your bottom off. The mosquitoes will be thick as bees and no telling how many snakes and spiders will be all over the place. You can forget that crazy idea."

"I will not. It's the only thing that will work and keep my family believing you and Lim are not just going off on a drinking spree. Now get your coat on, we're going out to talk with Lim."

Stella went back to her mother's bedroom to tell her where she was going. "Mother, I'm going with Bubba out to Lim's. Be back in a little while."

Bubba heard her father say, "Good. Maybe we can get some sleep."

Lim was just finishing breakfast when they got there. He was surprised by their untimely visit, but invited them in saying, "Bubba, what are you and Stella doing out so early?" Then with a smile, he added, "Or did you two stay out all night?"

Everyone sat at the table and Lim offered them coffee. Bubba, looking a little sleepless refused, "Been drinking that stuff since before daylight. All right, Stella, tell Lim what you told me and see how far you get."

Stella told Lim her plans in detail. When she got through, she smiled at Lim and pointed to Bubba. "Bubba thinks it's a crazy idea, but I'm a big girl now and can help more than both of you think."

Lim sat silently thinking for a long pause. Both Bubba and Stella looked at him and waited for his answer. Finally, after going over the pros and cons in his mind he said in a dry serious tone, "I think the girl has more sense than you and I both. If she can get her parents to go along with the deal, she's cut in."

Stella broke in, "I'm not cut in on the deal. Bubba and I will share his part." Jumping up she went over and hugged Lim.

Bubba sighed. "If it weren't so early, I'd have a drink."

Lim got up and went into the kitchen bringing back a bottle and three glasses. "When it gets too early to have a drink, I'll quit."

Stella refused, but Bubba and Lim had an eye-opener as they discussed their plans.

Lim laid out his ideas. "As soon as Stella gets her parent's approval, you and I'll go to Baton Rouge and meet with Mr. Breckinridge. He's holding back the main part of the information until he finds out if we're going to sign a contract with him. If the information looks good, we'll come back to Taylorsville and start making our plans. We've got a lot of equipment to buy. There's not but one thing I want us to agree on."

"What's that, Lim?" Bubba asked.

"If we decide to go into this, even if it takes a year, let's don't let any of us get discouraged and give up. We know it isn't going to be easy, and there's going to be times when some or all of us will want to quit. When that happens, one of the three of us is going to have to do some talking. We can't give up without exhausting every possibility."

Stella interrupted. "We'll all shake hands on it. What Lim says is right. I'll agree."

Bubba stuck his hand out. "I'll agree."

The three shook hands and sealed their promise.

Chapter 14

Leaving Lim's, Stella snuggled up to Bubba. "Now do you see how I can help?" she asked with a cozy smile. "You and Lim would never have figured out how we could have gone to look for the treasure."

"I sure do," Bubba replied humoring her, "and now smart girl, the fun starts. All you have to do is sell your mom and dad on the deal. I'm sure glad it's you and not me having to make the sales talk."

Stella laughed and replied, "Yeah, I've been thinking of how I'm going to explain it. First, I've got to sell Mom on the idea, and then we'll both have to start on Dad."

Bubba was laughing as he pulled up in front of Stella's house. "As I said," he offered, "I'm glad it's you and not me that has to do the talking."

Stella reached up and gave Bubba a peck on the cheek. "You know, there's been a lot worse things we've talked about," she said as she opened the door, "but as you know, we got 'em washed out. See you tonight," she added with a wink.

Bubba watched Stella as she went up the sidewalk open the door and wave. "That Stella's some cat. If anyone can work Mr. Ranking, she can."

Stella's mom was washing dishes at the sink when Stella entered. "Well, love bird; did you get all the problems worked out with Bubba?" Mrs. Ranking asked.

Sitting down laughing, Stella replied, "Most everything. We've still got a couple of minor obstacles to get over."

Mrs. Ranking poured herself a cup of coffee. "You want a cup, Dear," she asked Stella. Stella absently shook her head as Mrs. Ranking picked up her cup, brought it over to the table and sat across from her daughter.

"I've been drinking coffee since four this morning. Believe I've had enough."

Mrs. Ranking took a sip of hers and sat the cup back in the saucer. "All right Big Girl, I know when you've got something on your mind and need to talk. What is it?"

Stella smiled and reached across to hold her mother's hand. "You almost know my thoughts, don't you Mother?" she asked. Not giving her a chance to answer, she continued, "Mom, you better brace yourself. What I'm fixing to ask you is probable going to put you in minor shock." Stella knew that what she was going to suggest was more than likely going to put her into a full-blown tizzy fit.

Mrs. Ranking looked at Stella not knowing what to expect. Then a thought crossed her mind that she may not want to find the answer. "Stella, you're not in trouble are you?" she asked in a stern voice.

"Aw Mother," Stella replied laughing loudly, "you know it's nothing like that. No, but what I'm fixing to ask you might get you as upset as if I were."

Now Mrs. Ranking was thoroughly confused. "All right, you've stalled enough. What in the world has happened?"

It took Stella the next half hour to tell her mom about Mr. Breckenridge's visit, the treasure he had revealed to Lim, and the opportunity to find it. She took a deep breath and told her everything about the big decision they'd made this morning out at Lim's for her to go with them and look for the treasure.

Mrs. Ranking didn't say anything for a few minutes. She just sat there with a blank stare in her eyes. She quietly got up, poured herself another cup of coffee and sat back down at the table. She finally said, "Maybe it would be better if you were in trouble. You mean to tell me you're going over there and live in a tent with Bubba and Lim and that you think your father and I are going to agree to it?"

Stella, seeing how upset she was, almost wished she'd listened to Bubba and forgot about the whole deal. But for her mother to think that she was going to be living in a tent with Lim and Bubba didn't set too well with her. "Mom, that's not what I said. Lim and Bubba will have a tent to themselves and I'll be in a totally separate tent. Mother, do you realize how much money we're talking about if we were to find the treasure—not to mention how exciting an adventure like this is going to be? Mom, this is something you hear about or read in books. A chance like this will never come again. We've got to take it before someone else does."

Mrs. Ranking could see the desperation on Stella's face and in her eyes. "Stella, what about your wedding? You mean you're going to put it off?"

"Mom, that's how important this thing is," she replied quietly. "We're going to have to use all the money Bubba and Lim can raise to buy equipment." She reached over and covered her mother's hand with hers. "It's so important that we're going to put the wedding off for awhile, whether I go with them or not."

"Lord, Stella," Mrs. Ranking replied astonished, "it must be important. Your father is going to be more upset over this than he was about the wedding."

Stella jumped up and raced around the table, hugged her and said, "Mom, I knew you'd understand," as she hugged her tightly.

Mrs. Ranking was taken aback a bit and had the feeling that she'd been *took*, tried to explain that she hadn't exactly agreed, finally said, "Stella, I don't know how you do these things and I keep my sanity. I'll see if I can help you with your father, but you better let me break it to him first."

Stella hugged her again. "Mom, I knew I could count on you."

Her mother's reply was, "Yeah, you knew you could talk me into it. Now you're going to have someone help you sell it to your dad."

Stella laughingly replied as she picked up her coat, "Mom, Julia wants me to come over and help plan a get-together. We'll talk some more at lunch. You're not going to be using the car for a while are you?"

"No, go ahead. It's going to take me the rest of the morning to get my confused mind and sanity straightened out. Go ahead; I'll talk to your father. He's either going to agree to it, or kill you."

Stella kissed her on the cheek as she dashed out the door. "Better hide the guns, Mom," she called back giggling.

Sometime later, Bubba came by. He was totally unaware of what had happened when he got out of his mom's car and walked up to Stella's house. Stella watched and met him at the door as he walked up on the front porch. Opening the door, and with a big smile she invited him in whispering as she did, "Dad's in the den and wants to have a word with you."

Bubba started to turn and leave saying, "Oh hell, you haven't told him have you?"

Nodding her head, Stella replied, "Yeah, it wasn't too bad. He just threatened to divorce Mother and said he was sending me to a juvenile home and that he was going to kill you."

Bubba followed Stella into the den. "Has he got his shotgun in the den?" Bubba asked nervously.

"No, come on," Stella replied laughing. "He just wants to talk with you."

As soon as Bubba walked into the den, Mr. Ranking spoke. "Bubba, I just wanted to check and see if you'd lost your mind like Stella and her mother?"

Bubba flashed a shy grin. "Yes sir, Mr. Ranking, guess we all lost our mind and I can't blame you for anything you may think or say. In fact, Mr. Ranking, this notion she's got about going with us is so far out, I'm inclined to agree with you."

Stella snuggled up against Bubba and butted in, "Dad, you just wish you were going with us. Mom's told me about some of the things y'all did when you were growing up. This is not any worse."

"Maybe not, but back then at least boys and girls didn't go off on trips together. Most especially staying overnight."

"Daddy," Stella countered, "don't be talking that way. You know Lim's going to be with us."

Mr. Ranking sighed with a slight grin and replied, "That's supposed to make me feel better? That's one of the things I've been thinking about. Anyway, Bubba, I want to tell you how much I'm against the whole thing. I also want to say that Stella's Mama and I are reluctantly going to go along with this, but one mess up, and I'll personally come over there and get Stella and drag her home by her hair if I have to." In closing Mr. Ranking added, "Bubba, that ain't saying what I'll do to you."

When they'd walked out to the car later, Bubba opened the car door for Stella and said, "Boy, I'm glad that's over. For a moment there I thought he might have plans on sending me somewhere."

Stella reached over and kissed Bubba on the cheek as he got in the car. "Aw Bubba, dad's are just like that. They do more worrying than mothers."

"Yeah," Bubba replied, "you should have heard what my mother said when I told her you were going with us. She thinks we're all crazy. Me, you, your parents, and especially Lim—even on his good days, and she might be right."

Chapter 15

Walking into the Baton Rouge Delta Bank, Bubba and Lim asked a clerk if they could see Mr. Breckinridge.

"May I tell him who wishes to see him?" she asked sweetly.

"Tell him Lim Appleton from Taylorsville, Mississippi, Ma'am."

In a few minutes, she came back and said, "Come this way, please."

As they got to his office, Mr. Breckinridge met Lim and Bubba at the door. "Mr. Appleton, glad to see you, come in." Then offering his hand to Bubba he said, "You must be Bubba, Mr. Appleton's partner."

"That's right, Mr. Breckinridge," Bubba replied with a firm handshake and an even look into Mr. Breckinridge's eyes. "Glad to meet you, sir."

When they'd all sat down, Lim looked across the large mahogany table and got right to business. "Mr. Breckinridge, Bubba and I have discussed your proposition and we're very interested in giving it a chance. If the gold and silver is there, either we'll find it, or you can put it out of your mind. Won't anyone ever find it."

"Good. I've been hoping you'd agree. By the way, have you boys got motel rooms for the night?"

"No, sir, we figured we'd go back today."

"I think it may be wise if you could stay over," Mr. Breckinridge replied, "we'll have a few drinks and dinner and I'll explain everything I have concerning the treasure. There are a number of things we need to discuss. I believe we can have fewer interruptions if we handle the discussion at the motel."

Lim looking at Bubba who nodded. "Sure that will be fine, Mr. Breckinridge. We certainly have the time and would like to have all the information you have."

He handed Lim and Bubba a copy of their contract. "Read this contract over. If it's all right, sign it and I'll have one of our people notarize your signatures and we can get that part settled. Tonight, after we go over everything, we can tear up the contract if you decide against looking for the treasure." This brought an odd look over Lim's face. "The reason I need the agreement signed before I give you the information I have is because of the no disclosure clause I have in the contract. Being truthful, it is for my protection in case you decide not to look for the treasure."

"I appreciate that, Mr. Breckinridge," Lim replied. "I'd certainly do it that way if I were holding the key information as you seem to be."

"Good," Mr. Breckinridge replied, "look it over and see if we are in agreement. It is a very simple agreement, but I have learned over a period of time the best way for a clear understanding and to settle any misunderstanding is to have it in writing."

"We've just learned that lesson the hard way," Bubba interrupted. "I'll assure you written word seems to have a better memory."

Mr. Breckinridge laughed at Bubba's honesty. "I see you have. It's a protection for both of us as you'll see."

Since Lim was the legal mind, Bubba just glanced over it and waited for Lim to decide.

After reading it, Lim stated, "Bubba, it's just like Mr. Breckinridge agreed, the other night." Turning his eye across the table he continued, "Mr. Breckinridge, this is agreeable, we'll sign."

"Good." Pressing the intercom button, he called in a notary and they signed the contract. Lim handed the paper back and Mr. Breckinridge signed it saying, "Now I'll have my secretary call the Baton Rouge Motel and make reservations for you. It's located on the highway you came in on. Do you remember seeing it?"

"I saw it, sir," Bubba nodded.

"Fine, I'll pick you two up around six. We'll have a drink and dinner then we'll go back to the motel and I'll go over everything I have with you."

Walking out the back, Bubba spoke to Lim, "He sure gets to the point. You have to like the man even though he seems all business."

Lim was smiling when he got back to the truck. "Guess we'll just have to take him one dollar at a time. You never know what's in another man's mind, but he clearly seems fair."

"We're betting high stakes here," Bubba replied with a smile, "all we got. I sure hope we're not dealing with a nut that doesn't have all his cards."

Opening the pickup door, Lim replied, "Bubba, you got that right. Positive thinking is what you need. Remember what I said about shooting craps? Nothing different. The higher the stakes, the more exciting it gets. An old grabbling saying is 'you catch the big fish in the big log.'"

Bubba got behind the steering wheel and added, "Lim, treasure hunting gets you stirred up more than anything I've ever seen. I wish I could get the sure feeling you get about things. Somehow, not knowing for sure if any of this is true keeps bugging me. What if we spend all our money and it ain't no treasure there to start with? I never heard about any missing treasure being mentioned when we studied about the Civil War in school. All I heard was how broke the South was."

"Bubba," Lim answered, "during the Civil War lot's of money was raised by people donating or giving valuables, watches, rings, money, silver, land, whatever they had of value to the southern cause. I reckon' they figured if they didn't win the war that everything would be lost anyway. You're talking about huge sums of money, and especially when people start donating their personal possessions. Besides, many people had money. I can see where there could have been that much money stored in Vicksburg. There were many rich people in the South before the war. The reason you never heard of the stashed money in Vicksburg was because it was kept so secret. Even Jefferson Davis refused to put his orders in writing. The last thing he wanted was for the Yankees to know of the huge gold and silver holdings."

Bubba turned in at the motel and stopped at the office. "We best see if we can pay for the rooms. I bet a room will cost ten dollars a day."

"Aw, Bubba," said Lim, "after we find the Merrygold treasure, we'll be lighting cigars with five dollar bills. Didn't I tell you that you're going to have to start believing that you're going to win?"

Bubba answered with a smile. "Yeah, but it sure would help to have at least even odds. It'd even help if we knew for sure there ever was a treasure. Not to mention that somebody could've already found it. Besides that, the old Colonel, whatever his name was, that lived in the Old Soldiers' Home, could have been crazy as a Betsy Bug and made up the whole story."

Lim ignored Bubba's statement and got out to go into the motel office. "I'll be back in a minute. Let me find out what room we got. You see if you can find a coke machine and some ice while I'm gone."

Bubba spotted the machine but stayed in the pickup until Lim got back. "There's the coke machine over there. What room we got?" he asked as Lim sat down.

"Seven," Lim replied. "Must be on down past the coke machine. Here, take the key and drop me out at the machine. I'll get us a chaser and meet you at the room."

Bubba took the suitcases into the room thinking that it was a good thing Stella insisted that they bring them.

Lim came in as Bubba threw the suitcases on one of the beds. "It's almost five. That gives us time to have a drink or two before he gets here. You gonna take a shower?" Lim asked.

"Yeah. A shower'll feel pretty good right about now. Go ahead and fix you a drink, I'll get one when I get out."

Taking his shirt off and starting into the bathroom, Bubba remarked, "Pretty nice room. Two beds and all. What did it cost?"

"Not bad," Lim replied, "twelve-fifty."

"Ouch," Bubba replied wincing. "That's six and a quarter each."

At exactly six o'clock, Mr. Breckinridge knocked on their door. Both Lim and Bubba were dressed and ready, and didn't invite him in, just walked out and shook hands again. Bubba thought that Mr. Breckinridge would make a good politician by the way he shook hands.

Mr. Breckinridge took them to an exclusive restaurant where you had to have a key to get in. After a few drinks at the bar, the waitress led them into an elaborate dining room and they feasted on one of the best steaks a person could have, topped off by a floor show featuring scantily clad beauties.

It was after eight when Breckinridge pulled into the motel. Getting out, Breckinridge unlocked his car trunk, got out his brief case along with a round map tube, and followed Lim and Bubba into the motel room. "Lim, you and Bubba clear the bed and work some chairs around where we can see," he instructed. "We'll use it as our table."

Spreading the map out on the bed, he continued, "This is the latest map of the Mississippi River below Vicksburg." Then spreading out another larger sheet, he said, "This is the latest aerial photo of the area for five miles up and down the river around Carrier's Point." Weighting the maps down with ashtrays and glasses, he continued, "We'll get back to these in a few minutes."

He opened his brief case and took out a letter sealed in protective plastic. The handwritten letter was yellowed with age and worn so bad its edges were cracked. It was evident that the letter had been read hundreds of times. Handing the plastic encased letter to Lim, he said, "This letter was written to my great aunt who was Captain Fredrick Breckinridge's wife." He hesitated a second, then went on. "Before you read the letter, let me put it into the proper perspective.

Lim nodded his head and laid the letter on the bed as Breckinridge continued, "My Father was unaware of the treasure when he went to the Old Soldiers' Home in Gulfport. He'd heard that there was a number of old Civil War veterans still living at the home and thought that possibly someone there may have known of his Uncle Fredrick who'd lived quite a heroic life before and during the Civil War. He knew he was a Navy captain and died at Vicksburg. In fact, he had no idea he would be so fortunate as to find a person that personally knew his uncle. Anyway, at the Old Soldiers' Home he met a man named Robert P. Hampston, who told him the story of President Davis' message to General Pemberton and the part my great-uncle had in this unrecorded part of history. This, of course, interested my father, and he being a very thorough man, had affidavits made of the Colonel's conversation.

"Returning to Port Gibson, where we lived at that time, my father went to work trying to locate the personal effects of his aunt who had died a few years before. He remembered the story of her receiving a letter from her deceased husband soon after the war was over. The letter was delivered by a Northern gentleman that had been an officer in the Union Navy. That being so unusual is what made him remember it. The Northern man came a long way to deliver it and told Aunt Helen that he wrote it for her husband who had died a short time after he signed it.

"My father remembered his aunt showing him the letter and how she told the story of the Union officer telling about plucking her husband from the Mississippi River, badly burned and barely alive in his final hours. He told her of her husband's ship, the Merrygold, exploding, killing the crew and sinking a short time before his crew pulled him out of the river. His dying request was to write his wife and tell her his final thoughts just before he died and the captain promised to deliver it to her.

"Well, father remembered the letter and knew it had to be a family keepsake, even though it had no connection with the treasure. He made a search for it, searched every place he could think, knowing it had to be some place; his aunt would certainly not destroy it. Finally, while searching through an old trunk in the attic of his Uncle Frederick's house, he found the letter. Now gentlemen, I think this brings us up to the date of the letter you may read now."

Lim laid the letter on the bed where both could read it. The letter read:

To My Dearest and Beloved Wife, Helen:

Even though time and fate will surely end my life within the day, through the hand and pen of Captain Elton Townsend of the Union Gunboat, that has snatched my broken body from the death hungry waters of the Mississippi, this letter comes to you. In my last hours, my thoughts are of you. Your love, affection, and courage have given meaning to my life. Even though I cannot be with you in our remaining years, my prayer is that God will be with you and take care of you.

My words are to you; however, for the sake of the South the failure of my mission must be reported. I must place this burden on you my Dearest, please at your earliest opportunity, inform General Pemberton of my regrets of the mission's failure. The Merrygold was critically crippled with a water line hit during the run of the Union blockade. Reaching "Carrier's Point", where all efforts to repair the damaged hull failed, our cargo was unloaded to lighten the ship. Desperate attempts to deliver information to our rendezvous proved fatal. My regards to the General, by my signature, the South will survive.

My wife, Helen, my last thought will be of you and the happiness we have shared in the short time God has allotted to us.

My love always,
O
Fredrick IIIf
June 2, 1863

Lim looked over the letter again and caught the scribbled signature saying, "Your great uncle signed the letter?"

"That's right, but notice the Roman numeral "3" with the circle over it after his signature, this had no meaning. He was not even a junior and the circle above the three also baffled all of us. I wish I could have talked with his wife about it before her death. It may have been a sign or something personal between them. Also the "f" following the Roman numeral three, it undoubtedly was added by my Uncle Fredrick.

"Hmmmmmmm….," Lim mused, "it could have some bearing. Let's look at the map of the Carrier's Point. The letter definitely stated he unloaded the Merrygold there."

Taking the aerial photo off the top of the map, Mr. Breckinridge pointed to the large bend in the river saying, "This is Carrier's Point. There's a mile marker located here. Back in the days of the Civil War, it was a white washed cypress post about ten feet tall braced by a pile of rocks. Some rocks are still there, probably the same stones used to brace the old marker, however, now a concrete post has replaced the wooden one." Then, pointing to the curve below Carrier's Point, "Here on the lower side of the point a number of years ago we drove a well that has a pitcher pump on it. It may need new washers, but it was working all right three or four years ago. You might want to set up camp in this area where you can have fresh water." Sliding the aerial map back on top, he continued, "See this line where the lager timber starts about a mile and a half above Carrier's Point and extends below the point about the same distance. This land back to the Mississippi levy belongs to me. My father acquired it after he found out about the lost treasure. He bought close to ten thousand acres up and down the river at Carrier's point—on both sides of the river. The timber hasn't been cut since he bought it in 1910…

"I bet it has some fine hunting," Bubba interrupted.

"It does," Mr. Breckinridge replied smiling. "You'll not want for meat. There's plenty of deer, turkey, and squirrel. We allow a little hunting beyond the bayous that cut off the point. Where you'll be, we have allowed no hunting or any trespassing. You'll have the whole area to yourselves." Sliding the river map back on top and pointing with the pencil, he added, "Here, about three miles below Carrier's Point, is the sandbar where the Merrygold washed up. Of course there's no sign of it now."

After discussing as many things as he could, and answering all the questions he'd been asked, he rolled up the maps saying, "The letter I will keep, but if you need to see it, you may come to Baton Rouge anytime you like and look at it." Sticking out his hand and shaking both men's hands, he stated, "I assume the contract stands. It's getting late. I'll be at the bank if you need me. Good luck."

Lim answered Mr. Breckinridge as he walked to the door. "The contract is fine. We'll be getting our supplies together shortly. We should be in Vicksburg within a week or so. Mr. Breckinridge, there's a question that has been bugging me and I wonder if it has come to your mind."

"What's that, Lim?" Mr. Breckinridge asked.

"I know it's getting late and you need to go, but I can't help but wonder why did Colonel Hampston, I believe his name was, keep the information about the lost treasure to himself for all those years?"

Mr. Breckinridge turned from the door and replied, "That's one of the questions I asked my father and he said Hampston answered the question when he first went to see him at the Old Soldiers' Home looking for information about his Uncle. Let me sit down, Lim, this is going to take a little while to tell."

Going back to the chairs, Lim asked if he would like another drink.

"No, I think I've had enough for one night," he replied as he sat in the chair. "I've got a big day tomorrow. The bank examiners are coming and they can give you a headache without drinking. Let me tell the story about Hampston and make sure I get it exactly as my father told me." He took a deep breath and began. "When my father asked him if he may have known Captain Fredrick Breckinridge, the Colonel didn't answer at first, acting like he'd never heard of him. My father insisted that he should remember him because he was a Captain in the Confederate Navy and a close friend of General Pemberton's. This must have jogged his memory because he suddenly became deceptive in his remarks and asked of my father's connection to Captain Breckinridge, and why he was seeking the information. Remember, at this time, my father was totally unaware of any Confederate treasure, or of his uncle running the Union blockade during the war, even how his uncle died. Well, Lim, little by little my father was able to get Hampston to talk, and suddenly out of the clear blue, he told him the story of the Merrygold's alleged cargo. Finally, he told my father that he'd never told the story to anyone before because he, General Pemberton, and all those connected with the secret mission were sworn to secrecy. He said that it'd been so long since it happened that he didn't feel like he was breaking any trust to tell it now, especially since the war was over and everyone connected with the story was dead except him. Maybe it'll help the families of those brave men to rest easier if they know what had happened to their loved ones." Mr. Breckinridge got up to go.

Lim sat back for a minute and thought over the incredible story he'd just heard. "Not too many people have the will power the Colonel had."

Mr. Breckinridge walked toward the door, stopped and turned back to Lim. "This world could use more people like him."

Lim went to the door, and watched the long black car turn around and disappear out of the motel's driveway. Turning, he said, "That's quite a story. Fits Breckinridge to a 'T.'"

Bubba poured some coke in a glass and looked up at Lim. "Gives you an eerie feeling, don't it? I mean it's almost like it's a part of history that was never meant to be recorded. I don't know why, but it gives me the creeps, like all the souls of the ones connected with the Merrygold and the lost treasure are somewhere nearby looking down, or up maybe, just hoping that their secret will never be found. It's like we're doing something wrong looking for the treasure."

Lim came over and sat at the table across from Bubba. He didn't say anything for a while and you could tell by looking at him that he was in deep thought. Finally, he reached over and replenished his drink.

"I never thought of it like that. But ever since that little man came to my house, I've had the same strange feeling, but mine's been a little different, like we were part of the story. I don't know, but it's strange. When I read the sworn testimony, I felt like I was standing with General Pemberton when he received President Jefferson Davis' message. Makes me wonder about reincarnation. Maybe I *was* there."

Bubba gave him a comical look and both men burst out laughing.

"Whatever this feeling is, Bubba, the void, or the missing part that makes sense of all this is somewhere," he said with growing excitement as he waved his hand through the air to help make his point. "Maybe our destiny in life is to fill that void, or at least find the missing part."

Bubba got up, stretched and said, "Lim, I'm getting sleepy. We won't find the answer tonight, but I got the same feeling you do. We're going to find something. I feel it deep inside like I just know it's going to happen. What it's going to be, I guess only the Good Lord knows."

"Bubba," Lim answered as he sipped at his drink, "you can count on that statement being true. This whole set-up seems to me that we were destined to be part of it. Whatever happens, I got a feeling it's going to be a doozie. Does it suit you to leave around 6 o'clock in the morning?"

"Suits the hell out of me," Bubba replied.

Chapter 16

Lim and Bubba got into Taylorsville around 3:30 the next afternoon.

"Get with Stella," Lim told Bubba as he dropped him off at his mother's house, "then if y'all can, come to the house around dark-thirty. I'll get Jennie to cook us a meal and we can get started on our plans."

Bubba's mother met him at the door and hugged him. "Stella called a short time ago. You better go call her."

Bubba got Stella on the phone and filled her in on the meeting with Mr. Breckinridge, finishing with, "Lim wants us to come out to the Big House and eat supper. Tonight, we're going to start making plans and working on an equipment list. Suit you?"

"Is that all you got to say?" Stella wanted affection more than information.

Bubba didn't know what to say. He never could figure women out. "Stella, I haven't been gone but a couple of days, but I did miss you."

"That's better," Stella replied laughing. "I'll see you tonight."

"Mom," Bubba said as he hung up the phone, "sometimes I wonder what makes women tick. One minute they're as mad as a setting goose and the next minute everything's like peaches and cream."

Bubba's mom answered with a smile, "Just hope for more peaches and cream. Men have their problems, too. Life needs a lot of peaches and cream."

Bubba picked Stella up early. Naturally, they didn't go straight to Lim's, petting was more on their minds. Bubba stopped by their usual parking spot which made them late getting to Lim's.

"Love birds always takes they time gettin' places," Jennie joked. Sometimes it seemed like Jennie was as happy about Bubba and Stella's romance as Bubba and Stella were. "Mr. Lim's in the living room mixin' up some mess. You two better join him. I'll have supper on the table shortly."

Lim gave Stella a hug when she walked in. "Bubba," he remarked to his younger partner leaving his arm around Stella's waist, "it looks to me like you got all the treasure you need right here."

"Yeah, I sure thought about that while we were down there making the rounds with Breckinridge."

Stella got her two cents in laughingly, "I don't know if I'd trust Breckinridge any more than I do you two."

Jennie saved the day by calling them to supper.

After the meal and Jennie had left, Lim spread the maps out on the dining room table and went over everything he could remember with Stella, word for word telling her about Captain Frederick's letter to his wife even the part about the unusual signature.

"Mr. Breckinridge sure was holding back the aces," she remarked when he'd finished. "That treasure's still there somewhere. From the sound of the captain's letter, he must have been trying to tell General Pemberton where it was, yet trying not to arouse the suspicions of the Union captain that wrote and delivered the letter. He wanted it to sound like just some letter from a dying man."

Lim followed up her thoughts. "I believe you're right. I'm sure he wanted to write his wife, but I believe he was desperately trying to tell the General where the treasure was. The letter did say he was trying to meet the rendezvous. Maybe that was his way of giving the information."

Bubba broke in, "Yeah, he wasn't planning on the boat catching fire and blowing up or whatever happened. In desperation, he used the letter to his wife. I'm like you—the letter says more between the lines than you think, like some kind of code or something."

"Yes," Stella offered, "knowing he was dying, he sure kept his head."

"Stella, you're right," Lim agreed. "The old captain was smart as a whip even when he was dying. I imagine he did most of his thinking about what to say in the letter while he was floating in the river hoping some boat would pick him up."

Then Bubba said, "I don't know why, but somehow the whole thing gives me a strange feeling, like being in a cemetery."

Stella snickered. "I guess I shouldn't tell this, but I dreamed about the treasure the other night. It was a strange dream all about General Pemberton, Colonel Hampston and Captain Breckinridge. All three were dancing around a big treasure singing and waving their swords. The strange part was what they were singing."

"What in the hell were the fools singing?" Bubba asked.

"Over and over they kept chanting the words, 'You'll never find it. It's ours and we're going to keep it.'"

"You two keep imagining those crazy things," Lim added, "and you're going to start seeing goblins and ghosts."

"Lim," Bubba said with a worried look on his face, "Stella's dream brings out the same feeling I've been having, like we're looking for a haunted treasure."

Lim tried to change the subject. "Okay, you two, cut out your silly thoughts. We got a treasure we're going to try to find, haunted or not. Haints, goblins, or what, we're going down there and find that treasure if it's there. This kind of talk is for people that are touched in the head." Handing a blue-back tablet to Stella, he said, "Stella, you write down the equipment we'll need. We'll add to it, but what we can think of now, let's get it down. Me and Bubba will go to Memphis in a couple of days and start getting it together. And no more haints and goblins."

Stella smiled knowing that Lim was superstitious. She glanced at Bubba and started writing down the equipment as Lim and Bubba called it out. The list included everything from tents to life preservers, metal detectors to cooking vessels, and aqua-lungs to picks and shovels.

As the list grew longer, Bubba said, "Boy, it's gonna take a pile of money to buy all this."

"That's right," Lim replied. "And we're going to need an eighteen-foot boat and motor. We could use my boat and motor but it really is too small for the Mississippi. I figure we best pool our money and buy everything out of that."

Bubba tried to estimate the money he had left and said, "Let me see, Lim. I got about four-thousand dollars I can put in."

"That should be enough with my four," Lim answered. "If we need more, I got a couple thousand I can add to it."

Stella added, "There's a good bit of the supplies I can get at the house. If we run short on money, I've got some, too."

"With what we've got," Lim replied, "we should be all right. But if we're going to go into this, let's give it all we got. Get everything we'll need. No need of doing it half…," he smiled at Stella, then added, "halfways." Stella nodded her thanks at his gallantry. Lim continued, "You can't win if you're not in, and you're not in if you're afraid of your money."

The next day, Bubba and Lim went to Memphis and started buying supplies. By the end of the week, two pickup loads of supplies had been purchased, plus two boats and trailers—both loaded with supplies. Lim's porch looked like he was having a yard sale. To keep people from getting too interested in talk of looking for treasure, they decided to tell any curious people that a Louisiana firm had hired them to look for artifacts on the Mississippi River. This worked out well and even Mr. and Mrs. Ranking went along with the scheme.

I guess one of the highlights was when Mr. Ranking told Bubba he was going to let one of his men take his cattle truck over to Vicksburg with a load of their equipment so it wouldn't be necessary to make more than one trip. This made Bubba feel like he was finally getting to be one of their family.

The next couple of weeks passed like a couple of days. Everything was finally purchased and early on a Saturday morning the two trucks with the equipment left Taylorsville. Getting into Vicksburg around noon and finding a place to launch their boats, they decided to take two loads down the river that afternoon set up camp, and haul the rest the next day. Mr. Ranking's driver knew he'd have to spend the night and agreed to stay with the truck while they were gone, keeping an eye on what they hadn't moved down the river.

Around two o'clock, the excited treasure hunters pushed the heavy loaded boats out into the swift current of the Mississippi—Bubba and Stella in the larger boat and Lim in the smaller. Both motors cranked and ran smoothly, and in a matter of minutes, the boats were in the open river and on their way.

Looking back up the river as the boats went under the Vicksburg Bridge, you could see the town jutting out over the bluffs. The same thought was probably in each of their minds. This was the same town, the same river, the same journey the Merrygold had taken. The only difference was this was May 15 and two in the afternoon. The Merrygold had steamed out in the dark of the night a couple weeks later, close to a hundred years ago.

The trip down the river was beautiful. Lim pulled his boat alongside Bubba and Stella and all rode in silence. Each in his own mind taking in the magnificent scenery, thinking about the past, and what lay ahead in the future. Both boats gave way to the far side of the river as a tugboat pushing a string of barges slowly ground its way up the river pushing a two-foot wake of water across the river.

Crossing the wake Lim shouted, "We'll have to remember not to get too close to those big boys. Up close that wake could turn a boat over." Reaching in the cooler in front of him, he pulled out a fifth and took a straight drink. Pitching the bottle across to Stella as he got through, he hollered, "Give Bubba a drink. He may need an eye opener."

Bubba shook his head. "Don't need one, Lim. I'm all eyes now!" he yelled.

It was a beautiful spring day. The sun's reflection caught the green budding trees and the full bloom of the dogwoods gave a colorful background to the snow-white sandbars that glistened like large fields of diamonds. Stella, with the wind blowing her loose blouse, reflected the beauty of the surroundings as she pointed excitedly to the scenic wonders. Pride lifted in Bubba as he thought of how beautiful she was and even though he didn't want to admit it, how glad he was she made the journey with them.

The scenic beauty, the excitement, and never-ending thoughts of treasure expelled the passing of time. Each bend of the river held a new subject, from flocks of geese flushing around the endless sandbars, to deer and turkey either scampering for cover or standing motionless and observing the strangers passing through their territory.

Stella pointed to a coon that darted up a sheared off bank and called back to Bubba, "We must have seen every kind of animal there is!"

"A good sign we're getting further from civilization," Bubba called as he dodged the boat around a floating log.

The sun approaching the timbered horizon as Lim glanced at his watch, swung his boat in close and hollered across, "We're getting close. Watch for a heavy timber line on the left side of the river."

Rounding the bend, Stella pointed to the long curve with a high point jutting from the twisting river. "That must be Carrier's Point!" she yelled to Bubba who turned the boat to the east side of the river and followed the heavy foliaged bank. The second-generation growth was almost like a rain forest. All the trees were two to four feet through with little or no undergrowth. At places, the river had cut into the steep banks undermining some of the massive trees and toppling them into the swift river. The large root-laden stumps clung to the high riverbank like the fingers of a drowning man.

Rounding the rocky point, the historic mile marker glistened in the afternoon sun. The timber gave way to the rocky ground of the point for a good seventy-five to a hundred yards, leaving the bald knob sticking out in the river with the shining mile marker standing like a lighthouse to give warning to the passing river travelers. History lay unrecorded in the mystery of the many it had saluted, even the Merrygold.

Chapter 17

The swift current of the river cut along the base of the barren rock bluff exposing large slabs of rock that had sloughed off in years passed. The shining bald knob defied the angry undercurrent forming dangerous whirlpools that whipped along its rock base devouring everything in their whirling grasp Across from the point, a long silvery sandbar followed the river for more than a mile, disappearing as the river turned west which gave the illusion of switching the sandbar to the opposite side. Lim, taking the lead, guided his boat along the edge of the treacherous point instructing Bubba to watch the whirlpools! They could sink a boat.

"We'll circle the point," he yelled, "the water should be calmer on the back side." The swift current eddied in front of Lim as he guided the boat to a stop at the foot of a long bending willow protruding over the calming waters.

Bubba and Stella's boat floated in next to Lim's. "Is this where the well is supposed to be?" Stella asked Lim as Bubba wrapped the rope around the large willow.

Lim pointed to the timberline along the top of the rocky incline. "Somewhere in that tract of timber. It shouldn't be over a couple a' hundred yards."

Each took a load of supplies and excitedly scrambled up the rocky incline that quickly changed to large towering oaks, sycamores, pecans, and cottonwoods. The clean shady woods were breathtaking.

"It's so pretty!" Stella exclaimed to Bubba as they stood in awe of the scenery, "It's almost like the pictures you see in a magazine."

Bubba laid his load of supplies down. "It could almost make a person want to just stay here and forget the rest of the world. If a person owned this, he wouldn't need to be searching for a buried treasure."

"It is so beautiful," Stella said again, "not far from the way the Good Lord first made it."

Bubba put his arm around her and commented as a squirrel darted across the shaded undergrowth, "Looking at this makes you understand why the Indians fought so hard to keep it."

Lim broke in, "You two daydreamers bring your gear. There's the well over there."

It was after sun down when they finished unloading the boat and got the tents up. Lim finished putting the washers in the well as Bubba and Stella gathered wood for the night's campfire. They would fix their camping area better as time went along, but with the two sleeping tents, storage and cook tent and a wood table nailed between the two big oaks next to the well, the camp was pretty well set up.

Supper was light, consisting of weenies, pork and beans, sardines, and coffee. Finishing the meal, they punched the fire up and sat by its warmth swapping tales of the day's happenings. Stella snuggled into Bubba's arms, while Lim sat across the fire leaning against an old log. The stories continued into the night. The subject finally got around to old Captain Breckinridge and his crew—not a good subject for the first night in camp, but one thought would bring on another and before it was over Bubba had told of the eerie feeling he had of the captain and his crew. Then Stella added to the story, telling of her dream and how real it had seemed.

Lim laughed it off. "I guess everybody gets strange feelings around a cemetery and places where people have died or been killed. Maybe their spirits are still here, I don't know. But there's one thing I do know, crazy talk like you two keep dragging up ain't good for you and if you two don't stop letting your minds wonder we'll all be sleeping in the same tent. Now forget that talk and leave your goblins and ghosts here at the fire. We got a big day tomorrow. Let's go to bed." With that, Lim got up and went towards his and Bubba's tent.

Stella's tent was maybe thirty yards or so from Lim and Bubba's with the cook tent in between. Each of the three had his or her own thoughts as they drifted off to sleep listening to the gentle breeze sifting through the large trees. In the distance, an owl called and another answered over near the point. Gradually, the night sounds came forth. Crickets began their nightly chirping while the frogs on the river joined the chorus. A whippoorwill came forth with a sharp "chip flew out of the white oak," and far off a red wolf wailed in with a long mournful howl. Each strange sound harmonized, blending with the peaceful night. A limb, slipped loose by the breeze, dropped to the ground frightening an animal that scampered away simultaneously quieting the night like closing a door.

Suddenly a wild scream shattered the peaceful surroundings followed by the shrill snort of an alarmed deer. The screams came again, then another, then another. Each scream echoed with the bolting deer's snorts.

Lim threw his bedroll back and hollered, "What the hell is that?"

Bubba tried to get out of his bedroll and only succeeded in getting entangled in its folds and rolled out of his cot onto the tent floor. "Something's got Stella!" he yelled in a shrill, hysterical voice.

The screams came again and again. Bubba yanking his pants on and fumbling in the darkness finally found a flashlight. Then almost knocking down the tent, he stumbled out and ran around the cook tent shining the light on Stella's tent as he ran. The tent was bulging and bouncing from one side to the other with the wildest screams you can imagine going on inside. Suddenly the flap flew open as Bubba momentarily stopped in front of the tent. Out rolled Stella, her long flannel gown almost over her head.

Seeing Bubba, she jumped up and flew into his arms screaming, "There's a monster inside the tent!"

Bubba was so surprised that he couldn't do anything but hold Stella with one arm and his flashlight shining on the tent flap with the other. Then out darted the monster. Stella screamed again as the hairy thing sailed through the open tent flap, half scared to death, he darted between Stella and Bubba. The screams came again and Stella jumped up on Bubba's back coiling around him like a muscadine vine.

Stumbling and cussing, with no shirt, no shoes, and only a pair of pants on, Lim finally managed to stagger to the scene. His hair was bushed out and fell across his eyes like a tangled rag mop. He held a double barrel shotgun in one hand and the lantern above his head with the other.

"What the hell is going on?" he gasped.

Bubba wrestled with Stella trying to uncoil her from around his neck. "Ain't nothing, Lim. Stella tried to scare a hairy monster to death." Surveying the scene, he couldn't keep from laughing. "The poor thing sure jumped on the wrong person. I bet it's still running."

"What the hell was it?" Lim asked trying to catch his breath.

"A damn coon got in my tent," Stella replied with an embarrassed, "go-to-hell" look.

Lim walked over to the fifth bottle on the pump table and answered with a chuckle. "Hell, for a moment I thought old Captain Breckinridge's haint was in there."

Settling Stella down with a drink, the three again continued their night's rest. Lim and Bubba chuckling to themselves as they crawled into their sleeping bags. Stella was so mad and embarrassed it was almost daylight before she finally went to sleep.

The quiet morning awoke with the loud gobble of a turkey that had roosted a short ways from camp. Lim slipped out of bed, eased over to Bubba's bunk, and shook him. Bubba, half asleep, asked "What is it Lim?"

"Did you hear the turkey gobble?"

"No, I think I just got to sleep."

"Well go ahead and sleep. I'm going to get the gun and slip out there and see if I can catch him coming off the roost."

"Okay, but don't hurry back," Bubba grunted as he rolled back over.

It was dark as Lim got the shotgun and eased outside. A lazy smoke covered the ground from the smoldering fire forced down by the heavy morning dew. Lim, picking up a few sticks of wood, punched the coals up and laid them across the fire.

Suddenly the gobbler cut loose a series of gobbles, answered by another gobbler not far away. Marking the area of the gobbles, Lim loaded the gun and eased past Stella's tent, laughing to himself as he remembered the previous night's excitement.

The pink sky slowly turned a brilliant red as morning broke and with the breaking of day, the forest slowly awoke. In the distance, a crow gave his sharp caws answered by an owl. Not far away, the gobbler announced that he was king, so close to Lim now that he almost shook the trees. Picking out a fallen log, Lim eased up beside it and sat down. The gobbler, unaware of the intruder in his forest, gobbled again. A hen circled from a nearby tree and gracefully sailed to the ground not over twenty yards from Lim. She clucked a time or two, and then worked her way across the open forest. The flap of wings turned Lim's head as the gobbler left his perch, set his wings and glided to the ground a few feet from the hen. Bursting into full strut, he shook the air with a loud gobble. Following the hen, he walked behind the trunk of a hackberry tree. Lim raised his gun and touched the trigger as the massive bird cleared the tree trunk.

Stella heard the shot. She hurriedly dressed and ran from her tent. Bubba was boiling a pot of coffee on the fire. "I heard a shot. It was so close. Who could it be?" she asked looking worried.

Bubba calmly took the spewing coffee pot off the fire, walked over to the small table and filled two cups, handing one to Stella. "Lim's gone coon hunting. Seems he didn't get much sleep last night."

Stella was slightly taken aback by Bubba's remark. "Cut your fooling and tell me what's going on?" she said with an unsure grin.

Bubba glanced back and saw Lim coming through the opening behind the tent. "There's Lim now, ask him."

Lim came around the tent proudly holding the bird out to Stella. "Thought I'd get supper."

Stella hesitantly held the bird by its wings and commented, "Lim, it's beautiful. How did you know where to go?"

Bubba walked over and held the turkey by its neck examining it carefully. "It must have been following a coon. Boy, its fat as a butter ball." He handed it back to Stella. "Cook of the Appleton treasure hunting camp, please clean this magnificent bird and prepare it for our supper."

"Me? You must be kidding!" Stella exclaimed. "I've never plucked a chicken in my life, much less a turkey."

Lim added his part to the tease. "Aw, it's not hard. Just get some boiling water and scald it. The feathers will come right off. After you get the feathers off, split it open on the bottom side and pull out everything you can."

Bubba broke in, "Be sure to save the gizzard and liver for giblet gravy."

Stella laid the bird on the table trying to be as good a sport as she could. "And what will my two great hunters do while I'm cooking their royal supper?" she asked whimsically?

Lim laughed as he hugged Stella. "Just got to tease you a little after last night." This solicited a dirty look from Stella.

While Stella finished washing dishes at the pitcher pump, Lim went over his plans with Bubba. "We'll take both boats back up the river and bring the rest of the supplies down. We may have to make two trips. If it's okay with Stella, she can stay and straighten up around camp. The lighter the boat the faster we can travel."

"That sounds like a good idea to me," Stella said as she walked up. "Besides that, I don't want you two watching me getting the feathers off that bird."

Bubba broke in, "We were just kidding about dressing the turkey. I'll do that before we leave."

"You will not. I'm a big girl and it's time I learned how to dress and clean game. We may be eating a lot of it before we leave here."

Bubba looked at Lim who nodded his head in approval with a smile. He gave Stella a hug as he started down to the boat saying, "Lim, come on. We got a big day. Looks like Stella has everything under control here."

"Stella, load that old double barrel. We'll see you sometime after noon," Lim said with a smile as he walked away.

"Don't worry about me," Stella replied with a smile and a wave. "I can take care of myself. I don't expect many visitors will be dropping in."

A short time later Lim and Bubba cranked the outboards and left the eddied bay for the swift current of the river. Stella was standing on the bald knob waving as they rounded the point and headed up the river.

Lim pulled close to Bubba and shouted, "Open her up but watch out for floating logs. It's going to be slow going against the current. Try to hold the inside of the bends. That way we can dodge some of the swift water. It's going to take three and a half to four hours regardless."

It took three-hours and forty-five minutes to get to Vicksburg. Pulling into the dock, Mr. Ranking's hired hand saw them coming and backed the truck down as close as he could. After loading all they could on the two boats, Lim told the young man to try to find a place to park his pickup at either one of the gas stations or garages while they were gone.

"We'll be back for the last load about the middle of the afternoon," he explained.

The trip down the river was without mishap with both men enjoying the beautiful scenery and perfect spring day. It took less time going back with the current than it had coming against it.

They reached Carrier's Point around one o'clock. Lim pointed out the mile marker with Stella standing on the point waving. As they rounded the rocky point, she turned and ran to meet them.

It took them a few minutes to unload the boats and grab one of the sandwiches Stella brought them, then they left without going to camp. Bubba joked for Stella to keep an eye out for coons as he pushed the boat off, then dodged a well thrown rock as he turned the boat up river.

Lim laughed as he backed his boat off the rocky shore. "We'll see you around dark," he called. "Do you need anything from town?"

"No, everything's fine," Stella called back as Lim turned up river. "Y'all be careful. I'll have supper ready when you get back."

Catching up with Bubba, Lim shouted, "Open her up, Bubba. If we push it, we can make it by dark."

As before, the hired hand saw them coming and had his truck backed down the ramp when Bubba and Lim pulled in. Not wasting any time, they loaded both boats, thanked the hired hand for his help and were on their way back down river in less than a half hour.

"We're making about as good time as the Merrygold," Bubba yelled over the sound of the motors as the speeding boats passed under the Vicksburg bridge.

"Probably are," Lim called back with a knowing nod, "but the cargo is a little different. Maybe it'll be the same when we come back up the river."

The sun was sinking behind the willowed horizon as Bubba tied up to the leaning willow. Both men were tired and whipped and glad the full day was over.

"Look at that," Lim remarked as he got out of the boat, "Stella has carried all the supplies to camp. She's some girl."

Bubba smiled, "Guess my idea about bringing her along was about the best idea we've had."

Smiling, Lim replied, "That's some statement."

Carrying a load of equipment, they started for camp. Walking around the tents with their load, both stood in amazement. Over the fire with a metal rod stuck through the middle and resting between two forked sticks, was the prettiest roasted turkey either man had ever seen. The small table was set with a candle in the middle, then to the side on a smaller table the whiskey bottle, three glassed and a chaser.

"Well, I'll be," Bubba said. Then he almost dropped his armload of gear as Stella came out of her tent with a fresh outfit on. "Great hunters that have traveled the mighty waters of the Mississippi," she said with a slight bow, "fix yourself a drink and have a seat. Dinner will be served very shortly."

As she pressed by, Bubba swatted her across the rear, "Stella, you're something else."

Bubba began slicing the turkey as Stella brought the Dutch oven to the table and opened it. Looking at the steaming beans, onions and potatoes, Bubba exclaimed, "Stella, this looks more like a Thanksgiving meal. You're some cook."

"You're just trying to get on the good side of me. I never cooked with a Dutch oven in coals before. Sure hope it tastes as good as it looks."

Lim passed his plate to Bubba who put a large helping of turkey on it. "Whoever thought of bringing Stella on the trip was some smart person," Lim said.

Bubba handed Lim's plate to Stella who loaded it down with vegetables. "Thank you, Lim," Bubba replied immodestly.

All were laughing as Stella and Bubba finished serving their plates. Then, as usual, things got quite as the eating began, which is a pleasing sound to any cook.

Full and content Bubba and Lim retired to the fire while Stella started cleaning up the dishes. In the distance, an owl called as Lim stuffed tobacco in his pipe and lit it with a burning stick from the fire and declared, "What a day!"

The next day was spent fixing up the campsite. Wood had to be cut and an eating and worktable had to be built. A rock furnace with a wire mesh grill was constructed from the fieldstone lying about and wires strung for lanterns—a general clean up and repair around camp finished out the afternoon. As the sun set behind the willowed horizon, Lim and Bubba went back to the bayou behind the point and seined some carp, small perch and crawfish. Returning to the river, they put out three throw lines with about ten hooks each.

As dark claimed the daylight and the full moon rose over the forest, the three watched the lingering coals disappear, discussing their plans. "Tomorrow we'll map the area and start looking for the treasure. What do you think of starting with the metal detectors and cover every inch of the Point for at least a couple hundred yards, or even back to the bayou. We know the Captain and the crew couldn't have crossed the bayou, but without knowing how much time spent at Carrier's Point, it's hard to tell how far off the river they may have taken the gold and silver," Lim explained.

"That sounds good to me," Bubba answered. "But what if it's buried a couple of feet deep or more, will the detectors pick it up?"

"I'm sure it will, being such a large quantity as it is. Anyway, at least we'll eliminate one possibility if we don't find it."

Stella broke in, "I don't believe it's buried. I believe it's in the water, maybe right down there at the leaning willow where our boats are parked."

Lim walked over and poured himself a drink. "Could be anywhere. There ain't but one thing to do and that's check every place we can think of. It's going to be slow, but we're going to try and search every possibility. There's one thing I'll bet on, it's within a half mile of us right now."

Bubba sipped his drink and thought to himself, 'At least Lim is willing to bet on it being here, and he don't make bad bets.'

The next day, Lim and Bubba ran the throw line while Stella fixed breakfast and pulled in a nice eight-pound flat-head catfish, which was proudly brought back to camp.

Stella saw them coming, took up the eggs and walked to meet them at the top of the bank with the skillet still in her hands. "We'll have fish tonight. That's a big one. Come on and eat breakfast. Y'all can dress the fish while I clean up the dishes."

Gathering their equipment, the search began by tying cloth flags to mark the areas that had already been searched. The bald knob was soon covered with the red marker cloth. The rest of the afternoon, the search included the timbered area back to the big bayou.

Stella cooked a light lunch and kept them in water as the search continued. Around mid afternoon, she brought coffee and cookies and called them in for the afternoon break. "Coffee's poured. Come rest a spell. We're probably going to be here for a while. Don't want to wear yourself out the first day."

Lim agreed wholeheartedly as Stella handed him a cup of coffee. "You're not only good with the metal detector; you got a head on your shoulders, too."

Bubba said, "I still think my idea of inviting her was a good one."

Tired but not discouraged, the three ate the golden brown fish as night descended, reminiscing over their unsuccessful day. Bubba pitched a cleaned fish bone into the simmering fire and joked with Stella. "You may not be able to find the buried treasure with that metal detector, but you sure whopped that old cotton mouth over the head with it."

Laughing in turn, Stella replied, "At least tomorrow when we work the bayou side we won't have him to contend with."

"That's for sure," Lim added. "What do you two think? After we finish the Point, we start with the scuba equipment along the edge of the Point and finish the east side, say for a quarter-mile in either direction from the point?"

Bubba helped himself to another piece of fish. "Lim, that sounds fine with me. How do you plan on using the scuba equipment with the water as muddy as it is?"

"We'll just have to stick iron probes into the mud every two or three feet. It'll probably be buried under the sand. However, if it's there, it was dumped all in the same place. It'll be in a pile and we have a chance of hitting it. Everything we do is going to be slow, but if we keep a map of our work, we'll eventually eliminate one possibility after the other. The main thing we want is when we check an area to be sure we checked everything."

Stella added, "We've got enough work in front of us to last a month. Don't you two forget about food. One of these days we're going to have to get our great hunters back in the woods hunting."

Lim got up and went over to the worktable, fixing a drink. "That's smart thinking, Stella. You know fish ain't my main dish. Maybe I should go kill us another turkey or a mess of squirrels."

Bubba put his two cents in. "Ain't too far up to Vicksburg. A big old chunk of steak would go pretty good. Of course, Stella could leave the tent open and we could have coon."

The meat situation was resolved a few days later. Bubba and Lim were scuba diving along the edge of the point while Stella was cleaning camp. Suddenly a wild scream came from the camp followed closely by a gunshot. Lim yanked on the nylon rope tied to Bubba, who was under water probing the bottom of the river. Another scream came followed by another shot. Not waiting, Lim started pulling Bubba to the top explaining as his head popped out of the water, "Get that stuff off quick. Something's happened to Stella up at camp!"

Lim left Bubba at the boat and took off up the bank running. Bubba caught him as he went over the crest. Running to camp, he called for Stella who was nowhere to be seen. Lim was so out of breath that he could scarcely talk when he rushed up.

"Stella, Stella," Bubba called frantically, "where in the hell are you?"

Lim finally caught his breath and asked, "Where the devil is she?"

"I don't know," Bubba answered, then called again.

About a hundred or so yards from camp, Stella answered as she waved her hands for them to come to her. Both men started running, Lim struggling mightily and gasping for breath. It was all he could do to keep up.

Reaching Stella, Bubba yelled, "Stella, what in the hell happened?"

She casually leaned the double barrel against a tree and pointed to the gray form lying in a brush pile. "That crazy thing almost tore up one of the tents before I could get to the gun."

Bubba walked over and saw the wild hog lying in a brush pile. "Lim, this thing's huge! He must weigh a hundred-fifty pounds. Look at those tusks!" The wild hog had three-inch tusks rolling up on both sides of its mouth. Pulling the hog out of the brush pile, Bubba remarked, "Looks like he must have died of fright. You didn't scream at him did you?"

"Seems I heard a little commotion before the shot," Lim said as he hugged Stella.

"Would the two great hunters take the game back to camp and butcher it before we elect a new hunter and a new dish washer?"

Excitement was high before they got through with the hog butchering, so were the butchers. Sitting around the campfire that night eating the tender ribs that Stella had broiled over the mesh grill, all was well with the campers.

"Maybe Bubba would be better as camp cook," Lim said as a way of congratulating Stella. "I believe you and I can keep plenty of fresh meat in camp." This caused Bubba to eye them both suspiciously.

For the next couple of weeks, the search included everything on the Carrier's Point side of the river, and then moved across to the large sandbar. With the metal detectors and probes, the search ran from the waters edge to the willow thicket.

Unsuccessful on the sandbar, the search continued using the scuba equipment in the water along the shoreline. Nothing was found but an old plow point, one metal can hook and a few old whiskey bottles.

Stella brought up the idea that maybe the cargo was dropped off above Carrier's Point or possibly on the sandbar below the Point. The next couple of weeks these areas were searched with the metal detector, obtaining the same discouraging results. However, a horseshoe was found which Lim nailed on the large pin oak above the pitcher pump.

"The horseshoe is a good omen," Lim said when he'd finished nailing it up. "Our luck is going to change."

Tired and disgusted after another week of the fruitless searching, Lim suggested going back to Taylorsville for a week or so to get more supplies and rest up. Everyone agreed, and the following day was spent closing camp. The non-perishable food items and supplies were hung in trees well out of reach of the animals.

Hiding the smaller boat, everything was loaded into the large boat and the trio left for Vicksburg, each with his or her own thoughts as the white mile marker faded in the distance.

Is there really a hidden treasure? Could this whole thing be some type of hoax or mistake? What about the old Colonel at the Old Soldiers' Home in Gulfport, could he have just made the story up? There's no proof or record in the courthouse or anywhere in history that the Merrygold or any boat ever ran or ever made any attempt to run the Union blockade. Also, there was no record of gold or silver or any money being stored in the Vicksburg bank for the cause of the South, even with most of the bank's records being destroyed, there should have been some records, even a rumor if nothing else. Could it be possible that there was this vast treasure and only President Davis, the captain that delivered the message, General Pemberton and his personal aid, Colonel Hampton, had held the secret? If it really did happen, could old Captain Fredrick have dropped it off miles up the river or did he have it on the Merrygold when it sank, scattering it, God knows where along the muddy river bottom? What are the odds of finding the treasure? Will it be a thousand to one? Maybe a million to one? Like a royal flush, the odds of hitting it are almost impossible, yet if the cards are in the deck, who's to say?

Disillusionment held their thoughts, but behind this disillusionment, each of the three held the same positive feeling. If the treasure was there or not, not one of the three was ready to throw in the towel.

Chapter 18

Taylorsville looked good. Stella's mother couldn't believe how tanned her daughter had gotten. Lim and Bubba gave the bream a try over on Stogner's. The only days they missed fishing was when it was raining. Those days were spent getting clothes and supplies ready for the return trip to Vicksburg.

Lim spent most of his spare time reading everything he could find on the siege of Vicksburg. His research turned up no ties or clues to the alleged silver and gold contraband, nor could he find any historical reports of the Merrygold or her mission of running the Union blockade. Disappointed in his research, he told Bubba and Stella that he wanted to go to Gulfport and see if he could get access to any records of the Beauvior Confederate Soldiers' Home or the Beauvior Cemetery records. Bubba and Stella agreed this was a good idea, but suggested it would be best to check the Beauvior records this winter. Both felt their time would be best spent looking for the treasure now while the weather was still good.

Lim agreed. "You're right, but the research is needed if for no other reason than for self assurance. I also want to go to Vicksburg and check the historic battlegrounds, museums, and records of the courthouse. Somewhere there has to be a record of the Merrygold and her captain."

Bubba and Stella both agreed with Lim. "Let's go back and give as thorough a search as we can and if we don't come up with something, we can spend the winter doing research."

"We've had all the rest we need," Lim said. "Let's go to Memphis tomorrow and start getting supplies. It'll be cold in a month or so. We need to get as much looking done as we can."

"All right Lim, I'm ready to go any time you're ready, but I'm lost as to where to search. Have you come up with any new ideas?"

"Not many," Lim replied thoughtfully. "We never did check the old bayou where we seined the bait and I want to go to Baton Rouge and have another look at the letter old Mr. Breckinridge wrote his wife. I can't help but believe it holds the key to the whereabouts of the treasure."

Stella wanted to go to Memphis with them to get the supplies, which was agreeable. They left early the next morning and were in Memphis when the stores opened.

On the way back from Memphis, the truck overloaded with supplies, Lim, trying to be thoughtful to the lone female in the group, asked Stella, "I know staying over on the river is mighty hard on a man much less a woman; If you want to stay in Taylorsville this time, it will be understandable. It's going to start getting cold and it's going to be pretty rough."

Stella turned to Lim, her eyes showing that sharp flash Lim had learned to avoid, "You two may think you can go off and leave me, but if you do I'll come over there and swim down that river and bust every bottle of whiskey you have."

"That settles it, Stella's going back with us," Bubba laughed. Lim agreed.

The next day was spent packing and getting final arrangements made to leave for Baton Rouge the following morning. That night, Jennie cooked a big pot of spaghetti and Bubba and Stella came over for supper. Of course, drinks were in order and everyone was excited talking about their return trip to Vicksburg.

Jennie came in to call them to the table saying, "If you treasure hunters have time, come eat! That old pot of gold you're looking for's been there a long time. I'm sure it'll be there when supper's over."

After the meal, Bubba and Stella stayed and talked awhile until Jennie came in to get Lim to take her home.

Bubba got up as she came in the room. "Lim, we got to leave. We'll drop Jennie off on our way."

Lim handed Jennie a couple of bills. "You two go home and get some sleep. I'll be by early."

"I'm so excited I'll never go to sleep," Stella replied excitedly. "Might as well keep Bubba up. He could go to sleep in a tornado."

"That shows you who has a clean conscious," Bubba said as he opened the door to leave.

Lim set his clock to go off at 4:30am, but before it alarmed, he was up, shaved and had his first cup of coffee. It was still dark when he pulled up to Bubba's house and flashed the headlights. Day was breaking as he and Bubba got to Stella's, who was sitting on the porch steps as Lim turned the pickup up the drive.

Bubba slipped her bags in the overloaded truck and whispered, "You're up early, or didn't you go to bed?"

Stella answered as she slid into the pickup next to Lim, "I went to bed, just didn't sleep a wink all night."

Stopping only at a truck stop in Jackson for coffee, then in Natchez for lunch, they were at the bank in Baton Rouge before three o'clock, and were greeted by Mr. Breckinridge.

"You people still with it? I haven't heard from you in so long I was about ready to come see if you were drowned or something."

"No, Mr. Breckinridge," Lim replied warmly, "we have been steady at it but haven't been too successful."

Mr. Breckinridge's eyes flashed from Bubba to Stella then he said, "You're not ready to give up, are you?"

"No sir," Lim answered, "we're still searching, a bit disillusioned, but we're still at it. Came out for some supplies and to get a few days rest. In fact, we're on our way to Vicksburg now. But before we went back, we wanted to come down and touch base with you and have another look at Captain Breckinridge's letter. Somehow I get the feeling that letter holds the key to the treasure."

Mr. Breckinridge rose from his chair, "It's in my safety deposit box. It'll take me a minute to get it. I also got a new aerial map of the area last week. I'll get that too," he said as he left the room.

A few minutes later Mr. Breckinridge returned and handed Lim the plastic sealed letter. "Have you found anything that might tie in with the Merrygold or Captain Breckinridge and his crew?"

Lim studied the faded letter, then replied, "No sir, we only found an old plow point, a can hook, some logging chains and one horseshoe."

Like Lim, Mr. Breckinridge replied with a smile, "Maybe the horseshoe is a good luck omen."

Lim handed the letter to Bubba and Stella and laughingly replied, "People can joke about omens if they want, but Lady Luck shines on those that believe."

Standing, Lim shook hands with Mr. Breckinridge. "The letter puzzles me. I wanted to look at it again before we went down the river."

Mr. Breckinridge agreed. "I guess I've read it a thousand times thinking each time the answer was there."

"Did you tell Lim or did I just think it up, that your father remembered Captain Breckinridge's wife telling about receiving the letter?" Stella asked.

"That's right, Stella. I told Lim that my father told me a number of times about the stranger from the North delivering the letter after the war was over. It was quite a story as she, Aunt Helen, was so sure he'd been killed instantly when the Merrygold blew up. Of course, Aunt Helen was seventy-five or eighty years old and my father was just a young boy. She knew nothing of the secret mission in which her husband was involved. Probably never did know about it. The message probably never got to General Pemberton. I'm sure the General thought the gold and silver went down with the Merrygold. Just happened the Captain owned a small plantation somewhere below Port Gibson and she was living there during the siege of Vicksburg completely unaware of her husband's death until after Vicksburg surrendered."

Lim interrupted, "We best be leaving. It's a long drive to Vicksburg and it'll be dark before we get there. Mr. Breckinridge, keep believing in that horseshoe. We're going to find that treasure if it's there."

"I'm like you, Lim," Mr. Breckinridge replied with a smile, "horseshoes, black cats, dove calls in the morning, broken mirror, all have an affect on me. Maybe it shouldn't, but it does. You'll never see me walk under a ladder. I don't know if I'm superstitious or what, but I do know I get a strange feeling when I'm confronted. Maybe it's because I like the challenge of a gamble but I'm also a positive believer."

Lim laughed loudly. "There's plenty to be said about believing in yourself. In fact, I believe positive thinking makes its own luck. There's one thing for sure, a positive thinker will last longer than a negative thinker."

Stella interrupted, "And it's a whole lot easier to work with one who believes the Merrygold treasure is real than one that puts your mind in doubt."

"That's for sure," Mr. Breckinridge replied. "Most people would have been ready to call it quits by now. In fact, that's exactly what impresses me most about you folks. If you need anything or if I can help, let me know."

Lim drove the same pace back to Vicksburg, stopping only in Natchez again to eat supper, getting into Vicksburg after dark. Bubba made the remark as Lim turned into the Vicksburg Motel parking lot, "Glad Stella had sense enough to make reservations. Late as it is, we'd be sleeping in the truck if she hadn't."

Lim answering as he got out to go into the motel office, "I'll see what rooms we got." He came back a few minutes later and said, "Rooms 5 and 6, just to the right down a couple doors. Bubba, pull on down. I'll walk."

Rising early the next morning and eating breakfast at the motel, the first stop was at the garage to get the boat out of storage, then Lim drove up to the river ramp, unloaded the pickup and had the truck back in the garage before good sunup. The happy treasure hunters were going under the Vicksburg Bridge as the sun rose over the sleeping town.

They arrived at camp a little after noon. It surprised them how quickly they got the camp re-equipped as well as the day it was first set up. Bubba and Stella slipped off and killed three squirrels for supper while Lim stayed at camp studying the new aerial map.

As Stella cooked supper, Lim and Bubba went over plans for the next search. Both men agreed to search the willow brake across the river with the metal detector. If this proved fruitless, they would move the search to the sandbar up the river.

The willow brake was better than a half mile long. Their search ran for a hundred and fifty feet in the thick willow underbrush, the full length of the sandbar. No need to say, it took quite a time to cover the area. On top of that, they found an old boat hull buried in the sand which got them excited, but after a couple of days of digging enough of the rotten hull had been uncovered to satisfy their minds that it was built much later than the Civil War and had no connection with the Merrygold treasure.

A month passed. The searching of the willows and the sand bar up the river proved nothing except that there was no need to look there again. Dejected and tired, the trio decided to go into Vicksburg, rent a motel, wash their clothes, take a good bath, and enjoy a good meal. Also, Lim decided that a few supplies were needed.

The trip into Vicksburg did rest them up and a change of scenery for a couple of days helped. However, on Sunday, they were back at camp ready to give the search another try.

After breakfast the following morning, Lim suggested a search of the bayou, "It's down low now and a good time to check it. Who knows, Ole Breckinridge's crew could've carried it back there and dumped it in the slough. That way it wouldn't have to be buried." Bubba and Stella agreed, but warned that the slough was alive with snakes.

Leaving camp for the bayou, Lim agreed saying, "We'll have to be double careful. A snake bite could be mighty bad this far from a hospital."

By noon, a probe of the biggest portion of the bayou had been made and nothing found, but a few snakes and a turtle or two. Dejected, but determined to check the bayou, a quick break for lunch was taken. Muddy and tired, disillusioned but still determined, the search of the slough continued that afternoon. I guess this was when things started turning dark. Lim was probing around a large cypress tree about five feet in front of Bubba when he let out a yell, "Snake got me on the leg!"

Making his way to the bank, Lim crawled out of the muddy slough. Bubba, right behind, snatched Lim's britches leg up. The cottonmouth was still wrapped around his ankle, his fangs buried in Lim's leg. Grabbing the snake, Bubba yanked its squirming body from Lim's leg and slung it halfway across the slough, wrapping it around a sapling as it hit.

Not knowing what to do, Bubba hunched down over Lim's leg slapping his mouth over the two bleeding fang marks and began sucking the blood and poison from the wound. Stella came running up and cuddled Lim's head in her lap softly crying.

Of course, everybody was excited and scared and Lim wasn't going to have any part of that. "Hell, you two think I'm going to die or something? Let me get up, we best get to camp."

"Yes, and head for Vicksburg," Stella stated.

Bubba looked up, his face as muddy as his clothes and smeared with Lim's blood, told Lim, "You ain't going no where 'til I suck the poison out of that leg."

Lim looked at Bubba and said, "Hell, you keep on and I won't have any blood left. Put my belt around it and let's go."

Hurriedly Bubba strapped Lim's belt around his leg above the knee. Getting up to Lim's objections, he threw Lim across his shoulder like a sack of potatoes and headed for camp. Stella tried to hold Lim's head as Bubba half walked and half ran. Not stopping at camp, as Lim wanted to get a drink, he carried Lim straight to the boat.

Hollering for Bubba to go to the boat, Stella stopped at camp and picked up a couple of towels, a quilt and pillow, not thinking to get a change of clothes. She got to the boat almost as quick as Lim and Bubba.

Lim sat on the edge of the boat and asked Stella, "What's all that for?"

She didn't answer until she got the quilt and pillow fixed in the bottom of the boat, "It's for you to lay on."

Wobbling, Lim got in the boat. "You'd think a little old snake could kill you with all this carrying on."

Bubba gave the motor a couple of yanks and hollered for Stella to push off and hop in. In a matter of minutes, Bubba had the speeding boat passed the big rock point, headed for Vicksburg. A little over three hours later, he was pulling the boat up to the ramp in Vicksburg. Stella stayed with Lim while Bubba went to the garage and got Lim's truck.

Lim refused to lie down in the back of the truck, so everyone got in the front and Bubba drove to the hospital.

"You'd better slow this thing down," Lim cautioned Bubba. "Won't none of us get to the hospital if we get killed in a car wreck."

"Listen to him, Bubba," Stella added siding with Lim, "before you do have a wreck."

Bubba ignored them and drove on. Pulling up in front of the Hospital emergency room, he replied, "Now what was it you two were saying?"

Stella jumped out and helping Lim said, "Forget it, come on and help me get Lim inside."

Lim's leg had swollen as big as a watermelon as the nurses laid him on the emergency room table. Luckily, a doctor was in the building and in a matter of minutes, he had started working on Lim. Stella and Bubba waited impatiently outside the operating room, pacing the floor and pestering every nurse that came by, asking how Lim was doing. Finally, Lim was brought out and rolled down the hall to a hospital room. Stella walked beside Lim, holding his hand as Bubba held back and waited for the doctor to come out of the operating room.

When the Doctor finally emerged, Bubba flooded him with questions. "Doctor, how does it look? Is he going to be all right?"

"Well, Son," the Doctor began, and then paused; "you are his son?"

"No sir, a good friend, business partner you might say," Bubba answered.

"I believe he said his name was Lim, anyway, he's going to be a sick man for a few days. That must have been a big snake from the looks of the fang marks."

"Yes sir, it was pretty good size, but...but, he'll be all right, won't he?" Bubba asked hesitantly.

"I feel like he will. That leg's going to swell some more but let's hope we don't have any complications. If not, he should be up and going again in a couple of months," the doctor explained.

"You mean it will take that long?" Bubba asked.

"That's right, son. It may take six months. Just be thankful he's alive and hope he doesn't lose his leg."

"Gosh, I didn't know a snake bite was that bad," Bubba said.

"Oh, yes, snake bites can be extremely serious," the doctor replied.

Walking to Lim's room Bubba thought about what the doctor had said. 'Hell, it'll kill Lim if he knew that he's going to be laid up for two or three months. I best not let him know, at least for a while.'

Bubba walked to Lim's bedside. You could tell that Lim was feeling bad but he was still able to sport a smile. "Bubba," Lim said smiling, "the doctor said you probably saved my life, sucking that poison out and getting me to the hospital soon as you did. Just wanted to thank you."

Bubba grinned and replied, "Lim, ain't nothing to that talk, but your leg could use a little scrubbing."

"Speaking of scrubbing, you two look like two mud balls," Lim said then laughed loudly. "Go find a place to clean up and come back tomorrow. I'll be all right."

Bubba and Stella argued that they were going to stay. Lim held up his hand and said, "Either you two go or I'm going to have the nurse give you a bath." He managed a mean look.

Stella kissing Lim on the forehead said, "Come on, Bubba. Looking at you would make a well man sick. We'll be back first thing in the morning."

It was late and there was no place open to get extra clothes, so the motel was their only option. Stella washed Bubba's clothes in the bathtub, and Bubba, wearing the wet clothes, took Stella's clothes down to the all night launderette while Stella stayed in the motel room wrapped in a bed sheet.

Around midnight, they went to a truck stop and got something to eat, topping it off with a bottle of beer. Stella's mom would have been proud of how the night in the motel went—Stella slept on the bed and Bubba on the floor. Early the next morning they went to the hospital and checked on Lim.

His leg was swollen twice its normal size and had turned an ugly black; however, the doctor assured them that this was not unusual, and Lim was probably over the worst part.

As Bubba and Stella walked into the room, Lim told them, "You two go on back to Taylorsville. I'll be all right. You can come get me in a few days. We'll go back to the Point and find that stuff. I'm not going to be in here over a couple more days."

Bubba didn't want to let Lim know how long it was really going to take for him to get well. "Lim, we're going back to the Point to check everything out. We'll be back tomorrow and decide then about going to Taylorsville."

Stella kissed Lim saying, "We'll see you tomorrow."

Lim grinned and said, "If I'd known I'd get all this attention, I'd have let a snake bite me a long time ago."

Stella and Bubba spent the next seven days at the Point, coming to see Lim most everyday. Finally, the doctor agreed that Lim was well enough to go to Taylorsville but he was going to have to stay in bed or around the house for a month or more.

"It's going to be spring before he'll be able to get around on that leg," the doctor said sternly.

Discouraged and worried about Lim, Stella and Bubba went back for the last time, closed camp like before and brought both boats back up the river. After making arrangements for storing the boats for the winter, Bubba and Stella went to the hospital and told Lim they were taking him to Taylorsville.

"Like hell you are! We're going to camp!" exclaimed Lim.

The doctor came in catching the heated conversation and told Lim in no uncertain terms that he was going to Taylorsville.

"I'll go for a week or so then we're going back to camp," Lim agreed reluctantly.

Bubba stopped at a pay phone and called Breckinridge to tell him about the snakebite and of their decision to go to Taylorsville for the winter.

He was both surprised and concerned about Lim. "I wish I'd known Lim was in the hospital," he said showing genuine concern. "I would have come up to see him. At least I could have sent him some flowers or something."

Bubba recognized Mr. Breckinridge's concern. "After we found out that he was going to be all right, Lim said there was no point in bothering you. Mr. Breckinridge, we'll be gone for a few months, more than likely the rest of the winter, but we'll be back as soon as Lim gets straightened out."

"That's fine," Mr. Breckinridge said. "Take all the time you need. We'll extend the contract, if necessary."

Before leaving town, Lim made them stop and get a bottle. "A drink ain't going to hurt me. I always heard it was good for snakebites. Besides that, it's been almost two weeks since I had one."

Stella and Bubba laughing with Lim, agreed and said, "Maybe we'll join you."

Chapter 19

Nothing unusual had happened around Taylorsville other than the routine burglaries. The mayor's car had been stolen and there had been a couple of Saturday night stabbings. However, with Bubba and Lim back for the winter things had every expectation of picking up. Even Sheriff Tate and Deputy Hodge perked up their ears a notch.

It may have been Lim's leg that slowed things down but things ran pretty smooth for over a month. Bubba had gone back to work part time for Morris. Then, just before Christmas, with Lim's leg about well, he invited his gambling buddies down from Memphis for a weekend card game. One of their big time cronies from Chicago came with them and all the gamblers got rooms at the motel. The honeymoon suite was rented for the weekend where they set up their bar, card table and a food table. Everything had been planned for an exciting weekend and as it turned out, it was.

Lim wanted to show the big town boys a little Southern hospitality, got one of his friends to kill some birds and had a bird supper out at the Big House on Saturday afternoon. Since the supper was a special occasion, Lim decided he'd put it on a little special for his six guests. Bubba offered to help Jennie wait on the table and be bartender, but wouldn't be one of the dinner guests.

Dinner would be served around 6:30pm. Bubba came out around 4:30 dressed in a white shirt and tie, and set up a bar in the corner of the dining room. Jennie, dressed in a white dress with a black apron, had started preparations for the meal around noon. When Bubba arrived, she had most of the meal ready except for frying the birds.

The long dinner table was set with a linen tablecloth and cloth napkins, Lim's family silver and crystal, along with crystal wine glasses—a large bottle of white wine in an ice bucket was placed at the end of the table. Everything was to perfection when the guests arrived. Bubba declared the bar open and started mixing drinks. Jennie came in with hors d'oeuvres as the guests moved to the living room.

After allowing time for a short visit, Jennie came in and stated, "Gentlemen, dinner is being served. Please come to the dining room."

Bubba seated the guests, then poured the wine. As custom, he let Lim taste the wine first. Lim welcomed the guests and blessed the food stating, "Gentlemen, welcome to our humble abode." Then, "Lord, thank you for our blessings and for the food we're about to partake." In conclusion he said, "As you know, Gentlemen, times have been pretty hard, but we're glad to share what we have with you."

Quietly the fidgeting men began to smile and then laugh as Jennie sat a large platter of food on the table followed by Bubba with two pones of cornbread. Jennie's platter contained turnip greens and pigtails. Smiling she said, "Eat up, gentlemen. Dats it."

The laughing changed to ah's and o's as Jennie and Bubba returned from the kitchen with large plates of fried quail, mashed potatoes, and homemade biscuits, followed by peach cobbler and sorghum molasses for dessert.

Just before dark, the gamblers moved locations to the motel, leaving most of the cars at Lim's, and using Lim's truck and a couple of smaller cars to haul people to the motel. Too many cars might be suspicious, especially to Sheriff Tate. Around eight o'clock the game started.

Saturday night nothing unusual happened other than Lim dropped two hundred dollars and ended up with too much booze to drive home and spent the last few hours of the night sleeping on the couch. Around one o'clock Sunday afternoon, the game started again, and as planned it ran into the night.

Since Bubba had taken Stella to the fish house on Saturday night, he had a chance to slip off and watch the game on Sunday night, while Stella and her mother were at church.

It was close to midnight when things started popping. Lim was dealing and the high-powered gambler from Chicago caught a pat hand. One of the Memphis boys had two pairs and Lim held three fours before they took their draw. The Chicago dude was well ahead in the game. He had almost picked them clean on Saturday night and led off with a hundred dollar bet. The two pair hand raised a hundred. Lim looked at the stately three fours and decided he'd let the raisers handle the betting and just called. Well, the Chicago slicker bumped the hundred-dollar raise a hundred and his Memphis crony called. Lim called and said, "Cards?", as he pitched his hundred in.

The slicker touched his cards on the table and said, "Pat." He pitched in two hundred before Lim and the other man got their cards. Lim dealt one card to the two pair and snapped two cards down for himself.

The two pair shuffled his cards a couple of times then cupping his hand squeezed the corner out, hesitated, then looked at the two hundred bet and pitched his hand on top of the wrinkled bills, saying, "Too rich for me!"

Lim waited until one card had finished, then made his move. He cupped his cards and slowly eased the corners apart just enough to see the top numbers. The three fours slipped by then a ten. Slowly squeezing the last card, his eyes caught the corner of the fourth four. Not blinking an eye, he laid the hand down looked at the pot, then slowly counted his money. They were playing table stakes, which means you bet the money in front of you. Lim had four-hundred-seventy-five dollars, which he slid to the middle of the table. "Raise two six bits."

The city slicker's eyes popped out on stems saying, "I didn't like the way you dealt them cards," as he counted out his two-hundred-seventy-five dollars and threw the bills into the pot. He laid his hand down and said, "Jack's full, over tens."

"That dog won't hunt," Lim said as he spread his cards out for the slicker to read. "Four little fours." Lim calmly reached and began dragging the pot. He lifted the corner of his face toward City Slicker and looked the man dead in the eye. "Mister, I didn't savvy what you said about my dealing."

City Slicker's eyes were flashing as he watched Lim stack the hefty pot. "I said one of those cards came from the bottom of the deck."

He shouldn't have said that! No sooner had the words left his mouth than Lim's eyes flashed to his Memphis cronies as if to say, 'what have you brought down here?' He slowly got to his feet. City Slicker was still sitting in his chair. He should have stood too. Lim came with an around house lick that could have knocked a mule down, catching City Slicker full in the face sending him and his chair tumbling backwards. Now the real action started.

City Slicker ended up in the corner upside down. When he finally uncoiled himself, he came up with a .32 automatic. Bullets went everywhere and so did people. Out windows, doors, under beds, anywhere there was a hole.

Sheriff Tate had already seen Lim's truck parked across the street from the motel and knew some hanky panky was going on. He had Deputy Hodge watching it and before the smoke cleared from the shooting, Deputy Hodge was in the motel room putting on hand cuffs, Bubba included.

The fine wasn't so bad as Lim had won a pretty good chunk and paid his and Bubba's fine of a hundred a piece. What was bad, the sheriff put them all in jail and held them there until up in the afternoon on Monday. The worst part came when he let them out. Stella met Bubba at the jail and gave him his ring back along with some awful ugly words.

This time breaking up with Stella was different. Mr. Ranking had agreed to the marriage, the treasure hunt, everything was built around their getting married. Like Lim stated when he was so down before, he should have gone and got married, not waited. If you love a person, marry her. If you put it off, more than likely you'll regret the day you did. Odds were you'd never marry her at all.

Bubba tried everything but Stella wouldn't talk to him. She wouldn't even come to the phone when he called. He tried going though Mrs. Ranking but that didn't work. This time it looked bad. She wasn't budging. The marriage was off and that was all it was to it.

Lim did everything he could to get things straightened out between Stella and Bubba, except what he should have done first.

He went over to Stella's house a couple days later, and caught her out front fixing to get in her father's car. Pulling in behind the car he called, "Stella, I want to talk to you."

Stella was a little taken aback by Lim's tone, but she walked back to Lim's truck. "Yes, what is it Lim?"

Lim thought it best to stay in the truck, so he gave Stella what she gave him when he and Bubba had their little problem. "Stella, you are about the most stubborn damn person I ever saw. You know Bubba is so in love with you he don't know what he's doing. I've already told you what happened down at the motel wasn't his fault. He was just as innocent as the preacher would have been, except the preacher probably wouldn't have been there. Now you show your butt so you'll never get things straightened out. Bubba's leaving. Said he was going to join the army."

Stella was really shaken at hearing this. It took a minute for her to get herself composed enough to answer, but she couldn't and began to cry. "You mean he's going to join the Army? Lim, you know I love Bubba; it's just that every time things get to running smoothly, all hell breaks loose. You know I don't want him going into the army," she mumbled through her tears as she absently turned and walked into the house.

Lim backed out of the drive and drove to Morris'. He pulled Bubba aside. "You call Stella and tell her I'm treating you and her at the fish house tonight."

Bubba started to argue, "It won't do any good, you must be crazy," but Lim drove off before he could get the words out. Bubba stood there thinking about what Lim had said for a little while before summoning up enough courage. "To hell with it," he mumbled just under his breath. "I'm going to call her. She can't say any more things than she's already said."

Sure enough, the call did the trick and before the night was over all three of them were pretty well slick and busy making plans to go back to Vicksburg. Stella flashed Bubba's ring like he'd just given it to her. Bubba going into the army was not mentioned, Lim may have just made that up, but who cares, it worked. As far as I know, Stella never mentioned it to Bubba, and Lim sure didn't. It was almost closing time before they left the fish house and all three were in such shape, a designated driver would have been wise.

Chapter 20

The next day things were running smoothly again. Bubba picked Stella up around six and the rejuvenated love birds went out to Lim's to eat supper. It was after the meal and Jennie had left, they were all in the living room sipping their drinks talking about their trip back to Vicksburg and the whereabouts of the Merrygold treasure. Some way the talk worked around to the snake biting Lim. Then Lim came up with this strange story about, of all things, a snake.

"You know Lim," Bubba said as he got up to get him and Stella a cold drink, "I've been thinking. You'd be safer staying in camp cooking and washing dishes. Stella and I will look for the treasure."

Stella went along with the joke saying, "That's right Bubba. Every morning before we leave, we'll check around camp to be sure there're not any snakes lying around that are liable to bite Lim, then it'll be safe for him to come out."

Lim took the ribbing with a laugh. "Okay you two, lay it on, but the only reason that snake didn't get Bubba in place of me was that you two were over there courtin' in place of working."

Everyone was laughing and enjoying themselves so Lim, in a solemn, tongue-in-cheek expression, said, "I'm going to tell you two something that I swore I'd never tell anyone. In fact, it's such a strange story, I'm hesitant about even mentioning it. It's been bugging me for quite a while, I feel I've got to tell someone, and you two may understand and not laugh or think I've flipped, so I'd like to tell it to you. It's about a snake, and the reason I haven't told it before is because it's so strange I felt no one would believe me."

"Hell, Lim," Bubba interrupted, "what are you talking about? Tell the story! Ain't much you can tell about a snake except what color or how big he is. Everybody knows he'll scare you to death if he don't bite and kill you."

"See," Lim replied laughing, "you're already doubting me. This is the truth, at least I'm pretty sure it happened and if you're not going to believe me, I best not tell it."

"Hush, Bubba!" Stella cried exasperated, "let Lim have his say." Then turning to Lim she said, "I'll listen to you Lim, and if you say it happened I'll believe you."

This suited Lim, so he started with the strange story. "All right, I'm going to tell you two what happened, but I don't want either of you ever to tell anybody else. They'd think I was crazy or drunk like Bubba already thinks. Anyway, I was bream fishing down next to the beaver dam on the lower end of Stogner's. You know the dam, Bubba?"

Bubba laughed nervously not knowing if Lim was serious or not, said, "Yeah, I know the one, where me and you killed that big old cotton mouth under that old cypress."

"That's right," Lim responded. "Anyway, I was fishing at the same beaver dam, and the bream were hitting pretty good. I'd almost run out of bait, and I had a cooler full of bream, so, I decided I'd quit for the day and was rolling up my line, when I heard a limb pop over my head and looked up just in time to catch the limb across my forehead. Bubba, do you remember sometime last year when I came into Morris' Station and I had a Band-aid on my forehead?"

"Yeah, Lim, I remember. I also remember telling you that's why you shouldn't go fishing by yourself. I didn't think too much about the limb hitting you on the head then, as you didn't seem all that concerned, but I do remember you telling me."

Smiling, Lim replied, "I really didn't want to talk about it. I guess I was just embarrassed over what I'm going to tell you and Stella of what happened, and if you start making fun or laughing, I'll not tell you another word."

Bubba and Stella's eyes flashed back and forth, then Bubba said, "Hell, Lim, I don't know if you're putting me on or not. Go ahead and tell us what happened."

Lim started, "Well, that limb knocked me as cold as a dead turkey. Luckily, I didn't fall out of the boat, I just sort of crumbled over into the bottom of the boat. Don't know how long I lay there, but it must have been quite a while. In fact, I must have had a dream, hallucination, or something as I lay there. I heard this strange sound, or word…or something. At first, it sounded way off, then the sound became clearer."

Bubba butted in, "What sound are you talking about, Lim?"

"That's what I'm fixing to tell you and why I'm so hesitant about telling you or Stella, or anybody."

Stella got her say in. "Lim, if it was a dream, there's no reason to be ashamed. What happened? It can't be all that bad, if it's just a dream."

"Anyway," Lim continued, "the sound got clearer and it definitely was calling, 'Help! Help!' and the sound was coming from right there on the beaver dam. Well, not knowing what to think, I paddled the boat over to the dam and pulled it up on the bank. Getting out of the boat, I heard it again, not twenty or thirty feet away, so I started walking toward the sound. It was pretty muddy on the dam, I had to pick my way. The sound came again as I walked, only this time, it was a little different. It said, 'Over here, next to the broken limb.'"

Bubba and Stella sat in awe, wondering what Lim was going to say next.

"I walked over to the fallen limb," Lim continued, "and there it was…"

"There what was?" Bubba asked excitedly.

"A little red and black snake about three-feet long, squirming and twisting trying to get out from under a fallen tree limb that had him pinned to the ground."

Bubba and Stella looked at each other doubtfully.

Lim continued. "You're not going to believe this, but that little thing said as plain as we're talking now, 'Get this log off me. It's about to mash me to death.' Well, I couldn't believe it. There was a snake squirming in front of me and talking as plain as an English scholar."

Bubba broke in, "Boy, that whack on the head must've knocked you as cuckoo as a Betsy Bug."

With a slight grin, Lim responded, "Yeah, it sure must have, but someway it seemed as if I still had my wits and I wasn't going to have any part of someone making a laughing fool out of me. I didn't say a thing, except to myself, which I thought in place of saying, 'Yeah, somebody's pulling one over on me—got this set up and going to make such a fool out of me, I'll be laughed at everywhere I go. I bet a tape player is hidden under that log or some place close by. I better do some checking first.' Not paying the snake much mind, I walked back down the beaver dam, looked out into the woods…didn't see or hear a thing, except that snake hollering, 'Come back! Get this thing off of me! There's no one here but us!'"

"Well, I didn't pay that statement much mind either. I knew it had to be some kind of trick or something, so I walked back to the other end of the beaver dam passing right by the snake. It just lay there and looked up at me as pitiful as could be. Getting to the other end of the dam, I searched the woods with my eyes and ears, and saw or heard no one, except that little critter begging me to come get that log off his back"

Bubba and Stella didn't say a word. Their eyes just flashed back and forth like a pendulum clock.

Lim ignored their dubious looks and continued, "Suddenly, I realized that maybe the snake was real and was actually talking, or as of right now hollering. Then the thought came to me, if I could catch that thing, no telling what people would pay to see and hear it talk. Why, that snake was worth a fortune. I don't know why, but I said to myself, 'this snake is worth more than the Lost Appleton Heritage.'"

Bubba said, "Boy, Lim, are you sure you weren't having the DT's or something? This is some story."

Stella interrupted sharply, "Bubba, be quiet! Let Lim tell what happened!"

Lim continued, "With the thought of catching the snake, I walked back to the log. The snake was still squirming and twisting, and began begging me, 'Will you PLEASE get this log off my back!'

"Well, the next time you think about feeling strange, think of talking to a snake. I said, 'You're a snake, and snakes don't talk!' Well, that little thing looked up at me and said, 'You're hearing me, aren't you? Just raise the log and I'll crawl out from under it. I'm not going to bite you, if that is what's got you so flustered.'"

Bubba looked at Stella and shook his head.

Lim continued, "I said to myself, 'Hell, if I'm going to catch this thing I've got to get the log off,' so I reached down, lifted the log, and moved it over a foot or so. That little critter squirmed a couple of times and said, 'Boy, thanks a lot! That log was about to kill me! Now, let me see if I can crawl. I don't believe I have any broken bones.' Then it said, 'I'll just crawl a-ways and see.'

"Well, the snake started crawling with me walking right behind him. I sure wasn't going to let him get out of my sight. Crawling a short distance, it came to a narrow place in the dam and somehow slid off into the water. Squirming and twisting, it tried to swim, but couldn't. Looking up at me with its little shiny eyes, it said, 'You'll have to help me. That log must've broken something; I can't seem to swim.'

"Seeing that little thing squirming in the water, I bent down to pick it up. I really didn't want to touch it, but hell, I had to do something. Bending over, my hand was just a few inches from the little critter when all of a sudden— WHAM! It's unbelievable, but it must have been the biggest bass in Stogner's Slash grabbed that snake, knocked water all over me; the water even knocked my hat off. Then, as quick as he came, that fish was gone and that snake, too. I just stood there looking at the muddy water where the fish had grabbed it.

"Turning, I went back to the boat and sat down in the back seat, still in a daze. I don't know how long I sat there 'til my mind cleared."

Bubba said, "You what? Lim, you puttin' me on!"

Stella worked her mouth trying to say something, finally said, "Is that all of the story, Lim?"

Lim, with a slight grin, replied, "Not quite."

Bubba interrupted, "That limb done knocked you as nutty as a fruit cake! What do you mean, *not quite?*"

"Well, Bubba," Lim said, "I just sat there in the boat thinking and feeling of my wet clothes. At first, I thought they were wet because of the fish, then I decided that the limb must have knocked water on me when it glanced off my head and hit the slough, but there the limb was in the bottom of the boat.

"I was still in a daze, I guess, but I suddenly realized that the boat was pulled up on the beaver dam. That couldn't be, I was out in the slough when the limb struck me. Looking at my shoes, they were muddy and there were my tracks leading away from the boat."

Bubba looked at Lim and asked, "What you leading up to?"

"Bubba," Lim replied, "I was still woozy, but I got out of the boat and followed the tracks. They went right down the beaver dam to a log about the size of my leg that had been moved. I stood there for a second trying to get my head clear. It had to be the one I lifted off the snake. Then I followed the tracks some more. They went the same route the snake had taken to the narrow part of the dam where the fish had caught the snake, and unbelievably, the water was still muddy. I couldn't believe what I saw. I just stood there and stared."

Bubba couldn't stand it any longer, "What the hell do you mean, 'Just stood there and stared?' What the hell did you do?"

"I just stood there and swore that I'd never tell a living soul about this," Lim said with a slight grin breaking his face. "Then, I reached down, picked up my wet hat, went back to the boat and came home."

Bubba said, "You what?"

Stella said, "Give me that bottle. I think I need a drink!"

Lim pushed his glass over to Stella, said with a slight grin, "Bubba, I ain't puttin' you on."

Chapter 21

With Stella and Bubba back together, things ran more smoothly. However, a few things still bothered Bubba. One of those things was answered a few days later when he went out to see Lim.

Lim was in the living room sitting by the fire and called to Bubba as he walked up onto the porch, "Come on in, Bubba. I'm in the front room."

Bubba came in and asked Lim how he was.

"Getting around pretty good," Lim answered cheerfully. "Have a seat. I just made a new pot of coffee."

"You *what?*" Bubba asked dumbfounded. "When did you start drinking coffee?"

"Oh, every now and then I'll make a pot. Seems just about as stimulating as a drink in the morning. I'm going to the kitchen and bring back the pot and a cup."

As Lim left the room, Bubba noticed a Christmas card on the coffee table. Of course, Bubba couldn't resist, picked it up and read it. It was a simple card, but the note at the bottom of the card answered Bubba's question. It read:

> *I haven't heard from you in a long time.*
> *I just wanted you to know that I'll be thinking of you*
> *this Christmas.*
>
> > *Love,*
> > *Barbara*

Bubba quickly laid the card down as Lim entered with the coffee pot. Lim, seeing Bubba with the card remarked, "Bubba, if you get any fool ideas about being Cupid again, I'll break your neck."

Bubba was embarrassed that Lim had caught him reading his mail, but that didn't stop him from saying what was on his mind. "Lim, when the hell you going over to see that lady? She's crying her heart out for you."

"Bubba, that flame died a long time ago and there's no need for an old man like myself even thinking about trying to relight it. Besides, I'd hate for her to see this twisted old body and scarred face of mine." He sat for a few seconds with a far off look on his face then added, "Bubba, she was about the prettiest woman I ever saw. I'd rather remember her just like that and I sure as hell don't want her to see how I've weathered."

"Lim, you're about the most distinguished looking man in the country when you dress up. Besides, I imagine she's added a few years also."

"Bubba, you just push any matchmaking thoughts you might have out of your mind. That's all over and I want it left that way."

Lim had let him know in no uncertain terms not to meddle, but Bubba couldn't get it out of his mind. Anyway, remembering what had happened before, he sure as hell wasn't going to meddle with any more letters. Maybe one of these days, Lim would forget his pride and let his heart do a little thinking. Least the letter answered the question about what had happened. Maybe the letter he wrote didn't do that much damage.

Christmas came and Bubba gave Stella a pretty set of jade earrings. His gift from Stella was a wristwatch. They both gave Lim a bottle of spirits and Lim treated them to a steak dinner out at the Big House.

January was over before they knew it, so was March, and nothing exciting had happened. Lim's leg was about well and he started doing a little bird hunting, which gave Bubba and Stella plenty of time for their courting. Their thoughts and conversation were that the worst part of winter was over, and it's getting close to time to go back to Vicksburg.

Bubba was still working at Morris' station. Buying the place was out of the question now that his bank account was gone. In fact, their joint account contained less than a thousand dollars and it would take the rest of that to buy supplies for the trip back to Vicksburg.

Stella could see a change in Bubba and knew he was worried about losing all his money. She also knew he was too proud to think about marriage now, even though her father had shown more respect for Bubba and wouldn't stand in their way.

It was close to the middle of April when Lim came driving into the station. Bubba could see he was pretty excited. Pulling the truck up to the regular pump, he greeted Bubba with, "Fill her up, Bubba."

"How's the leg, Lim?" Bubba asked as he cleared the pump.

"Hell, my leg's as good as new. Me and the preacher killed a couple dozen birds this morning. Bet we walked ten miles. By the way, can you and Stella come over for supper tonight? I'll get Jennie to cook up a mess of birds and we can do a little talking." Then before Bubba could answer he said, "I've been thinking all winter about some more possibilities on the location of the treasure. Maybe if we put our minds together we'll get some new ideas. At least we need to start making plans to go back."

"I'll call Stella and see if she's got any other plans," Bubba answered. "I'm sure she don't, though. She's about to drive me crazy about going back to Vicksburg before our contract runs out."

"Good, I'll see you around six," Lim said, paid for the gas and drove off.

Jennie, as usual, had fixed a fine meal. Birds, mash potatoes, homemade biscuits and gravy, and a chocolate pie. Nobody could cook birds or a pie like Jennie. After the meal, Stella helped Jennie do the dishes while Lim and Bubba went to the living room to smoke and sip their drinks. A short time later, Stella came to the living room as Jennie went out on the porch to wait on Tobe.

Stella started things rolling. "You know you two ain't done a thing all winter but lie around and drink whiskey. There's a fortune over on that river and it's been lying there over a hundred years waiting on someone to come and haul it away. When are you two going to get off your bottoms and go get it?"

"You're right," Lim laughed. "Our contract will be out in May and we've got a hell of a lot invested. I say we start buying our supplies and get the show on the road. You can't kill quail talking about it in the house."

Bubba added his approval, "Well, I guess I can put up with a cripple and a girl that's scared of coons for awhile. Anyway, bird season is over now and Lim should be ready to go."

Lim poured Stella a drink and gave it to her holding his glass up saying, "Here's to the Merrygold treasure. This time we're coming back with it."

Stella seconding the toast said, "Come rain, high water or snakes, this time I'm betting with Lim that we're going to find Mr. Breckinridge's treasure."

Bubba added, "And Lim don't make no bad bets."

Giving Stella a paper and a pen, Lim said, "Let's get things going. Stella, start writing down what we need in the way of supplies."

Before Bubba and Stella left, the estimated cost of supplies had used up their bank account plus another five hundred Lim said he was putting in, to which Bubba and Stella objected "We agreed we would share everything on an equal basis. Let's see if we can't get by on what we got."

"Okay," Lim agreed, "if you two insist, you can cut where you can, but not the booze." Laughing, they raised their glasses again in a toast. The plan was set. They would leave as soon as the supplies were purchased.

The next few weeks were spent buying supplies, checking equipment, and getting ready to leave for Vicksburg. Finally, everything was complete and Lim's truck was loaded. They would leave the next morning, May 1.

Before daybreak, Lim picked up Bubba then went to Stella's house. She was outside waiting on them when they drove up. "Do y'all want to come in for coffee? I've got a full pot freshly perked, just took off the stove."

"Naw, Stella," Lim responded, "we need to hit the road. No need for us to come in. We'd wake up the whole house. We'll get a bite to eat somewhere on the way."

Around one o'clock that afternoon, they pulled up in front of Mr Breckinridge's bank and went in. After a short wait, Mr. Breckinridge came out and welcomed them, inviting them to join him in his office. "I was afraid you had given up on the search," he said as he offered them a chair. "All the trouble with you leg, I had my doubts if you'd be back. Are you doing alright now, Lim?"

Lim did all the talking. "Yes sir, Mr. Breckinridge, the leg's fine now, that old snake slowed things up a bit, but we haven't given up the chase. If the gold is there, we're still gonna find it. We're going to give it a hell of a try this time. It's time we had a little luck and drew a betting hand."

"Good!" Mr. Breckinridge responded confidently. "Can I be of any assistance? I haven't run across anything that I know of that will help, other than leaving you alone."

"There's one thing," said Lim, "we'd like a copy of Captain Breckinridge's letter to his wife. I can't help but believe he left an answer to the treasure in that letter. If we had the letter with us we could go over it and possibly break the code, if there is one."

Not hesitating, Mr. Breckinridge got up stating, "It's in my lock box. I'll get it and run you a copy. It'll only take a few minutes." Smiling he continued, "I don't have a drink I can offer you, but there's fresh coffee in the hall outside the door."

Stella followed Mr. Breckinridge saying, "I'll get the coffee."

A short time later Breckinridge returned with the copy. "I trust your confidence in the protection of this. If you will stay for the night, I'll be glad to treat you."

Bubba broke in this time. "We appreciate it but Stella's got a hang up about airing her tent out before dark, especially when the coons have been sleeping in it all winter."

"I'll hold that treat until you find the treasure," Mr. Breckinridge said, laughing as he opened the door. "Then we'll have a big one. By the way," he added as they walked to the door, "the contract we have expires around May 7, I believe. Let me get it and extend the time. A man's word is good for me, but I feel it best if it is in writing."

A short time later, the trio left Mr. Breckinridge's office with the new contract, extending the time for an additional six months. Arriving in Vicksburg after dark, they spent the night in a motel. Rising early the next morning and buying their last-minute supplies, both boats were packed and Lim's truck parked in the storage garage before noon. It was unusual, but everything ran like clockwork, even the outboard motors started without too much trouble. The trip down river was without incidence and they reached camp by mid afternoon. Things were working too good. Everything was pretty much like they'd left it. Its only permanent inhabitant was a copperhead that decided the cook tent was his winter domain. A hickory stick changed his mind.

It was a beautiful clear night and as Stella grilled their steaks, Lim and Bubba sat around the fire and swapped yarns sipping their drinks.

After supper, Stella joined in and the conversation changed to the lost treasure. Each one searched their minds for new possibilities, but could come up with nothing new. Finally, the subject got around to old Captain Breckinridge's ghost; this time in a more joking manner. Bubba didn't take things like that lightly and remarked, "You can joke all you want, but it won't change my feelings. Who knows, the Captain could be sitting right here with us listening to all our plans."

"Bubba," Lim broke in with a hearty laugh, "you think old Breckinridge keeps finding out our plans and moves the treasure every time we're about to find it?"

Bubba laughed. "I know you and Stella don't agree, but I still got my doubts about the old coot. I wouldn't put anything past him. In fact, he could have stirred up that old cottonmouth that bit you I got a feeling we were getting too close to the treasure and he had to do something."

"Well, that means it's probably stashed in the old slough or close by," Lim said. "If he didn't move it, we got a good chance of finding it tomorrow."

Stella, enjoying the laugh, said as she got up, "You two can stay up all night. I'm going to bed, haint or no haints."

They didn't waste any time the next morning after breakfast, Lim and Bubba started probing the old slough where the snake had bitten Lim. This time being more cautious and using screen wire leg protectors. Stella stayed at the camp giving it a good spring-cleaning.

Tired, muddy and finding no trace of the treasure, it was after dark when the pair returned to camp, dejected, tired and soaking wet. The days search was a failure, except now they knew the treasure was not in the snake-infested slough.

Stella had cooked ribs. As she took them up and spreading them on a large tray, she said, "Both of you could use a bath. Head for the river while I finish taking supper up."

The following day, the high bluff down the river was thoroughly searched. Finding nothing, the deep waters along the point received their attention. The dangerous whirlpools proved to be too risky and searching the point was abandoned for the sandbar across the river. Probing the sandbar took almost a week, and it too proved unsuccessful. However, a cannon ball was found which gave them renewed faith, but finding nothing to go with the steel ball, it was decided that whoever shot it was probably shooting at Indians, or possibly was fired during a skirmish with soldiers. It apparently didn't have anything to do with the Merrygold treasure.

The next two days, a search of the heavy wooded area up the river from the bar was conducted. Again, their search proved fruitless, other than a large timber rattler and fresh bear tracks that Stella would just as soon hadn't been found.

The next search was up the river at any point that would have been accessible by boat. The thought there, was that old Captain Breckinridge may have seen it impossible to go much farther without sinking and had decided to unload what weight he could and try to make it to Carriers Point to repair the leaking hull. The only good thing that came out of this search was no bear tracks were seen.

The month of May ended and the search had turned up nothing. It was the same on June 1; however, a fifteen-pound yellow cat was caught on their throw line, which made a good meal for the hundred-year anniversary night. Finishing the meal as the sun disappeared behind the willowed horizon, Lim replenished his drink and took his seat across from the dying campfire.

"Guess it was about this time, maybe a little later around nine o'clock, (the letter said the dark of the night) when Colonel Hampton and his soldiers loaded the Merrygold and she pulled out of Vicksburg," Lim said.

Bubba was sitting across from Lim sipping his drink and didn't say anything as Lim continued, "It's hard to believe that a hundred years ago this very minute what was going on such a short distance away. I bet the place was in some stir. No telling how many soldiers Hampton had getting that boat ready. Then right before she steamed out, the loaded wagon hurried down the hill with the gold and silver. The soldiers worked in the dark not knowing what a valuable cargo was being loaded. Everybody was hurrying hoping the Yankees would be too occupied with their evening meal to notice all the activity. I bet the boiler in the Merrygold was so hot it was ready to explode when the crew crawled aboard and Captain Breckinridge hollered, 'Cast off!' and the soldiers pushed her from the hidden mooring. Her old paddle wheels must have made some spray when they caught hold and she steamed out into the open river and headed toward the Union blockade."

Stella sat and listened to the conversation, her imagination going back a hundred years. A strange feeling caught her imagination just as it had Lim and Bubba. It was almost as if she was standing beside Captain Frederick Breckinridge watching the whirling paddle wheels. She could feel the trembling of the boat as it caught the current of the open river picking up speed with each turn of the wheels.

Lim continued, "Probably, the captain steadied the pilot wheel straining his eyes trying to pick out the dark form of the Union gunboats. I can almost see the boiler hissing steam and the whirling paddle wheels whipping spray above the double smoke stacks, and even feel the stripped hull trembling as it skimmed the choppy waves of the rushing river, picking up speed with every turn of the giant, whirling wheels. I can hear the captain yelling to his men to give her more wood and keep that boiler full.

"Rounding the bend of the river, the dark forms of the Union gunboats took shape. Captain Fredrick spun the pilot wheel, switching the Merrygold from one opening to the other. So close to the gunboats, the churning wheels sprayed the side of the massive floating fortresses. What was impossible was becoming possible, if the Merrygold's luck held, another two hundred yards and the bewildered Union gunboats would be behind them. In the open river, the Merrygold, with a full head of steam, would be miles down the river before the surprised Union blockaders could realize the speeding Merrygold had run past their blockade.

"The impossible was happening. The Merrygold and her precious cargo were going to make it. Yet it was not to be. Almost as if the sleeping gunboats were waiting for the daring ship to clear the blockade, their guns made sudden sharp flashes that illuminated the pitch-black night as ship after ship flashed their angry awakening like an electrical storm lighting the heavens.

"The Merrygold, illuminated by the devastating cannon fire, fought the river of hell with shells ripping the angry waters and missiles whining overhead, some exploding in front, some to the rear and side.

"Simultaneously the Confederates illuminated the river bluffs with their longest range cannons giving hopeless support to the struggling Merrygold as every missile possible was fired at the out of range Union fleet. Captain Fredrick fought the pilot wheel. His water-sprayed mates crammed wood into the boiler while shells and missiles rained in their hopeless path on a mission that was not to be. The odds ran out, suddenly a devastating jar; the Merrygold trembled and listed to the side as the river gushed through the gaping water line hit.

"The Captain yelled at the top of his lungs, 'Give her all the steam she has. Keep her nose up, then move port side and stuff everything you can in that hole.' Moments later, the bend of the river took the devastating hell. The cripple Merrygold had now only to fight the rushing waters of the river. It would take the stunned Yankees an hour to recover and have a gunboat in pursuit.

"An hour passed, then two, the exhausted crew bailing the uncontrollable water. The impossible was not in the book, their efforts were in vain. Captain Breckinridge yelled to his weary crew. 'There's Carrier's Point, if we can make the bend, we'll pull ashore and see if she's reparable.'"

Bubba and Stella were so engrossed with Lim's story of the hopeless fate of the struggling Merrygold that neither said a word for a long spell after Lim finished. Bubba broke the trance, "Boy, somehow it makes you feel as if you were on that boat with Captain Breckinridge."

"I had the same eerie feeling," Stella added, "like we'd moved back in time a hundred years and it was all happening again. Everything seemed so real that you'd think the Merrygold was down in the cove now with the Captain holding her steady with the paddle wheels all the while hollering to his mates to tie her off and to keep the bow above the water line. Then the captain and her crew taking their lantern and scrambling ashore to inspect the damaged hull. Everything seems so real that if you strain your eyes you might see flashing lantern lights."

"Or run down the bluff and see if you can help," Bubba added.

Lim made the comment, "The strange part of the story is it actually happened. Don't know if it was in all the same sequence we just described, but one thing for sure, a hundred years ago close to this very time the Merrygold was right down that bluff tied close to the old leaning willow."

Lim got up, went to his and Bubba's tent, and got the copy of Captain Breckinridge's letter. He came back and sat down. In the firelight, he read it again, thinking to himself, "It's dated tomorrow, June 2. Captain Breckinridge doesn't have but a few hours to live."

Stella yawned, awakened from her trance, as Lim came back and sat by the fire. "It's getting late," she said, "you two can stay up all night if you wish, but I'm going to bed. I'm so tired; I feel like I just rode the Merrygold down the river and helped the crew bail water all the way."

"Me too," Bubba said as he emptied his glass. "It must be getting close to midnight. You going to turn in Lim?"

"Naw, Bubba, I'll sit around awhile," Lim answered as he sat staring at the letter.

It must have been one o'clock in the morning when Lim walked out to the mile marker on the rocky point, lantern in one hand the fifth in the other. Sitting down against the mile marker, his thoughts drifted to the Merrygold. "She left Vicksburg about four hours ago, probably rounded the Point a little before midnight. The Captain, doing everything he could to keep her afloat, shifting the gold and wood to the off side from the hit. Nothing worked, probably still taking water, his men bailing like hell and still losing ground. No question he saw their hopeless condition and decided up the river that Carrier's Point would be the best place to try to repair the ripped hull. Knowing of the eddy water behind the point he probable docked her in the same place we got our boats. Then the Captain made his decision what to do after he surveyed the damage. That probably didn't take but a glance and he decided repairing the hole was useless. He'd have to unload the cargo. What would he have done then, those boxes with two bars to a box weighed a good hundred pounds each? Hell, he didn't have the manpower or the time to take it ashore. He didn't have any choice; he had to dump it in the river. But where? We probed every foot of that area where the boats are tied, from the Point to the bend of the river."

Lim was getting confused It wouldn't be where the Captain docked the boat if he's coming back to get it. The water's too deep. He said in the letter that he was trying to get word to the rendezvous where they could pick it up. He had to have put it in shallow water not over neck deep, probably three or four feet. Undoubtedly, the old Captain figured he could make it to the rendezvous without the weight of the gold and silver. But with it dark as hell, no moon, where would he have dumped it? It had to be in shallow water and he had to mark where he dumped it if he was planning to come back and get it. There was no way he would have just dumped it in the water.

Lim took a straight drink and sat staring into the darkness, his mind searching every possible clue. Then saying to himself, "Hell, that was his only choice."

The change of night was so gradual he didn't realize that the moon was creeping over the distant tree line until it was in full view, the crystal rays laying a streak of silver down the middle of the river. In awe, Lim stood up and looked at the moon. "I'll be damn! That's it! It has to be!" He let out a bear whoop worse than Stella with the coon in her tent did He grabbed the half-full bottle and lantern and started running across the bald knob, hollering to the top of his lungs, "Haints or no haints, old Breckinridge I done found your gold. Bubba, wake up Stella! Bubba wake up Stella!"

Bubba heard Lim yelling, jumped out of bed snatching his pants on and started running to meet him thinking something terrible had to have happened. Running as hard as he could, he met Lim stumbling across the point. Lim was so out of breath from running he couldn't tell Bubba anything. All Lim could do was gasp for breath. He couldn't say a thing. Bubba thought he'd had a stroke or heart attack or something terrible and tried to pick Lim up and carry him. Lim gasping and staggering kept pushing him away whispering, "Get Stella. Get Stella. I got it figured out. I got it figured out."

Bubba was getting nowhere with Lim and could make no sense out of his gasping conversation so he started hollering for Stella, who got to the fire about the same time as Lim and Bubba. Lim was having such a fit and was still so out of breath that he couldn't talk. This got Stella to screaming and hollering almost as crazy as Lim.

"What's wrong, Bubba?" she asked frantically. "What's wrong? What's happened to him?"

Bubba was dumfounded and just stood there watching all the commotion. Lim staggered around the campfire trying to catch his breath. Finally deciding he'd have to quiet the situation one way or the other, Bubba grabbed Lim up in his arms like a small child and started walking around the fire. Stella followed him as he circled. Lim held the whiskey bottle by the neck and hollered in a gasping voice, "I got it figured out. I broke the code. The old Captain's haint ain't going to fool us no more."

Stella snatched the bottle out of Lim's hand and took a straight drink herself. "Lay him down," she yelled at Bubba. "Hell, he knows where the gold is. We've got to do something where he can get his breath."

Bubba laid Lim down by the fire and finally got him quieted down long enough to pour a short drink in his mouth. Coughing and spurting whiskey all over them, Lim sat up with a smile on his bearded face as wide as the moon. He pointed up in the sky, "There...there it is!"

Bubba and Stella looked at the gibbous moon shining down through the trees, and then looked at each other, both sat in awe, speechless for a moment. Bubba broke the stalemate, "Hell, he's pointing to the moon. He's gone loco as a jackass."

Stella reaching for Lim's feet, "Help me. We better get him to bed; he's got D.T.'s, the fever or something."

Lim pushed them away and still so out of breath he could hardly whisper said, "Hell, ain't nothing wrong with me. Look at the moon. There's the answer. It's true! It's true! The old Captain can't hide it any more. I know where it is!"

Bubba tried to calm Lim down. "Okay, Lim, it's buried on the moon. We'll look there in the morning. Right now, we're putting you to bed and you're not getting anymore to drink, if I have to bust every bottle in camp."

Bubba's statement shook Lim about as much as solving the mystery and settled him down some. "Listen, you two goons," he whispered still so out of breath he could hardly get the words out. "The signature of the Captain, the Roman numeral III with the circle over it—it's the *moon*!"

This calmed Bubba and Stella down and suddenly they realized that Lim wasn't having a fit but..."Hell," both said in unison, "he's figured something out."

Finally, everyone calmed and had a drink, this time with chasers. Lim got his speech back. "Get dressed! We'll take the boat. I know where it is!"

You never saw anyone dress any faster. Lim was in the boat with the motor cranked when Bubba and Stella got there.

Turning the boat across the river, he gave it all it would take until they slid up on the sandbar across the river. Everyone got out of the boat and looked up the river at the moon's reflection. A glossy silver line followed the moon across the mile marker straight to the sandbar.

Lim pointed to the silver spectral, "Remember the old Captain's signature, the circle over the roman three? Well, that's the moon, the middle mark is the mile marker, and the three is for three-feet. It could be three fathoms, but that's too deep. The captain wouldn't have used fathoms because he knew the General would understand feet. That's why he put the little 'f' by the Roman numeral."

Bubba and Stella broke in trying to talk at the same time, "You mean it's right there in three feet of water?" they asked unbelieving.

Lim laughingly replied as he turned the bottle up, "Maybe not right there, but it's on that line somewhere. It could be on the beach or middle of the river. It's somewhere on that line. It just depends on how high the water was. The point didn't change and the moon didn't. Somewhere on that line, or mighty close to it, is the treasure." Lim pointed to the marker. "Old Captain Fredrick must have been as smart as a coon. He knew that if he unloaded the gold and silver bullion, it would lighten the boat and they'd have a chance of making it to the rendezvous. He also must have figured that if the rebels were going to come back and get it, it had to be stashed in shallow water, but deep enough to keep it out of the sight of the Yankees. Knowing this, he packed everything he could in the busted hull and headed the Merrygold for the sandbar. He probably made the decision coming across the river where to dump it. His big problem was where and how he was going to mark where he put it. That's when he noticed the moon that was just rising over the tree line. Putting two and two together, he lined the boat up with the mile marker and the moon, headed for the bar 'til she ran aground."

Stella broke in, "That must have been in about three feet of water. He unloaded the gold and lightened the Merrygold so she could float free. All he had to do then was head down the river and keep her afloat."

"I agree. His biggest problem was time," Lim added. "Trying to repair the hull he'd lost a half hour or more and he knew the Yankee gunboats were fast on his tail. Quickly, as his crew bailed water, the Captain dropped the bullion overboard. As soon as the bullion was dumped, the Merrygold floated free and old Breckinridge turned her down-river using all the steam she could take.

Pushing his luck, he probably over did it and the boiler ran short on water blowing the Merrygold to smithereens. The Captain was the only one that survived, and just barely at that. He probably found a piece of floating timber and hung on to it 'til the Yankee gunboat picked him up sometime the next morning."

Stella agreed. "That sounds reasonable to me. The Captain undoubtedly knew he was going to be captured and somehow figured a way to tell his wife where the gold was while he was hanging onto the piece of floating timber. It was a long shot, but it was the only one he had."

"I never thought of that," Lim said as he turned the bottle up and took a long pull. "He probably wrote that letter over and over in his mind a thousand times trying to figure some form of code that'd fool the Yankees. The old coot must've been some smart old man." Lim stopped for a minute and looked around, then said, "Bubba, get us something to mark where we're standing. There won't be any moon tomorrow during the day. We got to mark this spot."

Bubba went to the boat, came back with a paddle, and stuck it in the sand marking the line. It's a good thing no one came down the river around four o'clock that morning. They'd have probably thought that Indians were on the warpath with all the whooping and hollering Lim, Stella and Bubba did around that paddle.

It was after daylight when the celebrating threesome got back to camp, and probably wouldn't have made it back by then if Stella hadn't known how to drive an outboard motor. Then she had to threaten to beat them with the empty whiskey bottle before she could get them into the boat; she was still threatening as she got them up the riverbank and poured into bed. Luckily, she made it to her bed and they all slept until past noon. Stella, who had been in a little better shape than Bubba and Lim, got up first. Bubba smelled the coffee and stumbled out a short time later.

"I must have had a hell of a nightmare last night," he said with a thick voice. Stella didn't say anything; she just poured him a cup of black coffee.

"Hell Stella," Bubba went on, "that nightmare was so damn strong, I'd swear Lim told us where the gold is."

Stella smiled as best she could. "Drink the coffee. You didn't have a nightmare. You just got a hell of a hangover and keep your voice down, my head's on wrong, too."

After several cups of coffee, Bubba and Stella went out on the point and spent most of the evening letting the cool breeze and time have its effect. Over in the afternoon, Lim came alive and stumbled out of his tent.

"Y'all wake up! You two yo-yo's get out of bed. It'll be noon 'fore you know it. We got work to do!"

Bubba and Stella heard the commotion and came back to camp informing Lim that it was almost suppertime.

With the celebrating over, all three were up by the first gobbler call the following morning, and as daylight broke, were on their way across the river. Using the paddle as one marker, and the mile marker as the other, they drove stakes along the line from the backside of the sandbar to the middle of the river. The next plan was to probe the sand with a piece of reinforcing steel every three feet along the quarter-mile line.

As you might expect the probe hit rocks, old logs and stumps. Each time something was found, they would excitedly dig down and check it out This made their progress slow and it took quite some time just to cross the sandbar, but by the end of the following week, the first search had reached the last marker out in the river. Worn out and tired the weary probers went back to the starting point and moved over three feet and started again. Lim kept them pumped up by saying that since it was night; the captain was probably a few feet off.

Days passed then weeks, then a month. They'd made probes every three feet for fifteen or twenty feet on either side of the original line, and dug enough holes in the sandbar to hide a battle ship. Worn out, tired, and disgusted, the weary party went back to camp. Stella cooked a mess of young squirrels, topped off with the better portion of a fifth of whiskey. Dejected and whipped, Lim and Bubba kept their thoughts to themselves. Neither wanted to admit defeat, but each had the same thought; 'It's over. There's no treasure.' Finally, like whipped dogs, it was time to abandon the search, take their losses and go back to Taylorsville.

Stella thought of what Lim had said the day they shook hands in the kitchen at the Big House. Slowly getting to her feet, she turned to face her dejected partners. "I guess neither of you remember our agreement the day we decided to come on this treasure hunt. In case you forgot, it was not to give up, not to quit. Hell, we can be within a few feet of more money than there is in Mr. Breckinridge's bank. Are you two going to sit on your butts and let someone else stumble across it? Sure, we're tired as hell and searching for the treasure looks hopeless. I'll agree to that, but we're not whipped. Take the Stroader Well situation. It took months, but Lim, you finally figured it out. I know both of you'd feel better if we knew for sure that the treasure was still there and somebody hadn't found it. Well, it takes just a little reasoning, but to answer the last question first, if there was a treasure we know that no one has ever found it. I'm sure of that. If it'd been found, I don't care how many years ago, that would've been big news anywhere and everyone would've known about it. If the Union gunboat that picked old Captain Fredrick up found it, it would have been recorded in history. A stash of gold that big could not have been covered up. That eliminates one question. The other question is, was there ever a treasure? Well they found the Merrygold washed on a sandbar a few miles down river. That's part of the proof that there was indeed a treasure, a big part. It fits the description the old Colonel at the Soldiers' Home gave. Then there's the letter old Captain Breckinridge wrote his wife. What other proof do you need? The treasure is real. There's no doubt in my mind about that. Who knows, we may be within a few feet of it. Hell, we can't give up now. Something about the river had to change. A hundred years is a long time. I believe we broke the code. The treasure is still where the old Captain and his crew dumped it."

Lim reached over, poured a light drink and said, "Stella, you're right. Someone has to talk some sense. Sure, we're all whipped, but we can't give up now. Maybe something did change. Like you said, one-hundred years is a long time."

Bubba took the bottle from Lim. "Sure as hell wasn't the moon," he quipped and took a swig.

Excitedly, everyone spoke at the same time, "The point changed, or could it be the mile marker?"

"Remember the big rocks caved off the front side," Stella remarked loudly. "The point could have caved off twenty or thirty feet. There's no telling how much in a hundred years."

This put Lim's calculating mind to working. He stood up, sipped the last of his drink, and said, "Hell, if the point caved off even twenty feet, that would put us thirty feet or more off across the river."

This new idea gave new hope. Their spirits picked up, so did the ones they were drinking, but not so that it affected getting up early the next morning. With rejuvenated energy, they started where the search was left off the evening before, tired and worn out, but with renewed hope.

The first quarter mile line was completed with the same lack of success as the others. A bit dejected, the probing was moved over three feet and started again.

"Who knows, we may hit it the next try," Lim pointed out trying to keep their hopes up. "If not, we'll move over another three feet and try again. We got plenty of time and plenty to eat. We don't have a thing to do but keep trying. The only other option is to admit defeat and go back to Taylorsville. I'd rather stay here all summer than to do that. At least we've got a chance, even if it is like drawing two cards to an inside straight."

Bubba laughed as he stuck the iron prove in the soft sand. "Lim, you ever make a draw like that?" he asked.

"A few times, Bubba, if the stakes were high enough. I'll have to admit, it's bad odds, but I'd give her a try."

Stella took the probe from Bubba putting her two-cents worth in. "All I can say is I think the stakes are high enough. What we need is Lim's confidence and Lady Luck's smile."

Completing the second line, they moved over and started on another, each time growing a little more dejected.

"I feel like we're looking for something that's not here," Bubba blurted out. "A needle in a haystack would be easy compared to this. This is more like looking for a pebble in a mile long sandbar. Hell, the stuff could have been on the Merrygold when the boiler blew. Breckinridge's father's report said that a large part of the hull was missing."

"That's true," Lim stated, "but the Captain's letter said he unloaded the cargo. It couldn't have been on the Merrygold when she sank."

The days passed along with more stories and more stumps, rocks and logs. Completing the last probe around dark, tired and disillusioned, the weary searchers returned to camp and ate a breakfast supper of bacon, eggs, and Dutch oven biscuits. As Stella cleaned up and washed dishes, Bubba and Lim sat around the campfire almost too tired and dejected to talk.

Finally, Lim pulling on his pipe broke the silence. "What'cha say we take tomorrow off, go into Vicksburg, rent a motel room, wash our clothes and rest up a few days? Then, we'll come back and give the probing a good chance, if we don't hit something in a few days...say, a week, we'll go to Taylorsville and rest up a spell...about a couple of weeks or so?"

Bubba agreed. "I could use one of those big steaks, also a hot bath and a change of beds wouldn't hurt."

Stella came over to the fire and sat down by Bubba. "The hot bath and bed idea sure sounds good. I believe I could sleep a week."

The trip to Vicksburg was needed as Bubba said when they returned to camp. "Those couple of days in Vicksburg were like a two-week vacation. I'm ready to get with it, and I believe that tomorrow we're going to find old Breckinridge's treasure."

Stella joined in with a smile. "The rest did help. I don't know why, but I'm like Bubba. I got the same optimistic feeling. The sun's fixing to shine. It's a wonder what a hot bath and soft bed will do."

Lim got his two cents in. "You can't win, if you ain't in. This kind of talk is what we've been needing. You got to believe you're going to win, but right now we've got to hit the sack if we're going to find that gold tomorrow."

However, the next morning was not cooperating. It was a dreary, overcast day. Dark clouds had held back in the west most all morning, now they seemed closer. Everything was still, too still. The humidity was heavy and it looked like it would start raining any minute. Completing the probing across the sandbar and wading and probing until the water got too deep, they started probing out of the boat.

Bubba was working the rod from the front of the boat. He pushed it down to a foot above the water line and when he was sure nothing was there, he'd pull it up and moved over a few feet, jamming it in the soft sand. It sank about two feet and with a jarring thud stopped. Bubba didn't say anything, figuring it was another log or rock, pulled the rod up, moved over a foot or so and rammed it down again with the same result. Surprisingly, it felt like the same object he'd hit before.

Bubba looked at Lim and Stella and in a shaky voice said, "There's something down there, not a rock. It don't feel like a log or stump. It's something else like it's hollow."

Lim and Stella almost capsized the boat getting hold of the rod. Bubba went to the rear of the boat and started strapping on his diving gear. Stella and Lim kept moving the probe back and forth on the hidden object; the dark circling clouds overhead were the least of their worries.

"I'm going down," Bubba yelled as he eased over the side not taking the time to tie on his safety rope. "Hold the rod where it is," he instructed. "We'll find out shortly if it's a log or not."

As Bubba went out of sight, the Lord must have decided that this wasn't the day for them to find the treasure as heavy clouds began to cover the heavens. Suddenly, an intense bolt of lightning ripped through the sky, and it began to rain softly, then changing to a heavy downpour. It rained so hard you could barely see. Not satisfied with this, the Lord sent marble sized hail. Stella and Lim were fighting to hold the rod as the hail whipped at them like rifle shots. The winds came next making the waves waist high.

Lim hollered at Stella, "Put on the diving gear! We got to get Bubba in the boat or it's going to capsize! Why in the hell didn't he wear the safety rope! We got to get to the bank!" He looked at the darkening sky. The storm was raging so now that it was making it impossible to talk. "Hell!" he called loudly cupping his hand to his mouth like a megaphone, "it looks like a tornado's coming! We got to get to the bank. This river is no place to be when a tornado hits!" No sooner had he spoken the words, the rod pulled loose. Lim frantically jammed it back into the sandy bottom trying to hold the boat. Luckily, as the rod broke loose, Bubba came to the surface. He started to complain, but when he saw what was happening he made a beeline for the boat. Lim had it cranked by the time Bubba crawled over the side and flopped into the bottom of the boat.

Stella, sitting in the middle section in the bottom of the boat with a scuba tank strapped on her back screamed, pointing toward the sky as she did, "Look, it is a tornado, and it's coming up the river!"

Lim gave the motor full throttle and yelled, "Hold on! We're going to try to make it to the point!" The waves shook the boat from side to side, as water poured over the front. Lim frantically turned the water-swamped boat toward the Point, but it was too late. In a matter of seconds, the angry funnel cloud bore down on them. The huge funnel stretched from one side of the river almost to the other.

"We can't make it," Lim yelled over the screaming storm. "Bubba, you and Stella jump in the river! Stay under till it's passed!"

Bubba hesitated a second, looking at Lim like he'd just lost his mind. Understanding what Lim was trying to do, he yelled, "Stella, put that mouth piece in and jump! Swim underwater to the point."

Stella rolled over the side and immediately went out of sight. Bubba hesitated. Lim yelled at him. "Don't be a fool! Jump, Bubba! I'll ride her out."

Bubba didn't wait this time and rolled over the side. He went under for a few seconds, then came back to the top just in time to see Lim and the boat sail over his head.

It seemed like an eternity. Bubba forced himself to stay under thinking as he did how calm the water was, almost like it didn't have a current. Only the

Lord knew what hell was going on a few feet above his head. Saying a prayer, he came to the surface. His eyes caught the ugly form of the massive funnel as it left the river and disappeared across the heavy timbered bottom ripping a path a hundred yards wide. He looked for Stella and yelled, then for Lim, then for Stella again praying between yells, "Lord help me! Lord help me! Please don't let them die!"

It's a strange thing about tornados. One minute the world seems to be tearing itself apart, and just as suddenly, the waters grew calm, with just a slight hint of a breeze and the sun began breaking through the clouds making everything seem unreal. The ugly tornado was like a nightmare, almost as if it hadn't happened. He heard a faint noise, then a muffled call, "Bubba!" He looked toward the point and saw someone in the water, waving.

"Stella!" Bubba yelled excitedly and started swimming as hard as he could. When he'd finally reached the rocky shore, Stella was clinging to one of the boulders on the point.

"Bubba, where's Lim?" she cried as she slipped into his arms. "Bubba, where's Lim?" and she began to softly whimper.

Bubba pulled Stella's scuba tank off, flung it into the rocks, and pushed Stella up the rocky cliff trying to answer her as gently as he could. "I don't know. Maybe the Lord saved him." Then under his breath he said, "It's the only way he could possibly be alive."

Bubba left Stella at the top of the point. "Stay here!" he told her, "I'm going to get the other boat and find Lim." He didn't give her time to answer, just took off running across the Point and down the far side. He found the other boat, but it was wrapped around the stump of the willow tree. Bubba stopped only long enough to utter a curse, "Oh Hell!" as he eyed the crushed hull of the other boat, then started running down the bank of the river yelling at the top of his lungs. "Lim! Lim! Where the hell are you? Lim!"

Bubba ran and stumbled a mile or more down the river. He'd yelled so much that he could scarcely make a sound when he turned around. He didn't want to believe what he was thinking as he ran stumbling back to camp.

Stella had a fire going and a lantern she had found was burning on the table by the pump. It was all that was left of their camp. As Bubba walked up, Stella stood questioning him with her eyes. She couldn't bring herself to say what she was thinking and ran to Bubba.

"I didn't find him," Bubba said softly. "The other boat was bent all to hell. Stella, he's gone. There's no way he could have lived through that. I saw the wind grab Lim and the boat and sail it through the air like a pie plate. He's gone. Ain't no way he could have lived."

"There's no way we can go look for him tonight," Stella said as she led Bubba over to the fire making him sit down. "Maybe he washed up on shore somewhere. He had a life preserver on. He could be across the river."

All Bubba could say was, "He's gone. I know he's gone. God knows he's gone. Why didn't you and Lim leave me in the river? You saw the thing coming."

Stella took the lantern and rumbled around in some of the scattered belongings until she found a bottle. She came and handed the bottle to Bubba. "Here, drink a drink of this."

Bubba took the bottle, looked at it and set it aside. "Reckon I just don't feel I could get a drink down." He got up and went over to a piece of one of the tents that was wrapped around a tree, unwrapped what was left and brought it over to the fire. "Here, wrap up in this. I'm taking the lantern and going out on the point. Maybe I can hear him or he'll see the light. I've got to do something."

Knowing Bubba wanted to be alone, Stella wrapped the remains of the tent around her and sat down by the dying fire, too exhausted and worried to punch it up.

Bubba stopped at the mile marker and began to talk aloud to himself, "I should have known better than to make that dive. I saw the storm coming. If I'd had any sense, Lim would still be alive. Damn gold will make you crazy! It's almost like a woman. You just lose your reasoning when you get around either one." Bubba stood silently for a moment, then continued. "Ain't nothing I can do. If I had a boat, at least I could cross the river. Lim's body is probably on the sandbar or in the willow behind it. He could be alive…Hell, I'm going down and try to beat that old boat out. I might get it straight enough to paddle across the river. If I don't, I'm going to swim across it."

It was near midnight when Bubba finished kicking out the boat's sides. The gas tank was crushed, so he took the motor off and pushed the boat out into the river. It leaked like a sieve, but it would float. Pitching an old coffee can into the boat, Bubba kicked one of the board seats loose. "Ain't much of a paddle, but it'll do."

The river current swept the ragged boat down stream. Bubba held an angle and kept it going, hitting the sandbar a half-mile or so down the river. Hurriedly pulling the boat up on the sandbar, he grabbed the lantern and started walking, calling for Lim every hundred yards or so. Going up the river first, he stopped at the paddle marker. The moon had come up leaving a silvery streak down the middle of the river.

"Right out there's where the damn monster hit us," he said under his breath. "It slung Lim and the boat across this way. Hell, he could be anywhere. It could have thrown him into the willows behind the bar. I better check there."

Reaching the willows, Bubba called for Lim again. Still no answer, so he began breaking his way through the heavy underbrush knowing his search was as useless as the search for the Merrygold treasure. He stumbled and crawled through the wiry thicket for more than an hour. Finally giving up, he returned to the sandbar where he called again and again, but there was still no answer. Whipped and exhausted, he sat down on an old log and thought about Lim.

"Lim, why in the hell didn't you leave me in the river? I'd have been all right…Damn the gold! I wish we'd never heard of it…What we found in the river could have been nothing. Maybe a pile of rocks or a log, God only knows what it could've been. One thing's as sure as hell, all the gold in the world isn't worth what's happened. It's all my fault. I saw the dark clouds. I knew the damn mess was coming. It's the treasure. It's been there over a hundred years. Why in the world was I in such a rush?…I'm such a fool! The stuff sure wasn't going anywhere." Drifting off into semi-consciousness, his thought went to Captain Breckinridge and General Pemberton and the two men that were on the Merrygold when she blew to smithereens. "It's almost like they sent that tornado. Now they're probably dancing around on the sandbar laughing and whooping it up knowing their secret will never be found." Bubba stood up and shook his fist at the dancing spirits. "You can have the damn gold. Keep your secret forever! It's Lim I want, not your damn gold. Why did you have to take Lim? It was my fault he's gone! Why didn't you take me?" He hesitated as powerful emotions rose within his heart. He screamed again, "Dance and laugh all you want! I'm going to find Lim, and when I do, we're going to find your gold!" He screamed at the top of his lungs, "You're dead and your time is past! Go away to heaven or hell or wherever you're supposed to be! Go…go away…go!" Slowly Bubba gathered his senses. 'I must be losing my mind.' He turned and started back down the battered sandbar, its former beauty now tainted and ugly.

Bubba was almost out of his mind, kept repeating, "Lim, I'm going to find you. Lim, it's me, Bubba. I'm going to find you. I've got to keep going. He's

196

over here some place. I've got to keep going. Lim, I'm going to find you. Lim, I'm going to find you!"

Stumbling and talking to himself, Bubba made his way down the timber littered bar walking over and around twisted and broken trees. Passing the twisted boat, he stopped and hollered out…bewildered, "Did I hear something? Hell, I'm going crazy as a Betsy Bug." He called again and waited…nothing! He started walking, still talking to himself. "Maybe I'm dreaming. Maybe I'm dead. That's it!…I was killed in the tornado. I'm a ghost like the old captain. Hell, Bubba, you're losing your mind." Trembling and cold, Bubba stopped, shook his head, and then fell face down in the wet sand.

Drifting away in a hazy dream, he saw them coming. Captain Breckinridge and his two mates racing at him waving their swords, screaming and dancing and whooping it up. "We got the gold! We got the silver! We got Lim, and now we got you. We got the gold, we got…"

Bubba came to himself fighting the wind with both hands. "You ain't got Lim! You ain't got Lim, and you ain't got me!" Bewildered, he momentarily came to his senses and feeling the remorse and fear raging in his mind, he screamed again, "Bubba, you have gone crazy as hell! Wake up you fool! It's the storm! You're too tired! Get up you fool you can't stop!…Get up!" Suddenly, things got quiet and he heard it again. Bubba shook his head trying desperately to straighten his mind. "Hell, I know I heard something." Standing up he yelled as loudly as he could, "Lim!…Lim, answer me!…Lim!" Turning in each direction, he watched and listened. There it was again, way off. It had to be something.

Adrenalin raced through his body. There it is again. Picking up the lantern, he started running. The loose sand pulled him down and his lungs felt as if they were about to burst. He stopped and called again.

The sound was clear this time. He could hear it as plain as day, "Down here in the river."

Bubba let out a war whoop, "Lim! Lim!" and ran toward the river. The moon's glow reflected a dark form fifty to seventy-five yards out in the river. It was wrapped around a snag and bobbed up and down like a bream cork.

Stopping at the water's edge, Bubba called again. "Lim! Is that you? Is that you, Lim?"

"Hell yes it's me," Lim called from the river. "Who the hell do you think would be out here in the river? If you don't get a boat out here and stop me, I'm going to end up in New Orleans."

Bubba sat the lantern down and started running back up the sandbar yelling at Lim, "Hold on, Lim! The boat's up the river. Hold on! I'll be right back!" Suddenly, he wasn't tired any more. The loose sand was no longer a barrier. He felt like he was back in high school with nothing but the open field and a goal line in front of him.

Snatching the boat out in the edge of the water, he ran back down the river dragging that battered boat, thanking the Lord as he ran. "It's him! It's *Lim*! He's alive, Lord! Thank you! *Thank you, Lord*!"

Reaching the lantern, he turned the boat out toward Lim and called, "Hold on, Lim! Hold on! I'll get to you in a minute."

When Bubba got a good look at Lim holding onto that snag and looking like he was all right, he couldn't hold his joy any longer and picked at Lim as he paddled with the boat seat. "Lim, what the hell you doing down here hanging on to that snag? We've been holding supper for you at camp."

Lim answered as he caught hold of the boat, "Just get up here and help me get in the boat. I've been roosting on that damn thing all night. Where's Stella?"

"Back at camp planning your funeral," Bubba said with obvious relief in his voice. "We may have to have her's when she sees you."

"Thank the Lord we won't have any funerals for a while yet," Lim said as he worked his way into the boat.

Day was breaking when they finally worked the boat back across the river and tied up to the willow stump. Stella was sleeping by the burned out fire when Bubba and Lim walked into camp.

When she saw Lim, Bubba thought they were going to have to have that funeral anyway. Awaking, like in a trance, she looked at Lim and her mouth flew open like she was trying to speak, but couldn't. She jumped up and ran into Lim's arms crying, "Lord, Lim, you're alive! Lord, Lim, you're alive!" She hugged him, then held him back from her to look at him again like she couldn't believe what she was seeing. If they'd been able to find more of their whiskey, they'd have thrown one hell of a party. All three hugged, shouted, and embraced each other in joyous relief. It was some sight to see.

Finally, settling down by the fire, Lim poured the last drink from the scavenged bottle, saying, "I want to tell you both one thing. While I was hanging on to that snag, bobbing up and down in the river, I talked a long time to the Man upstairs." Lim stopped talking for a minute as he finished his drink. "That's something I ain't never done before. I told Him if He'd just let us live through the hell of that tornado, Old Lim would never let Him down. I also told Him if we didn't find that treasure, it was all right, too. In all my life, I never talked to the Lord that seriously before, and Stella and Bubba, I want you both to know He must have been listening."

Bubba nodded, "Lim, I did some talking, too. I guess He can hear you underwater too, 'cause every minute I was under there I was doing my part of the praying. Then, when I went crazy on the sandbar, I had a run-in with…" Bubba stopped and didn't finish that part of the story, he just added, "The Lord shook me back to my senses."

Stella hugged both Lim and Bubba and began to cry. "He answered all our prayers. I was praying all the time I was under the water, and when I came to the top and called and nobody was there, I really did some heavy duty praying. And last night, while Bubba was looking for you, Lim, I prayed so hard I can't remember all the things I promised. The main thing was that we'd somehow come through this awful tornado and be safe and unharmed. There's not a one of us that don't know He had to have answered those prayers."

Lim moved over to the fire and punching it up said, "I'm starving. Did any of you find any food?"

Stella smiled, "I found your old gun, a scattered box of shells and a can of flour. It's light enough now that if I had a hunter in camp, he could go kill us a couple of squirrels for breakfast while I whip up something to go with 'em."

"You two keep looking around for some coffee and a little salt and pepper," Bubba said as he picked up the gun. "I'll be back in a few minutes with breakfast," he called back over his shoulder as he walked off, "if you find any of Lim's whiskey, save me some."

Lim waited until Bubba disappeared into the heavy timbered bottom, then turned to Stella. "Stella, that's something else me and the Old Man talked about. You and Bubba been waiting too long to get married. When we get back to Taylorsville, whether we've found that treasure or not, I want you and Bubba to get married as soon as possible. That's more important than the treasure or anything else."

Smiling, Stella hugged Lim and kissed him on the cheek. "Thank you, Lim. No matter what, it's a good world and it's people like you and Bubba that make it better."

A short time later, a couple of shots were fired. Shortly afterwards, Bubba and Lim were dressing squirrels while Stella fried flour and water hoecakes in a broken handle skillet. Things were slowly getting back to normal.

Chapter 22

Not having any coffee with his meal upset Lim. "That does it!" he said as he stood up. "I can do without food and even a drink of spirits, but no coffee and no smoking is something else. You two get ready. We're going to have a search party bigger than for the Merrygold's gold. We got food, clothes, hammers, saws, axes—everything we own—scattered all over these woods and somewhere in it is a can of coffee, my pipe, and a can of tobacco."

"Lim," Bubba said quickly, "that tornado came up the river, hit the point and cut across the bald knob over there. It didn't take a single tree around camp, but it snatched our tents, clothes, everything we own right out of these woods— picked it clean. What the hell happened? You'd think old man Breckinridge did it himself."

"I reckon old Breckinridge didn't have much to do with it," Lim replied. "When a tornado hits it's like a giant vacuum cleaner sucking everything into the funnel, then the outside wind blows it to hell knows where; that's what happened to our tents and belongings. What we got to do now is start searching every place we can; in the trees, in the water, over on the sandbar, everywhere imaginable. We should find most of the heavy stuff. Keep everything you find. It's going to be a mess for quite a while, but with the Lord's help we'll survive. There's lots to do. First, we've got to build some form of living quarters even if it's nothing but a lean-to to keep out the bugs, the animals, and the rain." Lim started to say snakes, but thought it best not to bring that subject up. What's the old saying…talk about the devil?

The search began and by noon their inventory was growing. The search turned up two flashlights, posthole diggers, pots and pans, spoons, knives, hammer, a bucket of nails, the handsaw, ax, some sugar and salt, and a bottle of cooking oil. The sack of flour was wet, but hopefully it could be dried. Along with the flour, there was a canister of meal and even a few bars of soap. They even began to find things they didn't want to find, like four broken fifths of booze and a coffee can with no coffee, Lim's cot, broken beyond repair.

The trees were littered with clothes, pieces of tent, towels, socks, shorts—you name it. There was so much stuff that to look at it you'd think it grew on the trees in place of the leaves. All in all, they salvaged a large part of their belongings, but Lim's pipe and fixing's were not among them.

As dark descended it was time for supper, which consisted of another meal of fried squirrel, then they wrapped themselves up in the tent scraps for the night and went to sleep, too weary to talk, but happy and content just to be alive.

They spent the second day making a pole shelter and covering it with the remains of the tent. It wasn't all that cozy, but at least it kept them out of the rain and protected the things that had been salvaged.

While re-setting the camp, they kept a sharp lookout for boats coming up the river. The barges were too big to stop, but every so often a commercial fisherman would come by and it was hoped one could be stopped and a ride caught to Vicksburg.

Their second choice was walking out to the nearest highway, which Lim estimated to be three to four miles. This suited everyone, but only if a boat couldn't be stopped within a few days. Lim kept insisting that because it was spring the fish would be spawning making commercial fishing better and increasing their chances of getting a ride.

On the third day, a throw line was found, baited with spring lizard, squirrel and turkey innards, and then set out. Most everyday a fish was caught, and what wasn't eaten was stored in the live box. The one bottle of cooking oil didn't last long. Now their biggest problem was finding some cooking grease. Boiled fish was nourishing, but not the most desirable. Bubba supplied the cooking oil some days later when he killed a small shoat. The fresh meat was most welcomed, but especially the lard. Living was getting easier, but there was still no boat.

The week passed and it seemed that walking out was their best choice. It was decided that everyone would go because there was no need for anyone to stay in camp. The few things the tornado left weren't worth guarding. However, their luck changed that afternoon when a commercial fisherman came up the river running his nets. Flagging him from the point, he turned across the river and met them at the willow stump. He was going to Vicksburg, but he was going to be running his nets on the way up the river. Lim made the guy a sizable offer and he agreed to take one person, if that one person didn't mind riding with a boat load of catfish and buffalo. As a friendly gesture, Lim offered to help run the nets, which seemed to go over big with the fisherman.

Waving to his marooned companions, and reminding them that they weren't married, Lim promised to hurry on his mission, and loaded in with the fisherman. It took the rest of the day and on into the night to get to Vicksburg. The old fisherman must have had twenty nets stretched in every bend of the river all the way to Vicksburg. Lim knew the station was closed where he had his truck stored, and started walking, but finally caught a ride to the nearest motel, got a room, and took a long hot bath. He had to put the same clothes back on, but at least he was clean underneath. After the bath, he walked to a nearby restaurant and got something to eat. Returning to the motel, he washed his clothes in the bathtub and hung them out to dry overnight.

As soon as he could the next morning, he called Mr. Breckinridge and told him about the tornado wiping them out. Lim added that he thought they were close to finding something and asked if Mr. Breckinridge could come to Vicksburg.

Mr. Breckinridge hesitated just for a moment, then trying to conceal the excitement in his voice he said, "I'll be there by noon."

Lim smiled as he hung up the phone and went to the motel restaurant and ate breakfast. He caught a ride down town and picked up his truck. Stopping at a dry goods store, he bought himself a new outfit and spent the rest of his money on a newspaper.

"Lim, old boy," he said softly, "this is the first time in a long while that you don't have a nickel in your pocket." Reminiscing, his thoughts went back to the thirties in New Orleans.

He thought about going to the bank and seeing if he could get a check cashed, but changed his mind thinking that the bank didn't know who he was and probably wouldn't cash it. 'I best just wait for Mr. Breckinridge. He'll vouch for me' Lim reasoned.

At straight up noon, Mr. Breckinridge knocked on the door. Lim invited him in. "Don't have any coffee, or a drink to offer for that matter, but I do appreciate you coming up."

Mr. Breckinridge shook Lim's hand vigorously, "I'm sorry about the run of hard luck. From the looks of things, I would say you're having plenty of it. I'm sure glad all of you are all right. It's a miracle none of you were hurt."

"That's true," Lim replied, "at least we're alive. The good Lord must have figured somewhere down the line we could serve some purpose for something."

Mr. Breckinridge answered softly, "I've found He can do wonders myself. I guess you lost everything, huh?"

"That's right, boats, tents, supplies, everything, however, I believe we have broken the code. In fact, we feel we may have located the treasure." Lim's calm attitude disguised the importance of what he'd just said.

Mr. Breckinridge caught on immediately and almost came out of his seat. "The hell you say!" he exclaimed, "where…?" he caught himself, "I don't have a right to ask that question. You are doing all the looking, not me. What can I do to help? I suppose I shouldn't ask about the code either?"

Lim thought for a minute and looked the man over. 'What the hell. He's the one we're working for.' Lim answered Breckinridge's offer. "Even with the code broken, we're still looking We located something when the storm hit that we hope is the treasure. The biggest thing we need now is money. I need you to vouch for me at the bank. We're going to have to buy another boat and a few supplies."

"That's not necessary, Lim. I thought you might need some financial help before I left, so I brought some cash. Also, I got to thinking, I have a pontoon boat over on Eagle Lake. It's not too far from here. It will sleep all of you, has gaslights, cook stove, even a gas refrigerator. It even has folding cots and drop mosquito netting in the sleeping quarters. I don't know why I hadn't thought of it before. It'll take a little doing to get it here," he stopped, contemplated for a moment, and then with a determined look in his eyes, he continued, "start getting what supplies you need and I'll handle the boat. Right now, let's go eat lunch."

Before Breckinridge left town, he gave Lim five hundred dollars telling him, "Buy what supplies you need. By noon tomorrow I'll have the boat gassed and docked at the boat ramp, ready to go." Continuing, he offered Lim the use of his car, but Lim refused saying that he'd already picked up his truck.

"Mr. Breckinridge," Lim added as he got into his car to leave, "getting the boat and the advance should be all we'll need. Hopefully we'll have good news for you shortly. Maybe our luck is changing."

It took Lim most of the day to gather the needed supplies; a couple changes of clothes for himself and Bubba and Stella, some food, and last but certainly not least, a case of booze.

As promised, Breckinridge had his boat and an attendant at the dock when Lim arrived. It didn't take long to load the gear and advise Lim on the boat's operation. A little past noon he was on his way down the river about as happy as a young boy with a new toy.

Bubba and Stella were sitting on the bald-rock point as Lim eased the large boat around the point's backside. He waved to his marooned partners as they ran to greet him, arriving at the twisted willow about the same time Lim slid the boat beside it and tied off.

"Hell, Lim, I didn't know you was going to buy a yacht," Bubba shouted as he climbed on board. "We ain't found that gold yet."

"I'll have to admit," Lim replied, "it's quite a difference, but it didn't cost a thing. Breckinridge owns it and said that we could use it the rest of the summer if need be."

Moving their belongings wasn't much of a problem, most everything wasn't worth keeping and was abandoned in the woods. As the sun set behind the willowed horizon, the three happy treasure hunters were cooking saddle blanket steaks and drinking whiskey with ice and store bought chasers.

After the hearty meal, Lim smoking his new pipe, stated with a smirking smile, "Not bad, huh Bubba?"

"Real uptown," Bubba replied smoothly.

Sitting on the boat deck sometime later, talking and quietly sipping their drinks, each was absorbed in his or her own thoughts. A smile crossed Stella's face as she broke the silence. "Bubba, the other night when you and Lim finally got back to camp you made a statement that's been on my mind."

"What was that, Stella?" Bubba asked.

"Do you remember when we were each telling about talking with the Lord, you said something about going crazy over on the sandbar like you'd met someone?"

Bubba didn't say anything for a short spell, then with a shy smile said, "Me and Old Captain Breckinridge had a run-in. I thought I was a ghost like him…" His eyes flashed from Lim to Stella as he searched their faces hoping that they didn't think he was still crazy. "We had quite a row; its hell trying to whip a ghost, but it was either me or the Captain. One of us had to go."

Lim and Stella laughed with Bubba. "Who won?" Both asked in unison.

Bubba laughed nervously, then said, "It was a tough fight, but the last time I saw the old Captain he was hightailing it across the sandbar into the willow thickets."

Rising early the next morning with a feeling of excitement and anticipation filling the air, each believed they were close to finding the treasure. However, the feeling was short lived, none of the objects could be found no matter how many probes that were made, it just was not there. The tornado had taken all the marker poles, but they had to be in the right area as it was in water not over eight to ten feet deep. Each time they went back to the sandbar and probed the line past the ten-foot mark, nothing could be found, and there was nothing to do but start over again. This fruitless search kept up until well past noon when Lim suggested a rest to eat lunch and let their minds clear. Something had to be throwing them off.

Disillusioned, they ate lunch and sat for a while discussing their luckless search. All agreed that the treasure had to be here, but there was no sign of it; it couldn't just disappear.

"Its Breckinridge," Bubba offered as an explanation. "The old coot knew we'd found his treasure and now he's moved it."

"I agree," Stella said. "He's done this to us the whole time. Looks like every time we're about to find it, he snatches the rug out from under our feet."

Lim sipped his coffee. "Now, you two don't start your hobgoblin and ghost stuff. That treasure is still right where it was, we're just mixed up. Some way something must have changed."

Stella, looking at the broken willow stump setting close to the edge of the water said, "That's strange. You know that stump was way up on the bank this morning."

"I reckon it decided to move down to the river," Bubba replied sarcastically.

Then almost at once Lim and Stella cried, "The river has risen!"

Stella jumped up laughing. "No wonder we couldn't find the spot. The river must have risen three feet or more. If that's it, we just didn't go out far enough."

Lim went to the icebox, pulled the fifth out and said with a wide grin, "Old Breckinridge is sharp, but we done broke his code again. Crank this thing up. The sun's fixing' to shine."

On the second probing trip, Bubba located the objects. Staking the boat front and back and tying it off, Bubba made the first dive.

Following the iron rod down to the bottom, Bubba felt the smooth sand where the rod entered. There was a little current, so he tied himself to the rod and started digging with the short handled shovel, trying to scrape the sediment and sand as far away as he could. Excitement raced through his body with each scoop he made. Lim and Stella stood with heads over the boat rail watching for any signs from the murky water. Bubba's thoughts drifted as he dug,

'Probably just another log or piece of bridge timber.' He was down a foot, then two feet…and almost swallowed his mouthpiece when he hit a solid object. Quickly laying the shovel to the side, he began to dig with his hands.

It wasn't a log.

He dug faster. His heart almost stopped! It was a box, maybe a foot or so wide and a couple of feet long. Bubba dug down far enough to get his hands under it, excitement racing through his body. It was heavy! Lifting it to his knees, he rolled it out of the hole. He caught the rod and shot to the surface almost knocking himself out on one of the pontoons.

Snatching his mouthpiece away, he yelled, "Give me a rope! Better make it two."

Stella and Lim were both trying to talk at the same time, finally got an answer from Bubba about what he'd found.

"It's a wooden box—heavy as hell. Gotta be the treasure." Bubba didn't take the time to say any more, he just disappeared under the water pulling the ropes along with him. With nervous hands, he tied the ropes around the box, one on each end, then followed the marker rod back to the top. Swimming over to the boat rail, he spoke in a whisper as he climbed through the rails, "It's tied. Lim, give me a hand." Slowly, Bubba and Lim worked the heavy object to the surface, all three struggling with the slippery box, easing it onto the pontoon deck.

Yelling and jumping hysterically around the mud-coated box, they were so excited that no one thought to open it. All this action shook the boat so much that the box almost slid back into the river. The cypress box had copper bands tightened around it and was so preserved you could still read the words, "50 Caliber Musket Balls," burnt into the wood. With shaking hands, Lim cut the copper bands, and then slowly tapped the top board loose. You never heard such screaming and yelling in all your life as Lim lifted one of the cinnamon colored bars from the box. Stamped on the end of the bar it read, "Forty nine pounds gold." The celebrating started again. Everyone handled the heavy bar. Stella even kissed it.

With the celebration over, Bubba put his diving gear back on and soon had another box tied off; it was hauled up and set aside unopened. Bubba continued disappearing under the murky surface until after dark. Before long, there were eleven boxes stacked across the front of the boat with the same burnt markings, "50 Caliber Musket Balls."

Worn out and exhausted, Bubba crawled over the pontoon rail for the last time. "This is the last box. We'll probe more tomorrow if necessary, but I've probed with the shovel across the bottom for thirty feet in each direction. I believe that's all of it." It took a good ten minutes to slide the last box through the boat rails.

Lim and Stella helped Bubba get the air tank off with Lim talking to Bubba the whole time. Bubba stretched out in one of the deck chairs, too exhausted to speak, and Stella followed suit, plopping down in the next chair.

"You two can sit there in shock if you want to. I'm going to have a drink— a large one," Lim added.

It was midnight when Lim maneuvered the pontoon boat to the willow stump and tied it off. Lim and Bubba opened and checked all the boxes as Stella cooked a midnight snack.

The boxes contained exactly what Mr. Breckinridge's father had recorded in the sworn statement: "Ten bars of silver and ten bars of gold." The eleventh box contained fifty caliber musket balls with a small copper box packed in the center. Opening the copper box, Lim poured a half of a teacup full of glistening diamonds, rubies, and sapphires into Stella's hands.

Morning broke clear and beautiful. The sun's reflection made the clouds glow a cherry red as it slowly cleared the heavy timberline An owl hooted off in the distance and another answered from down the river. A crow lit on the mile marker post adding his sharp salute to the morning. A gobbler awoke the peaceful forest with a series of tree shaking gobbles.

"I feel just like that old gobbler," Lim said to Bubba as they sipped their morning coffee. "It's such a pretty world. It makes you want to shout your lungs out."

"Yeah, Lim," Bubba replied, "ain't' it a pretty world when things are going right. It's hard to remember even back a couple of days ago how everything looked so bleak. Almost like there wasn't anything left to live for."

"It's strange how quickly things can turn around," Lim said. "It makes you think that there's hope in most every situation. Guess ain't nothing quite as bad as it seems when it's happening."

"Yeah, Lim," Bubba laughed. "I've given a lot of thought to what you said about it's always the darkest just before day."

Stella came over and replenished their coffee. "You two talking like that makes one feel sorta sad about leaving here. This place holds memories we'll never forget."

"Reckon' old Breckinridge would sell us this point?" Lim asked. "Sure would be a good place to spend your last days. Maybe even make a good final resting place."

"We can ask him," Stella replied, "but it ain't going to be for a place to come and die. Let's see if he'll sell us part of it, maybe a few hundred acres. We'll build a summer house right up there where the camp was. You know there'll always be good hunting and fishing and what a place to spend a vacation."

"All right Stella," Lim said. "You've come up with another good idea. We should have enough money to make that deal. I'll ask Mr. Breckinridge as soon as we settle up. Right now, the sooner you get Bubba to untie the boat and push us off, the sooner we'll find out how rich we're going to be."

Bubba slipped through the boat railings. "Lim don't need to look for a last resting place for his weary bones. He's all ready shone me where the omega is going to be."

"Where's that, Bubba?" Stella asked.

"There ain't but one place he'll be comfortable and that's in the Appleton cemetery where his great-great-grandfather lay before we dug him up. He's the alpha and Lim's the omega.

"Get in here, Bubba," Lim yelled laughingly, "before we leave you."

Bubba untied the boat and gave it a push hopping on board. Lim slipped the clutch to reverse and eased it back, then switched it forward and turned up stream against the swirling current. Rounding the rocky point, you could almost tell the thoughts that were going through each of their minds. The white mile marker glistening on the shining point, the towering trees in the background and the early morning sun shining on the peaceful river: a memory that would be cherished as long as each lived. Like the end of a dream, the pontoon boat slowly disappeared up the swirling river.

It was noon when Lim docked the big boat at the ramp in Vicksburg. Bubba jumped out and tied to the nearest cleat. "I'll go get the truck while y'all start unloading the boat," he said as he hopped onto the dock. "I'll be back as soon as I can." A short time later, he was backing the pickup down the steep ramp. Bubba got out of the truck and chocked the back wheels.

"Let's leave the bullion out of the boxes," Lim instructed. "Just stack it across the back of the bed next to the tail gate. We'll put the boxes and our gear up front. If we don't distribute the load evenly we'll be fighting the truck all the way to Baton Rouge. Besides, it'll make it easier to unload when we get there.

Mr. Breckinridge said to secure the boat at the ramp when we got through with it. He gave me a number to call and said one of his camp members would pick it up.

With the pickup loaded and the pontoon boat secured, the three joyful treasure hunters crawled into the truck and Lim eased it up the ramp. Lim drove back to the garage where the truck was stored and stopped for gas. "Willie," he said as he got out, "fill her up with ethyl and check the oil. I'm gonna make a phone call. Be right back."

"Yes sir, Mr. Lim. That ethyl is up to twenty-four nine, but it'll sure make that Willis hum."

Bubba didn't wait for Willie to check the oil but got out and checked it himself as Willie filled the truck. Looking over in the back, Willie noticed the bars of gold and silver stacked across the rear of the pickup's bed. Not knowing what they were, he commented as Lim walked up, "Mr. Lim, them old bars make your pickup ride a lot better don't they?"

"Yeah, Willie," Lim replied with a wide grin. "I can't tell you how much better it rides."

"You gonna throw them old boxes away?" Willie asked as he squeezed the pump up to an even number. "I'll take them off your hands if you are. They'd make some good kindling."

"Naw, Willie," Lim answered as he handed Willie a five-dollar bill, "I guess we'll keep them. They hold a few memories."

"What about them old iron bars? Looks like you got a little more weight than you need. I got a scrap iron pile over there next to the station if you want to throw a couple out."

"Willie," Lim said, "it was a pretty hard job finding them. I guess we'll keep them, too."

"The gas is four dollars," Willie said looking a little dejected. "I'll get your change."

"Forget the change, Willie," Lim called to him, "I'm kind of in a hurry."

"Lord, Mr. Lim!" Willie exclaimed grinning, "You must have struck it rich."

Lim didn't answer Willie, he just drove off flashing a huge smile. Bubba and Stella were about to burst, but held their laughter until Lim turned the pickup up the street. Then almost exploding with laughter, it took the better part of the trip to Baton Rouge before they settled down.

You never heard such plans of how each was going to spend their fortune. Bubba was going to buy Morris' station. Stella was going to have a house with a swimming pool. "About all I want is a new pen for my dogs," Lim said laughing, "and a little polishing done on the Big House ending with a well stocked bar. His final comment as he slowed down for traffic light in Baton Rouge was, "There's one thing for sure, Taylorsville is fixing to have the biggest wedding it ever saw."

Stella leaned over and kissed Lim on the cheek. "Lim, you reckon we'll be able to get Bubba in a tux? Wouldn't he look good in one of those long-tail jackets?"

That made Bubba snort, "I'd just soon we eloped. Brother Layton can tie the knot just as strong without all that fancy stuff."

"You can forget that, Bubba," Lim replied sternly. "We're going to do this up right!"

Lim pulled up to the bank and parked in the "No Parking" yellow zone. "Guess it'll be all right to park here for a few minutes," he said as he turned the motor off. "You and Stella stay with the pickup. I'll go find Mr. Breckinridge."

Lim walked into the elegant bank, his looks in sharp contrast to his surroundings. Going to one of the tellers, he asked to see Mr. Breckinridge. The look he got made him aware of his appearance. He could well imagine how he looked—the three or four day growth of beard blended with his unattended clothes, in fact, this was the first time in weeks that he'd even thought of his appearance. Smiling as he thought of what the young lady probably was thinking, Lim said, "Ma'am, I wouldn't blame you if you called the police, but for now, just tell Mr. Breckinridge that an old tramp named Lim Appleton is out front and thinks you will be glad to see him."

The girl smiled and left. She couldn't have barely gotten in the back before Mr. Breckinridge came rushing out into the lobby with the gaping young lady right behind him. Lim answered Mr. Breckinridge's questions before he could ask, "We found it. Every cotton picking bar of it."

You talk about a spectacle, the bank president in his fine tailored suit hugging Lim in his dirty, weatherworn clothes. The bank customers, employees, everyone was gasping in amazement at the unusual spectacle, all thinking the same thing, Mr. Breckinridge has gone loony as a Betsy Bug. When the embrace was over, Mr. Breckinridge asked Lim where the treasure was. Lim put his arm around the little man's shoulders and replied, "Right out in front of your bank." Everyone thought Lim's reception a curious thing, but was amazed as the stately dressed bank president rushed outside with the bearded stranger.

Mr. Breckinridge rushed to the rear of the truck slapping Bubba on the back and hugging Stella as he passed. Standing up on the back bumper, he stared at the neat rows of metal bars. Quickly crawling into the truck bed, he pulled one of the heavy bars up on its end. "My god, you've found it." In his excitement, he jumped over the side of the pickup and stumbled into Lim as he came down. Grabbing both of Lim's arms, he looked up into the proud face, "Lim, I had faith in you. Somehow, I knew that you would find it. You are quite a man." Turning, he grabbed Stella and hugged and kissed her, then gave Bubba a big embrace. As if he didn't believe what he'd seen the first time, he went back and looked into the truck again so excited that he could hardly talk. "Let's get this stuff into the bank," he whispered, "there's a fortune in gold and silver out here. The whole world will know about this shortly."

Hurrying into the bank, Mr. Breckinridge returned with two employees and a couple of two-wheel dollies, which could carry about five bars each. As the bank employees rolled the last of the bars into the bank, a crowd gathered. Seeing the crowd, the police came by and asked Mr. Breckinridge if everything was all right. Then seeing Lim's old truck in the unloading zone, he asked, "Who's old truck is that parked in the "NO PARKING" zone?"

Mr. Breckinridge calmly replied, "They're making a deposit. It's all right."

Well, you'd think someone robbed the bank by the way all the people gathered, each with his or her own opinion of what was going on. Finally, after the gold, silver and jewels were stored in the bank vault; Mr. Breckinridge walked to the center of the bank lobby and called for everyone's attention. He motioned for Bubba, Stella and Lim to stand in front of him as he put his hands on Lim and Bubba's shoulders and addressed the crowd.

"Ladies and gentlemen, I know all of you are wondering what all this commotion is about," he hesitated as everyone turned and started listened, "these two gentlemen and this young lady have this day passed before you unrecorded history. History that would never been known without them. Before you, you have seen those dollies hauling those metal bars. Ladies and gentlemen, those were gold and silver bars. Could be worth over a million and a half dollars." The crowd began to buzz. Mr. Breckinridge raised his hand, "Ladies and gentlemen, let me present the people that have been in search of this lost treasure for over a year." As he introduced them, the crowd rushed around shaking hands and asking all kinds of questions. Finally, Mr. Breckinridge came to their rescue slipping them out one of the back doors telling them as he closed the door, "I'll have my secretary call the motel and make y'all reservations." Reaching the motel, Stella called her family and Bubba called his mother, who agreed to drive down together the next morning and see the treasure.

That evening Mr. Breckinridge came by, picked them up and took them to his favorite restaurant where he wined and dined them with the best in food and drink to be found in Baton Rouge.

"You three have certainly taken the whispering and gossiping off my back," Breckinridge said as he neatly folded his napkin and laid it on the table by his empty plate. "I've been searching for the Merrygold treasure for so long people were beginning to think I was some kind of a nut. Of course, I never did divulge all of the particulars of what I was looking for; therefore, there were all kinds of speculation and gossip about it. I think even the bank directors were getting a little worried, thinking that I had lost my marbles or whatever."

Lim laughed at that. "My suggestion is, Mr. Breckinridge, if any of them come up with any negative comments now, you just buy the bank." Lim waited until the laughter had died before he finished. "I've been whispered and talked about so much I guess I'm kinda used to it and never let that sort of thing bother me. I'm sure I've been accused of everything bad a person could do, like drinking, gambling, womanizing, and some probably think I escaped from a nut house somewhere. I laugh with them but let them know right off that what I do with my life is my business. This pretty well keeps the whispering behind my back. I don't try to hide what I do, nor do I try to attract people's attention to it. The thing is that most of what's said is close to being right. Of course, being a bank President is different from being an unemployed gambler, especially one who drinks too much and looks for buried treasure."

Breckinridge slapped Lim on the back with a hearty laugh. "The three of you finding the Merrygold treasure will turn some heads and thoughts, too. Some of those that have been doing all the joking and laughing will probably be thinking a different thought now," he declared as the dinner party broke up. Leaving the elite restaurant, "We'll meet in the morning at the bank when your family arrives. I'm sure they'll want to see the treasure."

The next morning Stella's mother and father arrived along with Bubba's mother, meeting them at the bank. Newspaper reporters came by in droves making it almost impossible to have any time to visit with their parents. Breckinridge entertained the group for lunch and invited them down to the bank that afternoon to discuss the assaying of the treasure. Stella declined, telling Lim and Bubba to go ahead. She wanted to visit with her parents.

Arriving at the bank, Bubba and Lim went to Mr. Breckinridge's receptionist who told them to go right in that Mr. Breckinridge was expecting them.

When seated, Mr. Breckinridge offered them coffee. "I went ahead and took the liberty of having the gold and silver bars checked for authenticity and a preliminary estimate of their value made. I hope that was satisfactory with you."

"That's fine, Mr. Breckinridge," Lim replied. "We'll leave all of that up to you. What did they come up with?"

"The assayers had to drill each bar," Mr. Breckinridge replied as he sat down behind his large mahogany desk. "Each bar checked better than ninety percent pure, which is good, especially for when it was cast. The jewels and diamonds were also of excellent quality. Now understand that the estimates given are subject to adjustment since it was done on such short notice, but still the estimated market value was over a million dollars. In fact, it's possible for the final tally to be somewhat closer to a million and half when more accurate tests are made."

Bubba interrupted with a sheepish, almost disbelieving look in his eyes, "Boy, I had no idea it'd be worth so much. Are you sure the appraisers didn't make a mistake?"

"No, Bubba," Mr. Breckinridge replied laughing. "The people that made the assay are very reliable. They are all certified by state and federal agencies. If there is a mistake it's probably on the low side, if anything."

Lim poured himself a cup of coffee, "What about the value to a collector? Do you think we should check with them?"

"I certainly do, Lim. In fact, I suggest we take some time and check all the sources we can to ensure that we get the best price. The only problem I can foresee is that we're going to have to hold up on making any commitments or sales until we get a determination from the government as to who has the legal right to the treasure."

This upset Bubba and he almost came out of his seat. "Mr. Breckinridge, you mean we're going to have a hassle over who legally owns the treasure?"

"I don't think so Bubba," he replied. "I've had my attorney working on this for years. He says that the Mississippi River has free salvage rights and there shouldn't be any problem over legalities. It's just something that'll have to be cleared before we dispose of it. It protects us, if you think about it. Once the determination is made and a judgement passed, no one could possibly have any claim to it but us. It'll probably take a month or more to clear the title, but I see no problem with that. We'll need that much time to check out different buyers and ways of disposing of it. If you're worried about money, I'd be more than happy to give you an advance, if you like."

Lim smiled, "An advance will be fine, if it's all right with Bubba."

"It certainly is all right," Bubba replied grinning from ear to ear. "I don't know about Lim, but I'm as broke as a run over mirror."

"And we're fixing to have a wedding," Lim added laughing. "That's going to require some cash."

"I figured you'd both probably like an advance. I'm sure your expenses have been excessive. Would twenty-thousand each be sufficient?"

Bubba almost choked at the sum. "That's more than sufficient for me. In fact, I can get by on a lot less."

Breckinridge looked at Lim, "How about you?"

Lim nodding, "That's fine. I'm like Bubba, twenty or less."

"Very well then, I'll have a couple of twenty thousand cashiers checks made out. You can take them with you. You'll need to sign an open note, if that's all right."

"Mr. Breckinridge," Lim said as he stood, "what about the boxes the gold and silver were packed in? We have a small museum in Taylorsville and if we could, Bubba and I would like to donate the boxes to the museum."

"Lim, that'll be fine," the banker nodded. "I'm sure they'd like reproductions made of the bars, and also of the jewels. I'll see what I can do on that score." After Breckinridge gave them their checks, they shook hands all around and said their good-byes.

"You know, Lim," Bubba said as he folded the twenty-thousand dollar check and stuck it in his wallet. "That Mr. Breckinridge is about the most thoughtful person I ever saw. It makes you feel good to be around someone like him, especially when he's handing out twenty-thousand dollar checks."

"Yeah, Bubba," Lim answered as he got into the truck, "I've come to appreciate him, too. I don't believe there's a selfish or greedy bone in his body. I bet that old son of a gun would make a pretty good bird hunting partner."

"You're not planning on swapping Brother Layton off are you?" Bubba asked laughingly.

Lim put the truck into gear and started back to the motel. "If he'll come to Taylorsville, I'll give him a try. Hell, I might even take him up to Bailey's."

The thought of Mr. Breckinridge at Bailey's made Bubba howl. "I'd say the two of you could give the boys up at Bailey's a run for their money. Might even drive one of those Cadillacs back."

"I don't know about you," Lim said as he pulled into the motel parking lot, "but I'm ready to get this show on the road. All these reporters and that crowd of folks is just not my cup of brew."

"Mine either," Bubba agreed. "Let's get packed and head for Taylorsville. I'll go tell Stella that we're getting ready to go. She may want to ride with her Mom and Dad."

Lim was packed when Bubba got back. Picking up his over night case Lim said, "I'll meet you at the truck. I'll go to the office and catch our bill while you finish packing. Make sure we don't leave anything."

Stella and her father were at the truck with Bubba as Lim walked up. "Stella," he said, "I thought you might want to ride back with your Mom and Dad."

Stella gave Lim one of her sharp looks, then replied sternly, "Are you kidding? I wouldn't miss this ride for Bubba's half of the treasure. Besides, if I don't go and keep an eye on you two, no telling where you'll end up. New Orleans, South America…"

With a slight grin, Lim dropped the truck down into low gear and flashed his eyes to Mr. Ranking. "It must be those wedding bells she's hearing. Bubba's not getting out of her sight for quite awhile."

Laughing, Mr. Ranking replied, "Lim, you may have something there. Y'all drive carefully. We'll see you in Taylorsville."

It was after dark when they arrived in Taylorsville, and Lim dropped them off at Bubba's house, giving them a tongue-in-cheek lecture. "Remember, you two aren't married yet. Bubba, you drive Stella straight home."

Stella laughingly replied as she got out, "Maybe I should leave Bubba here and drive his Mom's car home myself."

"She's talking big again," Bubba said to get his digs in too, "but it was her idea you drop us off here."

Taylorsville was some excited town for the next few days. Most everyone in town came to visit with either Lim, Bubba, or Stella. It got so out of hand that the city had a reception in their honor at the museum so everyone could get the story first hand. At the reception, Lim donated the empty bullion boxes. The mayor wasn't going to pass up an opportunity to give a speech, stood and recognized Lim, Stella, and Bubba and praised them for their contributions to the city and county, ending the speech with a statement that made everyone laugh with nostalgia.

"Maybe we should go back and dig up City Park again."

Chapter 23

Lim left the Country Club with his heart full of joy and gladness for Bubba and Stella, but heavy with the thought of the changes this would bring. He didn't stop at his home but drove on north getting to Bailey's around ten that night. Maybe a little gambling would lighten his heart.

Bubba turned west out of Taylorsville onto number 6 highway with Stella snuggled close to his side. She looked up at him and whispered, "Bubba, do you love me as much as you say?"

"Certainly, Stella. Do you think I would put up with all that screaming if I didn't love you?"

Reaching up, she kissed him on the neck then snuggled closer and they both rode for a ways without saying anything. Finally, Stella broke the silence, "You're thinking about Lim, aren't you?"

"Yep, I guess I am. I bet he's sitting at the kitchen table right now. Probably just poured a drink."

"I miss him, too. If ever a good person lived, he's one. Hey, I thought you said we were headed for New Orleans. This is the way to Clarksdale."

Bubba rode on in silence for a minute, then turned and smiled at Stella. "I just thought we'd spend our first night in Clarksdale. Maybe you and I might ride out and see Lim's old girlfriend tomorrow. Lim said he'd kill me if I wrote her again, but he didn't say anything about going by and seeing her." He paused for a minute, just long enough for Stella to see the mischievous gleam in his eyes. "I got a feeling that by tomorrow Lim could use a call from his old sweetheart."

Stella laughed as she reached her arm around Bubba's neck and kissed him, "Bubba, you know that's why I love you so much," she kissed him again, then added with a mischievous gleam of her own, "and I've got a feeling that tonight you're not going to be thinking about anything but Stella."

It was getting dark by the time Bubba turned in at the Clarksdale Motel. "Let's go in, change clothes and go get a bite to eat."

Smiling sweetly, Stella answered him as he got out, "Are you that hungry? I'd just as soon stay at the motel." She grabbed his shirtfront and pulled him through the window kissing him passionately.

Returning shortly with the room key, Bubba answered Stella's question with a smile, "Come to think of it, I ain't all that hungry," and returned her passionate kiss with one of his own, "for food."

Stella put the suitcase on the bed then gently slipped into Bubba's arms whispering, "Bubba, you know all those times I gave you your ring back;...well, I never meant for you to keep it. Now that it's on my left finger, as long as I live you'll never get it back."

"I hope one of these days I'll get used to your ways," he said as he kissed her.

Stella eased out of his arms. "Let me freshen up a little and I'll start you getting used to my ways."

As Stella went into the bathroom, Bubba opened his suitcase and pulled out a brown paper bag. Scratching his head, he picked it up and mumbled, "I don't remember putting this in there." Inside the bag was a bottle of champagne with a small envelope attached to its neck.

Bubba called to Stella through the bathroom door, "Stella, who put this bottle of champagne in my suitcase?"

"I didn't pack your suitcase, Sweetheart. Maybe your mother put it there. Is there a note or anything with it?"

"Yeah," Bubba replied as he opened the envelope and took the card out. "I'll give you two guesses who did it. It's from Lim and he says, listen to this, 'This marriage is the most important thing that ever happened in my life. You two have a good time and I'll see you when you get back...Lim.'" Bubba stopped reading then said, "I can't believe this. Listen to what he says next, 'I know you won't have time to think about anything else on your honeymoon, but I got something I need to talk to you about.' I'll be damn. Ain't that just like Lim?"

Stella came out of the bathroom about this time and Bubba almost dropped the bottle of champagne when he saw her in her thin negligee. Slipping into his arms she whispered, "Open that bottle. I'll straighten Mr. Lim out when we get home. He wrote that just to have the last laugh."

Chapter 24

It was noon when Lim drove up to his house and got out. Instead of going inside right off, he walked around to the back, his bird dogs jumping up and down at his side. Stopping at Pete's pen, he watched the proud bird strut around his harem. Picking up a shovel, he spoke to the strutting bird as he went into the pen, "Pete, I won't bother you but a minute." He went to the west corner and pressed the shovel into the ground. "Bubba would have buried it about here." No luck. He moved over a couple feet and tried again easing the shovel into the soft dirt. He felt a clank as the shovel struck the glass jug. Raking the dirt back, he slipped the two one-gallon jugs of corn whiskey out of the ground. "Ain't exactly like finding a buried treasure, but almost as rewarding," he said as he admired his handiwork and walked into the house.

The phone began to ring as he entered the house. He set the jugs on the kitchen table and reached for the phone then paused. "Now who in the hell could be calling me? Surely, it isn't Bubba and Stella. They should be too busy to talk to old Lim." Picking up the phone, he answered in a gruff voice, "Hello."

There was a short pause, then a soft voice said, "Lim...Lim, this is Barbara. How are you?"

Lim did the pausing this time having been taken completely by surprise and shock as he immediately recognized the other party. "Bar...Barbara?...Barbara Tanner?"

"That's right, Lim, its Barbara Tanner. I know I probably shouldn't call you but, you've been on my mind and I decided that right or wrong I was going to talk to you. It's been a long time but your voice still sounds the same. How are you?"

Lim was stunned, but did manage to reply. "Hell, Barbara, I don't know what to say, except it has been a long time...and your voice sounds good, too. But to answer your question, I'm doing all right. Just getting old as hell. My hair's turned as white as snow and my face is as wrinkled and scarred as an old shirt that needs ironing. How you been doing?"

Barbara laughed and the memories flooded Lim's heart. "Like you, I'm getting up in years. Changed in all the wrong places. My hair's white, too, and I got the wrinkles plus the pounds in the wrong places." There was a lonely pause, and then she blurted out on the edge of emotion, "Oh, Lim, I've missed you so much. I think about you more than I should probably tell. Lim, I've always felt bad about what happened and knew someday I'd have to face up to it. I know I did you wrong and I just wanted to tell you I'm sorry. You can't change the past, but if I *could* change things, I would have a long time ago. What happened, happened—and the way it happened was what was so bad. After I'd hurt you it was too late to have second thoughts, which I want you to know, I did, Lim, many times."

Lim was still in shock but broke in and tried to sooth her wits. "Barbara, you don't owe me any explanations. Like you said, what happened, happened. I was hurt because I was very much in love with you, but those wounds have healed, somewhat. Sure, I've thought about what happened a thousand times and wondered how things might have turned out differently if it hadn't happened like it did. Anyway, it was probably best the way it turned out, especially for you. You'd probably been a pauper today if you'd married me. I made up my mind that what happened was best and I'd just live with the memories. I started to call you after I heard you lost your husband, but I decided I was too old and weathered. I'd just get blown out of the saddle. A woman of your beauty would be courted by every bachelor in the Delta."

The soft voice on the other end of the line answered after a short pause, "Lim you'll never be old and weathered to me. I know I shouldn't have called, but I just felt I had to talk to you, and while I'm so bold and telling everything a lady shouldn't, I may as well tell you all of it. I'd love to see you. Why don't you come over?"

Lim couldn't answer right off because everything rushed through his mind, all the feelings of love, the hurt. Then he said, "Barbara, I'm too old to start over. I'd be outdated and out classed. We better leave it just like it is. You know I want to see you but the heartaches are behind us now and probably best to leave it like that."

Before he could say anything else, Barbara said in a quivering voice, "Lim, I knew I shouldn't have called," and hung up.

Lim sat at the kitchen table still holding the phone to his ear, his thoughts filled with the past. "Barbara," he moaned softly into the dead phone, "why in the hell did you call? You know I love you! Why did you have to call? I'm too old. I don't want you to see how I've changed…I don't think I could take seeing the shock and disappointment in your eyes when you look at what's left of this withered and worn out body."

The operator came on the line, "Have you finished your call, Sir?"

"Yes ma'm, I'm through," Lim replied still in a daze and hung up the phone.

Lim downed a stiff shot of the white liquor and gulped a mouthful of the chaser. "How in the hell did she get my phone number? I had it changed and unlisted…Bubba! I'd choke him if I could get my hands on him. He and Stella did it sure as I'm sitting here!" He smiled, "Hell, I can't get mad with them. I'm glad she called. Bubba and Stella knew I'd be lonesome. That was a hell of a thing for them to do on their wedding trip. They knew too well how my heart's bleeding. I still could choke Bubba, though."

Lim finished off another drink, then slowly picked up the phone and waited for the operator.

"Can I help you?"

"Yes, Ma'am. Could you give me Barbara Tanner's phone number in Clarksdale?"

After a pause the operator answered, "I'm sorry, sir, we have no Barbara Tanner listed. Is there any other name she may be listed under?"

Lim thought for a moment then said, "Hell, what was her married name, Whitehead? See if you have a Barbara Whitehead?"

After a pause, the operator came back on. "Yes, there's a Barbara Whitehead. Would you like for me to ring that number?"

"No, just give me the number. I'll call later." He wrote the number down, thanked the operator and hung up. For a time he sat and stared at the phone. "Why in the world would she call me in the first place? She can have any man she wants. From what I've heard, her husband owned half the county and left her a fortune when he died. I know she's probably the prettiest woman her age in the Delta. She has to be remembering me as a young man. I sure as hell know she don't have any idea what's left of me now."

Lim poured another drink and looked at the tiny beads dangling along the top of the clear alcohol. As he watched them slowly disappear he thought, 'What if I went over there? It took guts for her to make that call. She must still care. I know she once did.'

As if in a trance, Lim picked the phone up and gave the operator the number. It seemed like an eternity before Barbara's soft voice said, "Hello?"

"Barbara, I know you think I'm crazy as hell, but if the offer still stands I'd like to come over."

She answered almost before he finished talking. "Lim, I'm so glad you called. You know the offer's still open. I'll be waiting. Let me tell you how to get to my house."

Chapter 25

This looks like a good place to end this story. However, some unanswered questions should be answered. Like, what did the publicity do to Taylorsville? What happened to the Sullivan brothers? Lim, Bubba and Stella, how did their newfound wealth affect their lives? Who gave the anonymous gifts? Finally, did anyone ever find the Appleton fortune? In order to answer these questions, five or six years will have to pass.

Taylorsville prospered greatly, due in large part to the publicity surrounding Lim and Bubba. The population soared to over five-thousand in a few short years, a growth rate many big cities could wish for, which caught the eye of a couple of manufacturing companies looking for a new source of labor. The city expanded its boundaries, a new wing was added to the hospital, and the museum was enlarged. Now, not only did the museum feature a display about Lim and Bubba's treasure hunting exploits, but also Bruce Gilmore let them include his collection of railroad artifacts that he'd spent a lifetime collecting. Even the rails that were dug up from the city park during Lim and Bubba's first treasure hunting ordeal were there. They also added Don Hillhouse's Indian artifact collection, and many other things of interest the citizens had collected.

The city's newfound notoriety brought prosperity to the downtown business section, too. There was a new motel, both banks built new buildings and there was a new drive-in. Even Morris' Service Station changed. The old frame building has been replaced by a shiny, fully equipped, three-bay porcelain service station with one of those automatic car washes out back. The name over the door changed, too. It now reads, Bubba Davidson, prop.

In a new subdivision over close to the high school, one of the largest houses in the subdivision belongs to Bubba and Stella. A big ski boat is parked in the double carport and the back yard's all fenced off with a new kidney shaped swimming pool. To add to the picture, there are a couple of little ones playing in a sand box next to the pool. The boy's name is Lim and is the spitting image of Bubba and the little girl's name is Sue. Stella said that no child of hers would be named Stella. She looks just like her mother. Of course to me all young'uns look alike when they're that age, but what the heck, I know Bubba and Stella think theirs are the prettiest children in town. And believe it or not, a wonderful thing is about to happen to Bubba and Stella; they're supposed to graduate from college this spring. When asked about this, Bubba replied in his usual tongue-in-cheek fashion, "When the honeymoon was over and we'd had our fling, I reckon Stella and I both woke up and got our heads on straight. The University was only ten miles away, so why not give it a try? Of course, when the babies started coming along—it slowed things down a bit, but things weren't all bad. We had two of the best babysitters in the world, Stella's mom and my mom. I guess I can sum it up this way; we finally grew up. After all, school's not all that hard once you realize it's just a part of life. Like Lim says, 'You can't win if you ain't in.'"

The Sullivan boys came home. Dave's living with his ma and pa. Ben did better on his trip to the outer world. He brought back a shapely Cajun girl. The newlyweds are living over close to his parents in a nice home that Ma and Pa bought. As for any charges brought against them, there was never anything said. The city's insurance paid for the truck. I think they used the term, "Act of God", and said a tree fell on it. I guess a stump is part of a tree—right?

This gets us to Lim, and he's doing fine. He still lives in the Big House. He didn't make many changes in the old place. Put on a new coat of paint, had a new chain link fence put up so his bird dogs could roam the yard and wouldn't have to stay penned up. He did splurge and buy himself a new 4x4 Bronco. He said that he needed a new truck to pull his new boat and motor. "It just wouldn't look right to be pulling that shiny new boat with that raggedy old truck. As usual, he was anonymously helping those around him. He put a new roof on Jennie's house and had a butane-fueled heating system installed. I guess the biggest change is the new Cadillac you see parked at the Big House on weekends. It has Coahoma county plates, whose county seat is Clarksdale. Sometimes you can see that same Cadillac up at the Peabody in Memphis, quite often with Lim's new Bronco parked next to it. There's talk that a wedding date has been set. Anyway, the lady is sporting a new diamond that will put your eyes out.

The two anonymous gifts were just something extra that happened in Taylorsville, and came about in an unusual way.

Two or three weeks after Bubba and Stella's wedding, a big stake-bodied van pulled up to Bubba's station and wanted to know how to get to the

Friendship Baptist Church. Morris, who's now working part-time for Bubba, pointed up the street and said, "It's up this street, but there won't be anybody there. If you've got something to deliver to the church, you'd better call Preacher Layton. He'll come down and open up for you."

The driver of the truck agreed that calling was a good idea and asked Morris if he could use his phone. After looking up the number, he made the call. Brother Layton answered the phone and the driver told him he had the church's new organ and needed someone to open the church so he could start installing it.

Things got real quiet on Brother Layton's end of the line, and after a few seconds Brother Layton responded. "Mister, you must have the wrong church. We haven't ordered an organ. We just started trying to raise the money to buy one a few days ago. I wish you were right, but we haven't ordered one. You must undoubtedly have the wrong church."

The driver was persistent. "Listen, Preacher, your name's Layton, ain't it?"

"Yes, that's my name but…"

"Preacher, my delivery instructions said to deliver the organ to the Friendship Baptist Church, Pastor F.M. Layton. I'm at the right place and the organ goes to your church. You can use an organ at your church can't you?" he asked almost as if he were being sarcastic.

Brother Layton didn't say anything for a long pause, then finally he said, "Mister, I'm sorry. You'll have to take it back, we didn't order it. Does it say who's going to pay for it or who ordered it?"

"I don't know, Preacher, it don't say who ordered it. Maybe the Lord did. My worksheet says it's paid for, even the installation and freight cost. It's a done deal."

All Preacher Layton could say was, "It must be a miracle. I…I can't believe it."

The other anonymous gift came about when Roosevelt Morgan's house burned and he lost everything. Roosevelt and his wife barely got out themselves. In Taylorsville, like in many small towns, different ones started collecting money to help Roosevelt. Up at Preacher Layton's church, they passed the collection plate and raised a hundred and fifty dollars. In all, close to five-hundred dollars was raised and taken to Roosevelt. Of course, this helped and Roosevelt and his wife were very thankful, but five-hundred dollars wasn't near enough to replace their home. Even a small frame house like the one that burned would cost quit a bit to replace and Roosevelt was too poor to have afforded insurance. About a week after their house burned, Mr. John McLemore, who owns Taylorsville Lumber Company, drove up to Theodore Morgan's house, Roosevelt's son. Roosevelt and his wife had been staying there since the night their house burned. Roosevelt came out to see who had driven up and John called him over.

"Hello Roosevelt. I've been looking for you," he said as he offered him his hand.

"You doing all right, Mr. John?" Roosevelt asked as they shook hands.

"Been doin' fine, Roosevelt. You and your wife all right, I mean, under the circumstances?"

"Yes sir, we're doing as good as old folks can be expected."

"That's good Roosevelt. I brought some good news that should help you and your wife's feelings."

Roosevelt perked up with a smile. "What's that, Mr. John?"

"Roosevelt," Mr. McLemore began, "when I went to the post office this morning, I had a certified letter in the mail concerning you."

"You did?" Roosevelt asked perplexed. "What did it say?"

John, hesitating a moment, said, "Roosevelt, call your wife. I think she'd like to hear this, too."

Roosevelt went back into the house and in a few minutes came back out with his wife Hazel. "Morning Mr. John," Hazel said as she walked up. "What's all this mess Roosevelt's trying to tell me? Sure sounds mysterious like."

"That's true enough, Mrs. Morgan. Things ain't nearly as bad as they seem. It appears that you and Roosevelt have come into some good fortune."

"What's dat Mr. John?" she asked curiously.

John reached into his shirt pocket, retrieved a letter, and began to read it, as he handed Roosevelt a check. "Roosevelt, this check's made out to me, but the note that came with it says it's for you and Hazel."

"Lawsie me, Mr. John." Hazel took the check out of Roosevelt's hand and looked at it. "That thang says five-hundred dollars, don't it, or is that five-thousand?"

"That's right, Hazel, five-thousand dollars. The note that came with it said, "Use this money to build Roosevelt and Hazel Morgan a new house."

Roosevelt and Hazel started speaking at the same time, but Hazel was the loudest. "Lord, Mr. John, who could have done this for us? It must have been the Good Lord's doing."

"May have been," Mr. McLemore replied. "Whoever sent it didn't leave a name or a return address. Maybe it was the Lord, I don't know. I don't imagine He needs a return address and this letter sure didn't have one. I've seen Him do some mighty good things for people over the years. Y'all need to come on down to the store and pick out what kind of paint and materials you'll need to get started," and that's how the second miraculous event happened.

This about covers all the questions, except the one final big one, what happened to Old Limbrick Appleton's fortune? I'm sure you figured that out by now. For those of you that haven't figured it out, I'll tell you. All the indications are, and this may come as a total surprise, but it appears that Tobe found it.

All the time that Lim was looking for the Appleton treasure, Tobe was looking also, in his own quiet way. He must have finally decided that it was buried in the Appleton Cemetery just like Lim thought, except it was in a different grave. Anyway, Tobe kept going to the cemetery taking a shovel and hoe. People that saw him said he told them he was cleaning the cemetery. Of course, he never told Jenny what he was doing. Well, he cleaned it pretty well before he found the treasure. In fact, he dug up most every grave in the cemetery except Old Limbrick's grave, the one that Bubba and Lim dug up. He must have finally found it because one day he just up and comes home telling Jennie that he was leaving, and he did, undoubtedly taking the treasure with him. Jennie didn't talk much on this, but she did tell Lim the story one night when she was cooking birds over at the Big House.

"I don't know what happened to Tobe," she said. "Mr. Lim, he just came home one day about three o'clock, said he was leaving, that he'd had all the living like poor trash he was gonna take. I don't know what got into him, he just went into the back room, got that old suitcase you gave me, packed what few clothes he had and left. He never asked me what I's gonna do or nothin', just walked out the door and left."

Jennie turned the birds and stuck a pan of biscuits in the oven as Lim poured himself a refill. "Where'd he go, Jennie? You seen him since?"

"He went to Chicago. Roosevelt Morgan said he saw him gittin' on the Trailways bus the afternoon he left and he asked Tobe where he was going.

Tobe told him he was headed for Grenada to catch the Panama going to Chicago. Roosevelt said he had two suitcases when he got on the bus. I can tell you fer certain that he didn't have but one when he left home. To answer your last question, I ain't seen him since. Good riddance as far as I'm concerned. He was lazy. He wouldn't do no work 'cept'n a little piddling around the house. He walked around here actin' all secret like he was really workin' somewhere's. I don't know why he left, 'cept'n he had some of that roaming blood in his veins."

Lim just smiled at Jennie and said, "I've seen him up at the cemetery a number of times. What's he been doing up there?"

"Mr. Lim, you know as well as I do what he's doing up there. He's been looking for that fool money you thinks your grandfather Arthur may have hid. What he didn't squander away on them white trashes in Memphis."

Nothing was heard of Tobe for over a year until Sylvester's mother, Vera, came down to visit Jennie and told her a big story about Tobe. Jennie didn't say much about what she told but like everything else in a small town, it leaked out.

Tobe, so Vera said, was living in one of the biggest hotels in Chicago. He'd strut around smoking twenty five cent cigars, had two or three young women around him all the time, wore clothes fit to be buried in and drank nothing but the most expensive store bought whiskey he could find. She said he had his own chauffeur that sported him all over Chicago in a big black Cadillac and was known by his first name in most every gambling joint.

"Jennie," Vera concluded, "you never saw such a sportin' stud horse in your life. He don't have nothing to do with the likes of us, but he's sure livin' the high life in Chicago."

"Humph," Jennie replied, "he ain't never been nothing, especially no sport or stud horse."

It could be that Tobe had as much right to the Appleton's fortune as any of the Appletons. He sure had Old Arthur Appleton's traits.

I guess Jennie summed Tobe up about right when she said, "He's got that bad blood in him."

So, this is where we leave off this round of Lim's adventures. People like Lim, Bubba and Stella always live life to the fullest and leave behind many wonderful stories. Maybe one day I'll sit down to tell the rest.

CRIME IN FITNESS

by Richard Wood

The story reveals many of the true crimes in the fitness industry as well as a murder. The main character finds he is in business with someone who has been hiding his true identity. The evolution of the health club industry in the early 70's is displayed when Dubois starts as an instructor for a health club. Making mistakes along the way, he builds a chain of clubs in Texas only to lose them to a mentor. Finding another chance to do it right, he is shocked to find he has ended up in a similar situation. The man with the hidden identity offers Dubois assistance when Dubois finds himself at the scene of a murder. Numerous characters appear to be possibly responsible. The main character is also going through a serious time with his personal life as he and his wife try to have children. They find out that after many tests the only possibility they have is through in vitro fertilization.

Paperback, 150 pages
5.5" x 8.5"
ISBN 1-4137-1399-8

About the author:

Richard Wood got his start in the fitness industry when he went to work as an instructor for New Life Health Spa in Lima, Ohio. Becoming the youngest man to be voted to the position as director on the prestigious board of the Association of Physical Fitness Centers, he was active in the development of legislation regulating that industry. RichardWood333@aol.com

THE LITTLE BOY OF THE FOREST

by J.A. Aarntzen

Jack Thurston eagerly awaited his return to Black Island, his mother's family retreat in Canada's wild and pristine cottage country of 1929. Yet when the young lad of ten arrived, no one would have anything to do with him, not his grandfather, not his aunt and uncle, his cousins, not even his mother. He soon discovered that the physical world itself would not interact with him. He no longer possessed even the simple skill of opening a door. The only ones that took note of him were two eerie strangers, a haggard old woman and a creepy little boy that seemed to be always lurking in the shadows. When his grandfather suddenly took ill, Jack knew that these strangers were somehow connected. The urgency of his grandfather's condition demanded that he be rushed to the hospital at once. The worried and distressed family went along with the dying old man. They somehow had forgotten Jack. He was left by himself trapped inside the cottage on Black Island with nobody other than the two strangers who were trying to get in.

Paperback, 522 pages
6" x 9"
ISBN 1-4137-8055-5

The Little Boy of the Forest follows Jack's odyssey into loneliness and fear with his undying hope that one day his family will return.

About the author:

J.A. Aarntzen has been crafting tales of fantasy and adventure since 1978. *The Little Boy of the Forest* is his first foray into ghost stories and is his first published work. An avid enthusiast of nature, he lives in the Canadian hinterland with his wife, Laura, and his dog Sarah.

also available from publishamerica

DROPS OF DEW
by Ashok Sinha

Drops of Dew is a collection of fifty poems by Ashok Sinha written during the mid-60s and mid-70s. During this period, Ashok Sinha traveled from India to the United States where he was a student and, subsequently, a research fellow (NASA), respectively. The poems mostly reflect emotional response to this transitional phase and related reactions in terms of love, separation, anticipation, etc. with a Sufi-like quality where the object of love is often identified with God. An underlying tone of positivity is usually present in most of the poems. Also, there are poems that deride human fragility or social aberration with a touch of humor. The reader is likely to identify his or her feelings with the themes of these poems most naturally.

Paperback, 79 pages
6" x 9"
ISBN 1-4241-8120-8

About the author:

Ashok Sinha was born in India on January 8, 1943. After completing a master's degree in physics, he traveled to USA to join the University of Maryland, where he worked as a graduate student and, subsequently, as a post-doctoral research fellow. His interests include poetry/literature as well as physics/science. He has several books and publications in both areas, in English and in Hindi (his native language) to his credit.

available to all bookstores nationwide.
www.publishamerica.com

THE FINAL MISSION
GRANT AND LEE

by George Miga

It is 1870, and the nation is still badly splintered by civil war. Ulysses S. Grant, two years into a presidency tainted by scandal, struggles to unite the country. He believes only one man can help him convince the factions to bury the gauntlet—a man admired more in the South and North than the general who won the war—Robert E. Lee. Grant assigns his young security chief, Colonel John Spencer, to persuade a reluctant Lee to invite the President to the first reunion of the senior officers of the Army of Northern Virginia. Grant believes the symbolism of his standing with Lee in front of the elite of the Confederate military will help diminish the bitterness. Colonel Spencer, with the help of General William T. Sherman, the President's trusted friend, learns that KKK assassins will attempt to prevent the meeting by killing Spencer—and the President.

Paperback, 271 pages
6" x 9"
ISBN 1-4241-7987-4

About the author:

George P. Miga, a Crisis Management and Communications Consultant, is an adjunct faculty member of Indiana University Northwest's Graduate School of Business and Economics. As a manager for Amoco Corp., he worked on a project with former Presidents Ford and Nixon. He was a commercial charter pilot and newspaper reporter.